Spaizzzer

tree of Aeons

book one

aethonbooks.com

TREE OF AEONS
©2023 SPAIZZZER

Aethon Books
www.aethonbooks.com

Print and eBook formatting by Josh Hayes. Artwork provided by Fernando Granea.

Published by Aethon Books LLC.

Aethon Books is not responsible for websites (or their content) that are not owned by the publisher.

ALSO IN SERIES

TREE OF AEON - ONE

I'm Matt, and I died in a bus accident on my way home from work when the bus I was in was T-boned by a runaway speeding truck.

"You died, aged thirty-four years. Death on impact," an old man said nonchalantly. He reminded me of Santa Claus, a little bit anyway—it was the mustache and beard.

"Oh, I did?" I was in a plain white space. It reminded me of the scene where one of those actors played a god, so I looked at him and asked, "Are you God, and do I stand before the pearly gates?"

He looked thoughtful for a moment before he answered, "You could say that. I am one of the many gods. My name is Mozart, and I'm an administrator of the soul recycling and transmission system."

Mozart? What a name. I don't recall Mozart having a beard, though.

"Uh, soul recycling? Wait, that sounds like reincarnation."

"Yes. Very much like all those *isekai* stories you've been reading."

Oh! That's a good way to explain it. At that moment, I thought I'd hit the lottery, and remembering all the other reincarnation stories I read, I couldn't help but feel a little excited. Would I get to build a harem? I would like a harem. That would be quite a nice change from my single-ass self. Little did I know I was gonna be really disappointed.

"Oh, nice. So what am I to be reincarnated as? What special powers do I get?"

Mozart shrugged.

"Roll this." A big disc appeared with weird characters on it. It resembled a giant Wheel of Fortune, complete with different colors for each slice, but I couldn't make out what each of the weird characters meant. Mozart noticed my confusion, but he wasn't interested in elaborating further.

"What is this?"

"This is the 'Race' wheel. The result of your roll will tell you what you get to be in your next life. You could be a mosquito, a dragon, or even a minor deity."

"Hmm, why not a human? That's how it normally is for *isekai* stories."

"You didn't qualify." He glanced at something and frowned. "Humanoids are a special category."

"What do you mean?" There were six billion...no, seven billion of us on Earth!

"Based on the kind of life you led, you don't qualify to be reincarnated as a humanoid."

"But why? I could be a deity, right? Isn't that better than being a humanoid? Then why is being human so hard?"

"That's just how the rules are, and I won't reveal more. Arguing with me won't change things. Roll the wheel. You will be reincarnated based on the results."

I still couldn't comprehend what the words on the wheel were, so I looked at Mozart. More accurately, I stared at him. "Seriously? Is this a trick?"

He looked annoyed. "Just roll the wheel. Or you can choose to be at the very bottom of the pyramid: a mosquito. That's permissible. Or a small wall lizard or gecko. The kind that everyone kills daily."

"Fuck that. I'll roll the wheel." *Isekai* wall lizard didn't exactly sound appealing.

Just as I was about to roll the wheel, I stared at him again. I did recall dying in a bus accident on my way home, and there were quite a few others on the bus. Was I being singled out here?

"Erm...how are the other guys in the bus?" I recalled there were quite a few teenagers there. It's a route that passed by a mall, and it was late, so they were probably on their way home after an outing.

"Dead. They are going to be reincarnated as well. After you."

"Oh. So do they need to roll the wheel as well?"

"Nope. They will be reincarnated as humans or elves."

Hey, I am being singled out! That's quite unfair! "What? How come?"

"They've gotten special clearance from the gods that oversee the worlds you will soon go to. They have been selected to fight the invaders as 'heroes,' so they will start with extra perks and privileges."

"How about me?" *I want to be a hero, too!*

"The gods didn't want you. You're too old, and you just happened to get on the same bus as the kids." Mozart looked really annoyed. "Roll. The. Wheel."

Wait. I am collateral damage? That's ageism!

"Why them? Why do they get to be champions?"

"Because they are young, courageous, good-hearted, and have a desire to do good. Not yet tainted by the evils of society. Quite unlike you."

"Wait. So they chose kids?"

"That's the criteria the gods wanted, so that's what they get." He gave me the kind of glare that made me feel like shit.

"Damn." I gave up and rolled the wheel. There wasn't much of a choice. The man wasn't buying my attempts to get some leeway.

The strange wheel spun and stopped at a random word I didn't understand.

Wait. The word transformed.

Tree.

I could read it...somehow.

"What?" *Hey, this is not going the way I thought it would. I am supposed to get superpowers and get reincarnated. This isn't how I envisioned my reincarnation to be.*

"A tree?"

"Oh, yeah, trees have souls, too. I forgot about that option." Mozart seemed rather casual about it. "Trees are not bad, actually. Huge potential."

Before I could ask anything else, Mozart interrupted me.

"All right, off you go as a tree! Goodbye!"

Wooooooooooosh!

It was pitch black, and it remained so for quite some time.

I mean, it started, right? Is there a menu? A timer? An interface?

Then I saw it. A clock.

YEAR 1, MONTH 0

[You are Level 1 - Normal Tree.]
[Skills possessed.]
[Hibernate], [Germinate - Produce fruits or seeds], [Autopilot].

There was a floating menu commonly found in computer games right before me. *Hell yeah. I have skills, and I am level one.* Despite these humble beginnings, I thought, *Hey, maybe it won't be so bad. A tree can get to do awesome shit, too!*

Let's get to it! So I waited. I mean, was it supposed to be black and dark like this all this time?

Nothing happened, and I wondered whether maybe this dark space was some kind of loading screen. But then the time kept ticking, and a good two hours later, I was still in darkness. Nothing.

I didn't feel a damn thing. No sensation, no vision, and no sound, either.

It was still dark. Was I supposed to do something? I tried to open my eyes but couldn't see. No, more like, what were my eyes? Did I even have eyes?

I kept waiting. I didn't feel tired physically, but I did feel mentally exhausted.

Time moved.

The clock just kept ticking, and nothing freaking happened.

Darkness.

Black.

Black.

Black...

Frustrated, I tried using my skills. I eventually discovered I could think of what skill I wanted to activate. And so [Germinate – Produce Fruit]!

A pop-up appeared. *'Not the right season.'*

What was the season, then? That very thought triggered a change in the interface, and next to the clock, a seasonal calendar or indicator appeared. It moved slowly, with a small needle-shaped indicator pointing at 'winter.'

Curious of my other skills, I mentally selected [Autopilot], and another pop-up appeared.

[Autopilot engaged. Time-acceleration activated. Autopilot will automatically activate skills. Autopilot activated [Hibernate].]

I fell into a sleep-like state.

When I woke up, a good four months had passed on the clock. Yet the darkness remained.

At least the season menu said 'spring.'

[Autopilot has activated [Produce Fruit].]

Nothing happened. It was still darkness to me.

With [Autopilot] active, time passed quickly. At first, I thought I misunderstood the clock, but it soon became obvious that a second was actually equal to an hour, which was really convenient because there was absolutely nothing to do. I watched the time pass by quite quickly.

A year went by.

Then another year passed.

And another year.

Was it going to be like this forever? Was this the life of a tree? Why couldn't I even feel my own roots or branches?

YEAR 4

In the fourth year, a string of notifications appeared. It instantly kicked me out of autopilot.

[Amber Lee has died. You received a fragment.]

[Samantha Chandran has died. You received a fragment.]

[Peter Varoufakis has died. You received a fragment.]

[Hyuna Park has died. You received a fragment.]

[Reed Constance has died. You received a fragment.]

[Shah Rasul has died. You received a fragment.]

[Mai has died. You received a fragment.]

[Lee Kang Ho has died. You received a fragment.]

[Shane Andrew Fillon has died. You received a fragment.]

[Pink Fung has died. You received a fragment.]

[The Demon King Asmodai has been defeated.]

Oh, wow. At first, I didn't recognize these names, but when the demon king's notification popped up, that was when I realized the kids had won.

Yet, nothing happened.

Still darkness. I thought something would happen. Perhaps I'd see a prompt that told me our mission was complete, and we would move on to the next reincarnation, but nothing changed. I thought that might be the trigger for me to escape my darkness, that perhaps I was a prisoner cursed by the demon king, but there was absolutely nothing.

Time passed, and a few years later, more notifications appeared. Similar to the others, they just said, *Saita Maru, Mark Antoinette, Kim Possibru, and Samantha Charleston* died. I received a fragment with each.

What are these fragments?

YEAR 15

[Demon King Astaroth has appeared.]

Frankly, I thought I should panic, but trapped in darkness, there was absolutely nothing I could do. A string of notifications popped up a few months later. *Azares Fox, Sarah Cole, Pamela Seis, Lucy Braveheart, Winston Chow, and Roald Strump* all died. Cumulatively, I now had a total of twenty fragments.

It seemed to suggest they had been defeated by this latest demon king. Why else would they die?

YEAR 16

[The Gods have summoned twenty new heroes!]

Oh, God. More kids? I mean, they had to be kids, right? Also, twenty? Wasn't that huge overkill?

YEAR 18

Two years after the new batch of kids was summoned, the Demon King Astaroth was defeated, but another eleven kids died. So now, I had these thirty-one fragments—with their names—sitting in my menu. For a bunch of heroes, they sure didn't last very long against demons. Or were the demon kings just so powerful? And two years!

The demon king could've destroyed a huge number of things in two years.

I got the feeling this was a circle that never ended. Demon kings appeared, and the gods summoned heroes from Earth to fight them. So, over the next ten years, another five died, and their deaths seemed to be spread out, suggesting either they somehow fought and died, or someone or something else killed them.

YEAR 30

Another demon king appeared, Demon King Dantalion, and a short while later, another four heroes died. I received another four fragments, which then brought my total to forty.

At this point, it felt like a statistic. A year later, right on schedule, the gods summoned another fifteen heroes.

Sometime later, Demon King Dantalion was defeated, and of the fifteen summoned heroes, ten of them died. I received ten fragments, and this brought my total to fifty. Fifty fragments were quite a lot to track, so my menu and interface automatically changed such that the fragments now had their own dedicated screen.

After that, nothing much happened for about ten years. Later, Year 42 on the clock, another demon appeared, the Demon King Ezekiel. Amazingly, the surviving five heroes managed to kill the Demon King Ezekiel with only one of the five dying.

They continued this streak even after ten years when Demon King Furfur appeared. Amazingly, the four heroes slayed the demon king within a few months of its appearance.

YEAR 52

I was jolted out of the darkness, out of my [Autopilot], by an oddity. There was someone there. He shone like a lighthouse in a sea of darkness.

"Hello." It was a young boy. He was a small, petite child, probably no older than ten. He approached me, and I saw the features of his face. I was surprised I could see him.

"Hi." I was eager to talk, so I responded. Somehow, I was able to talk, and I wasn't sure how I managed it. It was like sending a telepathic message, and I was sure I couldn't do that before today.

"Oh my God, did you just talk?" he shouted and then ran in circles for a while. "Wait, everyone will think I am crazy if I tell them a tree can talk. Oh, wait! Of course, a tree spirit could talk. But wait, I need to keep this to myself."

I didn't reply to that.

"Erm...oh, yes. Do you have a name, O tree spirit? I am Indra, a young druid in training."

At that point, I wondered whether he saw me as a tree or as a person, but he referred to me as a tree spirit. "My name is Matt. Hello, Indra." He seemed quite happy. "May I ask how you are able to see me?"

"I have a unique skill. It is called [Soul Communion]."

"Sounds really special." It was actually more special than he gave it credit for, because it also enabled me to respond to him telepathically.

"Yes, it's quite cool! It allows me to see and talk to ghosts and spirits!" He beamed. "I notice them whenever I walk around, and they speak to me."

"Your skill is amazing."

"It is! And this is the first time I have spotted a tree spirit! It's late, but I'll come back." He nodded. "Let me just memorize this place so I can find you again."

"Sure, please come back. It is nice to talk to someone." I waved with one of my branches.

"Okay." With that, Indra left. It was strange to see a human-shaped, faintly glowing thing. That was the beginning of our relationship as friends. Indra would later come by every week, and we would talk at length, mostly about his training as a druid.

"Hey, this might sound quite weird, but, uh...can I ask for a favor?" he asked after a few months of knowing each other. At that point, I was really quite eager to please my only friend.

"Hmm?"

"Would you mind granting me a magical familiar contract?"

"What does that do? How does that work?"

"I will be able to summon a familiar to aid me in combat, usually in exchange for some of my mana."

"I would love to, but I don't think I can do too much. I am not sure if I have any combat powers, either." All I had now was the power to make seeds and fruits.

"It's okay, nobody I know has a tree familiar. I think it could be quite cool."

"Very well, then."

Indra mumbled something, and that was when I had a pop-up.

[Indra has requested to enter into a familiar contract. Do you accept?]

A menu to click yes or no appeared, and I mentally chose yes.

Indra smiled. "Yay! I have a tree familiar. This is so awesome. I bet nobody else has a nature-aspect familiar."

Little did I know then that I may have sent him to his death.

Later that week, he returned and sat next to me. "My teachers took a look at my tree familiar form, and now I might be going away for a long time. It seems the druid council wants to see more of my tree familiar abilities as they are rare. Of course, they also asked me to lead them to you, but I said I couldn't find you again."

"Oh. Good luck, then. Is it that special?" *Huh, why did he hide my presence?*

"Yes. It is quite different from the kinds of regular magical familiars I usually see. It has mostly defensive and healing skills. Familiars have a few variants. There are those summoned by way of a magical contract or those granted by nature's aspects."

"That's very interesting. You used my skills?"

"Yeah, I did. I used them a lot!"

Hmm. I didn't even realize he used my skills. It seemed like once I agreed to the familiar contract, I didn't really need to do anything. Of course, I wondered why my familiar was even useful and wondered what my tree familiar's skills would look like.

Pop

A menu appeared.

[Tree Familiar]
[Ironbark Skin], [Healing Fruit], [Lesser Natural Healing Boost].

My familiar contract skills were quite different from my own, or maybe the familiar form had its own skill tree? Could I get them eventually?

"It is to be my first time away from home."

"Are you scared?"

"Yes, but I think it is also an adventure! My mom tells me not to worry, though. I will be going with the town's lead druid to the capital."

"Sounds like fun. Spend more time with your parents before you go, okay? You never know when you will see them again." Since the day I died, the people I missed the most were my parents, followed by my friends.

"You're right. I should spend more time with my family. I should go." Indra nodded.

"Bye. Good luck with your trip. Stay safe."

Unfortunately, that was the last time I ever saw Indra.

YEAR 55

[Indra Sinahalia has died. Some of the experience acquired through use of the familiar form has been transferred back to you. You gained thirteen levels. A fragment of Indra's skills was transferred to you in accordance with the familiar contract. You have obtained unique skill: [Spirit Vision].]

[You received the skill [Limited Telepathic Communication].]

[You are now level 14.]

[You gained the skills [Healing Fruits and Seeds], [Inspect].]

Oh, dear. My young friend died, and now, as the effects of the skill were applied, for the first time in forever, I could see.

It wasn't the kind of sight that humans had. I was able to see the spirits of people if they were nearby, and the pitch-black background was replaced with faint outlines. It was as if I was looking at things through an inverted outline on Photoshop.

But I wasn't picky. I could see, and it was how I came to the realization I was in some kind of park, or perhaps someone's garden.

And there were people.

They were a distance away, but every now and then, they would pass. From a distance, they were all blurry blobs, kind of like a wisp, but once they were closer, the details improved. It was kind of like short-sightedness but for spirits.

I attempted to communicate, but most of the time there was nothing. It felt like they thought they were being disturbed by ghosts and fled for their lives. I was disappointed at how the people around me refused to communicate.

Sadly, very few people actually walked near enough for me to communicate with them. It seemed that I was placed quite deep in the park or garden, so everyone seemed so far away. At my present level, they pretty much needed to be next to me to hear anything.

So, nothing happened for quite some time...again.

YEAR 56

Another battle happened. There were lots of people in the distance fighting creatures. (They appeared as rough, moving shadows.) The battle seemed intense, and many of the spirits were extinguished, the battle spilling over into the park as well.

One of the human fighters stood next to me, so I got excited and took the chance to communicate. Maybe he needed help, and I could get him to agree to a familiar contract.

"Ugh, damned demons..." he said.

"Do you need some help?" I asked and noticed his breathing was ragged and he was likely wounded.

"Huh?" He looked around, one hand still clutching his wounds. He then looked at the tree. "Talking tree?"

"You need help?" I repeated.

"Ah, yes."

[Healing Fruit].

This was the skill to create a small fruit that gave some healing effect. A fruit appeared and dangled right next to him. He plucked it off my little vine.

[Familiar Contract].

The battle raged around me, and I figured they didn't have

much time. He needed to rush back, and the familiar contract was probably the quickest way I could offer help.

"Oh." He accepted and munched down on the fruit. His breathing quickly improved, and he nodded. "Thanks. I should go and help the rest of my team. Damned demons."

I didn't see that guy again after that, and ten days later, I got a notification.

[Semara Falk has died. You gained 1 level.] [You are now level 15.]

Was this the fate of life as a tree, to watch everyone else die around me? Little did I know then it would be very much so.

The soulless monsters, or demons as he called them, appeared every now and then after that day, and the people repeatedly tried to fight them off. Some days there were monsters everywhere, even around me. Thankfully, they didn't indiscriminately destroy everything, so they didn't attack me. I wondered what would happen if they did. Perhaps I would die.

The humans would come back and chase them away. This lasted for months as the battles ebbed and flowed, and then, eventually, the humans won.

A lull.

Then someone approached a few days later.

"Is this the tree?" He sounded unsure, and he looked like he referred to a piece of paper.

Hmm. "Yes?" I responded telepathically.

"Ah. It is! I am Starric, Semara's teammate. Before he died, he asked me to properly thank you for your help. Thanks to the power of your familiar, he was quite the hero."

"I see." *Hero?*

"Well, not a hero-hero but, yeah, a small hero. He didn't have much, but he asked me to bury his trusty sword next to you."

Starric dug a hole and then placed the sword inside.

"Would you like a familiar?" I asked while he dug the small hole.

"It is okay. I can't. My religion forbids me."

Ah, damn it. Religion.

After he left, a few days later, a spirit appeared beside me.

"Hi." It was that Semara guy, but he was a ghost.

"Huh? Why are you here?" I asked.

"Oh, I am just a part of Semara embedded in the sword. The real me died and passed on."

I didn't understand.

"It's complicated, but the sword has been by my side since my youth—the past thirty years—and so a fragment of me is in it."

"Oh."

"So how long will you be here?"

"Maybe a few more months. I will eventually fade away with time."

"And how do you know all this? Like...how do you even know about your original soul?"

"Oh, I-I just kind of know, I guess. It's like I get a message about it. The leveling system and all that."

"Ah."

With this copy of Semara next to me, we talked. A lot. Semara was a lot more knowledgeable about the world than Indra, so he had more to share. That was how I learned about the world I was in.

This world had many gods and religions, and magic was commonplace. Demons and monsters appeared frequently, and some speculated it was due to the proximity to the world of demons. Due to stellar movements and astronomical forces, the barrier that protected the world occasionally weakened, and that resulted in stronger demons entering the world. Which led to the periodic entrance of demon kings.

Different religions, strangely, had different ways of answering why the demon kings came.

I found this strange because they could ask the heroes who

met the gods, or even ask the gods directly. Perhaps there was a lot of confusion about why it happened.

Gods of the world responded to the demons by summoning heroes from another world. The heroes rose to defeat the demons and usually they succeeded, though it was at great cost. The world today had a few remaining heroes, and those had since fallen out with each other and now fought to be the most powerful ruler in the world.

Six months passed a little easier with Semara around as I eagerly consumed his knowledge, but the good times didn't last very long, and Semara faded away. I was alone, again.

YEAR 57, MONTH 1

On the first day of the year, a young elf kneeled before me.

"Oh, tree, I, Salada Stoppu of the elvish tribe, humbly request for the blessing of the tree spirit."

How did this random elf know of my existence? And his name is Salad?

"How did you learn of me?"

"Oh...erm..." He seemed a little embarrassed. "You have been listed in the register of benign lesser spirits by the local council, following reports by the army to the town council."

I am in a register of the town council as a lesser spirit. I felt like a botanical garden exhibit.

"Fine. Familiar contract?"

This time, recalling Semara's spirit accompanied me for six months, I added a condition.

"You must leave an item with a strong personal connection to yourself with me, and upon your death, your weapon should be buried near me."

He nodded and buried a small wooden chain next to my roots. "This is a small chain I made when I was a child. Is this fine?"

"Yes." Frankly, I didn't know exactly what the criteria were to recreate Semara's case, but I agreed. And then I offered him the familiar contract. Maybe I would gain a skill, too, since this was a game-like world.

He bowed and then left, happy.

I sighed and went back into [Autopilot] mode. *I wonder how long they'll live.*

YEAR 57, MONTH 8

Another elf came to find me. He was a boy by the name of Croissanta Fillings, and I offered him the same deal I offered Salada—the familiar contract—and he buried a small metal ring. Happy, he then walked away.

I wondered how long I would have to live as a tree.

A pop-up appeared.

[Trees are eternal if they don't get killed.]

No shit.

YEAR 57, MONTH 11

I gained a level! [Level 16]
But nobody died. Strange.

YEAR 57, MONTH 12

Somebody visited. He didn't respond to me, but he seemed to be trimming some of my branches. Since I didn't feel any damage or pain, I allowed him to continue. He collected the trimmed branches, picked up leaves, and left once he was done.

YEAR 58, MONTH 1

I had gained a level! [Level 17] With the level, I acquired a skill called [Self-Visualization]. Despite the skill's title seeming to mean something else, it just meant I was now able to look at myself.

That was the first time I could see all my branches and roots. I was actually pretty big, about the size of a small house. Being able to see myself, thinking I recognized leaves from the trees in my past life that could be used to brew teas, I wondered if the guy who trimmed my branches and collected my leaves was doing that with them.

Maybe that was why I was gaining levels?

YEAR 58, MONTH 2

Another elf, Corna Corrola, came and asked for a familiar. As it turned out, some elves had a thing for tree spirits. *So typical of elves. Tree-huggers.*

Anyway, I agreed and gave her the usual terms, but I also made a special request that she come back every six months and tell me what was happening in the world.

YEAR 58, MONTH 6

I gained another level, but nothing in particular happened. [Level 18]. I supposed that was a good thing. I kept wondering why I gained random levels. Maybe it was just a tree thing.

YEAR 58, MONTH 7

A human had come and asked for my blessing to heal his child from a disease it suffered.

"I am not sure whether I can," I replied, "but I can try. Bring them to me."

They returned with a small baby, probably around eight months old. He looked really sick as his spirit appeared extremely faint, flickering. I created a magical healing fruit with all the nutrients I could gather.

The man fed it to his child. The child still looked sick, and then they left, the man looking sad.

Three days later, he came back with the child. The child's spirit looked better. It turned out that the child had actually been suffering from a very bad fever, and my fruit had helped. The father was grateful as I'd been his last hope.

From what I had been told, due to the war against the demons, there were no healers left. Most of them died some time ago, and those who survived now served in what was left of the army of this country.

[You gained a level. You are now level 19.]

The man returned a few days later again with poop. Cow poop. He mixed it into the dirt. Fertilizer? Yet I felt nothing. I thanked my lucky stars I lacked the ability to smell. Though, since I was a tree, I presumed the poop would smell like...food?

YEAR 58, MONTH 12

Winter. Due to the seasons, the system restricted me from creating fruits. A different man begged for help, and he pleaded for his wife, but I couldn't, no matter how much I wanted to. I told him winter was the time when I couldn't create fruit.

So I told him to hang in there and return when spring came.

YEAR 59, MONTH 1

The man returned and cursed me. I guessed from his behavior that his wife didn't make it, so I didn't respond to his curses. Yet, after the exchange, I gained a level and a skill.

[Level 20]
   [[Minor Winter Resistance] – Grants ability to create fruit during winter.]

Yeah, that man would hate me if he ever found out.

YEAR 59, MONTH 2

A young lady dropped by and begged me to protect her husband. He would be going to war soon, to defend the country from a demonic rift that had appeared. Her voice cracked like she wanted to cry, but I was a tree so, in my mind, I could only empathize and explain I wasn't a god. I didn't have the power to provide blessings. I was just a tree that happened to live here.

"Is there really nothing you can do?" she asked.

"Does he want a familiar?"

She paused and thought for a moment. "I'll ask him."

The next day, a young man came, along with the young lady. "Is this the tree you've been visiting?" He glanced up and shrugged. "Doesn't look very impressive."

"Please, Andy, a familiar might protect you."

He shook his head. "Do you have no confidence in me?"

"It's not that, but if something can give you a bit more protection, will you not take it?"

Andy sighed and approached me. "This is so weird, talking to a tree, but hey, if you can hear me, may I get a familiar? Just so that my wife feels safer?"

I wondered whether having a familiar would offer any

protection, as they might overestimate their own abilities and end up taking more risks, but I offered a familiar contract anyway. The wife buried a small pendant in exchange.

"Oh, wow. There really is a spirit here."

"Just take it, Andy. Don't be stubborn. Think about whatever would happen if you died."

"Yes, yes." He accepted, and the couple left.

YEAR 59, MONTH 3

The man with the sick wife returned with something in his hand.

Oh, no. An ax.

He scolded and shouted for a while and started to swing his ax. However, I didn't feel any pain, and I realized that my trunk was really, really hard and tough. After some time, he gave up, cursed, and left. Through his curses, I learned that the town was named Moton.

I wondered how that other guy managed to even trim my branches.

YEAR 59, MONTH 9

A bad month, really. The month started with three deaths as the three elves all died within days of each other.

[Corna Corolla has died.]

[Salada Stoppu has died.]

[Croissonta Fillings has died.]

I gained fifteen levels after the three elves died. I was now level thirty-five, and I also transformed from a [Normal Tree] to a [Spiritual Tree]. My skills were mostly healing and defensive, but I also gained a skill called [Tree Rebirth]. I wondered what it did.

YEAR 59, MONTH 10

Death came to the town of Moton.

Monsters. They attacked the town every day, and as much as I wanted to help, nobody got near enough for me to grant a familiar contract. They fled, and in all that chaos, they were not about to listen to a random voice. Hell, they probably wouldn't even notice me.

Battles raged in the distance as the defenders lost to the demons. On the last day of the month, a notification sprang up.

[Arsene Emir has died. You gained a fragment.]

Oh. One of the heroes fell.

YEAR 59, MONTH 11

[Demon King Baal has entered the world!]

Moton, at this point, was deserted. There wasn't a single soul I could see with my [Spirit Vision]. I hoped they fled rather than died, but the past month's battle made that seem rather unlikely. Everyone who remained had died.

YEAR 60, MONTH 2

Monsters wandered everywhere, and some, these... demons, tried to cut me down but, thankfully, my bark and skin defied them, and these monsters gave up once they realized it was pointless. I never expected trees would be so strong.

YEAR 60, MONTH 9

The town of Moton was no more.

Oh, shit, I thought as I spied something powerful on the horizon.

Is that...a demon king?

He was huge. A massive presence the height of a fifteen-story building. Even at a distance, his presence burned, and I could see a soul, but unlike human souls that normally appeared a faint white in color, the demon king's presence was a bright red one and surrounded by a constant, burning, reddish fire.

He turned, noticed me, and walked toward me. He roared, and the earth trembled.

Oh, shit. I shivered and didn't even know how, when I had no sense other than vision! *What!*

He raised his arm and slashed.

An intense flame seared me like a massive pot of hot oil was just poured all over my body.

"Ughhhhhhh!" I yelped, but no one could hear me. For a tree, I was both amazed and frightened I could feel so much pain.

The entire top part of my body broke apart. It'd been chopped off! For a moment, I thought I saw a burning soul smiling eerily, and then it walked away. It must have been my imagination.

I was still overwhelmed by the immense pain, pulled in multiple directions, but...I thought, *I'll live!*

I'm still alive! I was just a stump now, but somehow, trees didn't die so easily! The demon king disappeared into the distance, and once he was out of sight, I fell into a kind of recovery sleep.

YEAR 65, MONTH 2

I 've slept for the past four years? I quickly tried to feel myself and realized I was still just a stump, but a few small green shoots had emerged from the edges.

There was a notification menu that thankfully recorded the string of messages I missed. The remaining heroes were killed, but amazingly, they managed to slay the Demon King Baal, or at least, I think that's what happened.

Also, I gained a level, which made me level thirty-six! I also had a title now.

[Demon King Survivor.]

YEAR 65, MONTH 8

The new shoots didn't grow very well. In fact, they survived no longer than a week and then died. But new ones would eventually regrow and take their place. I noticed my ability to stay conscious was correlated to how many shoots were out so, when a lot of the shoots died, I usually lost consciousness.

Despite my consciousness wavering, I noticed a random elven druid visited.

"Oh, old tree, are you still there?" He touched my stump and carefully inspected the damage from the demon king.

I'm not that old!

"Yes, I am," I replied, but he didn't seem to understand me. In fact, he didn't hear me at all.

I waited for him to reply, but he just stood there quietly. Eventually, he spoke.

"Ah...the damage must have really weakened you." He touched the stump and seemed to be using some kind of druid magic. "I can't do much to help, but this will make you feel better."

I felt invigorated, but only temporarily. That energy quickly drained away.

"The demon king's presence has tainted these grounds. That is why you are unable to recover. To survive when the fire still burns and the ground is corrupted shows you must be strong!"

I didn't sense the demon king's presence, but maybe my ability to see was impaired as well. As I still couldn't really keep myself awake for very long, I didn't dwell on it.

"I will help you, and that will include moving you out of these tainted lands," he said and then left. I wondered how he planned to move me.

YEAR 65, MONTH 9

A few men arrived, and all of them seemed old. Oh, and the druid from last month.

"This is the tree I mentioned. It is amazing it survived an attack by a demon king. And look at those flames!"

"Indeed. I believe the druid council would like to examine it further," another man said. He held some kind of wooden staff, and he stood right next to me. "These fires are interesting."

"Should we move it back to the druid council's garden?"

"Hmm, I would rather not. Let's not have the others discover this. Druidhome already has another spirit. I would rather we keep this between ourselves."

"True. It would be troublesome if the other group finds it. Where do you propose?"

"Am thinking either the Salah king's outer garden compound, the Ransalah's Adventurer Guild's garden, or the Temple of Gaya's garden."

"The adventurer's guild. I don't think they'd expect it to be there."

"I prefer the Temple of Gaya. Easier to explain why we are moving trees, especially with the reconstruction happening

there. The caretaker would want to have a look at this as well."
They voted, and eventually, they decided on the Temple of Gaya.

I didn't pay attention to the details because I wasn't able to maintain my consciousness, and my brain felt like it was splitting apart from trying to follow their conversation.

The five of them spread out in a circle and surrounded me. They mumbled some kind of chant, and then the earth around me shook and cracked. I found myself floating, and one of the guys took out some kind of sack.

Then it was just all black for me. Maybe they'd somehow sucked me into the sack or used some kind of druid tree-moving magic, I wasn't sure. Once my roots no longer touched any dirt or earth, I just lost consciousness.

YEAR 65, MONTH 10

"How is it reacting?"

"Better than expected. Its color seems to be returning, and the taint of the demon king fades, but the fires remain."

"Did I say how amazed I am that it can resist the demon king's fire attack, and also its corruption?"

"Yes, you did. But I think most druids would be."

"That's what makes it worth studying."

The guys talked, and I could still hear them faintly, but my consciousness faded away every now and then. They came over every other day to check on me.

YEAR 66, MONTH 2

I felt much better after time had passed, and I could stay awake. The druids still came over regularly, and I noticed they had been casting some kind of spell on me. I sounded like some kind of [Appraisal].

On top of that, they poked me with weird contraptions, and they seemed very interested in my stump, mumbling about the fires of Hell and stuff like that.

Still, I was too sleepy to think too much, and every time I tried, I'd get a headache.

YEAR 66, MONTH 3

"Is this the tree?" An old man came to visit. *Seriously, I'm really popular with old men. Is it a thing in fantasy worlds for old men to constantly poke at things?*

"Yes," a younger man replied as he joined him.

The old man touched my stump and appeared rather deep in thought. "From Moton, you say?"

"Yes. It survived a demon king's claws. The scars on the stump still flare a little with the demon's fires."

Wait, the demon king's fire was still burning my stump? I took a good hard look at myself with [Self-Visualization], and that's when I felt a surge of pain. It seemed that my skill [Autopilot] had cut off a portion of my senses, so I didn't notice I was burning.

[Status: The Fire of Baal]

Whoa. And ow. Ow, ow, ow.

It felt like touching a hot kettle, for a long time. Pain. PAIN.

[Autopilot]
[[Autopilot] suppressed the sensations from the burning surface.]

"These fires, have we tried using them?" the old man asked.

The younger man scratched his chin.

"The demon king will return soon. We can better protect ourselves if we know what we face."

"What do you have in mind, Caretaker?" the younger man asked.

"Can we defeat demons with their own power?" the caretaker mused, twirling the stick in the fire.

The question stunned the younger man.

"Caretaker, to use the demon's powers, that may be seen as witchcraft and even blasphemy. Best not to repeat it." The younger man shook his head.

"You are right." The caretaker sighed.

YEAR 66, MONTH 9

That month, more people investigated the endlessly burning fire on my stump. Usually, it was the same old men with different contraptions or spells, but more had come. The investigators did strange things. They doused me with holy water and extracted my stump surface.

They thought I was strong enough not to die from the fires, and not let it burn the rest of me, but not strong enough to extinguish the fire. My body continuously regenerated a fire-resistant layer, and that layer was replaced by another layer once the fires completely consumed the upper layer.

The Fire of Baal interfered with all my attempts to telepathically communicate. I suspected they heard something, but the fires must have distorted the details.

YEAR 67, MONTH 1

I t happened at night. A group of masked men snuck into the temple grounds. They were dressed like typical cultists, in dark hoodies and masks, and they carried weird religious items. How did I know? Well, they talked.

"This is it. The tree that carries the Fires of the Demon King." One pointed.

"So the rumors are true. The Temple of Gaya really experimented with demon fire."

"The master will be pleased."

He took out a kind of vase. At least that's what I thought it was because it looked like one from the outline. The cultists mumbled a kind of weird chant while the one holding the vase leaned closer to me. He popped the cork on top of the vase, and with a *whoosh*, it sucked all the fires into it. *Since it had a cork, did that make it a wine bottle instead?* I wished I could see properly and not just the outline.

"All right. Let's go."

A few guards came by then, a little too late.

"Stop! What are you doing?"

Why did guards always spot the bad guys when they were done?

"Let's split!" the cultists shouted.

They fled in different directions and then disappeared into the distance.

[The Fire of Demon King Baal removed. Negative effects on some of your passive recovery, skills, spells, and abilities removed.]

Oh, thank you, cultists. I hoped I didn't meet a demon king again.

The next day, I heard voices of the priests and other temple guards.

"Who is behind this?"

"The fires are gone!"

"Did you hear me? Who is behind this?"

"Anyone able to collect the fires of Baal must be affiliated with the demons. Perhaps the demon cultists."

No shit, genius.

"Ugh. No one spotted them?"

"Where are the other guards?"

"Dead. We found a few of them in the alleys."

With the fires gone, I was no longer an interesting specimen. Nobody came over to visit again, and solitude returned.

YEAR 67, MONTH 5

Without the Fires of Baal interfering with my recovery, I regrew a proper trunk. I also felt more energetic than before.

YEAR 67, MONTH 8

"This is the tree that has a seat!"

I was now like a small tree, with a stump stuck at the side. In a way, I looked like a chair. Or maybe a stump and stick combo.

Some people would come over and sit, but most ignored all my familiar contracts. I wondered why, and then a pop-up explained: *'Believers of Gaya cannot accept familiars of nature and are naturally resistant to telepathy.' Ah, that explains why everyone rejected me.*

An old man approached me in one of the last few days of the month. Once again, I seemed to have a thing with old men.

"Hi, tree," he said.

He looked a little crazy. His soul appeared really messed up from its cracked and lumpy appearance.

"I am dying, and I am looking for a place to be buried. Can I bury myself here?"

I had no idea how to respond to such a question. Seriously. Should I say, yes, please, or should I tell him no? I tried to speak, but he didn't seem to hear me.

He touched my growing trunk.

"Yes, I think I will bury myself here."

Uh. Okay. He made the decision, so I guessed that's that. Maybe he'd end up a spirit like Semara.

YEAR 67, MONTH 9

That same old man came again and sat on me and then fell asleep. He didn't wake up, and his soul faded. He was discovered that evening by the temple guys. By then, he was dead.

"Oh, dear. The crazy old man really did die here," a young temple initiate complained.

"He's been telling the caretaker he wants to be buried here," another initiate responded.

"Call the caretaker."

Soon, the caretaker returned and sat beside the old man's corpse. "Old friend, I will bury you here as you asked."

The two initiates complained, "But, Caretaker, he is not a believer. What gives him the right to be buried in the temple grounds?"

"He *was* a believer. His three sons fought valiantly against the demons—as a part of the warriors of Gaya—but their death made him curse us, curse the temple for bringing doom to his family, so he stopped believing. In his dying days, I believe he came around."

"Ah, if you say so, Caretaker."

The next day, they dug a hole next to my roots and buried the old man. Strangely enough, he wasn't in a coffin. I wondered whether they had such a culture here. Come to think of it, I didn't recall ever seeing coffins, not that I would have given where I'd grown. Still, a part of me felt relieved I wouldn't get chopped up to be made into coffins.

YEAR 67, MONTH 10

"Hello, tree spirit."

"Oh. Hello, old man." The old man had actually transformed into a spirit, even though it took a week. I wondered what took him so long. Was there like some kind of incubation period? "Did you wait long?"

"No, I just appeared today. My, I'm quite surprised to see a tree spirit here."

"So, you didn't know I was here?"

"I just liked the location. It seemed like a nice place to be buried, protected by the temple and next to a tree that had survived so much."

"Uh-huh. How morbid. Thinking about where to be buried. That sort of thought never crossed my mind."

The old man's spirit shrugged. "You are a tree. Death must be a strange thing for you."

"Hmm. Never mind. Why are you here, and why didn't you move on?"

"I want to. But I have a lot of regrets. So much...anger and hatred. Frustration for the temple of Gaya. Anger at the gods and demons. Anger at how weak I was to let my children die."

"Huh. You're self-aware about it."

"Must be a foreign concept for trees with no family."

I understood it quite well, but I chose not to interject.

"Life and death. To lose your children to monsters. To flee when your children are fighting. Do you know how much I regret it?"

"No. Tell me, then, why did you flee?" He wanted to vent, so I gave him the chance.

"To protect my younger children. I ran with their wives, their kids, my grandchildren."

"Then you did your part, no?"

"No. I felt I should have been the one fighting while they fled. An old man like me, choosing to run instead of fighting. That torment, it burns me."

"Is that considered running? Sounds pretty honorable to me, and if you stayed and fought, would it have made a difference?"

"Maybe. I am much older, but when the demons attacked many years ago, I could hold a sword well. I was much higher level, and I had better skills. It was wrong for them to entrust the protection of their wives to me. I, the dying old man, should have been the one fighting and holding off the demons while they made their way out."

"They must have believed you could protect their wives and kids better than they could."

Hey! I didn't sign up for spirit-counseling. If this guy is going to vent at me for the next few months, I am going to [Hibernate].

"So what? I should have knocked some sense into them."

Ugh. I needed to cut this guy off.

"You are dead. Let it go and move on."

"No! I cannot. I must not. I spent the last few years thinking back to that day when we parted in Olbast. I should have stayed, and they should have left. Thirteen years and, every night, I think about it. If I made a different choice. If—"

"You are dead now. You can't make a choice anymore."

"I am a spirit. There must be something I can do. Something I can change. That is why I am still here and not in the underworld. I believe Gaya is not so cruel as to force me to remain."

"What would that be?"

"I don't know!"

"Uh."

The old man, Gewa as I learned his name was, spent a lot of time being upset over the death of his three sons. I occasionally humored him, but I mostly ignored him and went back to sleep.

YEAR 67, MONTH 11

[Andy Schulon has died. You gained 9 levels.]

[You are now level 45.]

Oh, I totally forgot about that guy. The guy whose wife came and begged for protection. He lived really long!

"Have you heard? The South Army fell in battle against the demons." Initiates chatted in the garden, and with the levels, my vision and range of hearing improved. There was clearly a passive boost to the effects of skills just from becoming a higher level.

"The demons must be strong."

"You seem to be interested in the conversation." Gewa's spirit sat next to me. I was eavesdropping.

"Yeah, I am. Who's this Andy Schulon?" I was just interested because...well, he seemed...familiar.

"Oh, one of the more famous local fighters. He was considered mid-tier and was known for his defensive skills. He contributed quite significantly to a few battles with his healing and defensive abilities. His front-line combat support had saved many lives."

"Don't armies have mages and healers? What's so special about him?" Was that the hero? It seemed rather strange that a familiar could make such a difference.

"Mainly because he was on the frontline. Healers and mages can provide support, but they do so from the back, and there is usually a delay. Mages and healers can be in front, too, of course, but most mages lack close combat abilities, and that makes them vulnerable. Schulon was a fighter with a defensive mage and healer's abilities, so that was a good niche for him."

I found myself quite impressed by Gewa's analysis.

"Hardly, but every generation has to fight multiple demon kings and help their champions throughout their lives. Combat ability is a necessity. Almost every ten years, it's proven necessary."

True. I'd forgotten that multiple demon kings had appeared since I came into the world. What a cruel, harsh place.

"Hmm."

"A mage can cast shields that provide some reduction in damage as a passive enchantment, but someone like Schulon could create a wooden barrier to block or parry specific attacks. Both are useful but in different ways."

"Makes a lot of sense."

"So, why are you interested in Schulon, again?"

"Hmm. We used to have a familiar contract. I mean, I gave him a familiar a long time ago."

"Huh?"

Gewa's spirit paced around me, seeming to think. My statement had triggered some kind of eureka moment.

"So, you and he have a familiar contract. Does that mean you were the source of his rather unique defensive powers?" He looked at me with hopeful, curious eyes. He had never looked at me like that before, so it freaked me out.

"I...am not sure. But if it was some wood-based ability, I believe that was most likely from my familiar."

"I see, I see." Gewa circled my trunk, and it made me a little dizzy. Then he stopped. "Can you give your familiar contracts to more people?"

That was a strange question. "Where are you going with this?"

Gewa stared. It was weird for a spirit to stare. What was he even looking at? My trunk?

"What?"

He stared some more.

"Seriously, what?"

"You have power to reduce casualties in battle. Imagine if the world had hundreds of warriors with incredible defensive powers, we would see less death, and we would have higher-level warriors all around because they would all survive longer."

"Hmm."

"What 'hmm?' Am I wrong?"

No, Gewa had a point, so I wondered how many familiar contracts I could give.

[You can presently grant twelve familiar contracts. There are no familiar contracts utilized at the moment. Total number of familiar contracts increases with every level gained.]

"What are your concerns, tree spirit? Or do you not care about human lives?" Gewa pushed. "Grant more familiar contracts and let those with your powers protect more people!"

Why should I? Giving familiar contracts made sense because I gained experience from it, but...

Frankly, I didn't know why I was hesitating. I looked at Gewa and considered my response, but all the thinking gave me a headache, so I decided to take a nap.

YEAR 68, MONTH 1

"Your naps are really long."

"Time moves differently for trees like me," I responded, but then I wondered why I did. Maybe reincarnation meant an entirely new set of experiences in this world.

"So...familiars?" Gewa kept pushing, and I ignored him. I still wanted to think, and he mumbled something about me and my absurd timeframes, but then again, maybe I should take a chance.

A druid dropped by as we spoke. "Ah, you are doing well." The new part of my trunk had reached a reasonable size now, right next to the stump. The surface of the stump was still charred black, but it was healing.

"Hi," I reached out telepathically.

The druid startled, and he looked around. "Is...is anybody there?"

"No one. Only me, the tree."

"Huh?!" He stared at me. "You...talk?"

"Yes. Do you want a familiar contract?" I could be blunt like that.

"Uh...no."

Okay, maybe I was a little too blunt.

"Are you a tree spirit?"

"Yes."

The druid paced. "So, what kind of tree spirit are you?"

What...what kind of question is that?

"Uh..."

The druid looked puzzled. "Ah, I mean, like, are you looking for help with breeding or spreading your seeds, are you the type that wants special nutrients or fertilizer, or do you want help with pests? Tree spirits are usually not chatty. And they only give familiars to those who have done a great deal of service for them, like after helping them through a difficult winter or battling a horrible disease."

Oh.

"So, do you need help with something? Is that why you are offering familiars?"

Hmm.

The druid circled a few more times. "I heard you survived a demon king's attack. Maybe you need help with your wound. Is that it?"

Wait. Stop. Talk to me, don't put words in my mouth. I tried to talk to him, but it seemed he was caught in some kind of monologue and just presumed I needed help. Why? Couldn't he hear me?

He stood over the stump. "Your wounds are fully healed, though. Ah, tree spirits, always being so vague and needing us druids to guess what you need."

"Wait. WAIT!"

"I know, I will give you some time, and I will come back next month, okay? Trees need time to think, right?" The druid walked off.

"WAIT!" *Oh, come on!* I was literally shouting, and he just walked away.

"Are druids normally so dense?" Frustrated, I looked at Gewa.

Gewa shrugged. "Druids tend to be stuck in their own world. Mages. Magic is everything, and it consumes them."

"But druids aren't mages?"

"They are to me."

YEAR 68, MONTH 2

The mood was tense. Soldiers covered in injuries and wounds came in by the cartloads or were pushed into the temple as I watched from the garden. I imagined blood everywhere and the foul stench from the dead and dying.

Or maybe it was just the newer initiates. They constantly complained about how strong the smell was.

"How many more?"

"A lot more, Caretaker," an initiate responded. The caretaker was like the lead priest of the Gaya temple, and he handled most of the administrative matters.

"Demons?" The caretaker perched over an injured man, using some kind of healing ability.

"Yes, Caretaker. Beast-type demons, about a hundred from the rift," an initiate explained while he assisted the wounded soldiers. Another initiate nearby helped support those who could walk. The injuries were bad. The soldiers groaned, shouted, or screamed.

Initiates put up tents in the garden and sorted the wounded according to the severity of their injuries. Those who needed less immediate attention were relegated to the garden. So quite a lot of the wounded and their caregivers were nearby, well within the range of my abilities.

"I didn't lose a limb," one injured soldier vented at the guy next to him. "I had a scare when the demons lunged for my arm. Thanks to the other guys."

"First battle?"

He nodded. "I-I just froze when that beast roared like that. I didn't expect that."

"Their roar has a [Fear] effect. You are lucky to receive just a few cuts."

"Yeah. Just a gash. It will probably heal and be a manly scar later on. Maybe you can get girls with it," another soldier added, trying to lighten the mood and downplay how bad the wound was.

"Girls don't like scars," one of them countered.

"Says who? I've met girls who like scars. They say it looks really tough, and they feel safe when they see it."

"No way."

"You guys are disgusting," a female soldier commented, and then she turned away and faced a sleeping female soldier.

"Hey, we didn't die facing those beast-demons. Cut me some slack. I am just happy to live another day."

"Yeah, yeah." I was sure the female probably rolled her eyes at that.

"Did you kill any of those beasts?" a soldier asked the others. There were about thirty of them in the courtyard, and they rested in the makeshift tents. Most carried a mix of light scratches or gashes. They wouldn't die, but they needed medical attention to prevent disease and infection.

"No. Their hides are so thick. If I had one of those magic swords, maybe I would have gotten a kill or two."

"Your skills, did they not work?"

"They did, but they're not enough."

"When do you think it's our turn?" one of the soldiers who could walk asked as he sat next to another soldier.

"Once the heavily injured ones are dealt with," an initiate answered as they handed out water and some light food.

"Yeah. We understand." The soldier nodded. "How bad is it in there?"

"Bad. Quite a few will not live through the night."

The soldiers glanced at each other. They sighed, but most were probably secretly relieved they made it out mostly fine.

An initiate looked at me. "Oh, I think that tree produces fruit every now and then. It is edible, so feel free to take it. We're short of regular food."

"Ah."

I produced two or three small peach-like fruits per week, but if I wanted to, I could trigger a small bloom to produce more fruits overnight. I felt like helping, which would hopefully lead to some familiar contracts.

The next day, I produced ten small fruits, all with a mild healing effect. The soldiers didn't hesitate and consumed them.

"Tastes kind of bland."

"Feels like I am eating some kind of disgusting forest herb."

"If you don't like it, you can starve your ass instead." One grateful soldier smiled.

I felt a bit slighted at the comments, and I realized I didn't have any skills that enhanced the taste of my fruits. Such human aspects should be considered, after all.

"I feel a bit better, though. I think the fruit has a healing effect..." [Appraisal]. One soldier held up his half-eaten fruit, and he looked at it inquisitively. There were skills like [Appraisal], too, and I wondered how it compared with my [Inspection] skills.

A loud horn blared, so loud my trunk vibrated, and my leaves rustled.

"Oh. That is not good..." Some of the soldiers looked at each other. "Another attack?"

"Looks like it." The soldiers who were capable stood. "We should go."

An initiate ran out. "No, you guys must rest. Going there with your injuries will just make it worse."

"But I am fully healed." A few of the men with light injuries had recovered as a result of the fruits.

The initiate looked at them and noticed their recovery. "Let me...let me get the caretaker to verify before we let you out. I can't sign you out without his approval."

The soldier nodded. "Yes, yes. Normal tracking procedure. Please, hurry and get the caretaker. The army needs our help if this attack is anything like the previous one."

The initiate ran and called for the caretaker. The soldiers glanced at their fellow soldiers.

"You guys better eat more of that fruit, then. Need you people back on the field once you are fine."

"Yeah." The soldiers shrugged. "Stay safe and don't get killed."

"We won't."

At that point, one of the soldiers walked close to me. "Hey, thanks for the fruit."

Since he was beside me, I pounced on the opportunity and immediately offered a familiar contract. The pop-up startled the soldier, and he stared for a while. "Oh. Okay." He accepted the deal, and then he looked at the other soldiers. "Hey, go and say thanks. You might get something."

Some of them laughed and walked away, but two others came over and gave me a pat on the trunk. Similarly, I offered both a familiar contract, and they accepted, after their initial shock.

"Hey, did the tree just—"

"Yes." The other nodded.

"What happened?" Those who were still injured were curious because they saw the startled expressions on the three soldiers' faces.

"This tree gave each of the three of us a familiar contract."

"Really?"

"What does it do?"

[Ironbark Skin]

One of the soldier's skin glistened a brownish shade. "Some defensive skills and healing skills. It is a tree familiar."

"Hey, this is useful." The soldier right next to me tapped my trunk lightly. "Thanks."

"Everyone! Those who say they have healed, please, let me check. Come over." The caretaker arrived and examined the soldiers.

He was surprised, but they were healed, so he let them go.

"Thanks, Caretaker."

The recovered soldiers left, and those remaining, about twenty, looked at each other. After a while, they started talking again.

"You think this tree can give us a familiar contract?" One of the injured soldiers approached.

"I still can give a few more, if you guys are not believers of Gaya," I replied to him telepathically.

"Ah!" The injured soldier lost his balance and almost fell. "I-it talked!"

"It did? I didn't hear anything."

"I-it talked into my head!"

"What did it say?"

"Uhm. I think...I think it said it can give a few more contracts if we are not followers of Gaya."

"Huh. But we are in a Temple of Gaya? Is this tree not a Gaya's spirit?"

"I'll go call the caretaker again."

The caretaker approached and then looked at the injured soldier. "You said this tree can give familiar contracts if we don't believe in Gaya?"

"Uh, yes."

I attempted to reply but was repulsed by some telepathic barrier.

The caretaker looked at me and then touched my trunk.

[Detect Evil] and [Detect Spirit].

His eyes widened. "It really *is* a spirit." He looked at me and then summoned an initiate to fetch some materials while chewing on some kind of leaf.

[Ethereal vision].

"Hello, tree spirit." The caretaker looked at me, and then he noticed Gewa next to me. "And you, too, old friend."

"Hey." Gewa smiled.

"Hi."

"Who and what are you?"

"I am a tree."

"But you have a spirit. That is rare."

That contradicted the statement I received from Mozart. I thought he said only trees of a certain size had spirits.

"Yes. I do have a spirit, but I don't know whether I am rare."

"You told the soldiers you cannot give them familiars if they are believers of Gaya?"

"Yes. Your believers will reject a nature familiar."

The caretaker thought for a while, and then he said, "Hmmm...must be the scriptures. Our god allows us to use only certain familiars."

He then looked at the soldiers. "Any of you not believers?"

"I'm not." A soldier walked over. "Not yet, at least."

"Can you give him a familiar contract?" the caretaker asked me. "I will inspect the familiar, and that will greatly help me assess what I should do."

I offered the soldier a familiar contract as the caretaker chewed a different kind of leaf.

"Accept the contract and open your menu. Oh, and eat this leaf."

The soldier nodded, accepted the familiar contract, and munched on the leaf the caretaker handed him. Seriously, did they have weird drug-like leaves in this world? Wait, they must have. It was a fantasy world.

Then his menu appeared for all to see. It was far more complicated than the menu I had. I wondered how I could see it, but I just could.

[Tree Familiar Level 1.]
[Element: Earth and Wood.]
[Rank: Nature Aspect.]
[Alignment: Neutral.]
[Active Skills: Ironbark Skin, Healing Fruit, Minor Regeneration, Wood Shield]
[Passive: Damage resistance, Improved Healing, Earth Magic and Wood Magic Enhancement]

Hey, there were more skills than I remembered.

"So, is the tree evil, Caretaker? Should we revoke the contract?"

"No, probably not. It is just not aligned to Gaya."

"Trees have alignment as well?"

The caretaker shrugged. "No idea. Still, you soldiers can accept the familiar if you want to. I think it will be helpful for the battle ahead. As for me, I need to go talk to some druids."

YEAR 68, MONTH 3

"Move it somewhere else," the caretaker said.

"Yes, Caretaker. Is this really necessary?"

"Yes. I brought this matter up with the temple leaders, and the conclusion is that we, as a temple, cannot accept a spirit that doesn't accept Gaya in our compound. It would be perceived negatively by the common folk if a tree in our temple tells them not to believe in Gaya."

"It is just a tree." The young initiate seemed rather baffled by it.

"I would have chopped it down if it was just a tree, but it is not just a tree but a spirit tree. One that has been helpful, and I don't see a need to destroy it. So moving it to a neutral location would be better."

The temple initiate and the druid next to him both nodded. "Understood."

It didn't take long for them to decide. Other druids came over, surrounded me, and once again, they moved me.

"The caretaker says you're a spirit, so we've got to move you," the druid said apologetically. "We will be gentle, and you will not come to any harm."

Before I could respond, they chanted, and the earth shook. My roots departed from the dirt and earth, and I lost consciousness.

Seriously, moving was really annoying.

YEAR 68, MONTH 4

Freeka.

I was moved to a small village with about fifty or so inhabitants. Elves. All of them.

It seemed to me that the presence of a spirit tree didn't go well with a lot of people in the city, so the druids decided to move me out into the villages. A spirit not aligned to the main religion of the world was seen as heretical to some.

But one's loss was another's gain. The elves were happy to have a tree spirit in their small village, and I could tell their joy from their daily conversations. The leader of the village spoke to the druids and requested I be placed in the center of the village, apparently for my protective powers.

Whatever those were.

The elves were quite chatty, and I met the leader of the village, a middle-aged man, Ricola.

"A tree spirit is good fortune for our small village."

He gave off a pleasant feeling, so I immediately offered him a familiar contract the moment I could. I wondered then whether it was a skill the village chief had.

"An honor, oh, tree spirit."

"If anyone else wants a tree familiar, please, let me know," I said.

"Certainly."

I ended up giving all my remaining familiar slots to eight more of the village's warriors. It helped them to protect the village.

YEAR 68, MONTH 5

Ricola's wife, Laufen, was pregnant. They came over and asked for my blessing. I responded that I couldn't give blessings, but if they were to fall sick, they could come to me for some healing fruits.

YEAR 68, MONTH 6

The elven kids decorated me for a festival of the earth. The elves in this world were a little animistic. They believed in spirits of nature, and their god was the nameless great mother of nature. Yet it wasn't as if all elves believed in the same gods.

"Trees are spirit of nature, so this festival is also dedicated to you." An older female elf, Casshern, led the ceremony. She took the role of the master of ceremonies as she was a living record of elvish traditions.

They ate fruits and vegetables, and some hunted meat. They prayed to the earth for a good harvest, a good hunt, and protection against demons, monsters, and humans. They had some kind of fermented sap, which made them high, and they danced through the night.

YEAR 68, MONTH 8

The tax collectors from the Kingdom of Salah paid a visit to the elves of Freeka.

Ricola paid with what little gold or silver coins they had. Some of the elves in the village sold their excess foods in the city for coin, just to raise funds and pay their taxes.

After the tax collectors left, Ricola sat next to me and complained, "These tax collectors are bloodsucking leeches. We get no protection from the army, yet we are forced to pay taxes lest we suffer the wrath of the kingdom's tax enforcement force."

"Ah. Do you have demons here?" I suddenly wondered how elves dealt with demons.

"Oh, tree spirit, we do fight demons. But demons are usually drawn to places with many souls for them to kill. Sparsely populated places like our village are mostly spared from their wrath, or so we believe. It is only when the demon king arrives, when the elves throughout the continent gather to fight it, or used to."

"I see."

One of the elf children ran over and knocked on my trunk. "Hey, tree. Do you think you can give me a familiar?"

Ricola patted him on the head. "Brislach, please don't

disturb the tree spirit. He has given all his familiars to the adults."

Brislach pouted and walked away.

"How's Laufen doing?" I asked, even though I saw with my [Spirit Vision] that she was well. The skill was quite good at telling the overall health of a person because a weaker person's spirit tended to wobble, fade, or blink.

"She is well. It's been a few years since the last birth in our village. Everyone looks forward to it, especially Brislach and Wahlen. They cannot wait for someone younger than them to appear."

YEAR 68, MONTH 10

I t was harvest season before winter. This year's harvest was better than the last, and Ricola said it was because of me.

I couldn't tell because I didn't see a skill that boosted harvest, but apparently, as the village head, he had a skill that informed him of the skills that affected the area. Maybe it was race passive for spiritual trees, so things just naturally grew a little bit better.

YEAR 68, MONTH 11

The elven villagers came over and chatted under the shade. I'd grown quickly, and now I was close to my size before I'd gotten chopped down by the demon king.

The ladies had their leisure time and activity under the shade. Things like sorting or cutting through their harvest or occasionally processing hunted animals. The elderly used my shade to teach the young. Some elves believed my presence improved learning, but I suspected that might have been a placebo effect.

I spent time listening to Casshern, too, and she recited some of her ancient history. She claimed a tree spirit was also a living record of elven history should there be no surviving elf.

YEAR 68, MONTH 12

Winters were mild. I produced healing fruits, but their effectiveness remained poor.

The men fought monsters during this time as it seemed winter came with its own set of monsters. Nobody was seriously hurt, so the mood was fine. One of the guys, Jura, was the village's best fighter. He was really good with a sword and a spear, and he was going to be level forty soon.

Laufen and the ladies would collect whatever winter fruits I produced to make tea.

YEAR 69, MONTH 2

Another festival to mark the end of winter. The elves prepared a fruit cocktail. The elves also came over to vent their frustrations, mainly about how things were done by other elves. Like everyone, they had small, petty conflicts with each other.

I generally just listened. I was no counselor. But listening seemed to be what they needed.

YEAR 69, MONTH 3

L aufen safely gave birth to a baby girl and named her Lausanne. The elves had a small party, and tradition dictated elvish babies be given the juice of a spirit tree if there was one.

I grew her a fruit with all the healing abilities I had.

YEAR 69, MONTH 4

One of the elves sat next to me and spoke of dire news. He returned from the nearest city from their bi-weekly market visits. Rumors had been going around that the demon king would descend soon, their once-a-decade disaster.

Human cultists had also emerged. Some professed to be able to control demons and had usurped control of distant villages, and some were puritanical zealots who couldn't accept other races. Bad news for the elves.

The focus remained mostly on the demons. A time for unity, it was said, as the demon king would rise once again to threaten the world.

To some extent, I wondered why cultists bothered when the gods consistently summoned heroes to defeat the demon king. It wasn't humans of this world who defeated them. The gods essentially obtained external contractors to do the dirty job.

"Will the gods summon heroes to defeat the demon king?" I knew from my records that it was what happened, but I had to ask the locals to be sure.

The elf sighed. "Probably. They always do."

"Why the sigh? Is it not a good thing?"

"Every time heroes descend to this world, we trade the methodical destruction of the demon king for the reckless destruction of the otherworldly heroes. We know what the demons want, but the heroes are unpredictable, and they are the worst rulers."

"Elves don't look at them as heroes, too?"

The elf paused before giving a measured answer. "The elves, as a society, are of two minds about it. There is a faction—well, no, not really a formal faction, but just a group—that believe in the gods' heroes, as they occasionally appear as elves, and these elven heroes are the gods' blessings to the elves. Another faction believes the gods don't want to summon the heroes, but because the destruction wrought by the demon king is too great, they have to. So heroes are a desperate response from the gods. A bitter pill for a horrifying disease."

"What do you believe?" I asked while I digested the fact.

"Neither."

Hmm.

"Has the demon king fallen to a hero or a fighter from this world before?" I wondered.

The elf stared at my trunk. I assumed he was deep in thought. Or maybe he thought I asked a stupid question.

"Legend has it that the demon kings of the past were all defeated by summoned heroes. So, no." I didn't understand.

"Oh."

Why couldn't the locals kill the demon king? They gained levels, too, obviously, so what made the heroes special? The gods must have given summoned heroes something that allowed them to slay the demon kings. Blessings?

YEAR 69, MONTH 6

A small group of soldiers arrived, so the villagers were tense. Soldiers were not a good sign. Ricola had talks with the captain of the soldiers, and it seemed the kingdom was gathering recruits to fight the demon at some strategic pass.

No one went with the captain as the village was already small. He wasn't happy, but after a while, they left. They had other places to visit.

YEAR 69, MONTH 9

Baby Lausanne started to mumble. She was really cute. I couldn't help but remember my own nephew back on Earth. *Ah, home.* I wondered how things were back there. The elves lived tough lives, but generally, they were happy, and many of the ladies enjoyed their time with the new baby.

YEAR 69, MONTH 10

I gained two levels when the men returned from their hunt, and I wasn't sure why. As I recalled, familiars only transferred experience when their holders died. So maybe the two levels came from other ways.

[Level 47]

The men told me they had to fight a giant beast, and thanks to my familiar skills, they succeeded.

I also gained two rather strange skills one morning, [Nourish] and [Secret Hideout].

[Secret Hideout] created a small room right beneath my roots. It fit two adults.

I wondered whether it was because the children, Brislach and Wahlen, frequently played hide and seek with my roots and trunk. Maybe they should play a bit more if that led to skills.

This year's harvest was somehow even better than last year's, and it seemed when I was around, the soil replenished its nutrients a little faster, so we went into that year's planting season with the ground more fertile than before.

YEAR 69, MONTH 11

Lausanne was feverish. I made a small fruit of healing, and her parents fed her the juice of the fruit. It helped a little, and her parents calmed.

Ricola also had an argument with the Salah Kingdom's tax collectors over the higher taxes, but eventually, he relented and paid. They argued over protections and all that, and I thought I briefly heard the tax collectors cursing the elves under their breath. Racism was a thing here. Or was it 'speciesism'?

YEAR 70, MONTH 1

The men reported more human armies on the move. The frequent movement disturbed animals close to them. They said it was generally rare for armies to move about when winter was still so strong, so the demons' attack must have been really intense.

Salah's armies often conscripted men who were poorly motivated and paid, and they were more prone to fleeing than actually fighting. To move them in winter wasn't a good sign.

Somehow, by just existing, I also gained a level [Level 48], and I finally obtained my first attack skill. I wondered whether it was due to my constant interactions with the villagers.

Oh, well, an attack skill! [Root Strike]

YEAR 70, MONTH 2

There was great unrest in the human cities, and among the elves, too. They looked into the sky every night, and Casshern, the old elf lady, explained it was an ominous sign. Six stars aligned in a hexagonal shape: the Mark of the Warp. According to their lore, the warp signified a weakening, a breach in the rift that separated us and the demon world. In other words, the demon king would soon return.

Some elves dismissed it as mumbo-jumbo as those signs didn't appear in previous iterations of the demon king. If I could sigh, I would, but all I could do was sway my branches. Or shake. I probably looked like a shaking tree.

"Worry not, the gods will look after us." Casshern nodded, and she sipped from a hot cup of tea. It was still cold this time of year. The thought of how hot or cold it was somehow made the system give me a new menu. It was a temperature bar, and it reminded me of weather widgets on my smartphone.

"How do you know for sure?"

"They always have, tree spirit. Legends have it that we have been invaded by demon kings since time immemorial, and every time, our world triumphed."

As financial advisors often said, past performance wasn't indicative of future returns, but I let Casshern continue.

"The stars. Despite the warp, in the distance, there is hope."

I wondered how the stars looked in this world. I couldn't 'see' after all.

YEAR 70, MONTH 3

Baby Lausanne crawled around and over my roots, and I got nervous every time she looked like she was going to fall. The feeling reminded me of my babysitting days. I wondered how my nephew was. Maybe he had grandchildren by now. After all, seventy years had passed.

On a more serious note, the men fought a few lesser demons while hunting, and the presence of demons so near to their home worried them, so they made some changes to their hunting practices.

"When the demon king was about to ascend, the elven nations summoned warriors from all over to take up arms and defend the elvish lands from the demon," Casshern explained. "Or, at least, they used to when the elven kingdoms had some semblance of duty to the world."

"Are we not in the elven nation?" I vaguely remembered not being in the elven nation, but since being relocated to Freeka, I had no idea whether that statement was still valid.

"We are not, tree spirit. But some of the men still feel a desire or a dream to answer the calling."

"Jura, perhaps?"

"Maybe. But while we are happy to let our sons and daughters choose whether they want to answer the call, the village is left with the consequences, and we have to figure out its defenses without our best fighters."

"Ah. That is indeed a problem."

"Yes, yes." She sipped her tea, and her wrinkly arms touched my protruding roots. I vaguely felt her, but my sense of touch was hardly accurate.

"How old are you, Casshern?" I suddenly realized I didn't know her age, but then again, age was just a number. In fact, after I asked that question, I realized how disconnected that question was from the previous topic.

"Ah. I am old, tree spirit, perhaps three hundred and thirty years by now. I don't remember the exact year anymore. But elves can live up to a thousand years, maybe even more. Humans, if they practice magic, can live similarly long."

Given her age, shouldn't she be very high level?

"So magic can extend one's life." Our conversations tended to drift far from where we started. I would ask about things I spotted along the way, and Casshern generally let me go off on a tangent. Perhaps she just thought it was how spirits thought and talked. Or maybe my mind was jumbled by being a tree.

"Indeed. It is a blessing and a curse. Live long enough to see so many demon kings come and go. They are as natural to this world as a typhoon or a massive earthquake. Long enough to see tree spirits die."

"Have you ever met other...tree spirits?"

Casshern looked to the night sky again, staring at stars I couldn't see. "Once. But when the demon king Astaroth ascended on my town, the tree spirit died."

"Ah."

"Tree spirits play an important role in a proper elven society. An elven village or town without one is nothing more than a temporary gathering of elves. So many elven towns never last beyond a century because they lacked a tree spirit as their guardian."

"Could you explain more?" I didn't really know what I'd gotten myself into when I transformed into a tree, so this was like crash course 101 on what a tree needed to do.

"For us, the wood elves, a large segment of us believe the tree spirit is the guide after death. A birth under the tree spirit's blessing will be stronger than one without, and on our deaths, we believe our souls will be guided by the tree spirit. Through it, we will return to our nameless mother. Our warriors are stronger, our druids wiser, and our walls sturdier. Our ingrained potential is best expressed when a tree spirit is present to channel our strength and guide us."

If I could gulp, I would. In fact, I felt like I needed a nap. I didn't think I could play such an important role.

"Tell me about the other tree spirits, Casshern. What are they like?" I was curious how those other tree spirits did it.

"The one I met so many years ago was rather imposing. Its presence dominated the town, and its protection allowed it to resist years of human and demon attacks. An elven town with a powerful tree spirit is like a strong fortress. The roots of the tree spirit merge and grow into the walls, transforming, reinforcing, and healing it from damage."

"And yet, it still fell."

"Yes. But not to any lesser threat. It fell to a powerful demon lord. A monstrous being shaped like a corrupted demonic dragon. It burned the tree and the entire town..." Casshern's voice drifted somewhat at the end.

"Oh." I survived the Demon King Baal. Didn't that make me super impressive? Or maybe I got lucky? I thought I got lucky because the demon king didn't press its attack and left after one strike. It just figured cutting me away and leaving its fire on me was sufficient to kill me.

So any high-level demon should actually be able to kill me fairly easily. After all, I was immobile, so dodging was out of the question. The only way I saw how I could really survive was if I had a powerful offense that I could slay the demons with before they got close or a powerful defense that I could shrug off even their best shot. Or, ideally, both.

I supposed if I was lucky, I wouldn't have to fight demons. But that was unlikely, given how frequent they appeared.

YEAR 70, MONTH 4

Humans came again. This time, it was a smaller group of four soldiers, led by a captain. They rode horses and were relatively lightly armed. Their armor was ceremonial in nature.

"The King of Salah has decreed that each village in his royal highness's domain is to dispatch five able-bodied men to join the king's royal demon-slaying army," the captain commanded.

"We cannot spare five men. If we send five, it means we will lose our ability to defend ourselves or hunt for food," Ricola replied, defending their position.

"This is not open for negotiation, villager. The king commands, and its people must answer." The captain's voice was stern, and he sounded like he had heard this excuse a thousand times.

"We cannot give five men."

"Then I shall mark your village as disobeying the king's orders."

"How about two?"

"No negotiations, villager," the captain spat out. "You will be marked if less than five men show up at Hammerhold Fort."

"Let me discuss with my fellow villagers."

"You will send five, or your village will be punished," the captain repeated.

The villagers huddled, and words flew. They spoke and argued, but eventually, Ricola faced the captain again.

"We will send five men," Ricola answered, "but not today."

"Not today, villager. Send your five men to report at Hammerhold Fort in two months." The captain nodded, passed them a letter. "Bring that letter along. Without it, your village is deemed not to have provided your men." The small group left on horses.

After they were gone, Ricola and the men kneeled before me. The decision bothered them greatly, and now they sought my counsel.

"Oh, wise tree spirit, do you have some words for us?"

Oh, damn. I was no great, wise tree spirit! I didn't know what to do during this kind of time! *Uh, wait. What should I do?*

"I don't know, Ricola. When do the men need to leave?"

"Hammerhold Fort is a month away, so a month from today."

In hopes of finding an answer, I took a nap. Soon, I had a dream.

Actually, it was a nightmare. I rarely got those in this world.

I saw a demon. A large demon. Lots of them. In my dreams, I saw them in color, in detail, and they reminded me of monsters out of video games. They were huge, dead people all around. Their path was one of destruction. Dead bodies, scattered all over the floor, burning forests, and a tree. A tree on fire, with corpses pinned on its branches. A large, monstrous demon walked through the corpses, its steps crushing every corpse in its way to a pulp.

I felt fear and shivered.

Was it coming for me?

The head turned, and its red eyes gazed at me.

At that instant, I was jolted out of the nightmare. A notification popped up.

[Demon King Andras has ascended.]

Fire. Death. Destruction. A thousand and one screams. It was as if the world screamed as one, and it was deafening. My imaginary ears hurt.

Casshern touched my trunk, and she felt like she was worried.

"You were shaking, tree spirit. What ill news do you bring?"

"The demon king is here."

"Oh. Oh..." Casshern's wrinkly old hands shook, and she cried out. The villagers all reacted in shock, and they rushed out of their houses and gathered around me.

Ricola spoke, standing before the small gathering of elves around me. "Is there something you wish to tell us, tree spirit?"

"The demon king is here."

Ricola froze for a brief second, then he took a deep breath and told the children to return home, leaving the adults behind. He then faced the rest of the villagers and repeated what I told him. The villagers looked at each other. Jura was the first to speak. "Then we should join the king's army and assist the heroes in crushing the demon king before it gets too strong."

Another man shook his head. "Only heroes can kill the demon king. The best the army can do is clear a path and take out the rest of the king's champions. But most will die on such a mission."

"Ah yes. But...but there are no living heroes left. The heroes died in their battle against Demon King Baal. Until the gods summon new heroes to this world, there is no way of defeating the king," the elf who usually traveled to the cities explained.

"So this army is doomed." Ricola sighed.

"Indeed. We should not join the army..."

"Would you rather face demons or what's left of a destroyed army? If we stay in our village, maybe a hero will emerge before we are attacked."

The villagers stood and argued till morning, but eventually, they arrived at a decision. "Thank you for your guidance, tree spirit. We choose to stay. The human kingdoms have never protected us, so we have no reason to listen to this king's demands."

I didn't really say anything to that, but hey, it seemed that was what they wanted anyway.

YEAR 70, MONTH 5

The men were hard at work building fortifications around the village. It would be difficult to hunt once the demons appeared more regularly. The demon king's presence had historically been accompanied by a surge in demons all around the world. It was just the way demon kings were with their ever-corrupting powers.

"Many will die," Casshern said, lamenting the demon king's presence.

"If there are no heroes, that would be the outcome."

"Every demon king has led to death. Countless deaths."

"Why?"

"Because it is so."

"Why no angel king?" I sometimes wondered why the enemies were always demon kings. Couldn't they be more creative? Little did I know that the demons were actually quite varied in terms of powers and appearance.

"That would be...*heroes*?" Casshern looked at me. I probably asked a stupid question.

YEAR 70, MONTH 6

An injured group of adventurers arrived at the village. The group of four fighters were all bleeding heavily, and two had lost an arm to what appeared to be a huge monster bite.

Ricola immediately brought them to me.

"Ugh..." Their spirit was weak, the sign of a person at the edge of death. What was normally a consistently strong white light now faded like a flickering lightbulb.

[Healing Fruit]

I created four fruits, and Ricola and another elf assisted with feeding them.

Their wounds stabilized, but the lost arm couldn't be repaired, not with my present abilities.

"What did this?" Ricola asked as he sat next to one of the adventurers and helped them eat the fruit.

"Demons."

The adventurers spoke of a new breed of demons—large, ferocious, and with teeth able to tear apart any creature. It sounded like hyperbole, honestly. Giants that walked on two feet with massive, magically reinforced jaws and thick, skin-like armor. Some had horns along their backs.

Ah, demons.

"Are all demon kings the same?" I asked Casshern, but she didn't know.

The adventurers' condition stabilized, at least physically. The two adventurers who lost their arms experienced emotional instability, and they lamented their lost future as adventurers. They would be nothing more than beggars now. It was so bad that Ricola separated the two one-armed adventurers from the others to prevent their negativity from spreading.

"Have we met any demons described by these adventurers?"

"I think these descriptions were pretty standard. Fangs, claws, scales, and horns."

YEAR 70, MONTH 7

The adventurers eventually fully recovered and left. The king's demon-slaying army had started their march for one of the heavily contested passes. The demonic rift was on the other side. News didn't speak of the demon king, at least not yet. Strange. Maybe they didn't get the message.

YEAR 70, MONTH 8

A raid occurred. A demon raiding party, if such a concept existed to them. One of the elves on watch spotted a group of thirty demons, led by a slightly larger demon. I called it an elder demon, but I suspected it was just a larger variant.

It wouldn't end well. The elves quickly assembled for battle. The young men and women without combat skills quickly retreated to the slightly fortified village hall. The demons were different from the earlier ones described by the adventurers. These were winged, and they wielded flaming axes forged from some kind of hardened demonic flesh.

The two groups fought, and the elves used everything they had. Every skill, every familiar power they had unlocked. I hoped it would make a slight difference. It was a long fight and led the battle as the strongest of the village. They fought hard, and eventually, they won.

They defeated the demons! But victory came at a cost. These demons were naturally tougher than elves. Even with the advantages provided by the fortifications, familiar blessings, and other tactical advantages, for every five or six demons killed, an elf died despite trying their best, fighting with everything they had.

I wished I could help, but the battle was fought mostly outside of my very limited range.

I saw their spirits fading in the distance, and I tried to reach out to them. *Hey, don't die on me.*

The injured retreated and limped closer, their spirits turning a deathly pale. Their wounds were too severe. My healing fruits couldn't do much, not at this point.

"Four. Four of us too many." Ricola kneeled next to their dying bodies. All of them were placed at my roots. I tried to help, with every single healing ability at my disposal, and it seemed like my branches drooped in failure.

The wounds were too serious, the bleeding too much. There wasn't much I could do, and I felt weak. Useless again. Casshern held the hand of one of the dying fighters. "Death comes to us all, but for some earlier than others. Death may come, but your spirits will never die. Oh, tree spirit, take good care of them."

I gulped.

The four passed on. I saw their spirits fade to darkness, and then there was a brief flicker of light at the end like the last hurrah of a match. They faded away, and their spirits drifted into the ground.

The mood was grim after that.

The men focused on repairs and sharpened their weapons. The women focused on their children. The loss of four men was too much for some, and the only way they could cope was to distract themselves.

At night, when the houses were quiet, some of the men and women came to talk to me.

"How do I move on? I knew him all my life. Things just cannot be the same, can they?"

I had no answer. I was just a tree spirit, and I had no words that could calm the hearts of those who had lost someone. I tried to be sympathetic, but I knew it was no cure for the holes in their hearts.

[Level up! Level 50! You gained the following skills: [Calming Voice] and [Haunted Tree].]

YEAR 70, MONTH 10

More demons attacked. Thankfully, the groups were small. The villagers fought hard, and they were focused. They wanted to avoid any more death. I saw Jura fight harder than ever before.

YEAR 70, MONTH 11

Death came.

Yet it wasn't from demons.

"Village of Freeka!" a roar broke the quiet morning. "You have failed to send what your king required of you. Five soldiers he asked, and you failed."

Ricola and the villagers, those who were up early, quickly woke everyone else. They had a hunch something bad was going to happen. The fact that soldiers came was clearly a sign.

"Elves. The king should have known that elven villages would have no loyalty to the king. Only humans know what it means to live under his majesty's protection."

A small section of the army was there. There were about four hundred men who were comprised of a mix of soldiers, knights, archers, and other fighters. They had insignias of the Salah Kingdom, and they wore the regular uniform and standard issue armor of Salah.

The army surrounded Freeka. There was no retreat, not with their large numbers. Ricola sighed. I noticed they must have taken out the elven sentry.

Ricola offered to talk, to explain. "The demon king has come. Without heroes, the army is doomed!"

"Hush, villager. No, let me correct that. Traitor!" Laughter came from the human army. They were confident, as they should be. They outnumbered the elves almost twenty times over. "I will not listen to your excuses. Those who dare defy the king will be punished."

The army didn't advance, not yet, so the women and children quickly hid. Lausanne, Brislach, Wahlen, Laufen, and two other younger ladies squeezed into the secret hideout beneath my roots. The rest, even the older women, grabbed whatever weapons they could.

"Are you ready, elvish scum? We are going to kill all of you now."

They came with arrows of fire.

The burning arrows rained throughout the village, and they exploded, spreading their flames. They were either enchanted or the archers had a skill that allowed their arrows to behave this way.

"The humans...they don't plan to fight us!" Jura shouted.

The burning arrows exploded midair like fireballs. The flames ignited the roofs, houses, furniture...everything.

More arrows came, and some of the elves tried to deflect them, but it was a fool's idea. There was no way it would work.

"We must break through while we can! That is our only chance!" Jura yelled and mustered the others. A large group of the elves followed his lead. They formed into a wedge, and they charged at the humans at Jura's direction. They all knew it was their only chance of survival. It was that or stay and be trapped in the inferno.

The elven villagers and the human army fought, and while some of them escaped, many died within my spiritual vision. Unlike demons, humans had levels and skills. This was an experienced force, one that had done this type of 'suppression' many times.

I watched in horror as the humans remained firmly outside my [Root Strike] range. The fires expanded, and it felt like a part of me was on fire. But these fires were mild, and they would not kill me. All they did was slightly singe my branches and leaves.

More fire arrows flew toward the village, and my surroundings turned into a blazing inferno. I checked in on the children and women now squeezed into my secret hideout.

They were shaken but still safe. My roots and bark protected them from the flames. They didn't feel the heat, and I suspected the secret hideout was a magical space. I felt relieved I could at least protect them.

The fighting intensified with the few elves who remained. They fought desperately, but then I saw Ricola retreat. He didn't charge through with the rest. Instead, he had stayed back to keep the soldiers away. He staggered, his footsteps unstable as he walked toward me. He was bleeding. His spirit was weak, and more than one arrow had pierced his body.

"Oh, tree spirit, I will soon leave this world."

I tried to heal him, but with multiple arrows and gashes all over his body, it didn't work.

"Please, take care of my children and my wife. Protect them from the demons...and these monsters, too."

"Yes, but don't die," I responded telepathically. I thought he smiled.

From the blaze, an armored soldier emerged. He held up a sword. "Why won't you die!" he shouted and stabbed Ricola.

Then he stabbed and stabbed again. Blood splattered across my trunk and bark. I was too stunned to react. What was this stupid human doing fighting elves when there was a demon king out there?

I felt anger and wanted to retaliate. The anger overwhelmed me, and I used my only offensive skill.

[Root Strike].

A root surged from beneath the earth. It impaled the soldier, and he died, eyes wide in surprise.

There was still fighting in the distance as the elves ran for their lives. Freeka burned in a firestorm. It was hot, but not enough to kill me. I was resistant to fire. Mortal, normal fires couldn't kill me.

I saw one of the elves as she took more hits than she could dish out. Yet she still took them, and she still walked, but her movement seemed unnatural. Her defiance wasn't enough, and she couldn't make it through the blockade, so she retreated. Wounded all over, she collapsed beside me.

"Casshern!"

"Tree spirit..." Two arrows were firmly planted in her chest. "I thought of choosing my place of death. Let me die beside you." She coughed blood.

This was madness.

Two human soldiers with spears closed in. They attempted to stab her.

[Root Strike]. I struck both first, and my roots impaled them, but I was still too slow. One of them had already used a skill, and a spear went through Casshern's chest.

"We will meet again, tree spirit. Elves who die with their tree guardians never truly die."

She collapsed, no longer breathing.

The fire raged on, and the battle came to its conclusion. The humans won overwhelmingly. One by one, the remaining elven fighters perished.

The battle was over, and the humans dragged the corpses of the elves to me.

"Hang them on this tree," the commander of human army said. I counted twenty-five bodies. Maybe fifteen or so had survived and managed to flee. "Then burn the tree."

"What about those who got away, Commander? Should we give chase?"

"Let them run. They will spread the word that disobedience has dire consequences."

The captain surveyed the corpses and walked well within range of my [Root Strike]. I felt as if I had a few more [Root Strike]s left in me.

In my anger, I attacked, two [Root Strike]s aimed at the captain. The roots burst from the ground, and though he saw them, he wasn't fast enough to dodge. He activated some kind of shield, but it wasn't much use. My roots struggled but still cracked through the barrier. One root pierced him right through the heart, and the other root struck his pelvis.

"A druid attack! Fan out and search for our attacker! There must be an elven druid still hiding!" the lieutenant shouted, and he turned around. Strange that he didn't suspect me, the tree. Tree spirits must be really uncommon.

He ran out of range. I felt as if I could still manage another [Root Strike].

I saw a bloody soldier who walked too close to me. "We should totally do this more often. Y'know, killing elves. Always hated these long-eared dudes."

"Rather than talk shit, why don't you find the druid?" another soldier said.

"Chill the fuck out, dude. The druid probably used the last of his magic to take out the captain. If he is still around, he's defenseless now."

"How do you even know?"

These people seemed really apathetic to the loss of their commander. Or maybe death was a common thing for them?

"True."

I saw the village was gone, replaced by a faint outline of rubble. The houses must have all collapsed from the flames.

"This tree is pretty sturdy, even though it's all charred and black," the soldier complained as their fires failed to burn me down.

"Let's just do what the commander said and impale the elves on the tree. Teach these long ears the power of humans," a soldier said.

"That's a little too much, man."

"You killed elves, too. I am merely enjoying the process. Seriously, think about it, elves on a stick like a barbeque."

I agreed with the other human, and with my last [Root Strike], I attacked him for entertaining such an abhorrent idea. I could comprehend war, but plain cruelty was a little bit too much. The root pierced through his armor and his heart.

"Fuck! The druid is still around." The soldiers looked around, and they quickly spread out.

An hour later, they returned.

"What should we do with the bodies?"

"Pile them up with the tree and burn them. Don't want them turning into zombies or food for the demons."

The humans stacked and piled the elves around me and then started a fire. It burned, and I felt helpless, but like the torches before, the fire didn't really hurt me physically, even though I looked charred. Most importantly, the six in my secret hideout were still safe and alive, spared from the heat of the fire.

Still, it stung.

The humans left after some time, deciding their raid was over.

The fire burned the corpses, leaving ash and charred bits of them behind. As the fire raged, the elves in the hideout trembled. I sensed their fear. Their bodies were weak and hungry, so I used [Nourish] to restore them.

So much death.

Was it my fault? Why didn't I ask them to send the five men to the army? A part of me wondered whether I had condemned them by not speaking out. But I decided I hadn't. I may have had a part in giving them the information, but they decided what to do with it.

But I was conflicted. Maybe I had some role. My lack of knowledge of the tensions between humans and elves, and my weakness and inability to protect those who gave me a place in their village and shared their lives with me, could well have played a role.

So many elves, all dead.

The fire burned into the night.

Death.

It stirred a desire, a fury, a need inside me. I felt like I had wasted the last seventy years in this world as a tree, that I had somehow lost my initiative and let things happen as they came. Everywhere I was, I was a bystander, with too little power to intervene meaningfully.

[Ricola Searwind and six others died.]

[You gained a total of 13 levels.]

[You are now level 63.]

[You have unlocked the next species change, upgraded from Spiritual Tree to Magical Tree.]

[Secret Hideout upgraded.]

[Camouflage and Illusions upgraded.]

[Spirit Collection upgraded.]

[Essence Harvesting obtained.]

YEAR 70, MONTH 11
(CONTINUED)

It was a few hours after the raid, and the bodies were a mix of ash and charred flesh. Freeka was destroyed. The inferno had engulfed all the wooden houses and halls. The six crawled out of the secret hideout after the fires burned out. Tears flowed. Laufen cried her heart out. So did Lausanne, Brislach, and Wahlen. The two younger ladies also squeezed into my secret hideout, Emile and Bellerive, or Belle as she was known, also wept for those lost and dead.

Death. The air stunk of it. The charred smell of burned bodies. The girls gagged whenever they accidentally got too close. It took all their willpower to not vomit.

"What are we to do now?" Laufen looked at Emile and Belle, who were in their teens. Their eyes were wet, their faces dirty from all the ash and soot. Everyone was covered in it. Well, more accurately, everything was *coated* in it.

"Keep Lausanne in the hideout. It is too dirty and dusty." Laufen sighed, and she held onto what looked to be a burned memento—Ricola's personal belongings. She was the eldest here, the only full adult left.

Emile carried her, and once the hideout door opened, she

gasped. "Uh, Laufen, the hideout looks different." The hideout had transformed once it was empty, the effect of my new levels.

Laufen shook her head. "Not now, Emile."

Belle was curious, and so she walked over, and she, too, gasped. "The hideout has definitely changed."

Brislach and Wahlen joined in. "It really has changed!"

A proper room. It was still small, but it was more comfortable than the space earlier and was about the size of a cellar.

"I gained a skill upgrade for [Secret Hideout]. I think all of you had to come out for it to reset and change into the new one."

The magical space was a creation of my ability, even if I didn't really understand it. It had grown wider and taller, and right in the center of the ceiling was a glowing fruit that provided a faint light. With more space, at least we solved one problem, which was the issue of shelter. The elves had a place to stay for a while. The elves nodded and said a prayer.

Lausanne was now one-and-a-half years old, and she could walk by herself. Brislach and Wahlen babysat her, while the three older elves went around, surveying what wasn't lost.

The three older ladies tried to recover whatever usable items they could find. They hoped that some managed to survive the blaze, somehow protected by the rubble above them.

But what was most important now was food.

"Are we...are we gonna starve?" Emile asked. "All our food is gone."

Laufen sighed, but then she steeled herself. She stood right in front of my black trunk. "Oh, tree spirit, are you there? Can you make some fruits?"

"Yes," I responded to her request. At the same time, my body quickly recovered from the fire damage. "I heard Emile's concerns, and you may eat my fruits. I will make more."

A few of my black branches displayed a burst of life, and their branches twisted and turned. New feelers grew that transformed to fruit. They might not be satisfying or tasty, but the fruit would deal with their hunger.

As they continued to search the rubble, the elves recovered hidden chests buried beneath the houses, a place where elves stored their most important items. Multiple chests survived. The fires somehow spared those items buried beneath.

In those hidden chests, they found clothes, weapons, money, and a lot of personal items.

They moved all the recovered goods to the hideout.

"Don't go too far, girls. We don't know how far the humans went," Laufen warned, still cautious.

They nodded and mostly walked around the remains of their village. I sensed their sorrow. Every now and then, they cried as they stumbled over something that reminded them of what was. They still needed to come to terms with the destruction. Soon, they returned.

Brislach, the little girl, asked, "Tree spirit, are you okay? You are all black." She played with Lausanne and Wahlen with some sticks and stones.

"I am recovering, Brislach. Rain will wash away these black stains."

"Uhm, why are the humans so evil? They killed us," Brislach looked at me as she asked. "Why did they do this to us?"

Ah, a question about the nature of man. If I could answer that, maybe I could win a Nobel Peace Prize or something.

"I don't know, but you must be stronger. All of us must be stronger."

Laufen, Emile, and Belle spent their time sorting through the rubble, and by the end of the day, everything usable was now in the hideout. I really admired Laufen's ability to just tough it out to get things done. Or maybe the work was her way of distracting herself from her loss. It didn't take long for them to fall asleep on the floor, exhausted.

As for me, I looked at each of my skills and abilities once again, testing out each and every one of them.

[Essence Harvest].

From the ashes, from the burned wood, faint energies emerged, and they joined together into a ball.

[Material Collection: Obtained Essence of Lesser Courage x 1, Essence of the Sword (minor) x 1, Essence of Spear (minor) x 1, Essence of Lesser Fire x 2, Essence of Death x 1.]

Oh? What do these do?

[Essences are a type of material used to permanently create and teach skills, enchant or imbue creatures and items, or combine them to create stronger essences.]

I pondered that as the night crept toward dawn.

The next day, a small pack of demons appeared. Without the walls and the fighters, and with the smell of death lingering in the air, it was no surprise demons gravitated to such places. Four demon hounds sniffed about. It was a tiny pack, but with only Laufen having any knowledge of combat, they fled back to me. Laufen had no confidence in taking them all on her own. Not at all.

"Run!" I told her. There was no need to fight. Laufen was afraid, but she wanted to protect the others. She stood at the hideout's entrance with her only weapon, a dagger, gripped hard in her hand.

"Hide, Laufen."

There was no need for her to sully her hand. Instead, I used four [Root Strike]s.

The roots surged from the ground and speared the lesser demons looking for the hidden elves. With my extra levels, I could use Root Strike more often. Three of the hellhounds died instantly. One remained barely alive, if such a concept applied to demons. Maybe I missed a critical body part. The root still impaled the hound, though, and it growled and seemed to be dying.

Laufen emerged from the hideout, and she landed the killing blow. With her dagger, she stabbed the demon's head. The events from the day before drove her into a state of rage, and she stabbed the hound's head repeatedly until the demon hound's head was a mass of holes.

"Arghhhhhh!"

"ARGHH!!" she shouted. The hound was dead, but she kept at it.

"ARGHHHHH! Die, DIE, DIE, DIE, DIE!"

"Laufen, sis, calm down." Emile emerged from behind. She was frightened.

Laufen panted, her breathing ragged.

"I-I am sorry, Emile. I-I just need to vent my anger, my frustration, and my sorrow at something."

Emile nodded. She walked up to the dead hound with its deformed head and kicked it. "Damn you, demons."

Anger. Maybe this was how they coped with grief.

[You gained a level. Level 64.]

Grief. We all had it. If I wanted to protect these elves and help them protect themselves, they needed to gain a lot of levels. In short, some assisted power-leveling was required.

YEAR 70, MONTH 12

Rain arrived, on the heels of winter, with no stockpile of food to tide the surviving elves over.

"Fruits." Laufen sighed. She was sick of them. The earliest she could start to plant crops was early spring. "And it is freaking cold outside." Her winter wear was destroyed in the fire, so they could only step outside for a short period of time before the biting cold got to them.

"At least it is warm in here." Emile nodded, trying to think positively. The secret hideout was naturally temperature controlled and had a small tap in a corner that supplied water from the roots below.

Freeka was now nothing more than a bare, flat area. The dust and soot were gone. The rains had washed it all away.

All of them, except baby Lausanne, made a familiar contract with me, and they attempted to hunt whatever animals emerged. But these girls and one young boy were inexperienced hunters, and so the animals all managed to run away.

So there hadn't been any meat. Only fruit, just like the day before, and the day before that. I wanted to help, so I got them to make a spear. I planned to test out the essences I harvested.

"I think it is ready, tree spirit." Laufen and Belle presented a spear, cobbled together from scraps, a wood stick with a large metal tip.

I inserted an [Essence of Spear (minor)] through my branches.

A small ball of light emerged from the lamp-fruit on the ceiling and then entered the spear. The spear vibrated slightly, then absorbed the ball of light.

"Laufen, how is it?"

"[Equipment Inspect]." Laufen helped with maintenance of weapons the warriors used, so her skill revealed more equipment-specific details than my general [Inspect].

"It grants a small boost to spear combat, so it is decent."

"Try using it?"

Laufen shook her head. "I think Emile should use it instead. I have a thing with spears."

"A thing with spears?"

Emile nodded. "She means she accidentally hurt someone a long time ago, and now she has a phobia when using spears."

"Oh. Emile, would you?"

"Yes, tree spirit." Emile grabbed the spear and gave it a few swings. She seemed comfortable with it, or at least her movements looked really fluid. But, then again, flashiness wasn't always a sign of skill.

"How is it?"

"Wonderful. I need some time to build an affinity with it, but once I do, I should be good."

"What's affinity?" That was a new term. I had to ask.

"Oh...erm...it is the familiarity of a person with a weapon. So, with low affinity, your reaction time, energy use, and overall ability is weakened. At full affinity, you could use it like an extra limb. We get extra damage, speed, and parry with high-affinity weapons, but getting new, stronger equipment doesn't mean it should be used immediately," Laufen explained. "We need to practice with it."

Affinity was one of those skills monsters like me didn't have.

"How do you know this?" It still baffled me.

"It's...combat basics. Everyone knows it when learning how to use a weapon. I think the only exceptions are the summoned heroes. The legends say Weapon King Valerian had multiplier affinity with any weapon he touched, instantly."

"Oh. What does that do?"

"I don't really know, but I think the stories say the weapons are able to exceed their own limits, and when he used them, the weapons often did things normally not possible."

"Huh." Reincarnators had cheat-like abilities. That was absolutely predictable. I wondered whether I could get one for myself.

Speaking of heroes and reincarnators... "Which of the summoned heroes were elves?"

"Our last elven champion was Roana the Druid."

"Let me guess, she controlled nature like a druid?"

"Yes. She was like the most powerful druid ever. Her power over the forests and tree spirits in the stories was incredible. The legends told of how every spirit of nature she met instantly liked and obeyed her. In the battle against the demons, she transformed an entire forest into an army of super-treants and called on an army of great beasts!"

"Huh." I felt a strange pain in my head. I had to learn more about this world's powers and creatures. The gap in my knowledge could be dangerous.

"Anyway, please practice with it."

Emile nodded, but she sounded a little sullen. "Okay."

Laufen gave her a hug. "It's just us now. I know you always thought you wouldn't have to fight, that the warriors would protect us..." The thought of having to defend herself really made her sad.

"Yeah. We all miss them."

"Yes. Yes, we do. But we must live on. Else their deaths will be wasted on us."

Emile nodded, and both girls had a moment together where they cried for a while.

YEAR 71, MONTH 1

Now, it was really cold. The elves mostly hid in the hideout, unwilling to face the frigid winds that frequently ravaged the valley. According to Laufen, Freeka was located in a valley, and so, occasionally, when the winds got strong enough to cross the hills on either side, it tended to grow even cold.

A large bear appeared outside. It looked curious at the disappeared village.

"Oh. There is a bear," I telepathically notified Laufen. She played with Lausanne and shook her head.

"It's too cold. We cannot catch it now..."

"Oh."

The bear came close, and it rubbed its fur against my trunk. I could kill it now, at this distance.

[Root Strike] x 4.

Four [Root Strike]s were overkill, as a well-placed hit through the chest would have killed it, but I needed the elves to kill it. If they gained some levels, they would be stronger and more useful. The bear screamed and roared in pain, but with the four roots that impaled its limbs, all it could do now was flail its head.

"Emile, can you come out with the spear?"

She nodded, and once she opened the latch out of the hideout, she yelled, "Oh, it's a brown bear."

Yes, Emile. I know it's a brown bear. At that point, I wondered whether it was possible to use [Essence Harvest] on a bear, so I did.

[Fragment of bear essence obtained. Collect multi-fragments to form bear essence!]

Ah, the whole RPG grinding mechanics. The worst part was, in most games, all those essences were useless. The bear struggled, immobile, and Emile stabbed it right through its head.

"Wow." Emile's hands shook from what I believed to be a mix of adrenaline and fear. "W-we have bear meat!"

Laufen and Belle came out of the hideout to assist her in cleaning up and processing the bear. More importantly, they cut away the pelt and fur, which would help them stay warm.

"Did you gain any levels, Emile?"

"Nope, but I did get a skill, [Spear Thrust]."

Hmmm. They didn't seem to be gaining levels that easily.

YEAR 71, MONTH 2

The elves seemed happier now that they had bear meat as another staple in their diet. Spring would arrive soon, and they couldn't wait to plant crops.

I took every opportunity to let the elves land the killing blow on any stray demon or monster that popped up. Despite my efforts, they still leveled slowly. I wondered whether I was leeching off all the experience, so I decided to change the manner of my training.

Instead of injuring the monsters, I used [Constrict], a new ability gained after disabling so many beasts.

I supposed there was some sentience in this system that tried to make things easier over time.

The first time I used it, Emile, Laufen, and Belle spent quite some time trying to kill a trapped lesser hellhound. At full strength and health, the hound could take a bit of damage, especially from unexperienced elves.

Yet it worked better, and the three elves progressively gained levels and skills.

"This is hard," Belle said, recognizing that, between Laufen, Emile, and herself, she was the least adept at using a spear, sword, or staff.

But it worked. The difficulty meant they learned, and so I knew it was the best way to level.

YEAR 71, MONTH 2, WEEK 4

"Is there a village here?"

"Must be a mistake."

A human merchant group passed by. "The map says there is an elven village." One of the merchants, an old man, turned his map around a few times, and he wondered whether he was reading the map wrong. "Come have a look at it."

Another guy walked over and peered at the map and nodded. "Yeah, this is the place. Freeka. Looks like it's not here anymore."

"There are just trees and rocks in this place."

"It looks creepy."

The merchant group comprised of eight people. They looked defenseless, but I doubted that was actually so.

At this point, I telepathically asked the elves, "What happens if you attack innocents?"

"Nothing much if you do it once or twice. Do it often, and you might get a criminal title, which makes it hard for anyone to go to town or cities where they have [Detect Criminal]."

That certainly didn't apply to a monster, right? Or maybe I would get a wanted monster title or something.

"Should I kill these humans?"

Laufen paused. "Uh...uh...no?"

From her tone, I surmised she was conflicted over her still very vivid hatred of the humans who killed her husband, but at the same time, these merchants had nothing to do with it.

"Never...never mind." She shook her head, but she squeezed her staff a bit. Maybe she really wanted to, but the part of her that was fair had just managed to hold on.

"It's a really creepy tree," one of the merchants said. "We should not get close. I sense danger."

"So, what do we do now? We are supposed to rest a day at the village before we go on."

"Let's make camp here. It is quite a nice, open space."

"Preferably some distance from that tree."

The merchants at least had the sense to set up camp farther up from the remains of Freeka, but that night, one of them actually walked up to me and stood really close.

"Why does this tree feel different?"

He was one of the older ones, probably in his late fifties. I couldn't tell for sure, but [Spirit Vision] seemed to suggest he was quite old. He carried a few small weapons at his side and seemed prepared for a fight.

"Are you some kind of rare wood?" He touched my trunk but then pulled back instantly.

He touched his palm briefly, then he tried again, placing it on my trunk.

"Is it really a normal tree?"

One of the effects of [Camouflage] was that I appeared as a regular tree. Otherwise, even animals with any sense of danger would not dare come close.

"Hmm...I feel spirits..."

"Danton! Get your ass back here and stop masturbating by the creepy-ass tree."

"Hey, fuck you! I ain't masturbating."

The old man turned and sighed, but he peed on my roots before he left. At that moment, I was tempted to kill him. He walked back to the group.

YEAR 71, MONTH 3

[You gained a level. Level 65.]

[You obtained Learning Aura.]

[Improves experience gain for those low-leveled. Improvement amount is dependent on the gap between your level and the subject's.]

All that 'guided' power-leveling led to a new skill. Despite my efforts, Laufen was only level twenty-seven, and Emile and Belle were level eighteen. Wahlen and Brislach were level six in totality because they were still too young to fight. Despite their levels, their classes and skills were mostly unrelated to combat, and only their recent levels and skills led to more survival and combat abilities. Humanoids had classes, and their levels were a combined total of all the classes.

Winter was also over.

The elves planted crops around me and were happy. The very act of planting was a routine they previously hated but now enjoyed because it represented normalcy. A return to what they once knew.

YEAR 71, MONTH 4

A familiar elf walked through the woods. Alone. It didn't take long for me to recognize the spiritual presence. *Jura!*

He looked like he had taken a trip through Hell. His left arm was gone, and his body was covered in scars. He walked up to me. "Tree spirit, you're still here..."

I told Laufen to wait, even though she wanted to run out and hug him. I just wanted to be sure this wasn't a trap. "Yes. How are the rest of the elves? How many others got away?"

Jura kneeled beside my roots, his voice defeated and sad. "I managed to safely send ten of them to one of the elf-friendly kingdoms. Demons, monsters, and humans...there were too many obstacles..."

"You have done what you could."

Jura clutched at his left arm, the one that was lost. "I wish I could do more. Is everyone dead?"

"No," Laufen said. She couldn't hold back, so she ran out and gave him a hug. "Glad to see you, old friend!"

"Laufen! You all are alive?" Jura wept, overjoyed to see survivors.

"Yes. Yes. We live. It's been really tough, but the tree spirit watched over us."

Jura entered the secret hideout, and he gave everyone a hug. Everyone was shocked but happy.

"I cannot believe it. To think some of you still live." Jura's voice broke.

"The rest died...horribly."

Jura nodded. "Things have not been well for us, either. Or anyone. Even the humans."

Laufen, Jura, and everyone sat in a circle inside the secret hideout. One of the girls was surprised at Jura's last statement. "Huh? What happened?"

"A demon king emerged during the depths of winter, and his swarm of demons crushed the king's army. A few human cities near the west rift have been destroyed, their people slaughtered. That made our escape difficult."

Laufen shook her fist. "Served those assholes right."

"The demons and the death that came after the demon king's ascent made our travel to the friendly kingdoms really challenging. With little belongings and no money, and plenty of other refugees, we were attacked...robbed. A few of us died at the hands of robbers and bandits who wanted what little we had left."

Emile and Belle both looked horrified.

Jura munched on a healing fruit and continued to share his tale of their life since that day. "So we had to fight other people and demons..."

A few riders emerged from the woods then, so I informed Jura, cutting their conversation short.

"I was followed!" Jura looked horrified at the idea he had led some bad people here.

There were six of them, and they looked like bandits, at least from their haphazard attire and lack of armor. "The tracks of the elf led here."

"I like his sword. I want it. Find him," one of the older bandits ordered.

"Where could he have gone?"

"And here I thought there was a hidden village of elves we could raid. We should have struck when we had the chance."

They were at the edge of my range, but then I asked Jura to come out.

He did, holding his sword.

"Taunt them," I whispered into his mind. "Stand next to me."

"Hey, scum. You want a piece of me?"

The bandits laughed. "So! There you are! I want your sword. Give it to me, and I might let you live."

"Dream on. Come and get it, you foul-smelling bastards."

The bandits charged.

Great. They were comfortably within range now.

Six [Root Strike]s shot out of the ground, stabbing each and every one of them. It killed five; only the leader escaped. He had some kind of magic armor, and the attack from the root merely knocked him off his horse, causing a dent.

"Ahcks!" He coughed as he landed on the ground. The armor bent a little. "Oh, you are some kind of druid, eh?"

Jura was visibly surprised as well, but he smiled. "Yes. Come and get me."

"Can you win?" I ask telepathically.

"Maybe. With one hand, I am not as good as before."

The two were in close combat now. The bandit leader slashed, and Jura dodged and counterattacked, but the bandit dodged again. They traded a few more strikes, seemingly evenly matched.

Jura coughed. "Ugh, you're pretty good, but if I still had my arm, I would have won this easily."

"But you don't." The bandit smiled and activated a skill. His body radiated an aura. "Now, you die."

Jura struggled to fight back and was cut.

"Aghhh."

I wasn't going to lose Jura now, so I decided to step in with all my remaining [Root Strike]s.

My roots impaled the bandit leader, his armor not protecting every part of him. Two roots shot through his thighs, one snuck through the gap between his leatherarmor and his legs, and another punched through the dent made earlier.

"Ugh...to think you still had a trump card..."

"That wasn't me." Jura stood and tapped my trunk as the bandit leader died.

[You have leveled up! Level 66.]
[Root Strike range extended.]

"Jura." Laufen asked him to sit. "Y-you should have beaten that guy easily."

Jura shook his head. "Not anymore. I have a curse. [Tormented Fighter]. It weakens all my abilities and skills."

"Huh?" *A curse?*

Jura sighed. "At first, the effect is mild, but as time goes on, I have nightmares every day, and now I cannot even wield my weapon properly."

Emile asked, "Can it be healed?"

"Maybe. Curses can go away in time, or if something breaks it."

Indeed, Jura later demonstrated how that curse affected how his skills were cut short, and he could no longer perform combos and chain-attacks as he once easily did.

"Tell me what you've seen out there," I requested. "Maybe fighting isn't something we should be doing now."

YEAR 71, MONTH 4, WEEK 3

Jura's daily routine became mostly talking with me, playing, and helping with the crops. I suspected the curse was something like mental pain and wondered whether my [Calming Voice] could help resolve it.

It seemed the curse was so bad that it actually interfered with his ability to use familiars.

Still, it was an extra hand around to help do things, and he seemed to enjoy having the kids around. He behaved like Lausanne's uncle and spent a lot of time playing with them.

Soon, the first batch of crops was ready for harvesting, even though they were just planted two weeks earlier. The speed of their growth was amazing. Having a lot of levels, I suspected Ricola was right that I had an effect on the crops.

"I am trying to train these girls in combat. What is the best way to do so?" I asked.

"Well, actual combat experience is the best. Next best would be practice battles."

"Why are they gaining levels so slowly?" I asked Jura, even though I asked the others before.

"I don't think they are slow. Based on what they have been doing, it seems they are gaining levels quite fast already!"

"Huh. Is there no way to speed it up?"

"If there is a tutor or a master, you could, or if they somehow got hold of any of the artifacts of the heroes."

"Artifact of the heroes?"

"Uh, yeah. I once heard Casshern talk about how the heroes' artifacts could cause explosive leveling and skills."

"Why?"

"No idea," Jura admitted.

YEAR 71, MONTH 5

Demons. A sudden surge in demons.

I saw them enter my field of view, and the creatures numbered in the thousands. At this point, Jura and the elves all hid inside the hideout. That was their only chance. Thousands of demonic hellhounds would sweep through, killing everything in their path.

"So many of them."

They approached me, but their claws and teeth failed to damage my bark.

Even as more demons swept through the valley, all I could do was watch. A large demon, one wielding a fiery ax, approached. It looked like an elder demon, and it noticed me despite my [Camouflage]. It swung its ax at me, yet the blade bounced off.

No damage.

Annoyed, the elder demon attempted to hack at me with the ax multiple times, but every time, the ax was turned away. Eventually, it decided that it had to move on, and they continued the march.

The army, the swarm of thousands of hounds and other kinds of lesser demons, filed past for a week.

I only had a limited number of [Root Strike]s, and so, since I had no way of killing a massive army, I thought that pretending like I was harmless was the best way to protect the elves. The elves had never felt so afraid in their entire lives, yet they were simultaneously amazed at how these lesser demons were unable to damage me. Every moment they wondered whether a demon would burst through the door.

"That's easily an army of twenty thousand!" Jura calculated once they passed. I didn't bother. I looked around and saw I was the only surviving tree as far as my eyes could see.

"The humans won't make it." Laufen sighed.

"If Freeka was still here, it wouldn't have, either." Jura nodded. "But, luckily for the humans, I only saw a few mid-tier demons. A massive army of low-tier hounds is probably something an army half the size can handle."

Later that month, a bigger demon appeared, taking the same path as the hounds had earlier. It was a large, lizard-like creature, resembling a gigantic Komodo dragon but with red horns and eyes.

"That's an elder demon." Again, all the elves hid, and I secretly thanked my lucky stars that we had [Secret Hideout].

It saw me, and it stared. It was monstrous, about the size of a three-story building. It was bigger than me and tried to bite me, but its fangs couldn't get through the bark of my trunk. Then it opened its mouth and breathed fire. It felt kind of warm, but with my high fire resistance, it couldn't kill me.

Frustrated, it used its claws again, to no effect. Infuriated, it slashed and swiped with its claws, mixing in bites. Still, my somehow magically tough bark held. I was amazed by it. There had to be some kind of anti-demon buff at work.

Annoyed, I fired four [Root Strike]s. They pierced its thick hide, and it roared, biting and swiping at my trunk repeatedly. But, once again, its attacks did nothing.

"Tree spirit, how do you withstand such fearsome strikes?" Jura asked.

"I...don't know?" I suspected my [Demon King Survivor] tag

had something to do with it. Maybe it granted me resistance to demon attacks?

The elder demon was injured from my [Root Strike]s and seemed angry. It breathed fire again.

Nothing.

It attempted to bite me again, as if that worked before.

I launched two more [Root Strike]s, spearing it through the mouth. My roots somehow pierced through and sank into its head. The elder demon ignited into strange flames, and after the fire was done, all that was left were fangs and horns.

"Hey, why does it do that?" I asked Jura and Laufen, both ecstatic to survive an elder demon.

"I think that is the demon king's summon, not a demon-spawn. A creature mostly made of the demon king's mana. When slain, it reverts into its mana form."

"I see..."

[You gained 5 levels. Level 71.]

[You unlocked the following skills.]

[Rooting field]

[Local Rootnet Access]

[Poison Field]

Whoahhhh! More offensive abilities, except that [local Rootnet Access]. I wondered what it did.

YEAR 71, MONTH 6

[Attempting Local Rootnet Access. GrassNet found. Connecting.]

[Sunsunsunsunsunsunsunsunsunstepstepssunsunnightnightnightnight-nightsunsunsunsunsunsun...]

What the fuck is this?
[sunsunsunsunsunsun...] ad infinitum...
It instantly reminded me of a router that couldn't stop pinging. A constant message where the grassnet transmitted what it currently felt.

Damn.

[Disconnect from GrassNet.]
[You unlocked a new skill. [Create Rootnet Node.]]

Great, a pointless skill.

The elves spent a lot of time hiding as more demons passed through, this time from the other direction. Once the demon king appeared, it seemed the number one priority worldwide was fighting demons. At least on the continent where the demon king was. There was no peace until the demon king was slain because his very presence amplified the demonic rifts and caused more demons to appear.

For our little group, we would take the chance to attack if the size of the demon party was small, getting the elves to help take a few down or land the killing blows. If the size of the demonic party was too large, they hid since the lesser demons couldn't hurt me.

YEAR 71, MONTH 7

The huge army of demons that passed through over the last two months was now in retreat, which brought them through the valley again.

I took the opportunity to test out my new skills [Poison Field] and [Rooting Field], which effectively created a field with tiny roots that attempted to tangle and dislodge any passing monster. The same roots possessed tiny thorns with poison.

The hounds generally passed through unharmed due to their small size, flexible and nimble paws, and some apparent poison immunity.

Some of the mid-tier demons, though, were unable to avoid the tiny thorns, so quite a few took hits, and the poison caused a few of these demons to collapse to the ground. The field of roots then slowly cut the collapsed demons, and after some time, the roots finished them off.

All of this happened over a period of a few hours.

About a week after the demonic swarm retreated, an army of humans appeared, which I suspected to be a force pursuing the swarm.

"A tree..." an old warrior spoke as he rode on an armored horse. He rode up next to me and looked at my trunk. "Even when thousands of demons passed through here, nature survives."

Two other warriors rode their horses next him. "Yes, Lord Rajjiv. It is amazing a tree can live when so few trees survive the hound swarm." They surveyed the barren field around them. All the other trees had been either burned or destroyed by the demons, though signs of recovery could be seen.

"We make camp here, then. It is a good omen from the gods. Perhaps this tree is blessed."

They were a superstitious bunch, but it reminded me of the founding mythos of many ancient cities.

"Yes, milord."

The lord and his trusted lieutenants all camped within striking range, and the remainder of the army settled around them.

"What should we do?" The elves panicked slightly because a large group of humans triggered their fear and phobia. It was unpleasant to be reminded of human armies.

"Hide. We have enough food," Laufen insisted, not wanting to face the humans.

Lord Rajjiv sat next to me with a drink. "Oh, tree, I suspect you must not be an ordinary tree to survive. Perhaps you are a tree spirit like the guardian trees of the elven capitals?"

Perceptive!

"Ah, wait. If you truly are a tree spirit, proper introductions are necessary. I am Rajjiv Nung II, of the Kingdom of Nung. I am but a minor lord, and I am here to push back the demon army that has brought tremendous destruction to the world. Perhaps through some deeds, the king will elevate my status."

Hmm...I figured I should reply. "Hello."

He jolted in shock, almost spilling his drink. "Ah, you are indeed a tree spirit! Well met! The demons, have they passed through?"

He was smart, directly asking a question on military intel.

"Yes, a week ago."

"Hmm, a week. We were still too slow, after all."

"Why so?"

"We are trying to catch up to them, but if they are still a week away, we have not gained on them at all. How many of them? Would you know?"

"No idea. Maybe ten thousand?"

"Ten thousand. Hmm, we can still take that."

He took out a map, and though I couldn't see the writing on it, he pointed here and there. Things were all outlines to me still.

Maybe I can learn a skill to see normally.

The demon king was very far away, but he had multiple champions that led his forces against the world. It seemed that after the champions were slain, their demonic hordes scattered and weakened in terms of tactics and coordination, so removing the demon champions was a good way to reduce the threat of demons.

The champions were then given multiple lieutenants, such as giant elder demons or just massive demon beasts.

"What if you meet the demon king?"

Lord Rajjiv laughed. "Then we run. We run as fast as we can."

"Is fighting him that scary?"

"Unless you happen to have the weapons of the gods themselves or you hide a summoned hero, there is no chance to even win. Why fight a doomed battle?"

"Good point."

Rajjiv said his farewells, and the army departed a day later. He led his army and marched toward the demons.

YEAR 71, MONTH 8

Lord Rajjiv returned. He was injured, and so was his army. There was also a demon swarm on his tail.

"Set up camp. Defensive structures!"

The army set up a makeshift trench and wall, digging fortifications from the ground. They would have added spikes, but there were no trees left to make them, well, except me.

"Scouts. Where are the demons?"

"Should be here in three days."

The army spent most of their time setting up the trenches. They planned to trap the hounds so they could stab them easily with spears. Those with higher levels and skills would be deployed against the mid-tier demons.

In a way, a defensive battle against demons would be advantageous, but the trenches would overflow with bodies, and that defensive advantage would dwindle.

"I don't know whether we can survive this." Rajjiv sighed as he sharpened his sword. "The men must be ready to fight to their last. We beat them here, or the towns behind us will die."

"Fear not, Lord Rajjiv, reinforcements are on their way," one of the lieutenants assured him.

As the battle with the demons loomed, I offered Rajjiv a contract. "Rajjiv, do you need a familiar?"

He turned and looked at me. "Uh, yes, that would help."

I also grew as many healing fruits as I could, which the humans happily consumed. I felt a little conflicted that I was helping them, but at the same time, these were not the same humans who had slaughtered the elves. Meanwhile, the surviving elves continued to hide.

"What should we do?" Laufen asked while she carried Lausanne with one hand.

Jura sipped a cup of water. "With such a large human army, we should just stay here. It is safer if the size of the demon army is like what we saw before."

"Yeah. Just feels like all we have been doing is hiding." Laufen sighed. "Should we fight for a change?"

"No," I intervened. "Hide. I will protect you."

Seriously, just hide.

Three days later, a black line emerged on the horizon. Hounds. A lot of them. They charged like a tsunami approaching the shore.

"[Ironbark Skin]!" Lord Rajjiv shouted as his skill enchanted his nearby lieutenants. His lieutenants joined the line and barked their commands.

"Spears, ready!" The defenders raised their weapons, and they formed a spear wall.

The swarm of hounds closed in and soon entered the firing range of the archers. They unleashed a volley of arrows at the swarm, both physical and magical, but it wasn't enough.

"Spears! [Defensive Line]!" Lord Rajjiv shouted, and the soldiers felt a surge in strength, a hardening in their skin.

Some lieutenants and sergeants activated their skills, too, and the swarm smashed right into the line of humans. All around was death. Skewered hounds.

The battle continued. As the hounds, in their thousands, clashed with the army in close combat, the other demons swiped and growled at the humans. The defenders switched to short swords and engaged in close combat.

Still, the momentum and force behind the demon's charge was intense, and they pushed and broke the first line of defense. It was now a brawl for those up front.

"[Tactical Reorganization]! [Morale Boost]!" Rajjiv shouted as the line around him broke. The second line of soldiers stepped in and reinforced the line. More fighting, more blood, and more death.

The hounds outnumbered the army, so for a while, the demons appeared to be winning, but it could have gone either way. The second line fell back to the third, creating another wall of spears.

Rajjiv waited for the moment to activate his skill. Timing was crucial.

But help came, and the odds shifted rapidly.

A horn. Then a stream of charging knights on horseback, five thousand strong. They descended from behind the hounds, crushing them with their heavy lances.

"Hold it together, men!"

Lord Rajjiv lifted his sword overhead, and his sword flashed brightly. The flash stunned the army of demons briefly as the skill briefly bought time and allowed the defenders to regain some ground.

The charging knights lost their momentum, however, but a vanguard force held back the hounds.

Lord Rajjiv lifted his sword again. "Advance!"

There was another flash of light, and he stunned the hounds that glanced at it. The demons, somehow sensing defeat, started to flee. The knights gave chase after the laggards, while a small group of knights regrouped with the main force.

"Glad to see you, Lord Rajjiv," a heavily decorated rider said as he approached.

"Me too, Captain. You came just right on time."

"My pleasure. You seemed to have them in your hands anyway."

"Perhaps, but I would rather not gamble with my soldiers' lives. Your charge helped a lot."

"Let's burn the dead before they transform into zombies."

The humans gathered the dead and formed a mountain, then set fire to it. Cremation was one of the ways to prevent the undead from rising. As the fires burned, a huge creature appeared on the horizon. A large demon, perhaps drawn by the sight of the smoke.

The sight of it sent the army into a panic.

"A demon champion." Lord Rajjiv paled.

The hounds appeared beside it, but unlike before, they didn't charge at the human army. They waited, perhaps for a signal.

The demon champion was massive, the size of a large tower. It looked like a giant earth golem, but it was reddish in color and had spikes and horns across its body. It was like a grotesque mix of a golem, a hedgehog, and a demon.

It stepped closer, and with every step, the earth trembled.

"Oh, shit." I felt a shiver down my spine, as if it were a demon king. *Okay, that understated the presence of a demon king.* Maybe a lot less than a demon king, maybe one percent. The champion grew closer. Each step left a deep scar in the ground like a kaiju's massive steps.

It roared, and everything vibrated. Shockwaves reverberated in the air as it shook my leaves and branches.

"Order the general force to retreat. All our top fighters and mages gather on me. This will be a battle of champions," Rajjiv commanded. "Send a courier to inform HQ now. Tell them to gather heroes and champions if they don't hear from us in two days."

The regular soldiers were more than happy to retreat far away. There was no shame in running from a giant monster that could easily crush you underfoot.

"Together, with me," I telepathically informed Rajjiv. Together, I thought we had a chance. Somehow.

Rajjiv nodded. "Protect us, tree spirit."

The captain dismounted, and his force of riders mostly retreated as well. He gathered his highest-level warriors, healers, and mages. I offered him a familiar contract, too. In fact, I offered everyone a familiar contract, as many as I could, and I maxed out my limit.

The captain leaned in. "Tree spirit, do you have [Empower Allies]?"

"No."

The captain took out a scroll. "[Loan Skill], [Empower Allies]."

[You have been loaned [Empower Allies] for twenty-four hours.]

The golem approached.

The human fighters and lieutenants stacked themselves with all the buffs and healing they had.

The earth shook, and stones jumped at every step. Jura climbed out of the hideout, deciding this battle was one he should take part in.

"Huh?" The humans were surprised to see an elf appear from nowhere, but there was no time for that argument. The golem roared. It was within range, and it whipped its massive fists at the human forces.

Whoosh!

They dodged, but the punch had such force that it caused a small shockwave that caught some of the unprepared lieutenants. The captain activated [Quick Step], and that skill allowed those who were too near to dodge.

Jura joined the captain and his lieutenants in their attacks, but they barely scratched the creature. Normal sword attacks or arrows did no damage against its large and horn-covered body.

Slash. The humans attacked its feet, and those with [Leap] attempted slashes at its body.

The golem punched the ground, rattling the earth, and rocks flew everywhere. The flying rocks were like a scattershot. Some smaller rocks and stones still landed a hit, and it hurt.

One brave lieutenant tried to climb up its back, but the golem swept him off. About fifteen hits in, the humans realized the folly of attacking with regular weapons.

"Don't swing at it blindly. Reserve your strength for magical attacks!" Lord Rajjiv yelled, and I presumed his lieutenants had never faced a high defense and regenerating golem. Maybe he should have said that earlier, but he panicked when it attacked.

It went after the fighters again, but its bulky size warned of its intent, so they managed to avoid its attacks. Still, they had to account for the shockwaves and flying debris as well, which were harder to dodge.

[Holy Strike].

Lord Rajjiv landed a cut, and with the holy damage, it left a small tear.

[Energy Lance]. The captain lurched at the demon with a magically enhanced charge, and it ripped a small hole in the golem's stone side. But it didn't dodge, confident in its thick rock hide and regeneration ability.

The golem swung its large arms, and two lieutenants were caught in the path of the swing.

"Arghhh!" they screamed, coughing in pain.

[Empower], [Defense], [Ironbark], [Wood Shield].

I activated all the defensive abilities I had, and the golem's arm crashed against a protective barrier. The golem was right beside me, so it attacked, its fist crashing into me.

Ouch. I really felt that. It left a dent in my trunk.

Another punch.

My body twisted ever so slightly as the impact of the punch radiated through my entire body.

It punched again. This time, I activated [Wood Shield], and

the shield shattered on impact. But there was no direct hit to my body.

Jura and the humans kept using their skills, and their attacks barely scratched the golem, nothing went deep enough to actually hurt it.

It grabbed one of the lieutenants and crushed him in its huge hands.

The captain charged with yet another magical attack. Again, though, like all the previous attacks, it barely left a dent. "It's too tough. None of our attacks are breaking through!"

"There's still my special [Holy Charge] skill, but I don't think it's powerful enough to kill it." Rajjiv panted as he dodged a swipe of the golem's large arm.

The creature stomped, and the earth shook once more. Fighters staggered and lost their balance.

The demon followed up by throwing loose boulders.

"It can do that?" one of the fighters yelled in frustration, clearly annoyed that after dodging rubble, they now had to dodge boulders.

I activated [Wood Shield], and I managed to protect a few from the boulders, but not all. For three unlucky lieutenants, a boulder landed on them and crushed them instantly.

"Ugh. We are losing!" the captain screamed. If it kept picking them off, they would lose eventually. As it was, the humans could only harm it with skills, but the demon's regular punch could take any of them out.

A battle of attrition or endurance would be one they lost. The humans needed special skills that dealt significant, overwhelming damage.

The golem stomped again, shaking everything, including me. It roared, and a burst of flame emerged around it. A few lieutenants caught fire, but one of the mages cast a water spell that put out the flames right away. The mages attacked again with fireballs, but the demon was apparently resistant to fire.

Rajjiv stood next to me. "Tree spirit, do you have any strong attacks?"

Well, I only have one attack, so I used [Root Strike].

It hit the golem-demon right in the chest, and it broke a rock or two from its massive body. Despite doing more damage than anything else had, it didn't seem to hurt it.

The golem retaliated, punching me in the trunk again. My entire body shook, and another dent was left in my bark.

"Ughhhh." That really hurt. I felt like somebody just punched me in my gut and then some. I was a little drowsy and dizzy. Strange how a tree could feel that.

Pain. I suddenly recalled that feeling when I was chopped by the Demon King Baal.

The golem had smaller appendages on its back that swiped at any attackers, and though Rajjiv and the rest tried to take a chance to attack, their attacks mostly did nothing.

The human fighters threw more magic attacks at it, but they hardly did any damage.

"I have an idea." Rajjiv looked at me. "Everyone, cast all your support and boosts on the tree!"

"Huh?"

"Trust me!" Rajjiv shouted. He dodged a punch and then ran beside me. He placed his hand on my trunk.

[Holy Power], [Blessed Strike], [Demon Slayer], [Energy Burst], [Fatal Strike], [Heaven's Punishment], [Holy Blessing]. Rajjiv used a string of powerups on me, and I felt a strange surge of power and magic in my roots. He chanted and mumbled it out while he dodged the giant golem's attempt to interfere with it.

"The tree spirit's [Root Strike] on its own can damage the demon. With enough magical enchantments, it might be able to deal a strong enough hit to kill it!" he shouted and continued to channel some kind of holy magic.

[Imbue Holy Power].

I felt really lightheaded.

The captain nodded. "Ah! Makes sense!" He dodged another strike, and then he, too, ran to me.

[Energy Boost], [Piercing Strike], [Magic Damage III], [Attack Boost III].

Other warriors ran up to me as well, using their support boosts, [Power Strike], [Dodgeless Strike].

All the magical and skill enchantments made me feel really quite engorged like I'd drunk too much water or ate too much. It even felt like my roots were about to blow up. The earth shook, drawing my attention from the weird feelings.

The golem punched me again. *Urgh...* If I was human, I would have likely coughed up blood right then. The golem hit me again, and I felt my bark bend and buckle. *Pain.*

I felt like exploding, and I wasn't sure whether it was from all the magic or the blows.

"That's it, tree spirit. Give it everything you got!" Rajjiv shouted. I took a good look at the demon golem champion. In truth, it was nothing when compared to the demon king.

I summoned all the strength I could manage and released the accumulated magical energy within me along with my [Root Strike]s. They shot into the sky and pierced the demon golem.

Nine magically overcharged [Root Strike]s.

They tore nine massive holes in the chest and body of the demon golem, and it stopped.

Then it stumbled.

All the rocky limbs and extra appendages of the golem slumped like a puppet whose strings were cut. Then the massive golem shattered, crumbling to rubble, quickly turning to dust.

"The golem falls!" Rajjiv shouted. "Wooooooooaaaaaaahhhhhhhh!"

The human army roared. The hounds disappeared toward the horizon as they took their cue from the defeated champion. Rajjiv, the captain, and the remaining lieutenants gathered around me, but by then, a sense of relief and nausea flooded through my senses, and I just couldn't respond.

I felt really dizzy and drowsy. Everything went hazy and blurry...then I fell into a kind of sleep...

[Level up! You gained 15 levels! Level 86!]

[You unlocked the following skills – Dream Tutor, Wood Magic and Creation, Rhizofiltration.]

[The following skills have been upgraded – [Secret Hideout], [Root Strike range and quantity, Local Rootnets Access.]

A dream came over me. A dream that contained visions of what looked like my home world.

It began in a vast sea of stars like the Milky Way. A galaxy, a nebula in the distance. From the vastness of space, it zoomed in on a solar system, then a planet. Earth. Or was it? The dream didn't linger, so I couldn't take a good look, and then it moved again. The shifting scenes were too fast. The scene zoomed in on a hospital or a clinic. A doctor, a nurse, a child, and probably the child's family appeared. The child smiled and nodded. A few around him were crying. They hugged the child while it slept.

Then the dream zoomed out again, back to the view from space. Stars. Thirteen streaks of light, all from the planet. They shot up, then the view sped up, and the scene resembled a warp or a slipstream.

The path the lights took was twisty and wavy. The streaks of light bent, seemingly taking sharp turns without warning.

A white layer emerged around the streak of light, and just as it exited the slipstream, another black barrier appeared. It shattered, just like glass when the lights crashed against it.

A green planet appeared. Thirteen streaks of light flew toward it, but one of the streaks flickered, and it moved a little slower. It lost speed and drifted apart from the rest of the group.

It crashed into the planet. A little while later, the twelve remaining streaks of light crashed elsewhere on the planet.

[Twelve reincarnators have arrived!]

YEAR 71, MONTH 10

Two months. I've been asleep for two months?

The elves! What happened to the elves?

Oh, they're still here. The elves were alive, thankfully. I was worried about whether my fruit, [Secret Hideout], or [Nourish] would be disabled when I was asleep. Now that I had woken up, everything seemed to be...all right?

"Jura, Laufen, what happened?"

"Oh?" The elves jumped, surprised by my mental voice. "Tree spirit, you're awake!"

"Ah, yes, I've been sleeping for two months?"

"Yes. All of us were really surprised you didn't respond after that battle, and one of the captains mentioned it could be a kind of mana-sickness or just spiritual exhaustion," Jura said.

"Then?"

He gathered himself and then started to explain. "Oh, erm... the humans left after the battle. They wanted to talk to you, but they all left after waiting for a few days. Since the demon champion was defeated, it has been quiet around here. The hordes in this region were in disarray, and their behavior turned erratic. Other than that, there was nothing much. We mostly continued to hide, and we survived on your fruits. Your passive abilities like

[Nourish] continued to function, even when you didn't respond to us, so we knew you were merely sleeping."

"I see. That's great."

"Yeah. We've been keeping ourselves busy since then. We gained a few levels, too!"

Jura participated in the battle against the demon champion, so it made sense for him to gain levels. "Ah. How many levels did you gain, Jura?"

"Oh, levels. Erm...I think I gained four levels and a skill?"

Well, that was a big difference. Only four levels? Was it because I landed the finishing blow?

That battle with such a huge golem helped with my worries and really boosted my confidence. Even my [Tormented Warrior] had improved to [Tormented Warrior (mild)]. I thought if we could keep it up, I would lose the penalty completely soon enough!

Laufen and the rest shook their head—no levels for them. All they did was hide after all. If you didn't participate, you didn't get levels. Sounded fair.

In fact, the whole fuzzy logic behind leveling incentivized hard work and participation. It was probably designed by a schoolteacher somewhere to reward kids. *Laze off, don't take risks, and you get nothing!*

A few days after I woke up, I remembered I had new skills.

I had somehow forgotten about them in the days since I'd woken. It felt like a bad hangover, really.

[Wood Magic]

A wheel popped up in my mind. At the center of the wheel was a leaf shape. There were a lot of grayed-out skills and menus that grew out of that wheel.

Ah, I unlocked the magic type, and I had two skills under it. [Bind] and [Bloom].

[Rhizofiltration]

[This is a passive skill. Will extract minerals and other items via roots and automatically filter out negative effects in the ground.]

[Dream Tutor]

[May use dreams to learn and teach. Requires a collection of spirits, memories, and objects to unlock more 'Dreams.' Essences can be used to bestow certain skills via dreams. Target must be sleeping for the ability to kick in. If sleep is interrupted, learning may not be effective.]

I immediately tested it out on the elves once they went to sleep at night.

YEAR 71, MONTH 11

The effects of [Dream Tutor] seemed quite varied. It worked very well for Jura, as he gained a new attack skill. For Laufen and Emile, however, they seemed to feel a little lost. To them, the dream felt more disorienting and confusing than enlightening. Still, they said they were learning something. For the youngest, Lausanne, the skill merely gave her nightmares, so I chose to stop using it on her until she was much older.

Perhaps dreams were just scary when you were two or three years old.

Nothing much happened that month. It started to get really cold again, and the elves spent their time resting in the expanded hideout, which now had an additional room.

Occasionally, they would pop out to kill whatever creatures came too close.

[Power-Leveling].

I needed a skill like that.

YEAR 71, MONTH 12

[Melur Marin has died. You received a fragment. You have 56 fragments.]

What? That was way too fast for one of the reincarnators to die. It had only been just over a month since they arrived!

Were they in danger? Or maybe a conflict had broken out? I asked Jura to gather more information, but he wanted to be here with the rest of the elves.

"I don't think it's good for me to leave, tree spirit. It's better if we stay in this hideout. It really is the safest place with you around."

Oh, well. The nearest town was a human one, and maybe the elves wouldn't be so well received, anyway.

[Your root has harvested some materials. Raw Iron x 5. Do you want to disable all similar notifications?]

Oh. Okay.

Materials, like essences, were used to make stuff. This

creation process was part of my [Wood Magic and Creation]. The iron and essences got absorbed into the wood, and the wood then formed itself into the item I wanted to make. It was a slow process.

YEAR 72, MONTH 1, WEEK 1

I created a wooden ring, with iron and essence of lesser fire. The process was more like the ring grew within a tree branch, and once it finished, the outer layers of the branch peeled away to reveal the inner 'product.'

A pop-up appeared.

[Material compatibility is low. Effects are reduced by 50%.]

Ah. Laufen, being the resident inspector, then advised on its effects. Honestly, it felt like I was at a MasterChef competition waiting on Laufen's judgment.

"Boosts fire magic by a little bit, and there is some attack strength increase." Ah. Not bad. Maybe I wouldn't get disqualified this round. *I kid.*

Other than that, it was a whole lot of resting and the occasional monster.

[Woodcrafting upgraded.]

Oh, that's easy.

YEAR 72, MONTH 1, WEEK 4

D emons, a group of hounds appeared. I killed some, and then the elves killed the rest.

[You obtained a new skill – Power-Leveling.]

Ah, finally. The elves, other than Jura, gained a level.

YEAR 72, MONTH 2

Another quiet month. More demons, and more killing. More levels for the elves. Other than that, the elves really wanted spring to come. Winter was finally ending.

[Essence of Winter (minor) x 1 obtained. Essence of Cold (minor) x 1 obtained.]

Ah, auto-mode [Essence Harvesting].

My new discovery of the month was that harvesting/material type skills had an auto-mode. That meant that my cells extracted minerals without the need of conscious interference. It was like breathing. I shouldn't need to consciously do it, even if I could.

YEAR 72, MONTH 3

A few small bushes and trees started to grow in the general area around me, the remains of the previously destroyed trees now regenerating. The recovery of bushes and trees returned some texture and features to the previously destroyed valley.

Demons—or more accurately the hounds—appeared like locusts. Swarms of them, here and there. I killed those I could and ignored those clever enough not to come too close. I mean, it wasn't like I could chase them.

I am like a Venus flytrap, and I've got to wait for my stupid prey to come near. Maybe I can get a 'lure' skill some day in the future.

[You gained a level. Level 87!]

[Skills upgraded – Healing Fruit upgraded, Healing Vines upgraded]

[Obtained a new skill: [Solar Healing.]]

Oh. I felt like a bulb-shaped monster.

YEAR 72, MONTH 4

A horseman passed through, resting for a while under my tree. He slept in the shade and laid his head on my trunk. I dropped a fruit on his head.

"Ouch."

He grabbed it, examined it for a while, and then ate it.

"Thanks, tree." He rode off after his nap.

[You obtained a skill: Fruit Attack.]

Oh.

YEAR 72, MONTH 5

There were more demons.

Seriously, these things never ended. How did the locals deal with so many demons?

"The demons appeared on average twice a week, which was okay. When demons were actually terrorizing us a few years ago, they appeared daily."

Ah, wait, I kept forgetting my sense of time was different from the elves. Killing all the demons, though, gave me a new skill.

[Obtained skill: Root Surge.]

[Obtained skill: Lesser Demon Suppression Aura.]

YEAR 72, MONTH 6

It was time for a big harvest! The elves harvested their crops, and I noticed some of the trees around me had grown larger. It was quite unnatural to see them grow so quickly, but apparently, it was a common occurrence if there were tree spirits around.

I had grown taller as well, and I was now about the height of a four-story building.

They said that excess mana harvested by tree spirits (who usually didn't spend their mana) would be dumped into the land around it, and that turbocharged all other plant growth.

Thanks to [Wood Creation], all the elves were now equipped with weapons and armor I made. That skill had an upgrade, too.

YEAR 72, MONTH 7

One thing about life as a tree, I was immobile. Well, mostly, except when I got moved unwillingly.

So I really spent a lot of my time doing nothing. It was a waiting game where I hoped for things to happen. I wondered how all the other tree or rock spirits felt. How did they even stand it, just waiting? Out of sheer boredom, I usually tried to use my plentiful idle time to help the elves, by using my skills such as [Dream Tutor], [Power-Leveling], and [Wood Creation].

Currently, Jura was level fifty-four, Laufen was thirty-one, Emile was twenty-six, Belle was twenty-five, Brislach and Wahlen both were eleven, and Lausanne was still unknown.

Lausanne, the now three-year-old child, could talk reasonably well, but she didn't know how to access her menu. Maybe in a few more months she would be able to tell me what level she was.

"Tree-Tree." Lausanne walked around. Her steps were stable, even if it looked like she was wobbling half the time. She crawled up and down my roots.

Laufen rubbed her daughter's head. "Now, now, that's not how to refer to a tree spirit."

"Tree-Tree," Lausanne mumbled. "Tree-Tree?"

She pointed awkwardly at me.

"Tree-Tree." Laufen likely rolled her eyes at her daughter.

Yet it felt endearing.

I liked that name, and thus, I decided I should call myself that.

Tree-Tree.

YEAR 72, MONTH 8

A small group of young adventurers appeared—six of them, on horses. Heavily armed, their horses exhausted, they made camp next to me. It seemed like being the only tree in this vast field did seem to draw attention. There were smaller trees around us, of course, but they seemed to have missed them.

"I think that tree in the middle of the field looks nice."

"I think so, too. Let's go have a look."

These six adventurers stood next to me and examined my trunk and leaves. They also examined the smaller trees that now flourished nearby. They were a group of four girls and two boys.

One of the girls looked around, and she sat on one of my protruding roots, admiring the view of the fields. "It's a nice view, even though it's probably one made by the demons."

"Yeah, it's a good place to take a nap. There are still a few days left in our journey to the rifts. Let's enjoy the peace and quiet while we can," one of the boys said and stretched his arms out. He took out a piece of cloth, spread it out on the ground, and laid down.

"True," the rest of them agreed. They set up their camp next to me and rested for the night.

The next morning, a group of fifteen demons appeared in the distance, and I learned from Jura that these large, winged creatures were known as manticores. They made their presence known with a loud roar, and that instantly woke the adventurers.

Silly, these manticores. They should have kept their mouth shut and launched a sneak attack on the adventurers while they slept. The adventurers, though, seemed unshaken as if this was a normal occurrence to them. In fact, the adventurers had already set up some kind of magical defense, and a huge thunderbolt zapped the first manticore that intruded on their defensive zone.

A long-haired girl shouted some kind of chant, and an orb of red lightning floated between her two palms. The electricity leaped out of her two palms in a flash, and it zapped three of the flying manticores, frying them instantly.

They fell to the ground, charred.

The leader of the adventurers raised his war staff, and it instantly created a forcefield that blocked the manticores' acidic spit as they attempted to spray them. Immediately afterward, he chanted again, and all the manticores moved sluggishly as if they were trapped in some kind of thick goop.

The other guy then took out a contraption that resembled a very long rifle, and he fired a high-speed orb. It exploded in midair and blasted a few of the slow-moving manticores to pieces.

A short-haired girl who wore thin armor flicked something that resembled a handheld fan. In its wake, a huge gust of wind appeared, and the force of the wind shoved the manticores. They fell to the ground with loud thuds. The two remaining girls, both holding a pair of shortswords, rushed forward and slashed the grounded manticores to death.

One of the twin-sword girls sounded cheerful. "I gained a level, and I got a skill!" She jumped around, happy.

"Oh, what did you get?" the other twin-sword girl asked, tapping her on the shoulder.

"[Flawless Dodge]."

"Oh, cool. I didn't get anything." The guy who cast the force-field sighed, and he sat on one of my roots. He took out some kind of cloth and cleaned his war staff.

"Stop whining. You're already level seventy-five! I am just level sixty-three!" the twin-sword girl shouted.

Meanwhile, the mage girl harvested the remains of the manticore corpses alone, with a small dagger and a bag. After she went through a few of the manticore corpses, she noticed she was the only one doing it and glanced at her teammates. "You peeps not helping to collect the loot?"

The rest of them unanimously shook their heads. "You do it. We'll just ruin it."

The mage girl rolled her eyes. "Ugh. You know my ability works so long as I am around!"

"Ain't taking that risk!"

They bantered for a while and took a rest after they were done. They moved quickly, and with a wave of a wand, their camp was clean. Then they headed toward the demonic rift.

YEAR 72, MONTH 8, TWO DAYS LATER.

Five demon riders arrived riding hellhounds. They were clearly following the scent of the adventurers, and I wondered whether the hellhounds actually had a sense of smell. These demon riders looked like they were previously human, but their bodies had been corrupted by demonic forces and transformed. As they were once human, they still spoke normally to each other, the only difference being their voices.

"They were here." One of the riders patted the hellhound. "They are headed for the southern rift." The very fact they spoke the same language was very strange. Who were these demons?

Another rider examined the dirt and the remnants from the battle. "Six of them. They rested here for a day. They can't be far ahead."

"No sign of any injury. The mid-tier demons were insufficient to hurt them. We will need the elders." The rest of the demon riders nodded in agreement, and two of them chanted some kind of spell. It seemed like some kind of communication spell, but they spoke gibberish I couldn't comprehend.

At that point, I wondered whether I could beat these demon riders. "You think we can take them on, Jura?"

Jura shook his head. "They look like they have some of the abilities and skills of normal humans, so I am not sure of our chances. They could be very strong or just like a normal human. I honestly can't say, but if you ask me, our chances are not great."

I decided to let them go.

YEAR 72, MONTH 9

We felt a huge explosion in the distance. Then another.

And another.

The earth shook constantly, even though the explosions were so far away. The sky above us was filled with strange streaks of color. It wasn't a pleasant sign. *Is there some kind of high-tier combat taking place in the distance?*

"Tree-Tree, these explosions...they are growing closer."

We felt even more explosions, the vibrations only getting stronger.

In the distance, the earth ruptured, and rocks shot up.

Jura told me of two large flying creatures, each with some kind of elemental breath weapon. They attacked someone, but we couldn't make out who.

Then they came nearer, and we identified them. It was the six adventurers!

The earth shook badly, so my roots increased their grip on the earth, mildly reducing the shaking. There were more explosions and spells that crisscrossed the skies. The destruction sent huge plumes of dust into the air, creating a minor dust storm that blocked out some of the sunlight.

This was followed by even more explosions, and we saw the adventurers fall back.

The adventurer group retreated and simultaneously retaliated with ranged attacks. The two large flying creatures appeared to be some kind of demonic wyverns, and they were accompanied by a swarm of hellhounds and lesser demons. The lesser demons kept their distance.

The wyvern's elemental breaths dealt a huge amount of collateral damage.

Boom!

An explosion erupted right on one of the demonic wyvern's chest.

It fell to the ground, and the earth shook briefly from the impact.

"Ugh, yes!" The adventurers took the opportunity to run, and three of them seemed heavily injured. The remaining wyvern tried to follow them, but a nicely placed fireball from the mage-girl tore through one of its wings. The wyvern crashed and was unable to fly. Still, it seemed to shrug off the damage and chased after the adventurers on its two large feet.

Luckily, it was slower this way.

They ran toward my position, noticing a large group of demons appearing from the other direction. Hellhounds had the adventurers surrounded.

"Let's go to the tree. Let's fight there." The fan girl pointed at me, and they ran as fast as they could. For them, any cover was obviously better than no cover.

As the adventurers repositioned themselves around me, I sensed the gunner man and the twin-sword girls were all injured. Their spirits wavered and flickered. The twin-sword girls' spirits seemed as if they were engulfed in some kind of demonic fire or rot. I wasn't sure what I was looking at.

The hordes of hounds and lesser demons surrounded us. Only the lumbering demonic wyvern dared to approach, but that was after what felt like a moment of hesitation. I wondered whether these demons were intelligent. They certainly exhibited signs.

"They... The rest don't seem to be approaching?" The adventurers were too busy to notice.

"Huh? Great!" One of the mage girls was surprised, and she scrambled over to help her injured compatriots. "You guys deal with it. I need to look after them."

The wyvern roared, and then it charged. It was already injured from all the ranged attacks of the adventurers so, at that moment, I felt like I could get a good shot in.

[Root Strike].

A root surged out of the ground and stabbed it right in the abdomen. Some of its inner matter spurted out.

It wasn't dead—not yet—but the stab slowed it down.

Another two [Root Strike]s followed.

My roots hit the abdomen of the wyvern again, but this time, one of the roots pierced through and skewered the wyvern's chest. It fell.

The death of the wyvern scared the rest of the hounds and demons, the lesser demons still keeping their distance.

"Oh, wow." The forcefield man touched my trunk. "A tree spirit! We're saved!"

The mage girl shook her head, and she tried to look at her friends. "They are dying!"

"Bring them to me," I mentally said to her. She turned and seemed to hesitate for a moment, but then she nodded and used magic. She levitated all three of the injured adventurers and moved them beside me. One of my small branches reached out, and from that branch, a vine extended to touch them.

I activated my skills.

[Solar Healing].

[Healing Fruit].

[Nourish].

The wounds closed a little, and I sensed their spirits beginning to stabilize. Of the three injured, two of them recovered
easily. Their wounds and cuts healed quickly, far quicker than
normal. Yet, for the last twin-sword girl, she had a stab wound
that went deep into her chest. I couldn't quite believe it, but up
close, I saw some kind of demonic presence in her body, and it
gnawed away at her soul. She was in pain.

"Don't die." The mage girl held her hand.

The twin-sword girl smiled weakly. I kept using my abilities
to heal her, but the demonic energy interfered. For every bit of
healing, the demonic energy undid the effects.

"No." The mage girl held her hand tightly. "No, no, no."

The demons tried to approach, but without the giant one,
the rest were just small fries. The adventurers, led by the forcefield dude and the wind-wielder, easily defeated the remaining
lesser demons.

I extended my feeler-like vines and touched the wounded
girl on the head, activating my healing abilities. Her wounds
recovered a little, but once again, it lasted for only for a short
moment before the demonic energy reversed the healing, and
the wound opened again.

"The demons. Damn them! They used some kind of special
demonic rot attack, and the effects are still in her body. It's interfering with our attempts to heal her. We need to remove that
demonic rot, but all we can do now is keep her alive." The mage
girl cursed and then glanced up at me.

"We need to coordinate our healing. Let's cast healing alter-
nately so her body doesn't deteriorate too much."

With the other twin-sword girl and gunner healed, the
remaining four adventurers unleashed their fury and slaughtered the remaining demon swarm. The large number of hell-

hounds meant very little for the group of powerful adventurers. They were fueled by both anger and desperation. The demons' numbers dwindled before the might of the four healed adventurers, and I marveled at wave after wave of attacks. The hellhounds fled.

The battle was over, the demons either fled or destroyed.

Their focus shifted to the injured twin-sword girl as we supported her battle against the demonic rot inside her.

"It's not getting any better." Mage girl sighed as she explained to the remaining four. "We been trying to heal her..."

"We have to take her somewhere, to the town."

"No." Mage girl shook her head. "I don't have enough mana to sustain my healing over long periods, not yet. As it is, we won't make it back in time. If I stop now, the demonic rot will kill her within three to four hours. We can keep her alive because the tree spirit's healing abilities are giving me some breathing room to recover my mana."

"Huh..." The fan girl held the injured girl's hand as she slept.

I used a mix of healing and regeneration abilities to keep the injured girl alive, but I was still unable to remove the demonic presence that gnawed away at her body.

It was a stalemate in the constant battle between the healing forces and the demonic rot.

"Hmm. So, here's the plan. Three of us will stay. Then the rest of us need to find the others and find a cure for rot, or anyone who has any inkling of what sort of cursed power that demon champion used. We'll continue her healing. Together with the tree spirit, we can keep her alive. I will stay back to provide protection."

The three adventurers chosen to leave were the other twin-sword girl, the fan girl, and the gunner guy. They all nodded. "That seems to be best choice we have now. Let's go. There's no time to waste."

That was when it occurred to me that they never even asked whether I agreed to the plan, but it was fine. I supposed saving lives made sense. But since these adventurers would be there for some time, I asked Jura and Laufen to come out of the hideout.

"Huh. Elves." The adventurers were surprised, but they didn't seem hostile.

"We live here. The tree spirit said we should meet you." Jura and Laufen introduced themselves. "We heard your plan to stay with the tree spirit."

"Ah. We mean no harm. We needed the tree spirit's help to keep my friend alive," the mage girl explained. "I can't do this on my own. I'm not a healing-focused mage."

Jura and Laufen looked around and nodded. "Then, please, come in."

"Come in?"

The elves brought them into the secret hideout, and the injured girl was placed on the floor in one of the rooms.

At that point, a pop-up appeared.

[Do you want to initiate Life Support protocol?]

Oh. Okay.

At that moment, the room shook a little. Multiple branches and vines appeared around the injured girl, and some of those vines attached to her body.

"What's happening?" the forcefield dude asked. He seemed worried and reached for his war staff. "Explain!"

The mage girl stopped him. "The tree spirit is doing something. I think it's some kind of magical 'support' mechanism."

The vines and branches transformed and took the general shape of a hospital bed, and a few little wooden feelers attached to various parts of her body. They supplied a mix of condensed healing fruit juice and whatever regeneration ability I had to the injured girl. It also activated a minor version of my passive healing ability.

"It's like a," the forcefield dude and the mage girl looked at each other, "hospital bed."

"Thank you for helping us."

Jura and Laufen shrugged. "It seems the tree spirit agreed to help you. We just hope you're not like the other humans."

"Other humans?"

"Those who hunt us elves."

"Oh, we're nothing like that. We promise we won't bring you any harm. We just want to save our friend's life, and I pray we won't take too much of your time or space." The forcefield guy nodded and sat. Mage girl looked at her injured friend, and after a while, she too rested. Her turn would come soon.

"She's stable. The tree spirit used some kind of constant healing ability that's channeled through the vines and feelers connected to her," the mage girl observed and explained to the other adventurer.

Laufen passed them fruits to clear the tension. "What's your name? I am Laufen."

"Hendry." Forcefield dude munched on the healing fruit.

"Alexis." Mage girl took a bite, and she pointed at the injured girl. "She's Meela."

"Ah."

"This place, it is some kind of magical pocket dimension inside the tree spirit, right?" Alexis asked. She was interested in the whole theoretical basis behind magic and found it to be really fascinating, especially how magic worked and interacted.

"Uh..." Laufen scratched her head. She had never thought about such things.

"This space is much bigger inside than the tree is outside, and yet it wasn't underground. Thus, the only logical conclusion is this is some kind of pocket-space," Alexis explained, and to be honest, that was the first time I noticed.

Meela was still asleep. I used a mix of liquid healing fruit extract, fed to her via the vines. I would then occasionally use [Solar Healing] via a leaf located right above her head. Alive and asleep, she received the healing powers of me and Alexis at alternating times. Whatever it was, the demonic rot was pretty nasty.

Exhausted, both Alexis and Hendry eventually fell asleep, but they took precautions and activated a wide range of spells. They were careful and prepared.

[You gained two levels. Level 89!]

[Nourish upgraded. Life Support unlocked. Suspended Animation unlocked.]

Over the next few days, they waited for their three friends, but it was likely they would need some time to come back with any kind of cure.

Alexis looked in on Meela, making sure to check on her every few hours.

Hendry seemed restless, and he paced about, taking long walks around and occasionally talking to himself about demons and monsters. He would go on long 'walks' where he slaughtered any lesser demons he came across.

"Worried?"

"Yes." Alexis munched on bread she pulled out from nowhere. "I don't want to lose her. *We* don't want to lose her. It would be unbearable."

Laufen nodded and tried to reassure her, "Your friends will be back with a cure."

"I hope so."

"What did you fight that caused such a bad wound?"

"A demon champion. It was some kind of earth snake that seems to be corrupted by huge amounts of demonic energy. It had a special weapon, a condensed kind of venom..."

"A demon champion?" Laufen gasped, and her palms covered her mouth.

"Yes. We killed it, but not before another hidden assassin demon retrieved that special venom and stabbed Meela with it."

"Wow. Must have been a big expedition into the rift."

Alexis paused. "Yes."

"Demons. On the horizon." Hendry came back into the hideout. "A lot of them. Hounds and a lot of mid-tier creatures. Maybe they're hiding some powerful demons inside as well, so we should be careful."

"Huh? Demons can do that?" Jura was surprised demons were capable of such sophisticated tactics.

"Uh...yes." Hendry nodded.

Jura shrugged and then looked at the adventurers. "I think we should hide. Normally, they ignore us. Our tree spirit has all sorts of defensive buffs, and the demons can't scratch him."

"Tree-Tree," Lausanne interjected, and Laufen caught her. "It's Tree-Tree."

"Yes. Tree-Tree has all sorts of defensive buffs."

"Hmm, very well." Hendry retreated inside as the demon swarm approached. The demons fanned out, and they covered most of the area. Once again, they destroyed the regrowing shrubbery.

Some came close to me, but they mostly walked past. A few attempted to attack my large, thick trunk, but they couldn't even leave a scratch. Hendry seemed surprised when the swarm eventually left.

"It's really neat, right? That's how we survived so long out here." Emile smiled. Her words contained a little bit of bragging. "The demons just pass by us like...we are not there. And even when they notice the tree, they can't hurt us."

"That is so strange." Hendry sat as he admired the view outside. The demons couldn't see into the secret hideout.

Later, Laufen tried to initiate conversation. "So, how long you think it'll take?"

"For?"

"Your friends. To find a cure."

Hendry and Alexis both shook their heads. Alexis rubbed her chin and explained, "I'm not sure. None of us have any specific anti-demonic curse abilities. We don't even know the specific magical nature or the mechanics of the disease or demonic rot

Meela is suffering from. We'll just have to try whatever they bring back."

"Ah..." Laufen felt like she just asked a question that led to a technical question way out of her depth.

Then Meela screamed in pain, and all of them rushed to her side.

"Meela, are you okay?" Hendry and Alexis grabbed her arms, and Alexis used a diagnostic spell.

The constant cycle of alternating between healing and the destructive effects of the demonic curse had resulted in a surge of pain. As her body regained the senses of the healed area, they were immediately damaged again. The sensation accumulated and abruptly jolted her with intense pain.

"I don't have any kind of pain-reduction spells." Alexis sighed. "If only we had a pill or something."

Hendry shook his head. "Meela, you've got to hang in there."

Meela slumped back and lost consciousness. The demonic rot weakened her spirit, and I suspected it also contributed to her inability to remain conscious.

"Tree spirit, do you have any pain-reduction spells?"

"Hmm... No."

However, I wondered whether I could produce saps or materials that might be able to suppress the pain. I recalled from my world that there were a few medical products that were derived from plants.

[Tree's natural abilities discovered: Tree Extracts and Saps]

Oh, wow.

A menu popped up and displayed a huge list. Rubber, oils, poisons, fragrances, saps...

Wait. Found it.

"Pick some leaves and make tea," I mentally spoke to Laufen.

A small branch with odd-colored leaves appeared from the wooden walls of the secret hideout.

"Huh? Oh, okay, Tree-Tree." Laufen ran and got some hot water, quickly picked a few leaves off the branch, and mashed them into some kind of paste.

The process of making the herbal tea took about an hour. Once ready, they fed the herbal-leaf tea to Meela.

She yelped from the heat, but as the tea flowed into her body, it released a pain-suppression effect. Alexis grabbed the remaining leaf and examined it, just to make sure it was nothing dangerous.

"Ah..."

Meela fell back into her slumber.

They made the tea for Meela every six to seven hours to keep her comfortable. Her pain popped up every now and then, and the days passed.

YEAR 72, MONTH 10

Meela was still in a state of assisted living as her body continued to be affected by the demonic rot.

[Tree Saps and Extracts upgraded.]

Thanks to the constant use of the leaves for the pain-numbing tea, the skill leveled up, and now it was more potent and longer-lasting. Thanks to it, Meela could stay awake for about thirty minutes to an hour per day to talk, which helped improve Hendry and Alexis's moods greatly.

"Don't worry, I won't die." Meela smiled as she looked around the room. "This feels like a hospital. It's a familiar place."

Alexis shook her head. "We'll get you fixed up again, okay?"

Hendry frequently spent his time climbing up my branches, and sometimes, he just sat at the very top and watched the sky. That was apparently his way of coping with everything, with the situation they were in, trapped waiting while his friend was wounded and out of commission.

Apparently, the stars were beautiful, and there were more moons here.

Later that month, we had demonic visitors again.

"The demon knights." Hendry gripped his war staff. I thought they were demonic riders or rangers, but I supposed people would refer to the same things differently.

They rode hellhounds, and there were eight of them. They had an interesting mix of weapons—three with swords, two with spears, two with bows and arrows, and one with a staff. Alexis held him back. "No, don't. I know you can win, but we must hide. We don't want the entire demon swarm coming down on us. If the demon knights are killed, they may send champions here. The demon knights are looking for us, you know it. Hide. Not fight. Not yet. Not with Meela injured."

Hendry sighed but eventually agreed. The demon knights rode really close to me.

"Their scent fades here," one of the demon knights said.

"Some went that way...but not all of them."

"Two...maybe three are here."

They looked at me, and the demon knights raised their swords. Their swords flared, and the three of them slashed at my trunk repeatedly.

And...it felt like an itch.

The demon knights paused as their attacks failed. "Strange..."

To be honest, I had always found my defense against demons extremely strange, too. But, hey, I wasn't complaining. They slashed a few more times before the demon knight with a staff walked closer and cast some kind of spell.

[Detect Resistance].

Oh. There's such a spell.

The demon knight paused. "Oh. Oh, no."

The other demon knights turned and looked. "What?"

"This tree, it possesses [Immunity to Damage from Mid-tier and Lower-level Demons] and [Greater Damage Reduction from Elder Demons]."

I was shocked, too.

"How?" one of the demon knights asked. They stopped their attacks. They probably realized it was futile in the face of that sort of resistance. "It looks just like any other large tree."

At this point, I realized I probably shouldn't let these knights run, and a few [Root Strike]s surged out of the ground, right through the hellhounds and the knights. One managed to leap off their demonic hellhound, but still, the [Root Strike] speared his demonic armor.

These demon knights were not very different from humans in armor, so in an instant, all of them were dead, skewered by roots. They were probably tougher than regular humans by a little, but against my [Root Strike], these lesser demons were just like paper.

After the battle, Hendry and Jura asked, "Tree-Tree, how did you get your demonic damage reduction?"

"Uh..." I didn't know.

"Is it an item that you have?" Alexis asked. "There are some items that reduce damage from demons. Wards?"

At this point, the only unidentified items I possessed were the fragments. I attempted to take out one fragment, but an error popped up.

[Fragments cannot be separated. They're fused to your body.]

Oh, but I could move the body part where the fragments were all fused. It felt like my 'core,' if such a thing made sense for a tree.

"Alexis, Laufen, I'm going to show you something. Please, help me examine and inspect it."

They both nodded, and the roof of the secret hideout shook a little. The wooden roof twisted and moved aside in a circular fashion like the opening of the lens of a camera. It revealing a lantern-like object made of intricately shaped wood, with dozens of little lights floating inside. It pulsed in a regular fashion, with tiny flashes within.

"Oh, it's beautiful," Laufen immediately said.

[Inspect Equipment]. Laufen used her inspection ability and then shook her head. "I can't see a thing. It's just filled with unknowns and question marks."

"[Thorough Examination]."

Alexis had a far superior identification spell, and after she used it, she seemed to lose her strength and sat on the floor.

"Are you okay?" Hendry tried to support her. "What did you see?"

"I-I am." Alexis pointed at it. "I'm just stunned. That...that thing is your heart, isn't it?"

"Oh. I think so." It felt like this was my 'center.' They were inside me.

"[The Tree's Heart and Spirit Lantern]," Alexis started explaining. "This is the heart of the tree, adorned with the fragments of the fallen fifty-six. It gives the tree a fifty-six times multiplier to experience gain, up to six times damage multiplier against mid-tier demons, up to three times damage multiplier against elder demons, negation of demon armors and defense, immunity to mid-tier and lesser demons, damage reduction against elder demons, and significantly reduced damage from all types of fire."

Wow! All those fragments had a function after all.

Hendry paused. "Alexis, are you sure?"

She nodded.

"This is quite the game changer. We must tell the others. We can take this knowledge and revisit how and where the battles with the demons are fought. This ability essentially transforms this location into a battlefield with a favorable advantage for us. We can save lives!"

I wasn't sure whether I liked the idea of being a demon-lightning rod. Jura and Laufen said, "Tree-Tree, I didn't know you were so amazing."

Alexis looked at Meela, who was still asleep. "Tree-Tree, can you please move your heart closer to Meela?"

My heart-lantern moved, dangling off the roof via vines, dropping above her. A prompt appeared. "Do you want to absorb Meela Adams?"

I shook off the prompt and answered no.

Alexis looked at Meela's condition. "Hmm. It had no effect. The rot is still there. It seems the resistance cannot be shared by the glow. Oh, well."

I moved my heart back. At that point, I realized it was probably very dangerous for me to reveal my heart that way. If it was destroyed, would I die? I assumed so.

Now that I knew the source of my past effectiveness against demons was due to the fragments, that meant against non-demon enemies I was actually significantly weaker, and someone of incredible power like Hendry or the humans could probably easily destroy me.

[You gained 3 levels. You are now level 92.]

[Skills upgraded: Secret Hideout—healing chamber adaptation.]

[Obtained skill: Summon Insect Warriors.]

[Obtained skill: Super Anti-demon Root Strike.]

[Obtained skill: Customizable Branches.]

YEAR 72, MONTH 10, LAST FEW DAYS.

A delegation approached from a distance. It was the beginning of winter, and yet it was warmer than usual, so warm that I felt something was in the air. The warmth confused my leaves, and they shriveled up a little. Somehow, this warm air was 'rough,' and my trunk and bark felt a bit rougher as a result.

A delegation of soldiers, a hundred strong, carrying all sorts of materials and goods approached. An expeditionary force?

Were they friend or foe?

"Tree spirit," a voice called out, one I vaguely recognized. Once he got closer, I soon identified the voice as Lord Rajjiv Nung. "Hmm...is it still asleep...Jura? Jura?"

He seemed to be in far better condition than the last time we met. Maybe he'd gained some levels.

The elves hid, a little intimidated by the presence of so many men. I, too, shared that emotion and was on my guard.

"Should I go out, tree spirit?" Jura asked while Rajjiv called for him.

"Hmm..."

It was the best I could do. Would it be a good idea for Jura to hide? I turned to Hendry and Alexis. "Do you guys want to go out? It's a group of humans, so maybe they can help you."

Hendry shook his head. "We don't know them, so we'll watch how this plays out. However, we will help if needed. Our priority is still Meela and, by extension, your ability to continue to support Meela."

That seemed quite reasonable.

"Yes? What brings you here with a small army?" I telepathically spoke to Rajjiv.

Lord Rajjiv smiled. "Ah, you are awake! Great! We have much to discuss." He dismounted from his warhorse and walked closer, gesturing to my roots. "May I?"

"Yes."

He sat on the flat surface of the few protruding roots.

"So, since our last battle, the defeat of the demon champion at our hands greatly improved our king's opinion about how natural spirits could be a means to fight demons."

He paused.

"And so, we are wondering whether you are open to relocating yourself outside of our capital city."

"No." I hated moving. I had to be decisive in rejecting this.

"Ah, I suspected as much. Well, are tree spirits able to produce offspring or saplings that we could cultivate into a tree spirit? Would a branch of yours grow into a split version of yourself?"

Eh? Now that was a good question. I recalled producing fruits, and they had seeds, but they only seemed to grow into normal plants. If they did somehow grow into their own tree spirits, I doubted I missed their presence.

"Rest assured, we would take good care of your offspring or saplings. We only ask as it would aid us in battle."

Rajjiv made a very good point. Could I 'procreate' in a sense that allowed me to create other tree spirits? Or would my 'offspring' not inherit any of my abilities or qualities?

"I am afraid I am unable to produce any spirit offspring. So far, my offspring and seeds are just normal trees."

Yet? Or maybe I didn't yet know.

"Ah, that is disappointing but not unexpected."

Rajjiv stood and looked around the area.

"But that is not why I came all this way..."

Rajjiv took out a small map and pointed. I couldn't actually see the map, though.

"The demon champions. Three of them. They've gathered somewhere in the region nearby. We will set up a base of operations here and then attack the demons."

Huh? "No." A large army, here? That would be bad.

"This doesn't please me a bit, but sadly, it is not a choice, tree spirit. I am just the messenger. The king has decreed this land and its surroundings to be the staging ground for military operations against the demonic champions. We have the heroes themselves, and they are on their way. We are just the advance party to prepare this place for the upcoming campaign."

This news was unpleasant, but then again, what choice did I have? If a large army came, what were my choices? I wanted to protect the elves, but I knew I couldn't fight off an army. As much as I disliked it, I had to accept that this was reality.

"Heroes?" *Ah, the reincarnators!*

"Yes, the ones with gods' gifts. We are not sure when they will get here. The king said they are visiting all the kingdoms along the way."

Both Hendry and Alexis seemed particularly interested in the conversation.

"But they are headed here, and then they will go to the demon champions. They will slay them, gain levels, and then fight the demon king."

The reincarnators, I would like to see what sort of cheat-like abilities they had.

Oh, wait. That meant the days ahead would be a whole lot of

death and war. Well, from what I learned about this world, it had always been filled with death and war, so I should not complain.

The elves too shook their heads. From within the hideout, they could actually eavesdrop on any conversation next to me. Hendry peered out through a small peephole. "That man is from the kingdom?"

"Yes, Rajjiv Nung of the Kingdom of Nung."

Hendry shook his head. "Don't know him. Do you, Alexis?" Alexis shook her head, too. "Ah, I guess we will keep hiding, then. No need to draw unnecessary attention."

Laufen gave Lausanne a hug, and she looked at the rest. "Hmm. It sounds like there will be a lot of fighting. This place is going to be a battlefield again. It's just not too long ago we had so much...death."

"If I can keep you elves safe, I will," I assured her, even if I knew what would happen was going to be unpleasant.

Rajjiv, oblivious to the conversation within the hideout, motioned to his men to start work.

"Tree spirit, may we meet again under far better circumstances. Some of my men will remain here to set up the area for the coming battles." After the men rested for an hour or so, about seventy of them followed Rajjiv's lead, and they rode toward the demonic rifts. The plan was to spread out, monitor the demons' movements, set up magical markers, and be on the lookout for any large demon armies.

The remaining thirty or so men started to build a campsite, setting up multiple large tents. Farther out, they built a low fence, and they marked where the future army would be. These men appeared to be builders and mages. Some of them used magic to manipulate the ground and dirt, forming makeshift dirt walls and trenches.

Alexis and Hendry looked out of the peephole. "Heroes are coming?"

"Yes, that's what he said."

"Oh, wow. I can't wait to meet the heroes. I wonder what they are like?" Emile and Belle both seem quite excited to meet heroes, and that excitement caused both Alexis and Hendry to sigh.

"Have you guys met them?" Emile asked.

Alexis and Hendry glanced at each other. "Ah...yes, yes, we have."

"They must be handsome and dashing... Oh, wait, don't tell me, don't tell me. I want to see them for myself." Emile seemed somewhat infatuated with the concept of heroes. Hendry and Alexis smiled awkwardly.

"I think fairy tales and reality usually differ quite a bit."

Meanwhile, I activated my [Summon Insect Warriors] skill, and a few beetles appeared on my branch, hidden from the soldiers. They seemed rather tough, and they were mostly mind-less creatures mentally linked to me. I would need to test them in actual combat to know how they would fare in reality.

[Customizable Branches]

[You currently have three slots for customizable branches. The branches can be customized for specific functions, such as producing certain materials or essences, hosting certain insects or animals, or becoming some kind of accommodation (if the branch if sufficiently large).]

Ah. There's actually a long list of materials extracted and essences harvested, hidden inside a separate notification menu. I remembered that I selected the option to hide those notifica-tions, else I'd be overwhelmed by these notifications all the time.

Hendry chose to mostly stay inside. Occasionally, he wondered when his friends would return. Meela was also doing all right despite her body's constant battle with the demonic rot within. Alexis spent her time talking to Meela and also playing with the younger elves.

The older elves were still apprehensive of the humans, but the younger ones didn't hold such prejudices. Perhaps, not yet.

YEAR 72, MONTH 11, WEEK 1

An army of twenty thousand passed by. Half of them joined up with the camp, but from the chatter they created, it seemed they were meant to leave very soon. The other half marched on. They were headed for a location closer to the rift where they would set up smaller camps.

With the larger numbers came traffic. There were more messengers needed for certain types of communication. There was also a small group of dedicated mages, and their role was to facilitate long-distance, secure communication spells.

Winter, strangely, was delayed this year. It was still oddly warm. The weather was behaving strangely, and Alexis suspected it was the fault of the demons.

Refugee groups started popping up, the fallout of the demon raids that destroyed villages closer to the rift, at least, those that had not fled yet. The rift, as Alexis elaborated, was some kind of a flux, a rip in 'space,' and it joined our world with that of the demons. It expanded and sometimes moved, usually slowly, but under certain circumstances, the changes could occur really quickly.

According to Alexis, so long as the demon king remained in

the world, the rifts would remain open and expand, and after their death, the rifts would shrink and, eventually, close.

So a world couldn't wait forever for the heroes to slay the demon king, else the rift would expand drastically, and demons would appear all over the world. It sounded to me like the demon king functioned as some kind of bridge to the demon world.

YEAR 72, MONTH 11, WEEK 3

From the bits and pieces of information I gathered via eavesdropping on the refugees and the soldiers, no one knew I was a tree spirit. They presumed I was a normal tree that somehow survived in this place. Other than that, they never spoke about me, as they mainly focused on their own affairs.

Their lack of knowledge made me curious, even a little suspicious. Perhaps Lord Rajjiv had reasons not to share that information, and so I adjusted my assessment of him in my mind.

They also took credit for the defeat of the demon champion earlier and ignored my contribution. At first, I felt a little slighted, but after I pondered that emotion, I realized keeping myself unknown might be better.

"Should I reveal my presence to the soldiers?" I asked the elves and the three adventurers.

"Hmm, what would revealing that achieve, Tree-Tree?" Belle asked as she peered outside. Emile had talked about the heroes for some time now, and she wondered where in the world they were.

"True. I stand to lose more than gain." As a tree, I couldn't really move, so I couldn't run away.

"If you have powers, it's best to keep it a secret," Alexis said as she held Meela's hand. "People will seek you out for your power, and you will become a tool, not a person. Your power will define who you are to the masses."

"Fair point." She had sounded really sad when she said that. "Sounds like personal experience."

"It is." Alexis held Meela's hand a little longer.

YEAR 72, MONTH 11, WEEK 4

Another ten thousand or so soldiers arrived, and as with the earlier group, they didn't stop for long, continuing their march toward the rift.

Thanks to the constant upgrades and additions, the surrounding area was essentially a makeshift fort. The humans with earth magic molded a two-layer wall complete with towers and ramparts, staffing them with soldiers.

Traffic remained high, and refugees continued to stream in. The refugees didn't stay for long as there wasn't much food available. Most of the supplies were meant for the army, and even then, that was barely sufficient. The refugees continued to move on to safer and hopefully more prosperous lands. There were minor demon attacks, but they were only small packs of hellhounds, easily disposed by the army camped in this place.

From the chatter, I gathered new types of demons were appearing near the rift. Larger versions of hellhounds and a half-golem, half-demon variant. Perhaps the demon king had some earth-elemental powers since his minions displayed earth-like features.

I wondered whether this had something to do with the mild shakes and tremors we occasionally felt.

"Where are they?" Hendry was frustrated, though Meela's condition was still stable. It seemed he was eager to get a shot at the demons but was also torn with Meela's present condition.

"Our friends will come back for us," Alexis assured him. "It's fine like this. A bit of a break from all this killing, and maybe the heroes' power can help Meela."

Hendry scowled, but then he paused to think.

"You might be right, Alexis. The heroes' semi-divine holy powers might be able to counteract the demonic rot."

YEAR 72, MONTH 12

The heroes arrived, accompanied by an army of adventurers about three hundred strong. It was normal for heroes to have a huge group of tagalongs. These people sought the glory and glamor of an association with the heroes, but they were also the first to flee when shit got out of hand.

The heroes themselves, five of them, were three men and two women, and they looked no older than twenty, maybe slightly over. The gods chose young people for their demon-killing tasks this time, and in a way, that was better than choosing teenagers.

They rode into the makeshift camp, and one of them stopped and stared in my direction. Though I couldn't meet his eye, I sensed his probing gaze.

"Hmm. I feel a familiar presence," one of the heroes muttered and rode his horse closer.

"You were here before, hero?" an adventurer who accompanied him asked.

"No." The armored hero placed his hand on my bark, and I shivered. "Just...someone familiar... Hmmm..."

"[Hero's Sense]."

The hideout shook a little, and everyone freaked out. This

hero had some kind of magical touch, and my body reacted to it defensively.

The shaking caused Hendry to sigh, and he decided to go out and talk to the hero.

"Hey, hero."

"Hendry!" The hero's eye widened, and he stared at Hendry.

The adventurer next to the hero raised his sword at Hendry. "Eh? Who goes there?"

"It is fine. Lay down your arms. He is one of us." The hero stared at Hendry. "It's been a while—"

"Yes. Yes, it has. First, take your hands off the tree, and I might need your help."

The hero took his hand off immediately. "Well, nice to see you, again."

Hendry paused and sighed. "Nice to see me? I take it that means you stopped blaming us for her death?"

The hero shook his head. "I'd like to think we have come to terms with it."

"Really?" Hendry took a step back.

"We were all too eager, too excited with this opportunity, this chance to make something of ourselves." The hero walked closer to Hendry.

Hendry paused. "Really? Just like that?"

The hero placed his hand on his shoulder. "Yes."

And then he punched Hendry in the gut. *Thud.*

"Ugh! I knew it." Hendry groaned in pain, but he recovered quickly and threw a punch back. The hero dodged.

The adventurers stared. "Uh, hero, should we do something?"

The hero yelled, "No! This is between me and him!" They punched each other a few times, then it escalated, and they started to throw empowered punches that were more like flashes. Both attacked each other with their abilities. The adventurers stared at the high-speed exchange of blows.

A few more heroes came over. "Max! Stop this."

Two female heroines shouted, and Max, the hero, jumped back a few steps, and that ended the exchange of punches.

"Hendry!" one of the heroines seemed to cry a little.

"Hey." Hendry stopped and sat on one of my roots. The heroines ran over and gave Hendry a hug. "Been a while."

"We've been looking for you guys..." The heroine smacked Hendry on his shoulder. "Running off like that..."

At this point, the adventurers asked, "Uh...who is he?"

Max laughed. "Ah, yes, please ignore us. He is a *friend*. You guys go ahead. We'll need to talk privately with our friend here. We'll be fine."

Max explained, "You guys should not have left like that. We were angry, and we are still sad. There is still a lump in our hearts. But we are willing to let it go, for in hindsight, we had a part to play, too. We failed as well. We all did. I think a part of the way we acted is because we were angry at ourselves."

At this point, I was confused at what their conversation was about. Perhaps some historical bad blood.

Hendry nodded, his eyes a little teary. "Heh...water under the bridge now. Well, Max, as I was saying, I need your help. Do you still have anti-demonic powers?"

"Huh? Of course I still do. Why?"

Alexis, right on cue, came out with Meela. She was asleep and supported by Alexis's levitation. "It's actually for Meela. She's received some kind of demonic rot or maybe demonic poison. She's weak and battling internally, and she is currently supported by a whole lot of healing magic. It...it seems to be some kind of magic meant for...us."

The heroes gasped. "Meela..." Max ran over, looked at her, and held her hand. He then proceeded to use some kind of magical ability on her, then their bodies glowed faintly.

The hero chanted and mumbled a little, and his palm glowed like a monk trying to use some kind of mantra.

"[Heroic Touch]."

The ability caused Meela's body to glow in a faint light.

"Hmm. I can't remove it completely. It contains a strong taint of the demon king. You are right. This is made to kill us, and this...this makes this demon king more dangerous than ever." He sighed.

Alexis held Meela's hand, and I saw the demonic rot shrink as if fenced in by a ring of energy. Meela's eyes gradually opened.

"I can suppress and weaken the effect of the poison such that it will stop hurting her."

"Thank you," Meela whispered.

Max smiled. "Nice to see you, Meela."

These adventurers are reincarnators as well. Now that they were right next to me, I felt strange. Were these people from Earth, too? The kids, those few when I came so many years ago, they had all died. These people...well, a similar fate probably awaited them.

What should I do?

Should I also reveal myself as a reincarnator? But what good would that do? Didn't that just unnecessarily involve me in the demon war?

There was also the question about the [Fires of Baal] I previously suffered. How I was able to recover from it, and yet Meela failed to recover from her own demonic poisoning?

Why? Was it because the fires I had were just generic fires of the demon king, whereas Meela's demon rot was a customized poisonous cocktail meant specifically for reincarnators?

I had no answer to that, unfortunately.

At this point, I decided to wait and see. I mentally pinged Alexis.

"So...may I ask what is happening? Will you leave with them?"

"Ah...er... Right now, there are still three of us out there, looking for a cure. Maybe there is no cure, and killing the demon king is the only way. Meela is currently in no condition to fight. Her demonic rot is still present, even though its curse has been weakened by Max's counteracting holy power. Until we know more about how this will affect us in combat, we don't want to risk it."

Alexis paused and took a deep breath. "Meela's body appears to be fine, with no observable negative effects so far, but I feel there remains a high chance that the demon king's magic will still interfere with our divine gifts. So attempting to assault the demons without being at full strength feels like folly."

"Uh..." Alexis was more technical when it came to magic. "Sorry, can you repeat that in simpler terms?"

"Meela and I will stay back. We will wait for the rest of us to return, and then we will join up with Max and the group. The fact that the demon king has a special weapon designed for us is...worrying."

YEAR 72, MONTH 12, WEEK 2

News and reports of the demon champions came. The heroes, adventurers, and soldiers moved out and headed toward the rift.

Meela and Alexis remained. Alexis played the role of Meela's observer and monitored her body's condition. Periodically, Meela tried to use her abilities, and they discovered that with the demonic rot suppressed but still present, her abilities were weakened by about twenty to thirty percent. Alexis's hypothesis was right after all.

The camp was quieter as only about a thousand soldiers remained. These were the communication mages, the logistics coordinators, and a few guards to keep the stray demon hounds at bay.

YEAR 72, MONTH 12, WEEK 4

The heroes defeated one of the champions.

And then the next day, the camp was attacked.

Six large demons, part-golem, part-demon. These appeared to be lesser versions of the golem-demon champion, accompanied by tens of thousands of the new rock hybrid hellhounds. The bodies of the six demons were made of a mix of rock, magma, and flesh, and their synchronized steps shook the ground.

How did they appear so suddenly?

Three came from the front, and three came from the back. They had the camp cornered on both sides, and their sudden appearance sent the camp into a panic. Mages quickly sent out requests for help, but any request would be too late. Reinforcements would take some time to get to us.

Alexis and Meela looked at each other. "How'd they get behind us?" In fact, that question was probably on the mind of the thousand or so soldiers now trapped within the camp. However, at this point, there were more urgent questions to be answered.

The two demon forces marched on the camp, their footsteps

causing the earth to rumble. How did all the shaking from their steps go unnoticed before this?

I [Summon Insect Warriors].

My insect warriors appeared, crawling from my branches. Three of them would deal with the hellhound hybrids, and hopefully, they wouldn't die too easily. The humans screamed in surprise when they saw my giant insects, but they didn't attack them.

I surveyed the field of demons. I needed to save my [Super Anti-demon Root Strike] for the lesser champions. The guards got ready as the demons closed in. If they were going to die, at least they would die fighting.

The mages in the camp blasted magic spells at the golems, and the camp descended into a chaotic battlefield. The six giant demons were exceptionally resilient, and they endured volleys of spells and attacks from the mages, only suffering minor wounds and damage.

Despite Meela not being in her best shape, she could fight, and so both Alexis and Meela joined the battle. Jura fought, too.

In the battle, I witnessed the sheer overpowered-ness of these reincarnators.

Alexis activated her spells, and she released wave after wave of magical explosions, almost constantly attacking. Meela, even in her weakened form, could swirl and twirl, and her slashes went through the rocky flesh of the monsters like they had absolutely no armor on and were made of chiffon.

It was ridiculous that they swept through hordes of demons like nothing.

One large golem was destroyed after it took a fireball point-blank. Alexis's blast had destroyed its body in a single shot.

Another golem wandered a little too close me, and I took the chance to test out my new [Super Anti-demon Root Strike]. It shot out of the earth and sliced the golem in half.

Whoa! I felt pleased with myself.

Alexis blew up another large golem. Throughout the camp,

soldiers and mages battled with the hybrid hounds, and though the soldiers could beat them easily one on one, even one on two, the hounds had them outnumbered, easily ten times their number. So mages and soldiers died as they were overrun.

Even with Meela and Alexis's tremendous support.

Meela cut down one of the large demons with some kind of flashy slashing move.

My insect warriors seemed to be performing as expected. They were able to take down about twenty or so hellhounds before they were torn apart.

Alexis blew up another golem. Then another fireball from Alexis blew up the last golem. She really was the true MVP in this battle.

"We did it!"

Alexis turned her attention to the regular hybrid hounds and joined Meela and the soldiers in their demon extermination.

Then the earth shook, and sparks of lightning shot out from the rubble of the destroyed giant demons. The lightning connected to all the other remains, and destroyed golems floated in the air and joined together. Alexis sent a few fireballs instinctively, and it knocked some of the rocks away, but something still piled it all together.

The remains of all the fallen golems and hounds merged into a giant, six-story-tall centipede made of earth, covered in sharp, jagged rocks and stone across its body. In a way, it was part-centipede, part-golem. It charged the battlefield, crushing both allies and enemies alike.

Once it lost momentum, it tunneled underground.

"Shit." Alexis and Meela ran, their eyes darting everywhere as they waited for the centipede. "It could appear anywhere!" They looked around, but their eyes mostly scanned the ground.

The earth shook, and it shot out of the battlefield. It killed more soldiers and hounds, but their absorbed debris and corpses of the fallen hounds, growing larger still.

Yet the centipede didn't approach me.

In fact, the moment it was underground, I could pinpoint exactly where it was, and my roots formed a layer of reinforced earth it was unable to tunnel through.

I sensed it, digging from one side to another as it tried to get through my defenses.

I thought I could beat it. I knew from instinct that my [Root Strike]s were more powerful underground. But the centipede moved really quickly, its movement shaking the ground. If I could just get it to slow down, I was sure I could get a good hit in.

"Gather around the tree! The monster is unable to tunnel close to it!" Alexis yelled. She seemed to have arrived at a similar conclusion to mine. She activated a weird console like magic and called all the surviving mages to her.

The demonic centipede surged out of the ground again, and Alexis yelled, "Now!" The mages coordinated a magical blast at the demonic centipede, and a few large chunks were blasted off its hide.

The demonic giant centipede tunneled again, and I tried to follow its movement. It was still fast, but I noticed it slowed down for a moment before it surged upward. That was the best time for me to hit it.

It shot out of the ground again, killing more soldiers and hounds.

I took my chance and hit it with two [Root Strikes], managing to knock a few chunks away.

The centipede regenerated from our attacks, rocks knocked off pulled back to the whole, but I felt its magical energy balance dwindled each time it happened. If we wanted to defeat it, it meant eroding its magical power down to zero by repeatedly blasting chunks away.

It attacked a few more times as I tried to learn the timing.

By that point, almost seventy percent of the humans were dead, and almost all the demon hounds were destroyed or absorbed by the centipede.

The battle was between us and the centipede now. Then it split itself in two along its length, and both centipedes tunneled underground. Once there, the centipede reconnected itself and became one very long and lean centipede.

This time, it popped up out of the ground and used its now longer body like a whip. Its body slammed into the soldiers, mages, and also into me. It still couldn't tunnel near me, but the centipede attacked the humans around me.

My trunk shook when the centipede slammed into me, and some of the mages retaliated with a blast, knocking more rocks from it. It pulled back and curled in on itself like a snake, springing to attack the mages and soldiers.

"[Grand Fireball]."

Alexis activated her signature superpower—a blue fireball—and it barreled toward the demonic centipede, exploding on impact.

The centipede was broken and burned from the fire, but the momentum of its attack still pushed through, and it stabbed Alexis right in the chest, pushing her back, slamming her into my trunk.

"Arghhhhhhhhhhhh!" Alexis screamed as she was stabbed by multiple sharp rocks. Those same rocks burned from her [Grand Fireball], and it spread throughout the centipede's body.

The demon centipede flailed from the flames but refused to let go. It kept its head on target and pinned Alexis to the trunk.

Somehow, she still managed to cast another [Grand Fireball], creating a huge explosion right in front of it. It blasted almost all the rocks at the head of the centipede away, but a skeleton of super-hard rock remained, and it pierced Alexis's chest.

It flailed, but it didn't let go. It pinned Alexis's body to the ground.

I used [Constrict] and held onto the centipede so my [Root Strike] could catch it, and then I released all my remaining [Super Anti-demonic Root Strike]. They pierced the centipede, and this time, together with a third [Grand Fireball] fired from

Alexis at point-blank, we successfully depleted its magical energy, and it crumbled. Its body turned into a pile of ordinary rocks.

Alexis, though, exploded into a huge fireball, and then just as suddenly, a vacuum-like effect appeared as all the fires swirled back and merged, forming into a human shape. The flames died down and revealed Alexis.

"Ugh," she groaned, visibly drained. "I really dislike using [Body of Fire]."

Meela smacked her on the back. "That went swimmingly. Once again, we've proven that's why you're always the bait! Everyone aims for the mage!"

Reincarnators...

[You gained 8 levels. You are now Level 100.]

[You have evolved into an Ancient Soul Tree. The next evolution rank up is at Level 130 if conditions and materials are met. You can still gain levels without ranking up.]

[Your following skills have been upgraded: Life Support Chamber.]

[Healing powers upgraded.]

[Secret Hideout upgraded. Extra rooms, special purpose rooms, and hideouts unlocked. Customizable branches option now has External room.]

[Soul Absorption upgraded. Soul Realm unlocked.]

[Symbiotic Extension unlocked.]

[Essence Collection upgraded. Essence Mastery and Generation obtained. Customizable Branch Options now include Essence Generator.]

[Materials Obtained.]

[Essence of Giants x 1, Essence of Starlight x 1, Essence of Sword x 4, Essence of Knights x 1, Essence of Fire Magic x 1.]

INTERLUDE

Level one hundred, and the rank up brought changes and a lot of benefits. One of the key changes was a UI change. My perspective and interface became much more organized, and the details on all the various menus expanded. There were more tooltips as well, and information about my skills improved.

Size-wise, the rank up brought about greater size and range. I found myself twice as large—almost eight stories high—and my roots extended to cover a wider area. They also went deeper, which then led to my discovery of how the demons appeared.

Deep tunnels. The rock centipedes dug tunnels underground and used them to move their forces without being detected. They covered the entrances, these tunnels reaching well beyond my range, and perhaps even into the demon lands.

This seemed like valuable information. Perhaps I could trade something for it.

The sudden increase in my physical size overnight scared the humans, but they were too preoccupied with the dead to do anything about it.

With this new size, I had eight large branches, and the new skills allowed me to set some of them as an [Essence Generator], which automatically generated essences of the moon, the sun, and nature. These would later be used as materials for items and weapons.

I learned from the soldiers and heroes that common theories suggested demons were generally weak against stellar materials, like metals from an asteroid. But these were rumors, of course, and I didn't actually have stellar materials to prove it.

Back in my secret hideout, the healing room changed, and it transformed into the shape of a pod, large enough for a body to be fully submerged within.

It looked like those mad scientist labs where there were vats that cloned creatures. Perhaps, someday, I would be able to rebuild bodies. Next to the pod was a lab-like area, all located in a small underground room filled with roots, pods, and other things like a spawning pool.

I activated [Soul Realm]. I felt my consciousness shift, and I appeared in a vast space filled with little floating lights. These little wisps floated and swirled around, and...they seemed to whisper and chatter endlessly in a language I didn't understand.

"What is this place?"

"This is your soul realm, and this is one of the strongest powers of a spirit tree." A wisp floated before me. It was different from the other wisps in that it was green while the others were white. "Here are all the souls of those who have died in your vicinity. They lay dormant, resting, waiting..."

"For?"

"For their travel to the afterlife. Tree spirits, as the elves once advised you, are the beacons of souls, attracting those who died. You also function as a pitstop, refreshing the souls, and souls who are stronger are more likely to make travel on to the after-life, where they will re-enter the cycle of life. Your very existence here prevents the presence of stray ghosts, but in turn, the ghosts exist all within you."

I paused and looked at this green wisp as it explained all this to me. "And...you are?"

"I am Wisp, and I am a creation made from the combined souls who didn't make the cut for the journey to the afterlife, and my role is to support and guide the newly dead. I have existed within you from the very moment you transformed into a Spiritual Tree. You have many questions, and I will answer them."

He first guided me to a tree filled with little lights like fireflies in a swamp. "These are the souls of the recently deceased. The faint white ones are humans, and as you can see, it's currently mostly humans, but we can also see there are souls with different colors, and these are the mixed-race beings."

Wisp floated over to a black tree branch, with tiny little lights there. These lights were smaller than the other souls. They looked like little blinking sparks.

"These are the leftover souls, fragments and souls that have degraded, or some that just don't want to be reincarnated. At their current state, they have lost their identity and awareness, so they become nothing more than a shell. They can be used to create things, custom familiars, infused into weapons, merged together...quite versatile, actually."

After that, Wisp led me to another black branch that had split in half.

"This is the [Soul Forge] where you can make even more things with the remnants, but it's inactive at the moment as you need to either connect to a magical ley line or gain more levels so you can power it yourself. It connects to the pod in your secret hideout."

I paused and then asked, "Why is [Soul Realm] a powerful ability?"

Wisp twirled. "The soul is at the core of power in this world. It is the soul that gains experience and levels, and the body is just the expression of that extra experience and levels."

"But why do people train their bodies, then?"

"Because the body changes the soul. It is a feedback loop. A strong, healthy body nourishes the soul and vice versa."

"Okay. You said this is a strong ability. Why?"

Wisp paused and twirled around.

"Because, when you change a soul, you amend their destiny. A soul doomed for mediocrity could be remade into something far greater."

PERSPECTIVE – ALEXIS

The demon king was out for their heads.

Alexis knew it. She felt it. Every battle with the demons, their eyes seemed to contain a deep, feral rage, all directed at them. Was it just how they always looked?

Even when they were not fighting, it felt like she sensed where the demon king was. It was as if there was always a cold wind that came from that direction, but there was no actual wind.

After the constant ambushes and attacks, she suspected the demons sensed them, too. It was the only plausible reason why incredibly powerful demons always appeared where they were, and somehow, these demons were always able to strike when the heroes were apart.

"It's a coincidence, Alexis." Max waved off the idea. "They have hunter demons and demon knights constantly tracking us. That's why they know where we are."

Maybe.

But was it?

As a mage, she believed there was a logic to everything. Even underneath the veneer of magic, there was a system, logic. This system, even if it didn't make sense when compared to where she came from, possessed its own rules and laws.

Everything obeyed those laws, including the gods' blessings.

These blessings offered some degree of protection from demons, and they enhanced stats growth and boosted experience gains for easier leveling. They leveled way faster, achieving more in a year than the natives could do in decades.

These were common knowledge. Heroes always received perks. They found it easier to defeat the demon king.

Lately, during these occasional moments of clarity, she suspected the blessings did more than just that. They had another function.

She remembered her friends and how they came to this world. Some days, it was so hard to remember, but today, it came easily. She sipped on her cup of tea. They were headed for a café when a truck lost control. The truck and its container flipped sideways and slammed right into all of them.

After a brief meeting with the gods, they all woke in this world. Since then, they devoted themselves to this divine quest to slay the demon king, even if they took detours.

Why were they so engrossed with the goal? All the death, pain, and suffering they had seen, it all seemed to be just a side note. A number. The vast destruction around her, rather than affecting them emotionally, merely enhanced their resolve to destroy the demon king.

It was as if the heroes had been mentally altered, made to be immune to the destruction, and all that negative energy and emotion was deliberately funneled back to their goal.

Even Meela, with her near-death experience, went back to the battlefield happily as if her brush with death never really mattered.

Alexis hadn't realized this before, but lately, during these brief moments of clarity, when she reread her daily journal, she realized her own strange mental processes and noticed the way she reacted to these things.

"We're on the way back, Alexis," a communication mage passed the message.

Alexis nodded by way of thanks. The mage bowed and left. The heroes, those summoned by the gods, would converge.

Here.

Alexis scribbled on her journal.

Destroying the demon king aligned with her and her group's interest. After all, they were hunted by the demons. But a feeling of dread permeated her. The demons were coming for them.

The demon king would look for them, even before they were ready. They needed to hit level one hundred.

What would she do? What should be done? They couldn't keep running. Not forever.

She glanced up and looked at the tree. It was larger, far larger, now. And she felt safe. If they had to fight, this was the best place for it. If the plan was up to her, they would fall back and fight here.

Still, she thought about her suspicions. How did the demons find them?

She sat and closed her eyes. She stilled her mind and concentrated on her breathing. She felt the prickling senses on her skin and the beating of her heart.

She searched for a subtle signal, a presence beyond their own. Were they letting something out? Did they release signals or markers? Were they like a nuclear bomb, leaking radiation that shouted to the demon kings that this was where they were?

If the gods had a hand in this, how and what would they do?

If they could hide their presence, maybe, just maybe, they could deal the demons a surprise attack.

"Alexis, are you busy?" Meela asked.

"Ah." Alexis snapped out of her concentration. "Uh, yes. I would like some time."

Meela nodded. "Oh, okay." She sighed and walked away.

Alexis closed her eyes and tried again, but her mind's moment of clarity faded away, replaced by—

Demons. Anger. Destruction. Fire. Death. Fields of dead men. The voices of all the grieving humans. These voices said the demon king must be slain.

Alexis shook her head. Not again. All of them felt this every now and then.

As if the world reminded them of their duty.

She walked closer to the tree and lifted a small wooden teapot. She poured herself a cup and sipped on it.

And, somehow, the voices went away. For a while.

YEAR 73, MONTH 1

Jura stepped out of the green liquid pod in the lab. He was submerged in the pod daily as part of my experimentation.

"How do you feel?"

"Fine, Tree-Tree. Did you do anything? My status is unchanged..."

"No."

In truth, all I did was look at his body in detail. The first time he submerged, the pod flooded me with data and details. It was fascinating. I felt like a scientist, looking at the body of a person with an electron microscope and radio wave imaging machine.

It felt incredible to see every strand of fiber, the organs, the bones, and everything else. Strangely enough, this was also the first time I had an actual idea how Jura looked. All I had before this was my somewhat pixelated [Spirit Vision].

Another thing I spent a lot of time looking at was his soul. I studied it repeatedly and tried to understand how it interacted with his body. Initially, I thought it was like the source of a river. A person with higher levels had a bigger source, and the waters from this source flowed into each body part, then each body part expressed the energy as toughness and awakened magical properties.

In Jura's body, it felt like there was a polluted drainage pipe. This polluted drainage pipe released dirty water into the river, and so each body part was weakened by it.

I reached out to it, and I knew it could be fixed.

But I would need the right materials.

Later that evening, I asked Meela for her help. If I could see Jura's body with such detail, I wondered what I would find from the heroes.

This request made Alexis a little suspicious, so she insisted on being around as well.

Jura guided both to the new underground laboratory.

"This...this looks like..." Both had stunned looks as if they didn't expect to see something like this in this world. "A lab."

I recalled only the elves had ever been to this new room. This was different from the medical ward area Meela once rested in. Jura pointed to one open pod. "Please, if you don't mind, I'll need you to get into the pod..."

Meela glanced at Alexis briefly and then nodded. "Okay."

Jura smiled and left the two heroes alone. Meela undressed and stepped into the warm green liquid, and the pod slowly closed. The vines naturally formed a mask that allowed Meela to keep breathing, even when her entire body was submerged in the liquid.

Alexis stared on, but she looked like she was thinking. She also used some of her skills and monitored Meela.

Meanwhile, a torrent of data came into my mind, and it stunned me for a moment.

"How long will this take?" Alexis asked.

"About two hours, if I don't find anything unusual." I snapped out of my shock and started my investigation into Meela's body. I really wanted to know what made her tick.

First, physique. Her body appeared to me initially as that of a normal human, but on further investigation, her body had changed. She was already at least three to four times physically stronger than Jura, and this was before any magic spells that would further push her into crazy-strong territory.

Her skeletal structure was tough. It was as if she had an adamantine frame, and her muscles all stored tremendous amounts of physical energy.

Then I looked into her soul. Her soul was like a massive lake. There were two waterfalls that floated overhead in the aether, and its star-sparkled water flowed into the lake. There was a spring of water in the middle. These three water sources pooled and flowed downward like a raging river.

The water was murky, not clear like the others. I looked a little closer and noticed that right next to that spring was a small black whirlpool, and it sucked some of the water away. There was barricade around the whirlpool, made with some kind of energy, and this reduced the impact of that whirlpool, such that only a small portion of water was drained away.

"This is taking too long," Alexis mumbled and used some kind of magic. "Is she all right?"

"Yes. She's fine. A bit more," I answered. I could revisit the data later.

I reached out and attempted to sense that black whirlpool. I felt an ominous presence as my mental senses touched it. It was demonic energy, and it attempted to burn me.

Ugh.

I investigated the starry waterfalls instead, and I sensed a kind of unknown power...perhaps divine? Or was it astral?

These heroes, it seemed to me that their souls must have been modified by the gods that summoned them here. Their size and capacity far exceeded that of a normal mortal, at least, when compared to Jura. But I would need more samples.

Alexis looked nervous. She didn't seem to like Meela remaining in the pod.

"I am done." The pod's doors opened upward, its motion a reverse Venus flytrap. The waters in the pod receded, and Meela's eyes opened.

Alexis immediately grabbed her. "Are you okay?"

Meela rubbed her eyes for a while and said, "I feel pretty nice, actually. It's like a massage."

[Secret Hideout – Biolab upgraded]

Oh.

"Really?"

"Yeah, it is. You should try it."

Alexis shook her head. "Uh...never mind."

"Why are you worried? The tree saved my life. If it wants us to just dip into a pool..."

"No." Alexis turned. "If we are done, then let's go out."

The two reincarnators left, and I telepathically reached out to Laufen for her turn to dip into the pod.

I also tasked Jura with a request.

"Capture a demon hound."

"Capture?"

"Yes. I want it alive."

"Really? Its teeth can chew through any rope or net we have..."

A net appeared next to him. "Woven from my bark and fiber. This should last a bit longer. Use this as well." I handed him a wooden container that contained paralyzing sap from one of my vines.

Jura nodded and set out on his mission.

Around this time, message spells bounced back and forth between the heroes, and both Alexis and Meela left with the remaining army. From the news, one of the nearby cities was under attack from a demonic force, so the rest of the heroes changed their plans and headed straight there instead.

This was great because the elves finally got to have their space again.

J ura finally caught a hellhound. It was tough to catch one in a manageable pack, but he finally did it.

The hellhound lost four limbs, and it was barely alive.

"So, what do I do with it?" Jura looked at me quizzically.

"Bring in down to the lab."

Jura paused. "Inside?"

"Yes."

He gulped but placed the struggling hellhound into the pod. The rest of the elves looked on curiously. Laufen, Emile, and Belle were all ready for battle just in case the hound tried something.

My branches and roots moved to wrap and attach to the paralyzed hound, and its struggling stopped as my energies and saps flooded it. One of the roots administered a dose of sedation, and it was successfully knocked out.

Then I peered into its body. The body of a hybrid hellhound.

The first thing I noticed was the unusual nature of its body. It was a mix of strange but still somewhat normal flesh. However, there was a smattering of earth, mixed with a latticework of interconnected rocks. This mixture was present throughout its body but more frequently in some parts, like the area nearer to its skull and teeth. The type of rock appeared to be compressed stone that was magically augmented.

Then I took a look at its soul.

If the magic from Jura's soul was that of a water tap, and Meela's mana was a raging river, this hellhound would be best described as a dried watering hole. Parched, its body was devoid of the natural mana.

Instead, there was a small red fire that hovered right above where the spring would normally be. The small red fire emitted a kind of heat that powered all the magical augmentation throughout its body.

I reached out to touch it.

Demon.

I felt a pushback from that tiny fire. There was a wall.

I kept pushing, and the wall bent as it wasn't strong enough to resist me.

For a moment, I thought I saw a glimpse of a faraway place...

A red planet, a surface filled with fire and brimstone, and a large, glowing red stone.

Then the fire disappeared. At that moment, any sign of life that once existed in the hound disappeared as if somebody pressed an off button.

Yet the hound was still there. Its body floated in my pod, its four limbs still severed.

[You gained a level. You are now level 101.]

[Secret Hideout – biolab, upgraded. Additional pods now available.]

Two additional pods popped up next to the one with the floating hound.

Was it dead? Its body remained instead of disintegrating. Perhaps the pod interfered with its natural decay into mana?

Jura stepped back in as he wondered what the sound was that he heard, the two new pods appearing.

"It's fine. The hound's dead."

"Oh."

"Anyway, good that you are here. Dip in."

Jura paused but then nodded. "Uh, okay."

Two days later, a horde of hellhounds appeared, together with about fifty or so larger demons.

Whoever they were looking for, I knew their target wasn't me. However, based on the strength of these demons shown to me so far, I knew I could defeat this horde.

So I did.

I took the chance to use my new skills. A mix of [Root Surge], [Super Anti-demon Root Strike], and [Root Strike]. Jura also participated in the battle.

A few of the demons survived, and Jura assisted with capturing them for my experiments.

YEAR 73, MONTH 2, WEEK 1

[Rajjiv Nung has died. You gained 3 levels. You are now Level 104.]

[Obtained skill: Lesser Holy Enchantment.]

He died. That was strange; he was with the heroes. I would have thought he would be quite safe. Whatever killed him, it must have been a rather fierce battle.

That actually reminded me of the familiars I granted, and I activated a menu that displayed a list of them.

I had been neglecting them, so I called Jura and Laufen over and had both show me their familiar forms.

A familiar allowed access to the spells and abilities largely based on their grantor. They had gained levels. Jura's familiar was level thirty, and Laufen's familiar was level thirteen. These familiars manifested in many ways, usually dependent on the user.

When they did, a prompt appeared before me.

[Jura's tree familiar has reached the limit of Level 30. Do you wish to elevate the familiar to the next phase?]

Huh?

"How long did it stay at level thirty?"

"Oh! It's been at that level for quite some time already, since the attack by the demon centipede."

"Uh, why didn't you tell me?"

"I thought you knew." Jura rubbed his head.

Ah, dammit. Communication breakdown.

I reminded myself that I needed to get these elves to tell me more about themselves.

I mentally said yes to the prompt.

Jura's eyes flew wide open as he seemed to see something. "I didn't even know a familiar could rank up! Wow, I get to choose its next form!"

Huh. I knew too little about familiars.

Meanwhile, one of my branches was converted into a room with my skill, [Customizable Branches]. It functioned as a jail cell for all the captured hellhounds. On top of the 'dead' hybrid in one pod, I subjected the remaining hellhounds to more investigation.

So long as I didn't attempt to sense or snuff out the 'fire,' it would stay 'alive.'

YEAR 73, MONTH 2, WEEK 2

The ground buckled, and bits of rock and dirt flew in the air as the earth shook.

My roots attempted to hold on, but the shockwave that caused this was way too strong. Throughout the plains, the ground buckled as if the dirt was pressed together and pulled apart.

The earth shook again.

Jura rushed out of the hideout. I ordered him to look out for what caused it and retreat immediately once he saw it. A part of me felt...afraid.

The earth rumbled again.

The shaking didn't stop over the next few hours. As the day went by, we felt and heard explosions. Something was coming, a battle maybe. They had been fighting for some time.

The shockwaves propagated through the earth and gradually increased in strength. My rootnet was flooded with pain.

The rumbling continued even after sunset, and Jura ran toward us in the darkness of night.

"No good! Three demon champions appeared. The heroes are engaging them in battle, but they seem to be retreating this way."

"Three?" That was far too many! Fighting one almost killed me and knocked me out for weeks.

Shouldn't the heroes be able to beat them?

"Did you see the heroes?"

"Yes! They are retreating here!"

"Why?"

"I don't know. Maybe they are trying to lure them away from the cities!"

The explosions and rumblings continued. They seemed to be fighting even while retreating, so whatever they were running from kept up with them.

"How far?"

"A day!"

Shit.

"What should we do? If three demon champions are here, could you hold them back, Tree-Tree?"

"No. If they are anything like the earlier giant golem, I may not last very long. I can take a few hits, but it will only be a matter of time before it kills me."

"But you are stronger than last time." Jura paused. "Maybe you can take one. Maybe that is why they are coming this way. They need your help to even up the odds."

"Don't they have an army of adventurers?"

Jura shook his head. "I think they are either dead or have fled. I don't think any sane adventurer would want to battle three demon champions together. Only the bravest or most foolish of adventurers would attempt it."

"And the world expects the heroes to?"

"Heroes have special powers! They are different!"

"This doesn't make sense. I thought they already killed some of the demon champions. How did three appear out of nowhere?"

Jura paused. "I don't know. I am guessing the heroes don't, either."

The earth shook. More rumblings. They were going to be here soon.

"What's our plan?" Jura paced the room.

"If I remember correctly, a few of them can take one demon champion with no problems. So there must be more to it. How many heroes did you see?"

"I couldn't get a good look at them. It was too chaotic."

"Ah."

Three demon champions, if they were of a similar strength to the golem, would be a real challenge. They were going to arrive in about two hours, so the heroes must have had something in mind.

Were they wounded?

How would I defeat these demons?

I looked at the hounds in the lab, strapped to the pod.

"Jura, what's known to be effective against demons?"

I actually asked this before. I recalled the answer was that there were weapons created by the heroes that had special effectiveness against demons. There were also natural abilities like holy magic or star weapons like metal swords made from asteroids.

Did the demons have an off-switch like the hounds?

If I could extinguish the fire in their body, they would shut down. Okay, following that metaphor, if their source of power really was that fire, would water therefore destroy them?

And so I tested my theory out on a hound, pouring my mana through the connected roots. It entered its blank soul realm, and some of the mana evaporated in the process. Was this from the heat of the soul?

But after the initial evaporation, the fire shrank, and eventually, it was extinguished.

It worked for one. But from this single experiment, I realized it was far too slow and not as effective as a simple strike. A strike would have destroyed that hound using far less mana. And if a demon champion was larger and more powerful, my mana most likely would be insufficient to achieve the same goals.

The 'dead' hound's body cracked, and the rocks on its body fell off like it was shedding skin. And then it convulsed and vibrated. It twisted and turned against the vines and started to suck in mana.

My mana.

It twitched.

And then it stopped. I saw the body regenerated, the wounds healed, and its limbs and fangs regrew like some sped-up documentary. The rocks that once decorated its fur were replaced with a strange, wood-like texture.

A shiver ran through me.

"Jura. Lab. Now!" Jura immediately jumped from his resting area and ran for the lab, armed.

"Which one?"

The hound opened its eyes. And they were green.

[Hellhound forcefully adapted into your subordinate minion with your natural mana and has transformed into woodhound.]

"Wait."

Jura eyed the hound. It should have been an easy battle, but you could never be sure.

The pod opened, and the healed hound crawled out. Its eyes locked on and stared at Jura.

I felt a link to it, and I mentally commanded it to sit.

And it did.

It fed on my mana to survive, and I sensed that mana link between me and this woodhound. The feeling was familiar, similar to the links with my summoned insects.

Fascinating.

[Skill obtained: Natural Mana Overwhelming.]

But there was no time to waste. I didn't have an answer for the three demon champions coming my way. The earth rumbled and shook, and the explosions were now visible in the sky.

Think!

I reviewed the skills I had. Familiars, essences, souls, soul realm, a few root attack variants, saps, leaves that functioned as tea, wood magic and shaping abilities, healing powers, [Spirit Vision], a secret hideout with a lab and healing chamber, insect warriors, rootnet, barkskins, wood shields, and some other lesser defensive items.

Could I make souls and essences into a weapon?

[Soul Forge required to form high-efficiency weapons. Your Soul Forge is currently not operational.]

Ugh. Not that. How about essences? Could I convert them into a weapon?

[Currently, the essences can be converted into a single-use weapon.]

Fine. Combine them.

[Vessel required.]

I would want to use it together with my [Super Anti-demon Root Strike], so I formed a sharp, pointy piece of wood that would serve as the piercing edge of my roots. Essentially, this was the 'arrowhead' of my roots. The essences were then added to it, with a little of my energies, and it transformed into a sharp piece of wood.

The earth rumbled, and the elves saw streaks of lights in the distance.

"They are here."

The streaks of light were replaced by explosions, and the heroes zoomed toward me. They used some kind of speed ability, and as they retreated, they also dodged the explosions that seemed to chase them.

Three demon champions appeared: a large golem, a huge, horned-stone centipede, and some kind of stone turtle with spikes. They stood in the distance, surrounded by a horde of lesser demons, minor golems, and a few other lesser centipedes.

YEAR 73, MONTH 2, WEEK 2

Eleven heroes. They ran and left a trail of destruction in their wake. Explosions were deflected by their barriers. Fires held back by magical shields.

The heroes tried.

Magical thunderbolts and lightning blasts erupted, and lesser demons fell. They were fodder. There were easily tens of thousands of them, and only eleven heroes stood against them.

The fan lady twirled, and she muttered a kind of chant. The demons attempted to disrupt her, but the other heroes covered for her.

Swoosh. An air blast came from the sky, and hundreds of the demons were crushed instantly by the windblast. A giant blue fireball streaked through the demon swarm, and the blue flames roasted all in their path and then exploded. The ensuing inferno destroyed a few hundred more.

The giant tortoise demon stomped its massive feet, and the earth shook violently. A few dozen massive boulders flew toward the heroes at high speed.

A wall of light emerged, and the boulders disintegrated when they smashed into them. The lesser demons that ran toward the wall of light also disintegrated. It seemed to be an ability Hendry and Max used together.

The tortoise stomped its feet, and a few dozen more boulders flew toward the wall. They were close, and I could vaguely make out their voices.

"Ugh." Hendry and Max both winced. "It's using up quite a lot of mana. Alexis!"

The heroes drew closer. Meela dashed beside me.

"Tree spirit, please, aid us in battle!"

"What if I refuse?" I responded telepathically to all present. I knew it was a stupid question. They'd forced my hand.

"Then the demons will kill you, too," another hero said blankly as he dodged shrapnel.

"Fine. Do you have a plan?"

"Yes. Cover us for a while. That's all we need," Meela said.

The heroes retreated behind me and formed into a formation. They immediately started chanting.

The horde of demons charged and flooded the fields. They came down the valley like a wave, a scene from a war movie. My insects and Jura formed a protective layer.

All we had to do was keep the demons from the heroes.

The three demon champions seemed particularly disturbed by the chanting, and they joined the battle. The centipede, the fastest of the three, was unable to tunnel through the dirt due to my dense subterranean root network, so it decided to attack us directly. It charged and tried to ram into the heroes.

My wooden shields appeared and blocked the centipede's strikes, and they shattered on impact. But the shields caused the demonic centipede to lose most of its momentum and deflected it off its path. I took the moments when it seemed startled by the shields to throw a few holy enchanted [Root Strike]s at its side. They knocked chunks of rock from its body.

I caught its attention, and the centipede turned and rammed into me instead.

Wham!

I felt its sharp, rocky tusks smash into my trunk, and some pierced my bark. A bit of it cracked. I had all my defensive abilities active, so while it hurt, it wasn't fatal. I suspected my fragments helped reduce most of the damage.

Another [Root Strike] smashed into the centipede's body, and a big chunk of stone fell away.

The centipede's upper body twisted and rammed me again. *Wham!*

Three layers of wooden shields shattered, and I shifted my attention back to the heroes. *Whatever the heroes are planning, it better freaking work.*

The giant centipede rammed me again, and more of my bark cracked. I could take the hits, but not forever.

The demonic hounds and lesser demons charged, but a white dome appeared over the heroes.

They'd protected themselves with a magical barrier.

The smaller demons rammed the barrier but mostly bounced off. The demonic centipede's subterranean attack nullified, the lesser demonic spawns resorted to ramming and swiping at the dome with their stone thorns.

The larger centipede remained focused on me. It was slightly bigger than the previous one, but I had also grown. My larger form and levels resulted in additional power for most of my abilities. Jura and the heroes were right that I could hold my own against these creatures...for a while.

The golem champion moved into range, and it immediately targeted the heroes. It tried to punch the white dome.

[Constrict].

My roots shot out of the ground and ensnared the golem, and the tangle of roots held back its punch.

I then activated [Constrict] on the giant centipede. My roots surged out and wrapped it, and it retaliated, twirling around my trunk. It coiled, tangling my roots and vines. We were both stuck. Or more like the centipede was stuck.

It felt like a snake or a python, wrestling with a stick.

Some of my roots pierced its stone structure. My roots were good at going through such surfaces. Elemental advantage, I supposed.

The golem and centipede, despite all my attacks so far, were still mostly unharmed. All I managed to do was trap them in a thicket of roots and branches, and the giant centipede was coiled around my trunk. The centipede took a few more blows, and I gauged its strength as it wrestled against my vines and roots. It pushed and rammed, like it was a rhino rubbing its thick body on me. It tried to claw through my trunk with its horns.

But the trunk and bark held and took just a little damage, a crack here and there, but the pain wasn't overwhelming. It felt like a slap. I thanked the defense buffs and the effects of the demon damage reduction.

The demon tortoise was the only 'free' one, and it tried to bite through the vines that entangled the golem.

Sharp bites cut through the vines and roots and freed one of the golem's arms. The golem immediately punched the heroes' defensive dome with all its might.

Wham!

The white dome cracked.

Crap. That's bad. I needed to protect them a little longer.

[Root Strike]s stabbed into the underbelly of the tortoise and knocked it back a little. However, it didn't topple.

The golem raised its fists and readied its next full-power punch.

If the heroes had a secret weapon, now was the time. I used my [Super Anti-demon Root Strike] together with the essence-edge, and my enhanced roots slammed right into the golem's body. There was an explosion of starlight that left a huge hole in the golem's chest.

Yet, it still lived!

It punched again, and I created multiple massive wood shields to block its strike. The punch crushed through my shields easily and still managed to hit the dome. Luckily, my defenses had softened the blow significantly, and the dome only slightly cracked.

The giant tortoise rammed me instead and tried to bite me with its beak.

It tore a gash in my trunk, but it quickly healed.

The centipede tried to crush my trunk by tightening its coil around me, like a python was squeezing me. My roots, which also wrapped the centipede, drained its energy and mana.

What was taking the heroes so long?

The golem managed to free its other arms from my vines and threw more punches at the dome. Yet, despite the attacks from the tortoise and the centipede, I focused on the golem and created wooden shields.

However, only the first punch was weakened. The other few punches landed squarely on the dome, and it cracked even more.

The dome glowed, and I felt power and magic in the air.

It seemed I had done enough.

The dome pulsed, and the glow became brighter.

Whoosh!

Then the glow turned into a blinding light.

The dome exploded outward, and with it came a massive energy wave that swept outward and encapsulated the entire valley like a nuclear shockwave. The wave disintegrated all the demons in its path. In an instant, the battlefield was cleared, and the only demons remaining were the three champions.

Whoa, that's just too overpowered.

The three champions didn't escape unscathed. The giant tortoise's shell was half-destroyed and revealed its charred body beneath. The golem's arms and half of its head was destroyed. And the giant centipede's body was half-gone, the blast vaporizing its smaller limbs and spikes.

Yet, somehow, the rest of us were safe. It was clearly a special ability attuned to demons.

The heroes emerged from the dome with shining weapons, their bodies covered with an armor of light. They dashed toward the demon champions, and in just a few flashes of light, all the champions were killed.

"What the hell was that?"

Did I just tank three demon champions so that the heroes could activate some kind of overpowered transformation ability?

The heroes in their light armor form made such quick work of the champions that I found it hard to believe they were even demon champions in the first place.

The heroes regrouped. "Thanks for covering us. We gained quite a few levels from that."

Seriously?

Now that they weren't jumping or flying from place to place, I got a better look at the heroes' new outfits. From my spiritual view, their bodies glowed and reminded me of *Power Rangers.* Or maybe *Kamen Rider.*

"Meela, did you guys unlock some special ability recently?"

"Yes, we did! We got this special, uh...[Heavenly Form] and a few other skills. That big boom thing was our [Starlight Nova]."

Whoa. How do I get that kind of power?

"Meela, may I ask you to dip into the pod again?"

"Yeah, sure!" Meela said happily.

At this point, Alexis and Hendry grabbed Meela. "No, it's our power. We cannot reveal it. Don't do this."

Meela shook her head. "Both of you are being unreasonable. Tree-Tree just helped cover our butts because this skill activation initially had a ridiculously long chant time, and now you want to deny him a look at our power?"

Hendry and Alexis paused before they replied, "Meela, let's decide collectively."

Eventually, the heroes came to a compromise. Meela's argument won. Sort of.

"Here goes." Meela dipped in. The rest of the heroes looked on, some with rather concerned expressions on their faces. Alexis and the fan lady activated a magical ability, and Meela glowed.

"That's our insurance. If there's anything unnatural, we'll go in," the mage explained, and I deduced it was some kind of magical short-range teleportation ability.

Max shook his head. "If this tree saved Meela's life, and Meela has done this before, I really don't see why such precautions are necessary."

Hendry place his hand on Max. "Yes. Yes, he did. But this is our gift, and it is also our burden. It must be carefully guarded, and we were told not to be put under the knife or risk it getting stolen. Precautions are necessary."

Max frowned. "As if it is possible to steal our powers."

"We never know."

I sighed. These reincarnators were a pain, but whatever. "I'm not going to steal it. I'm just having a look at it."

Meela shook her head. "You guys, stop being paranoid. I want to do this, and we voted. I'll be fine."

One of the heroes poked in. "I don't see the issue. Our ability comes from the gods, and I highly doubt it can be easily stolen or copied or whatever. Just because you can see the schematics doesn't mean you have the tools and materials to create a machine."

Well, that was a very good point.

Meela was fully submerged, and the roots and vines attached to her. I sensed the data flowing into me, and so I peeked into her body.

What was most obvious was that the two waterfalls from the aether that once poured slightly sparkly water into the lake of her soul now poured a glowing liquid, and it sparkled with starlight. This was what they referred to as 'star mana.'

The black whirlpool had disappeared, and the water that flowed down into the rest of her body was strong, clear, and sparkly, no longer weakened. Now, it was pure with the force of a raging river. That starlight water poured and fed every part of her body and enhanced her body's strength even more than before. It was so unfair. It felt like witnessing an athlete with some kind of supernatural performance-enhancement drugs. In this case, the change in muscle strength and texture was permanent.

Using a car as the metaphor, the star mana was the special fuel that powered their tremendous destructive ability, their exceptionally large and powerful soul was the engine, and their body was the frame.

When I compared Jura or Laufen to Meela, it was obvious to me that Meela's soul was larger and more robust. The energy behind the spring was just far higher, and as a result, their displayed potential and performance was just absurd.

"Is it done yet?" Hendry asked after about an hour. They seemed really anxious, but perhaps they were unaware how long medical procedures actually took. However, I thought it had been long enough for me to gather all the data I needed.

"Yes." The hatch opened, and the liquid drained out of the biolab's pod. Gradually, Meela woke up and stepped out. She gave a little shake, her body wet, and then she yawned.

"That was a very pleasant nap. I felt like your healing energies were all inside me!" Meela laughed, and she looked at her worried teammates. "See? I am fine!"

Alexis and Max both used some kind of spell and nodded. "Yeah, she's fine."

Max looked up at me. "Apologies for our reservations. Hope you keep whatever you discovered a secret."

"Honestly, all I discovered was that your souls are large and robust, you have huge amounts of star mana, and the huge natural mana from your soul and star mana changed your body into these anti-demon king superhumans." I honestly oversimplified. I wasn't sure how the 'anti-demon' aspect manifested itself.

All the heroes paused.

"Really, that's it?"

"Star mana?" Alexis paused, and then she seemed to make an 'a-ha' action. "Hmm, that makes sense."

"What?" The others turned and looked at Alexis, the group's wizard.

"I mean, it explains why we have such success against demons. Star mana is rare, as the records say, known to be naturally effective against demons who are extraterrestrial in nature, and yet our body overflows with it. I-it never occurred to me that the special mana we all get access to is just star mana. It should have been obvious since our recent abilities have star-like names."

Alexis sat on one of the many root-benches in the lab.

"Did you see our gifts?"

"Hmm, I can't identify what was the gift without comparing Meela to another. It's from your differences I can identify what is what. Otherwise, I have to assume that is the norm for everyone."

"Hmm. That is true. You do need a control sample or reference to interpret the results." Alexis rubbed her chin.

"Alexis?" Hendry walked over.

"Hmm...nothing." Alexis left the lab, and eventually, all the heroes followed.

Once they were gone, I turned my attention toward the new data. It was all stored like a medical record.

I wasn't lying when I said I didn't know where the divine gift was and comparing two reincarnators with different gifts would be one of the easier ways to find them since one would naturally expect different gifts to appear and manifest differently in one's soul.

The heroes went back to their camp, and with magic, they created a transportable inn that allowed them to live in comfort, even whilst traveling. Ah, such magic would put hotels and inns everywhere out of business, but the hospitality business could count on their lucky stars as such magic seemed exclusive to heroes, and even then, only some heroes had the luck to get it.

Later that night, Meela came over.

"Hey, tree spirit. I-I just want to apologize for my team's

behavior. I'm not sure why, but we tend to behave like that. It's all about us and not anyone else. Everything feels like it is just to further the goal of beating the demons."

If I could nod, I would. In hindsight, Meela was right, and the heroes were pretty asshole-ish. But this was a shit world from what I had seen so far. I might be an asshole, too, someday.

"You saved my life, our lives, and helped us a lot. I think we owe it to you, and I am really unhappy with what my team did. Even Hendry and Alexis are suspicious, and I don't know why."

Meela paused and sat on one of my many roots. Some of them were flat on top now, and so they conveniently served as makeshift tables and benches.

"Can I make a deal with you? Once we beat the demon king, I'll come back and help you, even if I am not as magically clever as Alexis."

Hmm, I wasn't sure whether that sort of help was useful, but if I had to ask...

"Tree spirit, do you have any requests?"

Hmm. "Accept my familiar." I could gain experience if they somehow died—that would really help me. "In fact, can you ask everyone to take my familiar? It'll help me level up, and that'll be enough." These heroes were going to fight more demons in the coming days, so I might as well profit from it.

Meela nodded. "Oh, that is fine. Give one to me, and I can show it to the others and ask them, too."

I activated the familiar contract, and Meela accepted without a thought. She grinned. "Ooh, it's like a summon."

The next morning, Meela demonstrated her new familiar abilities to the heroes, and about half of them accepted a familiar from me. The other half had their reservations.

Oh, well, it was better than nothing. Six heroes with familiars and five without.

They left that afternoon.

Meanwhile, I received the experience and levels from the battle with the demon champions.

[You are now level 110 (+6 levels.)]

[Secret Hideout: biolab upgraded.]

[Wood Shield upgraded. Steelwood Barrier obtained.]

[Constrict significantly upgraded.]

[Absorption significantly upgraded.]

[Obtained tree ability: Subsidiary Tree.]

[Customizable Branches options expanded.]

THE HEROES' POV (ALEXIS)

After we defeated the three demon champions, we felt quite good about our abilities. We gained around ten levels each, and all of us were now at least level one hundred. We felt we were ready for the demon king.

[Heavenly Form].

We got that power when all of us hit level ninety, and now, after the battle with the three demon champions, that skill leveled up, and we gained variants of that power. Max, for example, had [Heavenly Barrier Armor]. For most of us, activating the [Heavenly Form] no longer required that stupidly long chant time.

Even the chant time became irrelevant since Freyas, our resident lady with a fan, gained a power called [Accelerated Chanting – Heavenly form]. It allowed all of us to enter into the form within a minute.

In some ways, it was stupid that the system forced us to work around a long chant time at lower levels, and then removed it once we crossed level one hundred.

But, in a way, it told us that the gods planned on winning and had equipped us with powerful abilities and skills.

But I didn't get it. If our powers were so good, why had so many heroes died in the past?

Meela sat next to me. "Still thinking about it?"

We left the tree spirit a day ago, and Meela seemed fine despite our initial disagreements on what we should have done with the tree's request. But I guess that was a trivial matter. After all, we had a common enemy. The big, bad, evil guy. The demon king.

"Yeah. Still bothers me."

"It bothers Max, too."

We were closer to the rift now, and we sensed it. It was there if we tried to reach out to it.

The next demon champion was last spotted guarding one of the rifts, and our goal was to destroy it, gain levels, and then approach the demon king with significant force.

Meela usually rode next to me. "Maybe it's hidden in plain sight. Something obvious."

Possible!

Along the way, some demons attacked, but we disposed of them easily. We were a group of high-level heroes. These small fries could hardly challenge us.

The journey toward the rift meant we faced more demons, and in a way, that was good. The more demons we got to fight, the higher level we became.

We arrived at the rift a few days later.

The rift was like a glitch in the system and appeared like something from a damaged LCD monitor. The beautiful view was jarringly broken by a large, unnaturally black gash across the sky that floated in midair. Demons poured out of that gap in droves. Thankfully, most of them were just lesser hounds.

The demon champion was a giant cyclops golem with multiple arms, and it functioned as more than just a guard. It issued commands to the new demons. It pointed, and the hounds went off in that direction.

We didn't hesitate. Attacking with our newfound powers, we crushed the demon champion easily. Max's star-mana powered [Starlight Smite] skill weakened it significantly in a single blow, and a few hits later, it collapsed.

"Holy shit, this level one hundred thing really trivialized the demon champion," Max said.

"Hah. Power creep, eh?" Freyas laughed. The rest of the lesser hounds didn't last very long. A few area of effect spells from us, and the fragile hounds died like helpless ants.

Still, the rift kept pouring demons out.

"Can we do something about it?"

Meela nodded. "I'll need help, but I think so." Meela started to dance in a rhythmic fashion, and her body glowed in myriad colors.

"Meela?" I sensed her mana, that special mana, and then something else.

"I had a dream," she pointed both her swords at the rift, and two beams of starlight shot out toward the rift, "when I was in the pod."

The lights smashed into the rift, and it looked like its energies battled the light.

"In the dream, I saw a rift close when heroes channeled their power into it."

The rest of us together, with our combined powers, quickly overwhelmed the rift's energies, and it shrank. It eventually vanished in a spark of light. The deserted, destroyed valley suddenly turned quiet and normal again.

Demon king.

We felt a sensation in our bodies like an ice cube just rolled down our backs. The demon king. It was coming for us.

We shared a few glances. "The battle is going to happen soon."

"How long do we have, you think?"

I felt it again, that presence at the back of my mind, always outside my peripheral vision. It knew where we were. Worst of all, it felt like I knew where it was, too.

Max and Hendry both sat. "I feel...maybe two weeks." Strange, I had the same number in my head as well. We all shared the feeling.

"What's our strategy?"

"Hit it with all we got. At range."

"It's going to come after us with everything it has, too."

"Then I suppose we should intercept it and catch it off guard."

"I could do that." I thought I might have just the spell for a long-range, homing magical spell.

It took a day's preparation, but we got into position. We sensed it clearly, and if we could accurately sense it, we could launch an attack on it.

Eleven of us concentrated our energies into a glowing white energy ball above us, and this was our 'opening act.'

[Neutron Comet].

It was a large building-sized ball of light that contained our charged energy.

It zoomed toward the demon king at high speed. The demon king was far away, perhaps a thousand miles, but the [Neutron Comet] was tuned to our 'sense' of its location, and somehow, I knew we could hit it.

The comet impacted, and the air trembled for a moment, even though the blast was so far away. Then we sensed retaliation.

A wave of boulders flew toward us, but we deflected them away easily.

Even though the demon king was still far away, we knew then we could hit each other. For two weeks, we attacked the demon king with comets, and it retaliated with the boulders.

There were lesser demons that came our way, too, but we crushed them easily.

Then we had visual contact. The demon king was now in range.

The Demon King Andraas took the form of a large flying fortress with multiple massive, spider-like legs. On its top half, there were multiple tentacle-covered buildings spread all over its body, and there were also multiple spires filled with alien eyes. It was as if a tentacled monster merged with a fortress.

It was angry, and it attacked.

[Demon King Andraas]

It unleashed a wave of rocks at close range, and these rocks were magically enchanted with demonic energy. Simultaneously, its spires and those alien-looking eyes shot beams of energy at us.

"This is it, guys. Let's go!" Hendry put up a magical barrier, and it cracked when the beams smashed into it.

The battle had begun.

We engaged the demon king at close range, and the deserted valley was instantly filled with beams of light, flying rocks, and our counter-magic.

I felt the air twist, and a jagged rock *swooshed* right past me.

I shivered.

The jagged rock broke into a million tiny, needle-like pieces of shrapnel when it was right next to me.

"[Body of Fire]." My body of fire burned up the tiny rock needles as a few other rocks flew my way.

I looked around and saw my fellow heroes. Each of us had different ways of protecting ourselves. Freyas, with her wind magic, surrounded herself with a constant layer of magically enchanted high-speed wind that shredded the needles.

"Help!" I immediately turned and saw our gunner. A massive tentacle tried to crush him as he sped across the land. He fired shot after shot at the tentacle, and it detonated, yet the half-destroyed tendril kept attacking and almost caught him.

"[Holy Thunderstrike]."

A bolt of lightning zapped the tentacle and paralyzed it. It was only for a split second, but it was enough to let our gunner escape.

Max's sword glowed with holy magic, and he slashed at the tentacle. The holy energy flooded the entirety of the tendril, and it blew up, spattering the demon king's blood everywhere.

"I thought they normally looked like...demons."

"Well, that's what the record said. But this demon king has been doing strange things from the start. It even has elemental hybrids!"

Hendry created a barrier, and we took this moment to enter our new forms.

The demon king roared, and its tentacles and legs flailed repeatedly at our defenses. I felt my heart skip a beat as the barrier cracked, and each blow of the tentacles made it crack even more.

I wondered whether we would make it, but we kept our chant going. A part of me watched the cracks as they appeared across the barrier.

Hendry nodded in relief when there was a flash of light. The armor complete, the barrier exploded outward, and a white flame burned the tentacles that flailed at the barrier. But still, the demon king was relatively unharmed.

Its massive spider-leg stabbed Max in the stomach at high speed. "UGH!" he yelled as he tried to push the limb back.

"MAX!" Meela's light sword swished and slashed the leg off, but a stab from the demon king was still a stab. He was hurt.

Max's blood dripped onto his sword, and he was in a frenzy. He climbed onto the demon king's leg still connected to the main body and rushed forward.

"We should get on the body!" Max yelled. "We're not going anywhere like this."

"Good point. There might be a heart somewhere we can destroy!"

Freyas called the rest of us to gather around her, and she swept her fan. In an instant, a tunnel of wind appeared and carried us onto the body of the demon king, the tentacle-covered castle itself.

The fortress was like a demonic playhouse, and there were tentacles everywhere, each house covered with those same alien-looking eyes. There were also giant spiders that roamed the fortress. The demon king was a freaking demon spider nest.

"Should we just blow up this entire structure?"

"If we can."

We attacked everything. The floor, the buildings, everything we saw. The tentacles and giant spiders attacked us, but they didn't do much against our barriers. These tentacles were somehow less powerful than the ones below it.

We eventually bored a hole right into the fortress itself, and we found what we wanted. One of the many hearts of the demon king. Max, in his fury, slashed it, and the heart blew up and splashed tons of black blood everywhere.

"One."

An army of human-sized demon knights appeared as we looked for the next heart. There were easily a thousand of them, and they were accompanied by the same demon spiders. They were stronger, but in our starlight forms, we still crushed them easily.

From there, it was a game of hide-and-seek. We looked for more demon hearts until we reached the one that killed the demon king.

We found the next heart in a tall spire, and it was our gunner who blew it up.

The third heart was hidden in one of the many buildings. The fourth was in a corrupted church, and the fifth was in barracks filled with demonic knights.

Was this demon king some kind of 'corruption' king?

Each time, there were more and more demons that tried to stop us. But numbers were relatively meaningless.

"How many hearts are there?"

"Nine?" It was a random guess...probably.

We found the sixth and seventh hidden in another set of buildings.

As we destroyed the hearts, the demon king lost the ability to fly, and the castle drifted toward the ground. More demon knights and demon champions tried to stop us, but we destroyed them easily.

The eighth heart was in what looked like a polluted market, and then, the ninth heart was in a corrupted garden filled with spires and tentacles.

"That's it?"

At this point, we were all drenched in blood and whatever gunk the demon king was made of.

We felt everything shake as the fortress crashed to the ground, yet the tentacles kept up their attacks. But unlike before, their attacks were nothing more than random flailing.

Then the entire castle started to crumble, and the remnants of the demon king's hearts floated to the sky and pooled into a black ball.

Meela laughed. "This is like a video game. It's not even in its final form!"

The tentacles, the eyes, the legs, everything melted into a black liquid floating into the sky, merging with the black ball.

We didn't intend to let it finish, so we launched ranged attacks at the black liquid and ball, managing to incinerate some of the liquid.

Then an eyeball appeared on the black ball.

The next form was a massive black eye. And it introduced itself with a wave-ray of destruction.

Max and Hendry joined and put up a barrier, but that ray destroyed it instantly. The ray burned us. Unlike before, this wasn't a focused beam but more like a shining light, and every-thing the light touched started to combust.

Even with our protective armor, it was painful.

But we kept attacking, and cuts appeared on its body, yet this thing seemed to be a semi-liquid that partly nullified our attacks.

Meela used a special ability and managed to jump on it. She stabbed it repeatedly with her two swords.

The eye closed and tried to turn and twirl repeatedly, but Meela's magical blades were too deeply embedded, stuck in the semi-liquid form. It tried to shake her off and flung her around like a ragdoll.

She was fine, though, and shouted, "There's something hard deep inside. I think we need to get it!"

That was the cue we needed, and our gunner took out a harpoon-like weapon. It fired a chained-harpoon and stabbed into the eye. I winced a little at the imagery.

He channeled energy through the chain into the eye, and then it blew up. Meela thankfully managed to jump away in time.

The eye, now destroyed, revealed a round red-black crystal.

And it pulsed.

Another pulse followed.

And it glowed.

"Oh, fuck me, it's going to explode."

All of us huddled together and activated our defensive and barrier spells. At this range, and at this distance, there was no running away.

The crystal blew up with the strength of a huge hydrogen bomb.

[Demon King Andraas has been slain.]

YEAR 73, MONTH 2

A few days after the heroes left, [Subsidiary Tree] unlocked thirty additional trees. Used together with my natural tree spirit powers to stimulate plant growth, a small forest emerged around me. Though all these new smaller trees look like separate trees above ground, they were actually a part of me. These subsidiary trees were linked underground via rootnet, and they served a few functions.

Each separate tree unlocked one customizable branch. They also collected a few resources.

The immediate impact from a small forest was, of course, happier elves!

Well, Jura was happy for a few other reasons. As a result of his involvement in the battle with the three demon champions, he gained a level, and more importantly, the level removed his curse. It seemed that growth could overcome such curses naturally.

The elves were happy mainly because the additional trees reminded them of a time before the burning of Freeka, before demonic stampedes razed this place to the ground. Freeka was once surrounded by forests, and the forests were once home to many natural creatures the elves hunted and many herbs they used extensively in their cooking.

I tried to regrow the surrounding area multiple times, but before the trees managed to grow big, there would inevitably be a demon attack, and these regular trees just didn't stand a chance. These subsidiary trees, however, seemed to inherit some of my resistance and defensive qualities, and so I hoped they would last a lot longer.

The thirty extra trees formed two circles around me, six trees in the inner circle and twenty-four in the outer circle.

"It feels like a wall." Jura looked around.

"It is meant to be a wall." Indeed, the layer of demon-resistant trees was my idea of a defensive formation like a basic rampart.

"These trees, do they do something?" Laufen asked as Lausanne walked by her side.

As we had three younger elven children, Lausanne, Brislach and Wahlen, I converted one of the inner trees into a playroom. The secret hideout for my main tree didn't have much space as it functioned mostly as the actual living quarters, the food store, the lab, and the medical area. Oh, and there was a small pool.

These elven kids had seen too much pain and death, and I thought maybe a proper play area would bring a greater sense of normalcy into their lives. I equipped the playroom with a small slide, a few different toys, and some racks and small chairs made using my wood-forming magic.

Ah, children, such innocent souls.

Eh.

I wondered how a child's soul would look, and Lausanne was still too small, but Brislach volunteered for the dip.

It turned out that a child's soul was quite similar to Jura's, with one notable exception. The earth, or the body, was soft. The spring that poured out water seemed inconsistent. Brislach's soul, at strange times, surged and then shrank. It was as if the soul itself wasn't yet stable.

"When do children start practicing magic?"

"Oh...it differs by culture..." Laufen and Jura sat around and explained. "Some cultures believed it was best to let the body mature before attempting to draw out mana, and so, for them, the exposure to magic would be quite late, like some started in their mid-teens. Some cultures believed it was better to be exposed early and let mana flow more freely in the body."

"And different societies expose them differently. It is not as if there is one standard way of doing so, and of course, the bodies of different people are also very different. People all over the world may learn the same spell, but the body's elemental prefer-ence and natural stats can change how that translates into the real world. In fact, the only somewhat uniformly agreed skill that appears the same way is the most basic of spells: spark! Even that, from what I hear, doesn't apply to heroes!"

Hmm. I supposed the shape of the body—the way that water flowed from the soul to the body—caused that difference.

Wahlen was next, and I saw more of the same. There were some differences in the details, but structurally, they were similar to Brislach.

Actually, I now wondered, what about me?

I was a tree spirit, but I definitely thought I had a soul, and I wondered whether it was possible to look at myself the way I peeked into others.

I tried, and...

Nope.

I couldn't see myself. Though I possessed a wide array of menus, indicators, and measures on these menus. Oh, well, maybe someday I would get some kind of reflection-ish ability. But then again, menus were supposed to be more accurate; after all, they quantified everything into a number or a 'status.'

But my recent experience with these souls did highlight some of the limitations of these menus and 'dashboards.' Numbers were rigid. Compared to my vision of one's soul, the ability to visualize the flowing water through the body, these visual experiences explained how everything was linked, and how the body interacted with the kind of energies it produced.

Anyway, back to the children, and my newfound tree-mates.

With thirty new extra customizable-branches, I reserved the innermost trees for the elves. With the inner six trees, one became a playpen for the kids, and two more trees functioned as extra rooms for the elves—and perhaps future visitors. This was to create some separation, and I wanted my secret hideout to remain secure. I left three more trees in the inner ring empty for now. This was partly due to the process of converting one occupied customizable branch to another type took a month, even though the first change from a blank tree took only a day.

As for the twenty-four trees of the outer ring, I designated one tree as a kennel for the woodhounds, fourteen for various extraction functions such as essences and minerals, and five trees served as housing for insect warriors. This spawned an additional fifteen insect warriors into my service. I left another four unused for future expansion. Perhaps I would get some kind of defensive option in the future, then I could assign these unused four to new roles quickly.

I designated quite a few of these subsidiary trees with customizable branches for essence extraction because Wisp claimed that essence was one of the key materials for the [Soul Forge]. Still, even now, the [Soul Forge] wasn't operational.

The [Soul Forge] needed a power source.

With the two rings of trees completed, the elves happily walked around and explored the place. This was an expanded 'safe area.' Jura immediately took one of the extra rooms, and the two young elves, Emile and Belle, took the other. Laufen and the children remained in the secret hideout.

Unfortunately, the only toilet and washroom were in the secret hideout. Perhaps a common public bath could be made later.

"Tree-Tree, will these rooms grow?"

"Maybe? I don't really know." I wondered whether these

trees could level up, because if they could, then I could give them more options. But I thought it was quite unlikely as they were connected to me. Didn't seem to make sense that these separated trees could have their own experience and levels.

"Ah, oh well." Belle shook her leg as she sat on her new mattress. In the room shared by the two elven girls, there were three single-sized beds and a few cabinets. It was a fairly large room, and there were windows with a view of the main tree. These rooms looked like they were carved out of the trees themselves.

Emile checked out her new cabinets. She was quite happy she could move her clothes out of her wooden chest in the hideout and into proper cabinets.

"You think the heroes will defeat the demon king?" Emile sat on the other mattress and asked Belle.

"Yeah, of course they will. They are heroes!"

"Not as good-looking as I'd hoped, though."

"Well, I guess history paints heroes with a whole lot of makeup!" Belle laughed and rolled on her new bed. The mattress was made with old clothes stuffed inside.

Emile stood and looked out one of the windows and saw a few of the new trees. They were home to the giant beetles and had hollowed-out trunks. A few of the creatures rested around their trees. The beetles were magically linked to Tree-Tree, even if they fed on the sap their trees produced.

She felt a little tingle, an instinctual fear. It was weird to be so near these giant beetles, but they were minions, creations of the tree spirit.

Jura walked in. "Ah, the design of the rooms is the same."

"Oh, hey, Jura."

"Settling in already?"

"Yeah. Finally, a space outside!"

"Yeah, tree spirits are amazing." I knew from the elves that there were other tree spirits around the world with similar powers, and some of these ancient tree spirits managed to elude the wrath of the demons by 'escaping.' They tell stories of how some of these legendary trees created mystical forests that were able to disappear temporarily. The methods the denizens of the world used to survive and outlast the demons were quite interesting. Some chose to disappear, and some chose to be constantly on the move.

YEAR 73, MONTH 3, WEEK 2

[Demon King Andraas has been defeated.]

[Maximilian Powell has died.]

[Meela Adams has died.]

[Hendrick Mathers has died.]

[Freyasian has died.]

[Gunnar Forrest has died.]

[Peters Schmiel has died.]

[Fang Wei has died.]

[Omar West has died.]

[Sally Ann Courtlass has died.]

[Reese Witherfork has died.]

[You received 10 fragments. You now have a total of 66 fragments.]

[You gained 4 levels. You are now level 114.]

[Tree Familiar abilities upgraded.]

[Skill: Defensive dome obtained.]

[Customizable branch option unlocked: Shield Generator.]

[Soul Tree range greatly expanded.]

It started with a set of pop-ups, and then I had a very, very bad feeling, and I asked all the elves to hide. They didn't know why yet, but they trusted my commands. I activated all the defensive measures that came with the higher levels, and indeed, there was something that came.

There was a small delay of about an hour after the notification, and then a strong wind swept across the entire area. It felt like the shockwave from a faraway explosion, and it brought searing, hot air. Thankfully, the winds had weakened considerably after all the distance traveled.

"What the hell was that!" Jura exclaimed as he watched the trees sway and almost topple from the winds.

"The demon king has died. And...I think some kind of massive explosion happened."

"Oh!" The elves clapped their hand. "That's great news!"

"And the heroes died as well."

"Oh. That's sad, but that's great news, too!" Jura frowned and then laughed.

"What? Why?" The other elves looked at Jura.

"Surviving heroes tend to create political chaos after the demon threats are nullified. Actually, quite a few of the human kingdoms and empires we see today are descended from heroes.

So, heroes, while necessary, create a whole lot of wars and fighting after that."

So, what next?

"What would you do to prepare for the next demon king?" I asked.

The elves paused.

"Uh..."

Wait. I thought elves being long-lived creatures usually planned things out.

Jura and Laufen glanced at each other. "Well, we concentrated on our day-to-day lives. Sometimes we worked, and sometimes we trained, or we would spend our time looking after the kids. We, uh, we don't think much about the next demon king. If it happens, it happens. The kings and emperors, senior priests, and all the rulers worry about such stuff."

Those words reminded me of people stuck in dead-end jobs, unable to see the bigger picture because they were just faced with deadline after deadline at work. They were so busy surviving they didn't have the capacity to think or plan for longer-term events.

"And even if we think about it, the demon king is so powerful that whatever plans we make aren't going to work."

Well, that's fair. If it's not something you had the ability to change, there's really no use worrying about it.

At that point, it was the children who spoke up. Brislach and Wahlen laughed and said, "If we could be heroes, then we could beat the demon king!" That was actually the idea. If we could beat the demon king, then we need not worry about the problems it created.

And I wanted to try that idea. Would it be possible to make someone into a hero? I wondered whether [Soul Forge] had that sort of ability, but first, I needed to get my [Soul Forge] online.

YEAR 73, MONTH 3, WEEK 3

The news of the demon king's death took a while to spread as not everyone possessed a nice notification in their menus like I did.

The elves said that where the demon king perished, the land was sometimes warped by the mixture of his demonic magic and the natural magic in the area, and this created a special type of mana crystal known as Daemolite.

Daemolite was a valuable resource as it could only be found at the sites where the demon kings died, and the number of mana crystals created after the death of each demon king was finite. It was highly valued for its ability to store mana in large quantities, therefore making it useful for high mana requirement spells, rituals, and generally as a source of power for large, long-range weapons. Adventurers also used them as a sort of reusable mana potion as they lacked the pain and side effects from using too many potions. The crystals stored the heroes' mana, which they could withdraw later on.

This meant the period immediately after the demon king's death was usually a mad rush to the site to harvest these minerals. It was for these reasons that some adventurers had a secondary mission given by their countries, which was to observe and inform their benefactors of the location of the demon king's demise and harvest these crystals.

It wasn't easy to mine such minerals, despite the fact these crystalline structures were usually scattered all over the surface. The dense mana pools usually attracted leftover demons, stimulated the spawning of large monsters, and had a tendency to generate unusual weather or environmental effects.

Daemolite was valuable, but what really got kings and countries to send large armies to seize control of the areas was for the chance to find a very rare object. The last remains of each demon king were supposedly small, finger-sized horns, known as the Horns of Eternity. Ground into powder and consumed, it restored one's youth, extended one's life significantly, and depending on compatibility gained access to a special type of magic known as chaos magic. That said, in recent times, no one had ever found one, and so they remained an elusive artifact. Some said only certain demon kings generated it, and some others said it was nothing more than a myth.

With this as our backdrop, we had our next human encounter.

"Airship!" The elves pointed to an object in the sky.

Oh, a magical airship. I was amazed that these things existed in this world after all. From what little I'd seen so far, this world mostly relied on land-based transportation, so I was fairly surprised by the airship. The airship was a small one, and it zoomed ahead quickly.

At this point, Jura looked up. "That airship..."

"Huh?"

"They belong to the Salah Kingdom that attacked us." It brought up memories of their cruel act, where they burned the entire village. I felt anger.

Ah. That was a kingdom I didn't want to benefit. I realized I couldn't attack it at range as my [Root Strike] certainly didn't reach that high. If only I had some kind of lasso. I would work on that for next time. Perhaps flying insects, too.

As I reviewed my arsenal, I thought about whether my fruits could possibly hit the airship if I fired them. Perhaps I could create exploding fruits, too, like explosive mangrove seeds.

I created a bunch of corrosive fruits, and right as it flew overhead, I unleashed a huge barrage of fruits. The fruits smashed into the underbelly of the airship, it shook in midair from the impact, and then it started to lose altitude like it was about to crash.

The airship shuddered, but somehow, they performed a controlled landing. The airship skidded to a landing, and then once it came to a complete stop, about six drowsy, partly injured men popped out.

"Huh? What the hell happened?" one of them asked as he staggered out. He seemed like a fairly experienced adventurer.

"We were attacked. Something hit us with these things." Another guy pointed at the remains of the corrosive fruits stuck on the bottom half of the hull. It was riddled with splattered fruit.

"There's only that bunch of trees. Do you think something is in there?"

"Of course it is. What else could it be?"

"Let's go check it out." The six men took out their weapons and approached the outer trees. They approached carefully, but once they got closer and all were within range, my roots surged out of the ground and wrapped their bodies like multiple pythons.

They screamed.

But my roots and vines were able to hold back a demon champion.

They struggled.

My beetles charged out and snatched their weapons. Some dropped to the ground.

Weapon-less and restrained, I wondered what I should do with them.

Kill them?

At that point, I wondered whether all men of the Kingdom of Salah were the same. Maybe these men were unaware of the atrocities their compatriots committed.

"Tie them up and interrogate them. Find out what they want," I mentally spoke to Jura.

Jura took my extra-strong paralyzing sap and fed all of them, except one. It caused the five men who had a taste of the bitter sap to shiver and convulse like they were electrocuted. They fainted soon after.

The last man, the oldest, and the one who seemed to be in charge, stared at Jura. "What the fuck are you doing?"

"You belong to the Salah Kingdom, and they destroyed this village some time ago. I'm just taking revenge."

The man's eyes widened. "I had nothing to do with it."

"Really?" Jura shrugged. "That's what everyone says. But I might spare your life if you're cooperative. Otherwise, I'll kill you."

The beetle carried the remaining five men into a wooden cell, one of the extra customizable branches. Essentially, it was a room but with no windows and a door that could only be opened from the outside. After all, as these were my trees, I had full control over who was able to access them. There were vines inside that held their bodies.

"So, do you want to cooperate?"

"Fine. What do you want to know?"

"Good."

The group of beetles transported the damaged airship and moved it to the space between my main tree and the sub-trees. I would take a closer look at it later. I found the idea of having my own airship appealing, even if I couldn't use it.

YEAR 73, MONTH 3, WEEK 4

The adventurers were still alive, and my routine involved putting them under the microscope. I observed certain differences in the human body compared to elves, and this was most apparent in the nature of the 'water' of their souls. The elves had a very slight greenish tinge to them, and it seemed to explain the elves' natural disposition toward nature-based magics and why it was harder for them to use magics that contradicted this natural disposition. Humans generally had clear, colorless water.

After a week of being in and out of the biolab pods, they had gone slightly crazy, and it seemed like they were hallucinating. Perhaps it was the sleep-inducing elements I injected into them via the nourishing branches.

"Are we going to keep them here forever?" the younger elves complained, but they still put up with it because they were monitored by beetles and restrained by the vines.

Well, I planned to dispose of them, eventually. But, for now, they were useful. If the [Soul Forge] was that powerful, I had to establish an understanding of what the soul was.

Jura grinned, a part of it colored by his hatred of past events. "I would like to fight them one on one."

Hmm, maybe I could set up a match between Jura and them and allow them to fight for their fate. But what if he lost?

No, if he lost, it would be a problem.

"Fine. If they win, they go free."

Jura gulped, but he was the best fighter the elf village had, even more so with all the additional levels from the recent battles.

"Let them know, one on one, if they win, they go free, and if they lose, they die."

The adventurers were more than happy with such a challenge, and so they agreed. So, the next day, the captain faced Jura just outside the ring of trees. I would still be able to easily kill them with a [Root Strike], so I wasn't too concerned.

The battle started with both the captain and Jura staring at each other as they readied their weapons.

"Start." Laufen was flanked by about six beetles as she started the match. She shook her head. To her, this was a silly thing.

The two men traded sword strikes, but it was soon clear Jura was a lot stronger. I figured as much, as my investigations into the human body didn't suggest anything special.

The adventurer tried a few dodgy tricks—a poison dagger, a random hidden weapon—but they all failed. Jura, as an elven warrior, had fought adventurers many times in the past, so such tricks were not new to him.

One slash from Jura, and the battle ended. All in, the battle was mostly posturing for a good three to five minutes. The actual fighting was shorter, barely two minutes and that was it.

So the human adventurers died.

YEAR 73, MONTH 4, WEEK 2

Peace and quiet. It was lovely. Rather than killing the remaining adventurers with a [Root Strike], I felt like trying something different. I used my root's natural [Absorption] abilities, and I drained them into nothing but a husk.

With the new weapons and items collected from the adventurers, the elves could practice different kinds of fighting, which they would eventually need.

It dawned on me that I would need new skills and abilities soon. One alternative to the [Soul Forge] was to power it myself, but that would require a tremendous amount of energy, and so I explored how to store energy. The system gave me a solution. It came in the form of a potato.

[Tree ability: create tuberous storage.]

[A potato that stores energy.]

One tuber for every customizable branch. In total, that was forty potatoes. My main body had grown and had room for ten customizable branches, and thirty for each of the subsidiary trees. These regular-sized potatoes were now my standard unit for energy.

The 'energy cost' of my [Soul Forge] activities would be measured in 'potato units' (PU). I suspected, as with all units of measurements in a world with game-like mechanics, they would go obsolete very soon. Maybe in a decade or two, I would be using MegaPUs or GigaPUs.

Aside from my experiments on energy storage, we noticed a group of returning refugees.

Displaced by the demonic invasion, these men and women sought to return to their old homes, to rebuild and to see what was left. Their expression was a mix of fear, excitement, relief, and worry.

I didn't blame them. Returning after so long, there was a lot to think about. They probably lost a lot to the demons, and yet they still wanted to return. They didn't approach us and continued their journey.

"I wonder how everyone else is, those from our village?" Laufen sat on one of the flat roots that linked the main tree to the other trees. Jura sat a small distance away, opposite her.

"They are now in the elven kingdom. I'd like to think they are fine." Jura nodded, but he was probably faking the optimism. Not many survived the journey and restarting their lives in a foreign land was hard, even with skills and levels.

"Do you think they will come back?"

"If they know what we have, yes." Jura patted the wood. It was like a table.

There were a lot of things I wanted to do. One of them was to make contact with other spirits.

I thought about extending the range of my rootnet, so I could find them, but it was a difficult exercise, and they were probably very far away. So it was important to locate other spirits and find a way to link up.

The elves didn't remember where the nearest tree spirit was, and it was possible that not all tree spirits were known. Rumors said those attuned to nature could sense their presence, and so I wondered whether I sensed my fellow spirits.

Then I got a call from Wisp.

"Hello." Wisp floated, surrounded by multiple other floating souls. They glowed like little balls of white light, and they orbited Wisp.

"Oh. Hi, Wisp."

One of the little balls stopped and floated right in front of me. "Tree Spirit."

"Huh?" Oh, was this like Gewa? I immediately took a better look and noticed this ball was different. Its glow pulsed, and the color was different, a slightly bluish tone.

"One of your heroes. Unlike the others, there is something that held it back from returning to the gods."

"So you are?" Heroes? Ah, well, heroes were supposed to be special. Their spirits belonged to the gods.

"Meela. Died."

How?

"Her soul is in pretty bad shape. Whatever caused her death had to be really bad. Souls, even those of the gods, naturally decay when they are unprotected, and so it's actually amazing this soul made the journey here." Wisp floated. "You'll need [Soul Forge] to repair her."

"Why?" I asked Meela's ball of light.

"Promise. Help. Tree Spirit."

"My guess was it followed the path of the familiars attached to it, or else it would have given up and returned to the gods. She seems to hold rather strong emotions of a 'debt' to you, so she returned."

Ah. It was a bit like Gewa, but for Meela, it was her promise. I needed to figure out how all this worked.

"Okay, will it decay further?"

"Nope. Now that it's in your soul realm, the decay has stopped."

"I see." It seemed to me that everything related to souls must start with a functional [Soul Forge]. "Can I ask what happened?"

"Demon King. Explode. Die." Meela's soul bobbed up and down.

Oh, okay.

"I think that's all it can manage for now." Wisp stopped me from going further. "You can talk to her again tomorrow. Her soul energy is exhausted, and she needs rest."

Meela moved away, and the other souls followed.

"The rest of these lights, are they the other reincarnators?" I asked, but I noticed the other souls didn't look like Meela's. They were ordinary.

"No. Just random souls that died within your range. You get a lot of these." They were drawn to me, kind of like a magnet.

"Don't these souls have information I can use?" If they could talk like Gewa, that meant I could get a constant stream of information, so long as people died!

"Maybe, but you need [Soul Forge] to squeeze it out of them."

"Seriously! Must everything be dependent on [Soul Forge]?"

"No, you can also get a skill, but you're not there yet. Spend more time in the soul realm, you might learn something." Wisp then whooshed away.

YEAR 73, MONTH 4, WEEK 4

Refugees! And adventurers. These two groups had somewhat aligned interests. Refugees wanted to return to their old homes, while adventurers wanted to check out what was left behind. From the many demon battles, those who perished sometimes left valuable items behind that were useless to demons. The adventurers needed the refugees' knowledge of their areas to help find where people used to live and the location of common haunts. Perhaps they were here to raid any abandoned castles.

We saw four batches of refugees, mostly humans, and then one odd lizardman. Too bad the lizardman didn't get close to our location. I would have loved to put him under the scope.

These groups mostly avoided me. It seemed a gigantic tree surrounded by two rings of trees must appear scary!

I did some thinking and came up with three categories of threats I needed to prepare for.

The first threat was the nearby kingdoms. The kingdoms would eventually want to restore their rule over the land, and they would come back and claim this place. If their army came here, I would need to be prepared to face an army easily larger than before. I would also need to include their adventurers as well, those who may see myself as a prize, a bounty, or a monster to be slain. It was likely there were kingdoms and adventurers that didn't see tree spirits as something that needed to be protected. My experience with the Gaya Temples said as much.

The second threat was the non-demonic monsters. I had it easy with my various buffs against demons, but with the demons gone, that meant we would return to facing the regular monsters. So far, I could handle most of the regular monsters, but if there were greater monsters, then I wasn't so sure. There might be dragons, or monsters of that level, which might now be attracted to my larger size. I wasn't convinced of my odds if a fire-breathing dragon came my way.

The last threat was obviously the returning demon king. From past trends, it seemed to be a ten-year cycle, and I wasn't sure whether ten years was enough time to prepare. I'll also wanted to know whether I could somehow influence the return of the demon king. Perhaps the rift size influenced the demon king's return or something. If I could figure out how to push the time back—even by a year or two—that might allow more options. Or maybe I could even push it back indefinitely.

The kingdoms were the immediate threat, of course, and I would like to get back at the Salah Kingdom more for what they did to the elves. I thought about how to deal with a conventional army and concluded that I would need a large amount of area effect abilities, a standing army of my own—perhaps in the form of a large beetle army or a large group of converted woodhounds—and also some camouflage or ambush-like abilities to take out unprepared forces.

The peace among nations was held together through fear of the big, bad guy, the demon king, and once it was dead, the cracks naturally emerged. The period after the demon king was usually followed by all sorts of rebellions, coups, power grabs, and so on.

Against this backdrop of political turmoil, I could offer

protection from demons as part of a strategy to gather supporters and rebuild Freeka.

Against non-demonic monsters, my hopes were on the elves, Jura in particular. I would need to get them to the point where they could handle regular monsters, but I would still be stumped if I ever encountered dragons or other powerful flying beasts. My existing anti-air options were limited or close to nonexistent, and my fire resistances may or may not apply against dragon fire, but I hoped I didn't have to find out.

For demon kings, I honestly didn't know where to start. First, I figured that needed data—what was written and recorded in books about the demon kings—so I wanted to find libraries, scribes, historians, and other trees of knowledge, if there were such things.

"Tree-Tree." Emile snapped me out of my thoughts. The elves could call out to me anywhere around my main tree, and I could receive it. The range of my telepathic communication widened with my subsidiary trees.

"Yes?"

"Can you put your smaller trees anywhere? Must they be next to you?"

"Good question." I didn't think about that at all. The moment I got the ability I just instinctively placed them around me.

[Subsidiary trees can be placed anywhere so long as it remains connected to your root network. Each subsidiary tree also extends your root network.]

Thank you, Mr. System. It was like a build-range thing commonly seen in strategy games. My subsidiary trees were essentially pylons.

"Why do you ask, Emile?"

"Oh, I thought it'll be cool if we could like...have a room to stay at the end of every day's journey. If we were on a journey.

I'm just daydreaming." Emile laughed and rolled on her bed. "Or maybe the trees could become a wall or something..."

Hmmm, spacing out the trees like electrical pylons was an interesting idea since my vision was shared by my trees.

"Or maybe they'll be like the magical twin-trees of the old Ellara. There were these two spiritual trees that were apparently twins, and they had a connected portal that allowed a person to move between the trees."

Well, thanks for the idea, Emile! Maybe I'll get there someday.

YEAR 73, MONTH 5, WEEK 1

I was trying to find out whether my leaves could act as some kind of energy generator since I discovered the potato storage. In a way, a solar-panel/battery combination. If this world was a game, I thought it should be possible, but I wasn't sure what I was missing to get them. There should be a more 'efficient' and higher output design and construction.

Leaves generated 'food,' and the tubers functioned as storage of the food, and if the leaves produced more, the tubers refilled quicker.

Maybe I was missing certain kinds of minerals.

I was also stuck with [Soul Forge], but this time, at least I knew what I was missing.

[To fire it up for the first time, 1,000 potato units (PU). Subsequent use depends on the type of forging or changes you are making.]

It was rather weird that the system used my terminology. I suspected it had some ability to adapt to our norms and indicators. Then again, if the system supported heroes coming over from entirely different worlds, surely it had some ability to translate words, norms, and jargon.

Anyway, from what I calculated so far, I currently had forty potatoes underground. Each of my trees generated 1PU, and my main body generated 10PU. So, if I combined my existing production and released my stored energy, I could hit 80PU.

920PU to go. I needed to figure out how to close that gap. The elves, using their mana, could each produce about 1PU to 3PU worth of energy. In the scheme of things, their contribution was relatively negligible.

I also compared the potatoes against the storage capacity of the Daemolite. I wanted to know why everyone was looking to get some.

"There are a fair few souls coming." Wisp bobbed and floated in my soul realm. Lately, it looked like a firefly park. I wondered whether there was a capacity. "No. There's no limit."

"If I kill someone, do I get their soul?"

"If they are strong and hold strong emotions against you, no. Otherwise, there's a high chance you would. Most souls lose most of their worldly bindings and don't really care what spirit tree or spirit being captures them."

"Why don't all the souls with my familiars float back to me?" I wondered whether he knew, but I suspected it was just random chance.

"There's quite a bit of...randomness involved. Proximity, luck, the manner of death, whether there are other soul trees nearby...a lot of things influence it. The ideal situation for you to absorb a soul is to repeat what happened with Gewa. In short, they need to die right next to you, on their own. Killing them or a painful death reduces those odds. In their case, their actual soul still needs to go on to their next life, but that waiting time is spent with you..."

"So will Meela move on to the next life, too?"

"She should, as it is the way of the world, but otherworlders are special. I am not aware whether their rules are different. In any case, the damage her soul received currently prevents her from moving on."

Ah, so there were plenty of souls unable to move on. A gruesome death sometimes damaged the soul and released dark energy that might create haunted places or manifest as evil spirits. Spiritual intermediaries, such as tree spirits, exorcists, evokers, spiritualists, or certain types of places of worship, came in to control such negative energies and managed these wayward souls.

YEAR 73, MONTH 5, WEEK 2

It was getting hot.

The small patch of crops the elves planted around the trees were doing well, their growth augmented by my presence. There were multiple wooden pots, made from wood magic, hanging around all the branches and also on the floor, and they contained herbs and local spices. There was also a small patch that cultivated edible potatoes and corn.

Harvest should happen soon, at least for this batch.

Now that we were a small forest of trees, Jura practiced his tree-jumping. Elven archers usually jumped from tree to tree to get into their firing position. Previously with only one tree, he didn't have anywhere to jump. It was also a little silly since he couldn't use a bow with his arm out of commission.

The kids wanted to follow what he was doing, but it was too dangerous, so Laufen kept them in the playpen. Lausanne was at that mimicry stage, and even with her size, she tried to climb the trees.

Also, one random day, I acquired a new skill, or actually an upgrade of an existing skill.

[Customizable Branches upgraded. New customizable branch option: Harvestable Products obtained.]

[Options are: Cotton, Maple Syrup, Oranges, Olives. Expanded options will be available with higher levels or when new types of fruit are studied in the biolab.]

Ah, man. I didn't feel like using the inner ring of trees or the main tree's available branches for that, so that left the four outer-ring trees for this function. So I asked the elves for their opinions.

"For us, we'd like cotton. We'll get to make new mattresses, new clothes, and new pillows. We already have rather tasty fruits," Laufen and Belle answered.

"If we see more travelers, maybe there will be merchants, too! Olives and syrups should sell quite well; we can get money!"

"Ah...money." Hmmm, that would be interesting.

I still wanted to leave some of the outer trees available, so I chose one of the trees for cotton and another for olives. The two chosen trees entered a sort of hibernation stage, and I sensed their inner body start to change. In fact, as I reached out to one, a pop-up appeared in my head.

[Transforming to produce chosen products, please wait three days.]

Ah, well, that's not long.

With the merchant thing, though, I assumed I would scare them if I spoke directly into their head.

"We'll do it," the three ladies, Laufen, Emile, and Belle, volunteered. "We used to buy and sell stuff with merchants, so I think we can handle it."

All right, then. Olives for sale.

YEAR 73, MONTH 5, WEEK 4

The two trees completed their transformation and started production immediately, and each tree produced one cartload of olives and one bale of cotton per week.

The elves needed a storeroom, so for now, they stored the harvested goods within the secret hideout. The cotton was rather raw, so the elves and kids helped with processing it into a more usable form, which would take quite a while. In some places of the world, magic was used to process these raw cottons.

As for the olives, they were harvested in their fruit form and would be pressed for olive oil later. The elves said these oils were rather expensive since they didn't grow everywhere.

The quality of these two produces was average, and I supposed that was because I just acquired the skill for them. Perhaps I would get the ability to produce higher-quality produce at a later date.

The arrival of the additional crops made the elves busier, and somehow, it cheered them up. It reminded them of proper village life where everyone had work to do. Even if it was tiring to clean and process the cotton or press the olives with the wooden press, the elves found purpose, comfort, and even pleasure in these chores.

Occasionally, there were still some stray packs of hellhounds and other monsters, but they were easily disposed of by the beetle group.

Then came an odd bunch. They were like adventurers but different.

"Ah, bless the nameless mother!" Druids! They seemed extremely interested, and so they moved closer. "These trees! They look untouched by the demon's destruction."

"Ah, indeed. The gods are kind for some lands are preserved!"

As the elves hid, Laufen shook her head. I was worried. Druids were not a group I liked to deal with, and I just remembered being moved twice!

"Who are these people?" I asked the hidden elves.

"It looks like there are people living here!" one of the druids muttered as the rest caught up.

A man wearing a strange wig, with a necklace of multiple tiny bones, claws, and feathers, looked and pointed at me. He reminded me of a shaman or witchdoctor, and he carried a wooden staff decorated with small skulls and bones.

"Spirit sign."

"Oh?" Another man came up next to him. He wore a long, flowing, white cloak and hood and resembled a priest. "That explains it."

"Shall we leave?" the shaman asked, and the others nodded.

"Yes, yes. This place doesn't need our help—"

"Wait! Wait!" the super-excited first guy interjected. "I think there are elves here."

"Yes. So?"

"Isn't there a bounty on elves?"

"No." The shaman shook his head. "No elf hunting."

"Don't let the king hear that," another of his companions chimed in as he rode up next to him.

"He's no king."

"Okay, okay. We're not having this conversation. Let's go, let's go." One of them got in between the shaman and the other member of the party and tried to break up their conversation. "We've got plenty more to do."

The shaman nodded, and they moved on.

I felt relieved to see them go.

YEAR 73, MONTH 6, WEEK 2

Shrubs and small trees grew around my circle of trees now. They had been growing since spring began, and now they formed another layer outside. Throughout the valley, weeds and small shrubs popped up, and the elves described how the entire valley now had a layer of greenery, mostly grass.

My presence contributed to this burst of nature and vegetation.

Then we saw people building roads.

A group of forty or so constructed roads using a mix of earth and fire magic, building across the valley. They were accompanied by cartographers and a group of guards.

"Let's mark this on the map."

"It's Freeka, isn't it? We should say it's uninhabited now."

"Yeah, what's left of it. But it looks like other than the destroyed forests, the general area is unchanged."

"At least that's a section of the map we don't have to change much."

"Yeah," the first man agreed as he scribbled on what appeared to be a large floating book.

I found it interesting to watch the mage-builders at work.

The earth mages formed bricks from the soil and dirt, and the fire mages used fire magic to cook the bricks. The other mages magically arranged and levitated them to where they were supposed to go. It was a continuous, ongoing process, and these tiled roads would contribute to faster travel for merchant wagons.

"But we do need to note down that giant tree. It'll be a landmark."

"Giant trees. Probably magical. To be investigated further."

And that was the end of it. They moved on, rebuilding roads that were previously lost.

In this world, the devastation caused by magic was incredible. Towns flattened, hills destroyed, and forests razed. But on the flipside, nature's magic also restored the hills and forests at a speed far faster than my own. There was also a greater power at work that repopulated empty lands with monsters and animals.

And despite the really huge number of deaths from every demon attack, it seemed the world's population was still rather stable. Not all continents were affected by the demon king, though it rotated its appearance between the continents. So the destruction was usually localized and contained within a particular continent. It was usually when the heroes failed that the demons gradually spread across the worlds. The demonic rifts would open everywhere, at least until the demon king was killed.

In my opinion, the presence of reincarnators and heroes made the natural denizens of the world...lazy. And selfish.

Because it wasn't their problem.

The heroes would deal with it.

The armies nearest to the demons were there just to buy time and reduce the destruction, but kingdoms across the oceans, on the other continents, would not send armies to their aid. I found my thoughts constantly returning to how the demon king was a regular 'disaster.' It was like a mega-hurricane that happened every ten to fifteen years, and if what Meela briefly suggested was true, they seemed to get stronger each time.

That didn't make sense to me, of course. If they always got stronger each time, and this world had been around for ages, surely the world would have been destroyed eventually.

That also led to the next question. What if there were no heroes? What if there was no 'next time?'

I hoped I wasn't jinxing it, but what if? Ah, maybe I should ask the gods. Could I talk to gods in this world?

Maybe I shouldn't think so much. I am a tree, right?

"Tree-Tree..." Lausanne said as she sat on my roots the following day. Ah, yes. I had gotten distracted. Baby duties. When the adults were busy with the olive press or splitting the cotton fibers, Laufen occasionally asked me to keep Lausanne entertained. Brislach and Wahlen were old enough to be given some tasks, but Lausanne, at three years old, was still too small.

"Yes?"

"Play time. Please, make a wood ball?"

"Oh, okay. Sure." A wooden ball appeared from a branch, and she grabbed it. She had many wooden balls, but she seemed to enjoy the newly made wooden balls the most. She said the surface was smooth.

"Ball."

"Yes. Ball."

"Balls are like round fruits. Like oranges. But smoother."

"Yes." Lausanne hopped around, carrying her wooden ball. She walked out of the hideout to the inner circle courtyard. The other elves were working with the wooden press.

"Can you make a big ball?"

"Yes, how big?"

"Bigger than the tree? Bigger than...the world?"

"Well, no. I can't make a ball that big," I said.

"Oh." Lausanne looked down.

"Can you make a treehouse? So I can throw balls farther?"

Well, I could make a mini-treehouse in her playroom. But then she was only three.

"Ah. Yes, I can."

No. Wait. I didn't have the skill? Then again, I could create a treehouse-like structure, it just would not be secured to the tree.

"Can you make one now?"

"Uh...no."

"Why not?"

"I need to prepare."

"Can you make stairs?"

"Yes." Where was Lausanne going with this?

"Can you make stairs between trees?" she asked.

That's like bridges, no? Should be possible, even though the trees were not linked.

"Mommy says I am growing. Are you growing, too? You are a lot bigger now."

"I-I think so."

"I think I am growing. I can reach for things on the table now."

"Yes, you are."

"How much taller and stronger can I grow? Will I be a hero someday?" Lausanne kicked the wooden ball. It was hollow and smooth so it wouldn't hurt much. The ball rolled onto another bunch of roots.

"Maybe like your mommy."

"Can I be strong instead, so I can protect Mommy and everyone?"

"Why not? If you work for it."

"Uncle Jura said not everyone has the ability to be a hero. He says we need to be born with the talent."

Man, Jura was a bit too much of a realist there. But then again, he was correct.

"I'm just telling her to not pursue the impossible. People are born with a ceiling to their ability. Everyone gets there and then plateaus off," Jura had told her once.

Really? Maybe his understanding was incorrect. But, then again, I wasn't sure, either. Was this world so fatalistic that everyone settled at a certain level? Was there a 'level cap?'

"I can, right?" Lausanne looked at me, hopeful. She wanted to be a hero, and I thought, well, maybe she could.

"Yes, of course."

She smiled, picked up one of the small sticks, and swung it around like she was fighting. She was a bit too young for that, honestly.

Laufen shook her head as she watched, but she didn't stop her daughter. She went back to work, sorting through the cotton threads. They made some kind of basic loom, but they needed quite a bit of manual assistance to make basic cotton into cloth.

YEAR 73, MONTH 6, WEEK 3

A large caravan passed by, and the elven girls waited along the road made by the earlier builders.

"I hope they are sure."

"No one's sure, but if we manage to get there first, we will be one of the first groups to reopen the old trade routes. And that will make us rich. The price differentials are huge!"

There were easily two hundred people in this group, with about a hundred horses carrying goods. I wasn't exactly sure whether they were actually horses since they looked slightly different to me.

"I wonder why they didn't just send airships."

"You know how expensive the power crystals are? And they take so long to charge!"

At about this time, their conversation was interrupted.

"Hello, merchants! Would you like to buy some oils and cloth?"

They turned, and Laufen and Belle were there with one basket each. One contained olive oil stored in small wooden bottles, and the other contained the processed cotton cloth.

Of course, just a small a distance away were my beetles, hidden in the tall, natural weeds. The two elves were well within my [Root Strike] range, so I could quickly intervene if anything happened.

"Elf?"

"Kill them. We'll get the bounty," one merchant said.

Laufen and Belle's faces paled.

"Shut up. The bounty is worth a lot less than our trade rights to the elven kingdom! Apologies, ma'am, please ignore my guild-mate!" he screamed back and smacked the merchant on the back.

One of the guards rode closer to them and signaled the merchants. I tensed up, but then the guard turned away. He was just there to check on them.

Two of the merchants approached the elves, dismounted, and inspected the wares.

"Hmm. I am surprised you have olive oils in this area. I don't see any olive farms or groves."

Laufen smiled and didn't answer.

"Hmm. The condition is average and storing them in wooden bottles is not ideal." The merchant took the hint and focused on the goods.

"Yes, we would like to also buy some bottles or vases, if you have them," Belle added. Olive oils were usually stored in vases, away from sunlight and kept sealed.

Another of the merchants joined the two. "Oils?"

"Your field of expertise." The merchants glanced at each other, and this one traded in all kinds of oils.

The merchant took out a small bottle. "May I?"

"If you buy them."

The merchant laughed. "Fine. I have six large amphoras empty. I'll pay for that much." He took out some coin and passed them to Laufen.

Laufen carefully inspected the coin she received. "Would you sell us a few of your large amphoras?"

The merchant shook his head. "I have no extra today. But I

will arrange for one of my men to ship some. You can pay my men, then. How many do you want to buy?"

Laufen looked at her coins again. "I think this can afford me...ten?"

The merchant laughed. "Yes. Ten is about right once you include the cost of transport. I will get my men to deliver ten, then. To this location?"

He looked around and jotted some notes into a book. That was probably his order or transaction book.

The amphoras were used to ship goods, usually liquids, over large distances. There were also wooden barrels and metal containers, but these amphoras made of clay were cheap and quite durable, which made them popular with merchants.

Laufen nodded. The merchant poured the olive oil from the wooden bottle into his glass bottle. He inspected the color, the smell, and then stirred it.

"Hmm. It's of average quality, but it is still rather fresh. I can sell them." The merchant made some kind of signal.

The merchant's assistants helped to pour the olive oil from the wooden bottles into the large empty amphoras at the side of the horses.

"How often do you make olive oils?"

Laufen paused. "Maybe once every three months? Except winter."

"Ah. You will have available supply in three months? I know some nobles will prefer fresher olive oils, rather than those imported from farther away."

Laufen and Belle huddled, discussed, and nodded at the merchant. "Yes. I think we can have two or three full amphoras by that time."

"Great."

The cloth had no buyers. Superior quality cloth was easily available around the area, so the one they had made wouldn't sell for much. It wasn't worth the effort of buying and reselling this average-quality cloth.

But, strangely enough, one of them asked about the wooden bottles themselves.

"These wooden bottles are beautiful. The surface is really smooth. Do you have a master woodsmith with you?"

They were made with my magic and not carved.

"That's a secret." Belle smiled. The merchants accepted this, used to people having secrets.

"All right, we should get going."

"One more thing... Do you have any vinegar stock for sale?" Laufen asked.

"Ah, yes. One small bottle?"

The merchants continued on their journey, and the elves now had some coin and a small bottle of vinegar stock. Laufen and the girls planned to make fruit vinegar with the extra healing fruits.

"Ah. Next time I want to ask for flour!" Belle sighed. "Too bad we had to buy the amphoras first."

"Bread?"

"Yeah. I want bread."

Jura laughed and ate some potato chips. The inner courtyard was full of potatoes. It was the elven staple around here since they didn't have vast farmlands.

"I'm fine with potatoes. They taste pretty good when fried with olive oil." Jura shrugged.

"Bread." Belle rolled on her bed.

Emile laughed. "We can trade for that next time. If we can get better quality stuff."

At first, the elves kept all the money, but I also wanted some, so after some discussion, the elves gave me a fifth of the coin.

"We didn't realize tree spirits wanted money," the elves collectively said as if it never occurred to them that a tree would ever want money.

"I may need to purchase certain items, so I want to start saving for it. Especially for the advancement of my...powers."

"Oh..."

Well, I would need money someday, so I might as well start saving. I would like to be able to trade, somehow. There would be goods or materials I'd need to buy since I couldn't possibly make everything myself.

The elves huddled and discussed this. I could hear everything they said, but they agreed. They mostly discussed what they wanted to buy and why a tree needed money, though in the end, their gratitude won out.

YEAR 73, MONTH 7, WEEK 1

The elves worked hard on the olive press. Since the cloth didn't sell, the elves focused their efforts on the olives instead. So some of the week's cotton was left unharvested.

A small merchant convoy dropped by to deliver the amphoras as agreed. The merchants clearly had a means of long-range communication.

One hot day that week, a group of six fleeing men and women arrived on horses. Some of them were injured, and they all had multiple arrow wounds. Some arrows were still right in their backs, and even the horses were injured.

Another group of ten cloaked men chased them. These cloaked men were injured as well but less so than the other group.

"Head for the trees!" one of the group shouted as they galloped.

The cloaked men chased, firing arrows in hopes of slowing the others.

I wanted to kill all of them. I was already suspicious of visitors, and here we had these armed folks. The six were so heavily injured they would probably bleed out if they didn't get medical attention.

"Who goes there!" Jura was on one of the tree branches with a spear on his hand.

One of the six, a female elf, shouted out something I didn't understand.

Jura, however, did, and he shouted, "Tree-Tree, target the cloaked men!" as he threw wooden spears at the cloaked men.

Since Jura said so, I launched [Root Strike]s.

Eight roots flew out of the ground like sharp spikes and struck the riders, and since they moved quickly, they pretty much skewered themselves on the roots. It killed them instantly.

The remaining two tried to pull back, but they were too close.

[Constrict].

Roots popped out and entangled the two. The small thorns and vines on my roots administered a strong dose of sleeping poison.

The six riders didn't look back, and they rode next to the outer ring. They hobbled from their horses.

One of them revealed a young baby.

Jura paused. I had a bad feeling.

"Huh?"

"Hold him. Please." His blood soaked the cloth wrapping the baby, and Jura reluctantly held the baby.

"Is this Freeka?"

Jura paused. "I suppose it's what's left of it."

"I see." The wounded treated each other, and they pulled out the arrows from each other's bodies, using healing potion on their wounds.

The female elf that shouted looked at Jura, her armor drenched in blood, and introduced herself. "I am Eriz, an aide and guardian of Yvon."

"Who is that?" Jura scratched his head. "And why do you know our passphrase?"

Passphrase? Ah, Jura and the villagers developed a passphrase to identify friendly people before this.

"Ah. Yvon, our lady and mistress, she...she said her brother is the village head here." Her wounds were recovering; the potions were working.

"Brother?"

"Ah, yes. I believe she mentioned his name was Ricola. Is he around?"

"He's dead." Jura held the baby awkwardly. The baby was tiny, probably less than six months old. "And, please, take this child back."

"Ah." Eriz paused and faced the other riders. "Do you have clean clothes we can change him into? All of ours are bloody."

Laufen stopped eavesdropping from inside the hideout and walked out with some clean cloth from the extra cotton stores, a bowl filled with paste, and some clean water. She took the baby from Jura and cleaned the blood from it. The baby was alive but weak and exhausted.

"Does Ricola have a sister?" Jura asked.

"Yes. I met her when we were wedded but have not seen her since." Laufen nodded as her hands cleaned the weak baby. "Is she well, in the human kingdoms?"

Eriz smiled. "The mistress is alive. But it is a challenging period now, with the king suspecting the elves of treason and the other princes finding every chance to remove us."

"Who is this child?"

"Uh, it is the mistress's baby."

"What?"

Eriz nodded. "It's inevitable. With the tension in the capital, the mistress requested her brother assist looking after her child."

One of the humans stepped forward and joined Eriz. "Please, raise the child as your own. We will return to the capital."

Laufen shook her head. "I cannot. We cannot."

Eriz paused, and the other human female came up. "Perhaps the two of us could stay back with the child? The guys can head back..."

She looked around.

"Will you guys accept us? As refugees?"

The other men nodded in agreement. "That is a good idea. The child is most attached to you, Eriz. This place feels safe and magical."

Eriz looked around, at the trees, and then at me. She stared for a while.

"The mistress has many good people around her. She would want some of them to ensure her child's safety," one of the men said. "I will stay, too, if you want."

"Can we stay with the baby?" Eriz asked.

Laufen paused. This was something she couldn't decide. Jura and her both went back into the hideout to discuss with the others. They eventually agreed because this was family. Laufen felt particularly conflicted because if this baby was indeed her nephew, she would feel bad if they turned him away.

"Yes."

Eriz, the human woman, Safran, and a human man, Pock, stayed back.

As for the two unconscious human attackers, they were kept in the wooden jail, where the adventurers once were.

[You have leveled up! Level 115.]

[Skill upgraded - Subsidiary Tree amount increased to 40.]

[Skill upgraded - Secret Hideout has unlocked - Tree-asury]

Ah. Treasury. And more trees! This leveling system was so convenient.

YEAR 73, MONTH 7, WEEK 2

The two humans were placed under the influence of strong hallucinogens, and they soon revealed that they served one of the princes of the Salah Kingdom, First Prince Wargo. The king was dying, so all the princes were positioning themselves to seize the throne.

Eriz and the mistress, Yvon, served another prince, Prince Galan, the third prince. Prince Wargo was a humanist, and that meant he was against non-human citizens of the kingdom. This recently made him a target of a botched assassination attempt by elves.

Prince Galan, surrounded by elvish and other non-human minders, thus came under tremendous scrutiny from the rest of the princes, all eager to eliminate the competition.

Yvon was a highly skilled administrator in the inner circle of Prince Galan, and so her baby was a vulnerability. The men suspected those on the other side wanted to capture the baby and force Yvon to defect to Prince Wargo's side. There were also suspicions about whether the baby was one of Prince Galan's many illegitimate children.

After I extracted that information from the two men, I used [Absorption] and drained their life away. It was a slow, painless death—at least under the effect of strong sedatives. They were deaths with few remains as their bodies turned into nutrients.

The elves were not comfortable with the new people so near, so for the first day, the humans lived in tents, while Roma, the baby, and Eriz stayed with Emile and Belle.

The next day, I spawned two of my new trees outside the second circle and made two rooms for the new arrivals. This surprised them greatly, especially Eriz. But the distance was necessary.

"This is a spirit tree?"

"Yes." Jura nodded.

They reacted strongly to the beetles as well. They jumped and almost wet their pants when a group of beetles crawled down the trees while they were walking by.

The beetles were busy. Non-demonic monsters multiplied often, so I frequently sent a group of them to kill these monsters.

YEAR 73, MONTH 8, WEEK 1

The newbies had been here for a month, and out of boredom, they helped with the olive press. The elves also gradually opened up and allowed them to participate in certain activities in their life. There were so few of them, after all. The merchants planned to arrive the next month, so the olives were stored in the amphoras.

Meanwhile, my beetles continued their monster hunts. These monsters appeared regularly, and I deployed them, and they brought back the bodies for my studies.

They fought many monsters, and through it, my beetle skill upgraded.

[Armored beetles upgraded to war beetles.]

The elves were right to suspect these new people. Eriz communicated with somebody magically, and she forgot that tree spirits like myself possessed the ability to see everything in the trees. Perhaps it was her mistress, but at least they were smart enough to communicate in code.

I placed my new subsidiary trees like pylons, in a circular fashion. Each was as far away as possible.

With the new trees, I extended my vision to cover a larger chunk of the valley.

Weirdly, this led to another upgrade.

[Subsidiary tree upgraded. You can place a total of sixty trees.]

The increase in [Subsidiary Tree] led to an equivalent increase in [Tuberous Storage] amount, so at sixty trees, plus ten with my main tree, I had a total of 140PU—still very far away from that 1,000PU.

There must be an easier way to do this.

"No good. We must go back. We must help!" Eriz shouted and startled everyone.

"What happened?"

"The king and Prince Wargo ordered a mass execution of all the non-humans."

"What?" Safran and Pock both seem surprised.

"How...how do you know?" Jura asked, his hand on a knife.

Eriz realized the horror of her statement, rubbed her head, and then sighed. "I have been magically communicating with Mistress Yvon. And now, there is a massive uprising in the kingdom by the non-humans."

Pock shook his head. "The king is mad."

"Prince Galan and Mistress Yvon have not seen the king for weeks." Eriz shook her head. "It may be Prince Wargo claiming to speak in his name."

"What does the mistress plan to do?"

"Escape. The army is too strong and organized, and fighting back is meaningless. She had been making arrangements for the rest of the non-human civilians to flee to the sympathizing cities or to the other kingdoms, but it seems the other kingdoms have closed their borders."

"We can go and help with the refugee traffic."

Eriz, Safran, and Pock all faced Laufen. "Please, take care of Roma for us. We must go. We will return."

"No. One of you needs to stay," Laufen insisted as Roma was still asleep on the bed.

"People are getting slaughtered. They need our help."

"And a baby needs her guardian."

Safran and Pock nodded. "She has a point, and both of us will be able to disappear easier as humans. Eriz, please stay. We will come back."

Eriz sighed. "Very well."

A few skills of mine upgraded after using them all this while.

[Secret Hideout: Biolab upgraded. Pods increased to 5.]

[Essence Collection upgraded. Extraction rate and speed improved.]
[Mineral Extraction upgraded.]

[Mineral Augmentation obtained. [Subsidiary Tree], and [insect warriors] strengthened.]

I had a large stockpile of essences and irons from the automated harvesting.

YEAR 73, MONTH 9, WEEK 1

Eriz updated everyone daily. She couldn't keep her anxiety to herself.

I stopped following after a week. To me, it was just people fighting and dying far away, and running, of course. It felt distant, and it was. It felt like listening to the radio, hearing the news about bombings or fighting in some distant land. It got tiring, and shit like this happened all the time in this world. I supposed I should feel for them since they were elves, but I personally only felt obligated to the seven elves under my care, and...that was it.

"Wisp. Any idea how I can speed up this process of getting enough power for [Soul Forge]? Isn't 1,000PUs a little too much?"

"I thought it was quite little. A small forest would have more than a thousand trees, easy."

"But that implies I have all the trees as a subsidiary tree!"

"Do you have to?"

"Uh. What?"

"I said too much." Wisp floated away. "I cannot give you that answer."

"Oh, come on."

"There are some things a tree spirit must learn on their own."

"Tree. Smart!" Meela bobbed in. "Tree. Good."

"Yes, yes."

Okay, so there must be a trick to this. So if I didn't have to have them all as my subsidiary tree?

Was it via rootnet?

I tried it on shrubs and trees throughout the valley.

[Local Rootnet Access connecting to nearby trees...]

[Connected.]

The familiar sound of spam flooded my notifications. Spam. So much spam.

Spam...

[Filtration activated].

But the important question was could I extract power from them?

[Attempting to connect. Energy Drain initiated. Rootnet function obtained: Treenergy.net.]

[Connecting to 64,500 grasses, 367 shrubs, and 141 normal trees, producing an estimated 18.4PUs. Normal trees produce 0.1PU, shrubs 0.01PU, and grasses 0.00001PU.]

Ah, I needed ten thousand normal trees to hit 1,000PU.

But!

It was very doable! The entire valley was within my rootnet! All I needed to do was actively use my tree spirit mojo and grow this entire valley into a forest like it once was.

I felt like dancing. Too bad I couldn't! *Weeeeeeeee...*
Now, I needed to work on my mojo.

YEAR 73, MONTH 9, WEEK 3

Massive! There was a massive burst in tree growth in the valley. The number of normal trees surged by three hundred in two weeks! If I kept this up, I would hit ten thousand normal trees by Year 75.

The elves were especially surprised to see the sudden surge in the growth of new trees, and what was once a sparsely covered valley gradually started to look dense again.

But there was a trade-off. My essence and material extraction reduced tremendously. Essence and materials were not extracted and were consumed in the creation of these trees. I saw this as a small matter.

During this week, the olive oil merchant came. Once again, that generated a little bit of coin. Despite an ongoing non-human genocide, it didn't stop merchants from conducting business.

Those who worshipped coin were probably the most devoted of worshipers. I left a path through the newly regrowing woods for the merchants and also an empty area for the trading to happen.

We made a small hut with wood magic at the empty area,

then the elves helped to make a wooden panel that read, "Freeka Trading Post."

Eriz continued to share the chaos of the kingdom. I occasionally listened and knew there was only sparse resistance as most of the non-humans chose to flee. These still felt like distant matters to me.

YEAR 73, MONTH 10, WEEK 1

More trees! Over three hundred more trees spawned and brought the valley's normal tree count to seven hundred sixty-two. This would be the single indicator I followed for the next year until this damn [Soul Forge] came online.

Animals returned to the forest. I felt it was strange how these animals appeared when they were not there before. According to the elves, there was a god that 'created' animals in the lands the same way monsters appeared from nowhere.

Well, it felt logically consistent. If monsters were just magical versions of animals, and monsters 'spawned' out of nowhere, the same global magic should apply to animals.

Maybe they were both creations of the same gods.

I wondered whether this god could make sentients spawn out of nowhere. Was I created in this world—no, reincarnated to this world—in the same manner?

In celebration of the return of animals, Jura went out on a hunt. He apparently spotted one of his favorite foods, deer or something like that.

There was a new mild annoyance, though.

Birds.

They made nests in my branches, and they pooped everywhere.

Some of them were brazen enough to attack my reinforced war beetles.

But they were just irritants.

"Tree-Tree use magic?" Lausanne asked, her language still not very polished.

"Yes, Lausanne. It will be a forest once more." Lausanne liked trees. She liked flowers, too, and some of the shrubs could flower. She liked the yellow ones the most. She said they looked like the sun.

"Wow. Teach me, please?"

"I can't. It's something I just feel. It's like a primal urge I just have to let out, and it happens."

It's true. My ability to spawn trees was something I did naturally, even if I didn't understand it. Once I activated it, it just happened. Weird tree spirit mojo.

Lausanne shook her tiny toddler head. "No, no. Do you know druid magic?"

"No, I don't."

"But best druids learn from Tree Spirits!"

"I-I can't. Maybe someday?"

Did I say she was too young? She's too young. I didn't think she should be learning magic at three to four years of age.

But I also frankly didn't know how to teach my kind of magic. It was ironic since I had [Learning Aura] and [Dream Tutor]. Couldn't I just 'dream-teach' the 'feeling' to them?

The boom in the valley's tree population led to my subsidiary tree skill getting an upgrade. It seemed the subsidiary tree ability was just linked to me doing tree-like things.

[Subsidiary Tree leveled up. Limit increased to ninety trees.]

[Some of your stored iron materials and essence of nature have been

consumed. Six inner circle subsidiary trees upgraded. They are now able to support three external rooms each.]

Progress!

I wasn't the only one improving. The elves, too!

The elves gained some skills in [Olive Oil Making], and Laufen already had [Trading] and [Coin Management] from her past experience, so she was the elves' primary treasurer at this point, assisted by Belle.

Sadly, bad news arrived from Eriz. The resistance spread, and the country descended into a civil war, with the humans overwhelmingly on one side, and the non-humans on the other, outnumbered and outgunned.

Prince Galan, their benefactor, was killed in an assassination, and their mistress was quickly framed. Without their patron, the non-humans fled in large numbers.

YEAR 73, MONTH 10, WEEK 3

[Rootnet is now connected to one thousand normal trees. Local rootnet access upgraded, range extended.]

The valley finally looked like a forest, and I was no longer easily visible from afar. In hindsight, I should have done that a long time ago. The cover provided by this forest of normal trees helped to hide my presence.

With my new increased number of subsidiary trees, I scattered about twenty across this new forest and made them as homes for my insect warriors.

This also increased my total war beetle population to seventy-eight. I now had a small army of beetles in my hands, and I felt like a commander in an RTS game. I wondered whether I could get an air force of some kind, perhaps birds or some kind of bees.

The beetles were occasionally attacked by the animals, but they were tough enough to shrug it off.

Anyway, air force. How could I lure new creatures? Why couldn't they just give it to me like the beetles?

YEAR 73, MONTH 10, WEEK 4

I saw elves, dwarves, treefolk, gnolls, minotaurs, centaurs, and lizardmen. It was the first time I saw so many typical non-humans. From my spiritual vision, they didn't appear how I imagined them to be.

There were maybe two thousand of them. I listened as they approached some of my farther subsidiary trees.

"How long do we have to keep moving?"

"As long as we need to. The armies are still after us."

The only thing that united this ragtag bunch of nonhumans were the humans. Once things settled, they would all split up.

"After this area will be the old demon king territories."

"Safer than being hunted by an army. There shouldn't be many demons, so it should be safe."

"Should."

I had a discussion with the elves on what they would do if these refugees decided to settle in the valley.

The view amongst my group was that they were not comfortable with them being too near, and that was defined as the two rings of subsidiary trees and the area around it. This space, to them, was still 'their' space.

Yet they understood the needs of these people, so they were

willing to share the valley with them. Perhaps these refugees could base themselves in another part of the valley. After all, with trees everywhere, it wouldn't be a problem in terms of cover or protection.

"There's a path."

"Should we take it?"

"Yes."

"No."

In the end, some of the refugees took the path through the forest, some decided to wade through the forest itself, and some went around. It took them a few days, and of the two thousand, around three hundred or so elves, treefolk, and centaurs decided to stay in the forest in the surrounding valley. As they were different races, they quickly split up and made housing in their own part of the valley.

For the others, the forest wasn't their ideal 'place,' and so they decided to continue their journey farther. The human army was still a little too close for comfort.

Thanks to the cover of the forest, they didn't know about me or the elves' presence yet. And that was fine. Some of them saw the Freeka Trading Post sign, though, and they probably wondered whether it was still used. After all, the merchants only came by quarterly, and it was coming on winter. To some, it was better to gather food and shelter before then.

"There are treefolk, elves, and centaurs in the valley?"

"Yup. The treefolk set themselves up near the small pond, the centaurs near the valley's slopes, and the elves at the far end."

"Whoa."

Treefolk. They were part-tree, part-human, and part-insect, apparently a creation of the nameless mother to give trees some variety. I examined them. Some of them appeared like walking trees, and some appeared like insects that disguised themselves as tree branches and leaves.

When these treefolk slept, their legs needed to touch the

ground, so they often slept upright or slightly tilted, their bodies leaning against the wall. To them, living in homes with multiple stories was a strange and uncomfortable concept.

They were the first to detect my presence.

When they slept, their feet extended small feelers into the ground, and this exchanged their bodily waste for nutrients. This led to contact with my roots...

[Foreign entities attempted to connect. Treefolk presence detected. Rootnet intercepting connection. Isolating...]

[Treefolk successfully isolated.]

"Huh." They were jolted from their first night of proper rest. "This place...the ground..."

A group of beetles appeared outside their makeshift settlement. The few warriors quickly took up arms, but there were too many, easily forty of these beetles.

"Hello, treefolk."

"Who goes there?" There was a de facto chief among the treefolk, and he stepped forth.

"I have been instructed to visit you. Welcome to Freeka. This is our valley," Jura said.

The treefolk looked at each other. "We see no Freeka, no settlement."

"Ah yes, razed by the Salah Kingdom. But some of us survive, protected by our guardian spirit."

"Guardian spirit?" The treefolk instantly connected the dots. "There is a tree spirit here?"

"Yes. He's been watching all of you. This valley is under his domain."

A few of them gasped, but the leader asked, "Does he want us to move away?"

"No. At least, not yet. We are just a greeting party. If there are no unpleasant events, our tree spirit will not take any hostile actions."

The leader breathed a sigh of relief. "As treefolk, we would be greatly honored to live in a land watched over by our ancestors."

"We hope so. Try not to chop too many trees down, and if you encounter any beetles, please don't attack them. They are the minions of the tree spirit."

The leader nodded. "Certain...certainly."

The beetles and Jura disappeared back into the night, and the treefolk quickly huddled together to discuss this revelation.

Back home, Jura looked at me. "Was that necessary?"

"Yes. It is important they know who they are dealing with, and treefolk seem like the ideal candidates to make that first contact. I won't want them randomly attacking my beetles."

Treefolk and elves apparently had an awkward relationship, and they were often tense with each other. Although in theory, both races shared the forests, they had different ideas of what an ideal settlement was like. Elves, especially the high and sun elf variants, preferred to build tall structures, carved from the trees, whereas the treefolk preferred to have vast, sprawling settlements that allowed contact with the earth at all times. Elves also had good night vision, whereas treefolk vision was generally poor, and they depended on a wide range of other senses like touch, gravity, and vibrations.

The elven refugee group were quick to start work. They built makeshift shelters, while a few of them used magic to bend and shape the normal trees into a house. It was a slow process. Whatever wood-forming magic these elves used reduced that tree's energy output in exchange for greater structural integrity.

The centaur group lived near the sloped areas of the valley, where there was a mix of shrubs and trees. Unlike treefolk and elves, they erected large tents, and they preferred to be close to the woods but not in them. Any trees in their vicinity were used to anchor the massive tents, and one of the taller normal trees became the center core of their chief's tent. The tents themselves were made of their leftover hair—mane and fur—cloth, and whatever animal fur or skin they could find.

"So, what do we do with the elves and centaurs?"

"Watch them. I've instructed my beetles to stay away, and since both elves and centaurs are at the forest's edge, it's still fine...for now. But once they grow, I will need to make myself known."

"It would be easier to let them know now, though, wouldn't it?" Laufen said. "If we wait too long, they might feel defensive."

"Hmmm...true. Let's be proactive, then. Jura, can you visit the elves?"

"Certainly."

Jura visited the elven settlement. Everyone was so busy working on their new place that they didn't notice Jura. He walked right through their makeshift, incomplete gates. These folks were not warriors.

"Hi, everyone!" he shouted, and everyone jumped in panic. They rushed for their arms.

"Who are you?" Even I could tell their posture and form were poor. They were exhausted from their long walk, and they just wanted to rebuild.

"I am from the Village of Freeka. It's a really, really small village, but we thought we'd still let you know we exist."

"Village? Freeka?"

"That unused trading post?"

"It's *rarely* used." Jura laughed and opened his hands. "I come in peace and want all of you to know a tree spirit watches over this valley. It is for his presence that a forest emerged so quickly after the fall of the demon king."

"What do you want?" a young elf shouted. Even amongst elves, the youth could be rude.

"Nothing much." Jura smiled, and thirty war beetles appeared next to him. Some of the elves yelped in fear. "Just know that this valley is protected and behave accordingly. Elves should already know how to behave in the presence of a tree spirit."

An elderly elf appeared. "Ah, I didn't know Freeka has a tree spirit. That is a pleasant discovery."

A younger man appeared. He looked like a warrior, and he glanced at Jura. "Are you the chieftain of Freeka?"

Jura laughed. "We are so few, so small, we have no need for a chieftain. But our tree spirit guides us and speaks to us. Our tree spirit sent me to greet you."

The elderly elf patted the younger man on the shoulder. "This is our chief."

"Well met."

"How do we find you?"

Jura paused. He didn't want to answer that.

"How many are you?"

"Less than ten."

"Then you should stick with us. We have more. Help us. Your war beetles, too."

Jura shook his head. "These war beetles, they belong to our tree spirit, and they don't listen to me."

The young chief shook his head. "I have never heard of elves who obey tree spirits. Tree spirits are our guardian spirits, but we are the true masters of the forests. Tree spirits follow the will of great elves!"

Jura smiled. "Ah, you are free to believe what you please. I am here to greet and welcome you to the Valley of Freeka. This is both a greeting and a warning. Know that the forest you see is under the protection of our tree spirit. You are free to test our tree spirit's patience and kindness if you feel that is a hollow threat."

The young chief winced.

Jura gave a gentle, polite bow, turned around, and left with the war beetles.

That was tense, but I had more free subsidiary trees. If necessary, I could place more of them closer to both the elves and the centaurs. This way, there would always a beetle group ready to respond to any uprising.

Next were the centaurs.

"An elf?"

The centaurs spotted Jura the moment he peeked out of the forest.

"Hi. I wish to speak to your leader."

Two centaurs appeared, one male and one female.

"We are the leaders. Speak, elf," the female said first.

"I am here at the request of the tree spirit of the valley to welcome you to Freeka."

The male one then spoke. "Are you here to threaten us?"

"Yes, and no." Jura smiled. Such negotiations were getting easier. "The tree spirit has reasonable expectations of proper conduct from the valley's inhabitants."

The female centaur looked at the male and whispered. The male centaur nodded and then turned to face Jura.

"A tree spirit, you say?"

"Yes."

The male centaur asked, "May we meet the tree spirit?"

"Yes. We will arrange a day for the chiefs to meet."

"Chiefs?" both centaurs asked simultaneously.

"Chiefs of the elves and treefolk, too."

"Ah. The other groups." The male centaur turned to look at the female.

"If we meet the tree spirit, we will decide whether to comply."

Jura agreed.

Eriz kept us updated about the fighting happening in the kingdom. Her mistress was trying to flee. But it was difficult when she was the main suspect and the target of widespread human propaganda.

Anyway, I was more focused on our new valley-mates, and I

wondered how to best use my additional [Subsidiary Tree] slots. If there was going to be tension, I wanted more beetles to fight off their numbers, and I had no indication of how strong the leaders and warriors were. Maybe they were as strong as Jura or maybe more.

YEAR 73, MONTH 11, WEEK 1

The number of normal trees grew to about fourteen hundred. Of the new groups, the elves and the centaurs eventually cut a few trees down to build their homes and other structures, but other than that, the growth rate was stable.

The new trees were clustered closer to me, and this increased the density in the middle of the valley. I didn't want to take away the kind of sloped spaces that the centaur enjoyed.

Eriz was upset and cried for days.

Her mistress stopped communicating with her magically, and she feared the worst.

Laufen, on the other hand, felt sorrier for Roma, the baby who was away from his mother. His body was still rather weak. I suspected he lacked nutrients as he had been apart from the mother. Laufen suggested we dip the baby in the pod so I could nourish his body and channel nutrients in via the vines and feelers.

Roma's small body was frail, and he needed to be constantly comforted by one of the ladies. Eriz was too attached to the conflict back home to properly care for him.

"Can you do something, tree spirit?"

"I'll try..." I thought about hospital incubation facilities. Perhaps my medical room or the biolab pods could be modified...

[Secret Hideout upgraded: Childcare corner obtained.]

[Childcare corner produces a special infant-friendly syrup, similar to baby and milk formula. Infant-syrup can be further upgraded with various kinds of materials and minerals, if available.]

Ah! The system to the rescue!

YEAR 73, MONTH 11, WEEK 2

The chiefs finally met. It was their first time in Freeka. Three from each of the three groups arrived.

The treefolk instantly prostrated themselves before me and sang from the moment they saw me. It sounded a little like aboriginal songs.

"What are they doing?" I mentally asked Jura.

"Some treefolk worship tree spirits. They are like a crazy version of elven tree huggers." Jura chuckled at that. "They are everywhere, after all."

The young elf chief glanced at the treefolk and shook his head. "It's just a tree spirit."

The elder elf next to him ribbed him with his elbow and whispered, "Shh. Not so loud."

"What? It's pathetic. It's just a very large tree with magic that supposedly absorbs our elvish souls. Spirit trees can't even protect themselves and need us elves to fight for them," he retorted.

The treefolk ignored his words and continued to sing their songs and hymns. It was rather pleasing once I got used to it.

The centaurs—the two chiefs and one older centaur that

seemed to be the shaman or mage of the tribe—were unperturbed by the acts of the treefolk and the elves.

"Hello," I spoke directly to their mind. "Please, stand."

The treefolk stood. It was like they jumped, how fast they moved. I thought their limbs must have had some kind of spring action in them. Not exactly...trees.

"I'm Tree-Tree, the tree spirit of Freeka. All of you are here because I'd like to set some ground rules, norms, and processes to conduct ourselves and minimalize conflict. Either with me, the elves, or each other."

I spent the whole night thinking about what to say, without coming off as too asshole-ish. I thought of starting it by saying, "I am Lord Tree-Tree of Freeka," but then again, I wasn't a lord.

The centaurs nodded. "So the purpose of this meeting—"

"I hope to tell all of you that the entire valley and forest is within my influence, and I hope we can all coexist peacefully. I have no intention of meddling in your respective affairs beyond what is needed to safeguard my priorities."

The young elf chief shook his head. "My priority is the safety and survival of my people. We may agree if it suits us, but I make no promises."

"What are your 'affairs,' tree spirit? Would it not be better to set certain boundaries of each of our territories?" The male centaur instantly, with a wooden stick, started drawing on the ground. I couldn't see it—my vision was, after all, a spiritual/magical one—but Jura helped to explain. In short, the centaurs claimed the entire left slope, the elves claimed the far side of the forest and a big piece of the lands after, and the treefolk got a circle around the pond. Anything not covered was mine.

At this point, I felt like a host that suddenly had guests, and now the guests demanded a room. Their boundaries still crossed with my roots, after the last expansion of the eight subsidiary trees. And I could still extend even farther. I didn't like that they carved up 'my' territory.

"That boundary drawn is nothing more than a 'designated area' for each of you, such that you don't unnecessarily create conflict. But this boundary doesn't surrender my claim over this entire valley. The entire valley remains under my care, as my roots extend everywhere. There will also be no chopping of trees beyond reasonable quantities."

"Uh…"

The elf chieftain shook his head.

Well, I wanted to grow the trees in the valley. It wouldn't help if all these new people chopped down trees, right?

"That is not reasonable. You are a tree spirit. Nothing more. What gives you the right to dictate what we do?" The elf chief stood forward. "We may need to chop some trees to survive, and we will need to hunt. If you restrict us, you may as well chase us away."

I paused. So did the centaur and treefolk. Strong words.

The elf chieftain turned to face the other chieftains. "Look. We are just dealing with a few elves and a tree spirit. I say our needs are more important. There are a few hundred of us! Why should this tree spirit and a few elves be allowed to say what we can or cannot do? I say we do what we want. It's just a foggy old tree."

We just started the conversation, and the elf was already so hostile. Why?

The centaur looked back at the elf and then looked at Jura and me.

They wanted to see my response.

It felt like the elf's words were intentional. He meant to provoke me, to test me, and pretty much force me, so a display of power was necessary. If I backed down now, I would look weak, and I wouldn't be able to protect the elves and my home from their ransacking. I couldn't allow that.

Although I knew force was right, I still felt reluctant. I wished these elves hadn't forced me. They were refugees, after all.

I felt like being nice. I mean, these elves, centaurs, and treefolk...well, they were all refugees. They fled from the non-human slaughter in their home kingdoms. But this sort of entitled behavior was unwarranted and unreasonable.

This was my home, and these were my people.

No. I was willing to be nice, but they couldn't push me too far.

A [Root Strike] shot from the ground, and it *swooshed* just next to the elf chieftain's head. The force of the roots created a small shockwave, and the elf chieftain fell.

The elves were shocked. They didn't expect that as Jura noted the elf chieftain's reaction was a mix of shock, horror, and probably fear, a sudden realization I could kill him.

If this was a test of strength, I thought I passed. The [Root Strike] made all of them sweat.

Jura smiled. He stood a little straighter and opened both hands. "Our tree spirit here has survived many creatures, including demon champions *and* a demon king. If you thought you could just walk in and do what you wanted to in this valley, you are wrong."

The centaurs shared an awkward, uncomfortable glance. The three treefolk instantly prostrated themselves.

The elf chieftain stood again. "How dare you!" He feigned arrogance, defiance, but from my vision, his spirit was uncertain, and his body shook.

"Should I hit the head this time?" I mentally transmitted to all of them.

He gulped. Everyone else was wary, and the centaurs took two steps back.

The elder stood in front of him as if he tried to cover for him. "No." He held up what looked to be a wooden buckler as if that would stop my roots.

"The roots can come from anywhere. You can't protect him. In fact, I can hit anyone in this valley."

They both gulped. Everyone probably realized that if they made enemies, they wouldn't leave this valley alive.

Jura stood and walked closer to the elf. "We understand you are refugees, and there are many of you. We want to help, and we want to share. But you cannot just march in and demand things from the caretaker of these lands. We will let you stay, but you must do so on our terms."

The elf chieftain grunted in frustration, "Ugh!" and stomped off.

The elder nodded. "I apologize. He is young and only wants the best for our people. I think I can convince our chieftain to obey your rules, and I will try to convince him that as the tree spirit here, this is your home, and we are guests. We can decide on the rest of the details later. For now, we will stop any chopping of the trees. We will speak again when everyone cools down. As you know, winter is soon to be upon us, and traveling now is a hazard. May we stay through the winter at least?"

Jura smiled and nodded. He then turned to me. "Is that okay?"

"Fine. You can all stay, as refugees, but if I see any unpleasant behavior or actions from your people, I will not hesitate to take any action I deem necessary."

The centaurs nodded, and I saw from their body language they were nervous. "We believe that is a good suggestion. We will meet again."

The treefolk rose from their kneeling position and walked backward, their heads still bowing. "As you wish."

They left for their respective areas.

"That didn't go very well." I sighed.

"I thought it went wonderfully." Jura shook his head. "Power is sometimes a great way to enforce peace. I think the chiefs, all of them, got the message that we are not one to be messed with."

"For a peaceful coexistence, to be forged by power and fear?"

"The people need a uniting force. 'Force.'"

YEAR 73, MONTH 11, WEEK 4

No news came from the other camps or the groups that went farther, but that was fine. More trees were growing, and I crossed sixteen hundred normal trees connected through my rootnet. My growth rate slowed down in winter.

The cold started to bite. The refugee elves, centaurs, and treefolk were hard at work. They gathered food, hunted the magically spawning animals, and collected and preserved fruits. The animals still spawned magically, even in winter, and apparently, some smaller forest foxes and bears reappeared once more. The refugees tried their best to hunt, with some success.

They lacked proper storage facilities, so the food wouldn't last that long. I thought some of them might have food preservation skills and abilities, and if so, their chances of surviving winter would be better.

Jura, too, hunted some animals for food, and thanks to everyone's combined efforts, we were going into the winter with a surplus in our food store and new warm clothing.

I was still very curious about the presence of these newly spawned animals, and I wondered just how they were 'created' and whether they had a soul.

So, out of curiosity, Jura captured a few of the new animals for my biolab. I would also really have loved to see how the centaurs and treefolk looked in the lab, but that would be for next time.

Eriz stopped crying, finally. Her mistress still had not contacted her, but I think she got tired of crying—or maybe she just had enough of venting. Roma also responded well to the infant formula, and the elves also gave it to Lausanne. Adding olives into the child-syrup maker produced a kind of nutrient-infused syrup, so I assumed the syrup maker had just created 'baby-friendly' food with whatever was given to it. In fact, Roma's weight stabilized, and he was starting to regain some of his lost weight.

Emile, Laufen, and Belle made some warm clothing with a mix of cotton and animal wool—kind of like a basic jacket—first, for the kids, and later, for the adults. They spent so much time that they got tailored as a class. Laufen cried when she got the skill as it reminded her of another lady in the village who used to make all the clothes.

So the start of winter was pleasant. The production of the cotton and olives reduced substantially in the last week, but quite a lot of cloth and olive oil was already made, and some cotton was even left unharvested.

YEAR 73, MONTH 12, WEEK 1

Tree growth was slow, and only about fifty trees sprouted in the cold weather. In fact, it was pretty awesome that they sprouted at all considering the biting cold. It wasn't freezing or snowing yet, but in a bit more it would.

At this slow, wintery tree-growth rate, my estimated time to reach [Soul Forge] was going to be delayed.

On the last day of the week, it started to rain. Cold, cold rain. It rained for the whole day and poured water into every corner of the valley. Some parts of the valley even started to flood.

Then came the winds, and everyone stayed indoors during this time. For the area immediately around me, my roots were able to quickly absorb the excess water, and so there was no flooding, but still, it was an unpleasant environment, so everyone gathered in the main secret hideout.

The main tree was the safest, but I had confidence in my subsidiary trees. They were all large, thick, solid trees, and they all shared my buffs to some lesser degree.

"I wonder how the others are doing..." Eriz sat about. "I mean...the centaurs and all... They just got here, and it's already winter. It's probably tough."

She was the most sympathetic toward the refugees, being one who assisted her mistress on such matters prior to this. Perhaps helping the refugees was how she wanted to repay her mistress.

Jura suddenly snapped his fingers. "Did we just harm them by stopping them from chopping wood? They...they might need it for firewood!"

These elves had it good. The secret hideout and customizable branches: external rooms were temperature-controlled and contained natural ventilation, and even water drawn from the roots, and so they were quite comfortable and warm all year round. As a result, they had little need for firewood. Any cooking they needed to do was by collecting dried branches, which regularly dropped from trees, and they had a healthy stock of that.

Elven and treefolk societies generally tried to avoid the use of firewood, except when really necessary. When they did, they usually tried a farming method where only branches were cut off. As a result, their conventional sources of warmth were either energy crystals, heating metals, or oils from the trees—either peanut, cashew, palm, or olive oils. Furthermore, thick, mature trees were able to retain heat quite well so the homes built within them needed minimal heating.

"Ah." I paused.

Oh.

I checked on the three camps.

The treefolk were fine as their bodies were naturally able to withstand rain and cold without much additional heating. From what I observed, they used their natural abilities to shape the trees into hut-like structures and smaller shrubs into fences, and that seemed to be adequate, for now. They didn't seem to really fear the rain, and they appeared quite fine with being drenched outdoors. Of the three camps, the treefolk were the only ones that didn't avoid the rain. In fact, some of the treefolk still walked around in the downpours.

The elves also used a kind of wood-magic and magically transformed the trees into housing, but their constructions were structured differently from the treefolk. As the forest was still relatively young, the size of the trees—and their trunks—were small, unlike my subsidiary trees, which spawned naturally large so they could fit a dwelling or multiple beetles.

As a result, the elves were not well-protected from the rain. They huddled together in the largest of their mixed treehouses and tents. They used whatever fur and water-resistant clothing they had and covered themselves. Despite that, some rain and wind still entered those shelters, and they looked uncomfortable.

The centaurs' massive tents were able to provide shelter from the rain, but similarly, they were also a little cold. From my tree-vision, some of them huddled inside those tents as a way to keep warm. The location they picked to perch their massive tents seemed to have little issue with the deluge as the water naturally flowed down the slopes not into their tents.

"Do you think they need food?"

"Hmmm. I don't know." I looked at the camps and saw their spiritual presence fluctuating. Maybe that's a sign of weakness? But then, everyone's presence fluctuated.

"Doubt it, they've just moved here for a month. I think it's more likely that what they have is barely enough to get by, and they probably have not built any cold cellars or chambers," Eriz explained. "Refugees may have some skilled builders, but they need resources, tools, and time."

"Should we help, if they need it?" I posed this question to the elves gathered. Of course, the manner of aid should also be carefully considered, but to be fair, we only had a surplus of dried branches, fruits, cloth, oil, and potatoes. The meat supply was relatively short, as the animals were still relatively recent appearances.

Lausanne was the first to answer, "Yes! Heroes help people. And I would like to help!"

Ah, this child had her head in the right place.

Eriz agreed while she rocked Roma to sleep. "They are refugees, and my mistress would have helped."

Emile and Belle both nodded as well. "I suppose a bit of support will help smooth things out between us? I mean...we do have quite a surplus, with the cotton clothes and all..."

Jura and Laufen agreed last. "Very well. A bit of generosity is also a show of strength."

"Then it is decided. We help, a little bit."

"How do we deliver all these things there in this rain?" Emile pointed to the cloth and food. It was a concern if these things got drenched.

I thought I might be able to do something about that. A bit of wood-forming magic would do. I activated [Wood Shield] but pointed them upward. The wooden shield functioned as a massive umbrella, and so the elves could load some of the extra cloth, small bottles of olive oil, and food onto the cloth bags at the side of the beetles. There were three beetles assigned for transport and utility duty, equipped with cloth bags and compartments at the side.

It was a strange feeling to see my first aid convoy go out, with beetles that hauled cloth, olive oil, and some potatoes and fruits covered by wood shields moonlighting as a massive umbrella.

"Hello, chieftains." Jura arrived at the edge of the centaur tents. They seemed surprised to see him pop out of the forest.

"Yes?"

"We would like to offer a gift to help your people tide through this first difficult winter."

The two centaurs, the leaders, rode out into the rain and saw the beetles.

"These are..."

"Cloth, some food, some dried wood branches, and olive oil, which you can use to maintain a small fire for lighting."

The centaurs paused.

Jura unloaded the goods and placed them at the side of the tent. I expanded the wooden shields, and they were as big as a tent. Naturally, these wooden shields could be massive. After all, they were my own protective skills, and they had to be my size. "It's a gift."

The two centaurs shared whispers and nodded.

Jura departed once all the goods were delivered, and the convoy returned to the main tree. The beetles' cargo was reloaded, and once again, they departed, this time for the elves.

The elves instantly drew their weapons the moment they saw Jura and the beetles.

"What do you want?" the elf chief shouted. He brandished a big sword and wore his armor. He especially covered his head.

Jura smiled as his sword remained sheathed at his side. "I'm not here to fight. We have gifts for you."

He didn't want to argue with the other elves or talk, really. The elf chieftain might want to argue or shout, so he just unloaded all the cargo, placed them by the side, made a quick explanation of what they were, and then left.

The elf chieftain was shocked, but then the other elves shamelessly grabbed the items before he could reject them. Survival came first. Pride could be decided later on.

Lastly, Jura made a similar trip to the treefolk. The treefolk nodded and smiled. "I believe we have little need for such items. We are well used to rain and cold weather, due to our heritage."

Jura nodded. "I see, but it is only fair we leave some for you as well."

"Actually...actually, we have a request to make, but it didn't seem appropriate in our meeting previously."

"What would that be?"

"A few of our children are sick from the long journey, and we'd like to know if the tree spirit has any healing items. We are willing to trade what we have for it."

Jura paused. "I'll need to check."

Later, Jura returned with a basket of healing fruits, and the treefolk promptly administered them to the young treefolk.

The long journey caused the younger treefolk to suffer from some kind of "movement-sickness"—a problem that went away naturally for the more mature treefolk. It was nothing fatal, but it triggered a bit of vomiting and temporarily delayed their natural growth. Still, as parents, it saddened them to see their children weak. A simple healing fruit was all that was needed to fix it.

As a gesture of thanks, the treefolk's elder gave us a small wooden box.

"This is?"

Inside the wooden box was a root.

"It's a medicine. It helps boost a person's strength. But only take it if you've never taken it before, else it's not so useful."

"Ah..."

Jura returned to the main tree with the box of medicine.

"Have you seen this before?" He showed it to everyone else.

"It's...a root?"

"Do we eat it?"

"Yes...that's what the elder said, but only if we've never eaten it before."

Eriz looked at it curiously. "Ah...it's looks like some kind of herb."

"Oh?" Herb? I would like to make that!

At that point, the root went into the biolab pod for analysis. After an hour, I gained a level.

[You've gained a level. Level 116.]

[Essence Collection upgraded.]

[Essence Infusion unlocked. Essence-infused fruits, leaves, and barks now available. Essence-infused subsidiary trees now available.]

[Biolab: Analysis of specimen completed.]

[New unique tree ability obtained.]

[Limited-series Tree-type unlocked, [Magical ginseng plant.]]

[Ginseng plant is limited to three growing plants at any one time (can be increased with level). The quality of the ginseng depends on the age of the root, overall health throughout its life, essences infused, mana infused, materials infused, the environment, and astronomical conditions, etc. Ginseng roots, when consumed, give permanent boosts to various stats, resistances, and abilities. Effect diminishes with subsequent use.]

[Warnings]

[Cultivating ginseng will slightly increase monster spawn rate.], [Ginseng plant doesn't share any defensive or support buffs of the main tree.], [Ginseng doesn't work on trees.]

YEAR 74, MONTH 1, WEEK 1

It was exceptionally cold. Compared to last year, it just felt much colder this year. Perhaps it was the demon king's influence that led to last year's warmth, but whatever it was, we didn't like the cold very much.

The rain was replaced by snow.

Only three normal trees were added to the valley. Three.

I sensed everything was just less active this season. The energy I received from my subsidiary trees also dropped, and the energy generated by normal trees dropped to a fraction of what it was previously. I supposed that the subsidiary trees and I were considered evergreen trees, therefore we could maintain a portion of our energy output. In the cold, it didn't seem like a good time to test out my new ginseng tree.

Of the three camps, the treefolk were best suited for the snow. They had a kind of quasi-hibernation state where their bodies slowed down tremendously, and in exchange, they gained a wide range of defensive buffs and also reduced their food intake. In fact, I really, really wanted to look under the bark of those treefolk.

The elf and centaur groups gathered at their biggest camps

and burned branches for warmth. The centaur elder had an ability that allowed him to fully extract energy out of the branches and that kept their fires burning longer. One of the elven men used an ability to keep warm air circulating within their temporary building. Among the refugees, some possessed cold resistance abilities, and for them, it allowed the elves and centaurs to tide themselves through the difficult weather, especially the biting cold at night.

"I am sure some of them would trade their goods to stay in these warm, cozy rooms," Eriz said while reminiscing about her time in the city. In palaces and cities, there were dedicated butlers and maids who possessed the ability to manage room conditions, to the comfort of their lords. Some mayors and lords even had a kind of [Soften Weather] effect that reduced their city's heating and ventilation requirements.

"Well, they had to piss Tree-Tree off, so that's not happening," Jura said. "It's already very generous of Tree-Tree to send gifts and let the elves stay."

"Are we chasing them away?" Lausanne asked.

I paused. Well, I thought they should go. The elves, at least. The elven chief was probably not happy I attacked him, and I had no clue whether the rest of the elves harbored the same sort of aggression. I would have to be wary.

"They tried to threaten us, Lausanne. If they are bad people, they should go."

"To prison?"

"No, just go away."

The cold also brought new creatures. White wolves and horned deer. The white wolves looked for food in the cold and snow, and I noticed a pack of about ten. They were large, about the same size as my already rhino-sized war beetles, and they were equipped with similarly huge fangs and claws.

I tried to command my beetles to intercept them, and a warning popped up.

[Beetles suffer significant movement and attributes penalty in snowy weather. Insects are not adept at winter combat. Half of your beetles are in a dormant state and cannot be awakened.]

Oh, man. Previously, it was just rain, but if it snowed, this happened? Oh, well, at least I learned about this now.

Back to the white wolves, and they had spotted the centaurs. *Food.*

I watched through my various subsidiary trees placed throughout the valley, and it felt like I was watching a documentary through night vision, especially with my spiritual sight, of a pack of wolves fighting with centaurs. The centaur leaders fought their best, but these wolves were huge, and some of the centaurs collapsed under their ferocious swipes.

It occurred to me that maybe I should help. And I wanted the experience. A specimen for the biolab.

Two [Root Strike]s flew out of the ground, through the snow, and into the belly of the largest of the wolves. The pack leader.

It growled in pain as the [Root Strike] clearly hit and shattered a few bones and punctured a few of its organs. The second [Root Strike] penetrated the wolf's rib cage and instantly killed it.

The sudden death of the wolf leader sent the pack into a panic, and they fled.

As the remaining white wolves fled, I noticed one wolf that fell behind. It was weakened from its injuries. Great. For the biolab!

[Constrict].

My roots successfully captured the injured wolf, and a paralyzing jab knocked it out. I sent a few of my active beetles to collect the paralyzed wolf.

Experience gains came from killing but also from learning.

Although less, I wouldn't be surprised if there were bookworms out there that were reasonably high level. One of the ways the nobles had an edge over the poor, I supposed, was that their means of gaining levels were wider, through literacy and learning through books.

YEAR 74, MONTH 1, WEEK 2

It'd snowed heavily, so I focused on more academic matters and analyzed the white wolf in my biolab.

This white wolf did have a 'mana spring' in its soul, but it was smaller than any of the humans or elves, though it was still larger than the smaller foxes or other animals captured.

Relatively, Meela was like Niagara Falls, a regular person was like a small waterfall, and a normal animal was like a small pipe of water. This white wolf was just like a bigger pipe of water.

Next was the body. The soul and the body had a symbiotic relationship and formed a feedback loop. A strong soul usually led to a strong body, and vice versa. But in the case of the wolves, their bodies were strong, robust, and full of natural energy, yet a small, almost nonexistent soul existed within. It was a common theme, I thought, and I wondered whether this was a feature of non-intelligence or their designated status as 'animals' or 'monsters.'

The body was exceptionally strong. A lattice of natural energy protected its bones and claws. There were little sparks of energy in its muscles and joints, a kind of residual mana? I recalled that I saw something similar in Jura's hands and also Meela's, but theirs was almost negligible.

I zoomed in.

Nothing. Maybe I didn't have the right tools or ability to identify it because I thought I felt magic of some kind. As I looked at the jaws and their teeth, I got a similar feeling. There was something here that I hadn't figured out yet.

Ah, well. After I went through every part of the wolf, I was still unable to crack the code. I decided to leave it inside the biolab, sedated.

I then asked Jura to go for a dip in the pod.

Jura's body no longer had the lingering effects of his trauma, but he said he hit a limit—a plateau—and all the monsters he fought no longer gave him any new levels. Jura was currently at level sixty-five.

His body was strong, and his soul seemed healthy, too. The body, the muscles, and the bones all look strong and healthy. Well, except for the left hand.

But as I continued to watch how the energy from the soul spring instantly got drained by the body, I believed Jura's intuition was right.

The soul seemed capped out. The amount of soul energy produced was just enough for it to be at the current level but no further. Like a country with an electrical power shortage, it needed to either have a more efficient use of energy or produce more power.

"How do we change this?"

Wisp twirled around. "The elf can have an awakening and find his soul strengthened."

"That can happen?"

"Of course. He could consider going on a quest out of his league, where he would struggle and then emerge triumphant. Such acts of heroism and pushing against one's limits are sometimes rewarded. Your evaluation of the souls is nothing but an estimate, and reality is an exponential curve. It is possible to climb up that curve."

Huh. Still, that implied that there was nothing much I could do at this time.

"With his strength, it would be quite a long time before you could do anything to his soul."

Meela butted in. "Upgrade. Body?"

Hmm. That meant I should get ahead of the soul-body feedback loop and try to first upgrade the body, hoping that somehow that dragged the soul along.

How could I upgrade the body? Stimulants? Surgery? Or maybe I should try fixing his left hand first. I wondered whether the natives of this world had techniques to upgrade a body. Actually, how did the ginseng interact with the soul and body?

YEAR 74, MONTH 1, WEEK 3

Less snow. Yay!

Some of my beetles woke from their dormant state, so now only a quarter were still dormant.

More trees, too! From a low of three new trees, I was now back to about ten additional normal trees per week. I needed to prepare for spring, and so I asked the elves to help, and they collected any seeds they saw. I then commanded the beetles to spread the seeds around.

The elves, with not much to do in the cold, spent most of their time working on some of the cotton.

Jura spent his time tinkering with the damaged airship from the Salah Kingdom adventurers, and by some fluke, he accidentally dismantled what appeared to be the power source of the airship, a basketball-sized crystal. The demon-residue Daemolite.

It was the first time I had seen one, so naturally, it went into the biolab.

[Biolab was unable to analyze sample. Analysis unable to proceed.]

Eh.

The rest of the small airship was made mostly with regular metals and wood. It was really this magical crystal and the network of enchantments and runes throughout the structure that gave it flight.

Perhaps by damaging its enchantments, it therefore lost its ability to fly?

Sadly, the runes and enchantments remained incomprehensible to me.

[Enchantment familiarity missing. Language not understood. Understanding of runic markings required.]

Ah, man. The biolab's ability to analyze non-biological items was crap. Maybe I would be able to develop a material lab someday.

The three camps kept to themselves. Some of the hunters from the elves and the centaurs continued to look for food. They foraged and hunted the rabbits and the small rat-like creatures that now also lived here.

Creation of animals was interesting, and I had been trying to catch it happening, but so far, I had failed. Every time I took the granular view of the entire valley, just to watch how these animals appeared throughout the forests through the 'vision' from all subsidiary trees, I would get a massive headache. If I kept forcing it, I would lose consciousness and wake a day later. I didn't have enough mental processing power to handle the load.

The closest I got was a rabbit that somehow crawled out of the snow. So, even if I could see, perhaps the system that spawned these animals had ways to avoid 'notice.'

YEAR 74, MONTH 1, WEEK 4

There was a freak snowstorm on day one, and after that, it was sunny! The snow was melting!

"My mistress is still alive!" Eriz shouted and jumped happily. "Your mommy is alive!" She hugged Roma and jumped, and the baby cried.

"Oh?"

"She's managed to escape with the rest of them, and they are headed here. They slipped past the last of the human settlements and the kingdom's hunters! So, maybe in a week or so, they will be here!"

Laufen smiled. "That's good. So where would you go after this?"

Eriz paused at the question. "What do you mean?"

"I mean...once your mistress is here, you all should have some plans, right?"

"Uh, I think we plan on staying here." Eriz rubbed her head. "Can we? I'll let the mistress know we have to obey your rules, and you are in charge. Maybe...maybe a spot somewhere in the valley?"

Jura rubbed his head. "No, no. Tree-Tree is in charge."

Emile and Belle nodded. "Maybe this is like...rebuilding Freeka?"

"How many of them?"

"Uh...she didn't say..."

Ah. More refugees to deal with. Okay, fine. I would have to handle this better than the earlier elves.

YEAR 74, MONTH 2, WEEK 1

It was finally the tail end of winter. Tree growth was recovering, and that was my focus from now on. I wanted to hit ten thousand trees by the end of the year. It sounded like a big number, but if there was one tree for every five meters, an area the size of one square kilometer would have forty thousand trees. Earth had somewhere around three trillion trees.

The beetles were busy spreading seeds, and when they didn't have seeds, they used broken branches they found. I would regularly channel all my tree-growing mojo to boost the growth rate.

The more I used it, the more I understood that it was more like an urge, and I got better at controlling it. It felt even easier as the winter finally let up.

"What are you doing, Tree-Tree?" Lausanne asked, all dolled up and wrapped in thick clothing. Laufen wasn't letting her go out without winter protection.

"Growing trees. A lot of them."

"Oh. I like trees."

"Why?"

"I like fruits. They are yummy. And I like leaves. They give shade."

"Ah."

I didn't recall telling the elves about [Soul Forge] but, oh, well. I supposed they suspected something.

The refugees and the mistress should be here soon.

[Your Subsidiary Tree skill has leveled up. Subsidiary tree limit increased to 120.]

[Secret Hideout - biolab upgraded. Autopsy table and precision tools obtained. Pods increased to 10.]

YEAR 74, MONTH 2, WEEK 2

The mistress and her band of refugees arrived. About four hundred strong—half warriors, half escapees—they were a mix of humans, elves, dwarves, and centaurs.

Eriz quickly stepped in to mediate. I thought she probably saw the early scuffle with the elves and wanted to avoid a similar conflict.

In fact, once they were right outside, she ran to meet them before they even entered the forest.

She knew I could observe them once they entered the forest. They spoke at length, and of course, she took Roma with her.

"Think they have good intentions?" I asked the elves.

"Nah, I don't think they got good intentions." Jura shook his head. "They just want some cover for a while, and probably cover from their enemies."

"But they know your secret password."

"So? When we designed it, it wasn't meant to give free access to a few hundred people."

"True."

In the end, the rest of the refugees waited at the forest's

edge, and only Eriz, Roma, and five others came in—two elves, two humans, and a dwarf.

One of the elves was a lady, and I sensed something... different about her.

She approached the edges of the trees, and she was the one who spoke first.

"I am the leader of this band of unfortunate refugees, here to seek the protection of the guardian of this valley."

"And why should I?"

"We offer you our services, our goods, and our knowledge, those who we can give. And we will keep our distance from you and your affairs."

"And?"

"We just seek safe passage and protection from the kingdom that seeks to hunt us down."

"I want no part in your conflict."

Mistress Yvon sighed. "I understand, but please, help us, tree spirit. There is nowhere we can turn to, and if you push us away, we may as well die. An army is coming our way, and we're too weak to outrun them."

"You have lured an army here?"

She gulped. "No. When we realized, we were already almost here..."

"And you still came here?"

"We had no choice. There is nowhere we can go..."

"Why should I not leave you to die?"

Yvon took a deep breath. "Because—"

"Enough. Eriz, you lured them here, so you have blame in this."

She paused and kneeled. "I'm sorry. I felt they... It's their best chance of surviving. The humans are slaughtering elves by the thousands, and...there's no openly non-human-friendly territory anywhere near the Salah Kingdom...except...well, except here."

I sighed.

It felt like I had been led into this conflict.

"How many are coming?"

"Six hundred or so, a mix of knights and archers on horseback."

Hmm. If I left these refugees out there, would they let us go? The fact was, I had three groups of non-humans already living in the valley, and if they were really hunting down all non-humans, they might very well just set the entire forest on fire.

This was maybe something I could handle if they didn't have someone at the level of the heroes.

I mentally reached out to Jura. He had been listening in.

"It's not much of a choice. I think we can punish Eriz, this leader of the refugees, and whoever lured them here later, but the fact remains that a small army has trailed the refugees and would suspect this forest is the non-human base of operations as we already have other refugees."

"If we defeat this army, what is to stop a larger army from coming here?"

"That's true. If we can somehow pull a feint, like...distract the army and lead them somewhere else..."

"These refugees can't outrun this army on horseback."

"True. And the army may not be a conventional force. They may have mages or specialists amongst them since they are chasing after this group. Can you see them, Tree-Tree?" Jura paused, took a seat, and tried to think.

I tried to reach out to the farthest of my trees and roots. I placed one subsidiary tree in that direction, and it extended my vision slightly.

And another subsidiary tree.

"Spotted." Six hundred men on horseback. I couldn't tell much, though, but if a conflict was necessary, I could drag them onto difficult ground. They were probably not aware of my abilities as a high-level tree spirit, and so they would march past trees without suspecting anything.

So I planted about twenty additional subsidiary trees, all of them containing war beetles, spaced and spread out in that direction so that it maximized my root coverage.

The army passed the trees. No action, as expected.

"The moment we accepted the first group of refugees, I guess we had already taken a stand in this conflict." Jura sighed. "Let me march to the three refugee groups and ask them to participate in combat."

He wasn't exactly right. The moment I had taken on the promise to protect these elves, when Freeka was destroyed, I had made the choice to protect this valley. An army marching on us was therefore an enemy, especially a human army that was going to burn up this area.

"Offer them."

"Huh?" Jura turned. "Offer?"

"If they are willing to participate in this battle, I will consider lifting restrictions and conditions on their stay here. This is their opportunity to show their worth to me in this valley and earn their right to stay."

Jura laughed. "Hah! A tree spirit truly is wise. To make these refugees fight!" Jura nodded and then headed off.

I turned to Eriz and Yvon.

"Get your men ready for combat. I have, very reluctantly, decided to join this conflict. Eriz, Yvon, and whoever suggested all of you come into combat, your punishment will be decided after this battle."

Yvon paused and nodded. "Very well. If we live to see tomorrow's sun, I'll take the punishment."

Of the three camps, only the elves refused to participate. It seemed that they had already decided to leave once the weather improved. The treefolk and centaurs both agreed, and they sent about twenty men each. Jura and about a hundred or so men from Yvon's group also prepared. The rest, the women, and the children all hid in the forest.

The army approached.

"Those stinking rebels! Is that their hideout?"

"Forest. Hah! It's so predictable that it is a forest! Elves!"

"They should have chosen a cave or something."

I picked up chatter as they passed a few of my subsidiary trees. I was watching them, looking for...special individuals.

"I don't feel so good."

"What, you feel like taking a dump? You can take a dump on the elves later."

"Did Lord Rovas say we can take prisoners? Elven ladies are hot."

"No. He said kill everyone. No survivors. Can't leave any of these rebel scum to breed."

"Ah, man."

"I hate this armor. Why'd they insist we wear military uniforms anyway?"

"We're legit now. Deal with it."

Just then, a burly man came around and smacked a few of them with a cane. "We're closing in. Mages, get ready."

A woman rode next to him. "Our target is Yvon, Prince Galan's corruptor. It is she who led him into this foolish non-human love affair."

"Is she hot?"

"She's got a way with words."

"Really?"

"Shut it. We can't let this group escape. If this is their base, let's take it all out."

"Okay, boss."

Hmmm. They just passed the second layer of trees.

"They will try to fight in the forest, though."

"No. We burn the forest. Anti-elf tactics 101. Why go into the forest and fight on their terms? Set the forest on fire, and we attack whoever comes out."

Funny, they just walked past a few trees. They should have attacked the trees, then.

"They have centaurs and dwarves, right? And they can run to the other side?"

"A handful. Not enough to make a difference. Another group has already gone on ahead to the other side of the valley."

"Ah! Such genius!"

"Mages, gather up and cast a few fireballs into the forest. Let's burn this forest to the ground."

Great. That was the cue I'd waited for.

Of the six hundred, about twenty stepped forward, and they channeled some kind of fireball. Right when they started, I acted.

[Poison Field].

[Root field].

Roots surged out of the ground and released a kind of toxic fume into the air. It wasn't fast acting but would work.

That was followed by twenty [Root Strike]s. All at the mages.

I hit eighteen, killing them instantly. Their armor, though metal, didn't hold up very well. The two remaining had some magical instinct and managed to break their fireball-chant in time to dodge the surge.

"Druids?"

Their horses panicked as the roots and the poison was uncomfortable. They wanted to run.

[Root Surge].

I only had two uses of this ability per day, but it was very useful as an area attack. Sharp roots emerged in the area around four subsidiary trees, and so there were roots attacking about half of the enemy force.

"What!" The [Root Surge], though, lacked the punch each individual [Root Strike] had. I reckoned they were about a quarter of the strength.

Some of the men activated their defensive abilities, successfully blocking the surge. But as an area attack, about a hundred or so died, so that was pretty good.

"Run, guys! We'll need to come back with a bigger army!"

one of the surviving mages shouted, using some kind of magic to boost his escape. "Whoever is protecting them is a very powerful druid, perhaps one of the great elven archdruids!"

That actually needed to not be said. Some of them were already running when the [Poison Field] and [Root Field] popped up.

I couldn't let mages run, though. So I shot a few more rounds of [Root Strike]s, and I killed one. The last surviving mage used a string of magical nullification spells. He was hurt but not dead.

"That cursed elf woman! She's got a backer! Must be one of the elven nations secretly meddling in our country's politics!"

"Retreat!"

I aimed a [Root Strike] at the leader, but it hit a magical barrier. It broke through it, but then a metal shield blocked the [Root Strike].

"You won't get my head that easily!" he shouted, and he activated a few magical and physical defensive abilities, then as he was about to turn back, a shout came from the forest.

"Charge!"

Yvon and the refugees charged out of the forest.

Honestly, if you were to ask me, that was a stupid decision. Why did she and the refugees charge?

Since she was charging, I activated all the war beetles hiding in the twenty subsidiary trees. Sixty war beetles appeared and charged into the chaotic mess that was the kingdom's army. The beetles killed a few, but with the stronger, more experienced soldiers, it was an even matchup. After all, these soldiers had skills, abilities, and probably some enchanted equipment.

The leader, though, smiled and shouted at Yvon. "Ah, you succubus! Decided to appear and fight, eh?"

Yvon pulled out a sword, used some kind of ability, and vanished, only to reappear a second later, right in front of the army leader where she attempted a stab.

He blocked her strike, and his magical barrier was broken.

"Hah! Not so easy!" He unsheathed his sword and leaped from his horse.

Both Yvon and the army leader traded blows.

Meanwhile, the rest of the refugees and the war beetles fought.

At this point, I stopped attacking and observed the battle.

"She's pretty good." Jura laughed, still sitting at the side, not joining the battle.

"Aren't you going to join in?"

"Soon. I'm just waiting for the trigger."

"Which is?"

"That woman. She's going to try something."

She charged up an ability as Yvon and the leader fought. Well, sorry, I was gonna have to ruin the surprise. Two [Root Strike]s impaled through her body, and she yelled in pain, "AGHHHH..."

Both Yvon and the army leader turned to see the woman with one root through her chest and another through her stomach.

The army leader looked at Yvon furiously. "Which country is helping you, you treasonous beast?"

Yvon shook her head. "None."

"Then explain this root magic."

Yvon paused. "I can't. I didn't know of it, either."

"Lies. Again."

The army leader activated an ability and slashed at Yvon at high speed. She, in response, activated something similar, and they were back at a stalemate. He slashed, and she parried, dodging successfully.

She panted, her breathing heavy.

"You can't beat me. You know it."

"I can try. Vengeance demands it."

He laughed. "I didn't land the killing blow, mind you. It was not me who killed Prince Galan."

"But you were there. And so, you must die." Yvon's sword glowed with a greenish hue.

"Oh?" The army leader laughed.

I thought I saw a few opportunities for me to throw out a [Root Strike], but eavesdropping on the conversation was a lot more interesting.

Yvon disappeared into a whirl of greenish light, some kind of sword-dance ability. The army leader laughed, glowed in purple, and he, too, disappeared in a purple-glow. The two appeared solely as sparks for the few minutes that followed.

When they both reappeared, the army leader looked unscathed, whereas Yvon had cuts all over her body.

"See? You can't beat me, and I will make you join Prince Galan soon."

Yvon shook her head and forced herself to stand.

"Where's that druid of yours, anyway? Ran out of root attacks?"

Well, I still had about fifty to spare. But I was more interested in watching. My beetles and the rest of the refugees were still fighting. A few of the beetles had been killed, but they had managed to hunt down the last mage. So, with the mage out of the picture, I was actually letting the rest of this play out.

About this time, forty additional refugees joined the battle— the treefolk and the centaurs. They waited for the right time as they didn't want to join the fight until Jura did.

"Oh, treefolk. That explains the root attacks." The army leader laughed. "I'll slaughter them after I kill you."

"Not if I have anything to say about it." Jura stepped in front. "Jura."

The army leader laughed. "Oh? I'm Waysorious Moffard. Also known as the Purple Blade."

Jura bowed. "Please, allow me to join this battle as I've been robbed of my prey." *Well, I killed the lady Jura wanted to fight, so...*

"Well, come."

Jura grinned and activated an ability, covering his body in a layer of wood.

They traded a few blows, and Jura jumped back. His wooden armor had multiple scratches, but he lived.

"Ah, I'm weaker with the sword. But, thankfully, my defense is a lot stronger." The wooden armor regenerated, and the scratches disappeared.

Waysorious laughed. "That armor of yours is strong, but if that's all you've got, you won't last."

At that point, Yvon stepped up, her body fully healed. "Well, what if it's both of us?"

Waysorious paused. "Ah..."

Jura activated a healing ability before they started fighting as Waysorious looked around and saw the rest of his men dying or fleeing. He started laughing maniacally.

"I see. I see. I'll be back, you cursed witch."

Yvon attempted to stab him, but in a flash of light, he disappeared.

"AGH! I should have known he carries a ring of escape with him!"

Huh. There's an item like that, eh?

Once the captain left, the rest of the soldiers didn't last very long. It seemed, without his presence, some buffing effects that he had faded away. Whoever was still fighting was quickly killed by the remaining war beetles, Yvon, Jura, and the rest of the refugees.

So the battle ended.

The refugees stripped whatever equipment or items they could from the soldiers and then piled the bodies up to burn. Yvon's bunch of over two hundred refugees lost about thirty or so men, whereas the forty treefolk and centaurs lost none, all thanks to a great element of surprise, [Root Strike]s, and war beetles.

War beetles had a [Taunt] ability, which tended to cause nearby enemies to attack them first, and that tanking effect helped minimize our casualties. Add the confusion from the [Root Strike]s and root surge, and the army seemed to be concentrated on fleeing more than fighting.

"Centaurs and treefolk, thank you for your participation in this battle. With this, I'm willing to offer you full rights to your designated areas and also such that each person may chop down one tree per year. Ration your wood accordingly. Treefolk, you may trade your wood rights if you don't need them with centaurs, but notify me beforehand."

The centaurs and treefolk nodded and returned to their homes. They were glad there were no casualties in their bunch, but they joined the battle late. I later overheard that the sight of roots surging out of the ground was rather scary. From afar, it looked like the earth itself decided to fight them. Which reminded me, maybe I should have a giant worm of my own, like the demons. A subordinate giant worm or centipede would be nice.

As for Yvon's group, they quickly buried their dead and healed their wounded. Yvon was frustrated, though, not that I cared. Her punishment was due, and Jura delivered the message.

"You survived. Now face punishment," Jura spoke in a small gathering.

Yvon sighed. "No way out of this?"

"Speak to the tree spirit."

Later that day, after all was done, Eriz and Yvon both stood right outside my main tree.

"So, what punishment are we facing?"

"Eriz. Did you know that you were putting everyone at risk by luring them here?"

"Yes, but it was the best decision."

"You. You intentionally wanted to get me involved in this."

Yvon shook her head. "Uh...to be honest, I didn't fully believe Eriz when she said there was a tree spirit able to protect us. And, from my point of view, we had to escape the human lands.

Wherever we go, we are going to be hunted, so, since my son is here...I thought coming here made sense."

She looked at Jura, and Jura shook his head. "Go on."

"Erm, whatever it is, I didn't realize there was a forest here, and I didn't think they would suspect this forest was a hideout for rebels. In hindsight, it is obvious, but when we were just trying to successfully escape, we...we didn't think that far ahead. So we decided to take a chance on whatever Eriz told us."

I sighed. How should I punish these people? She was trying to feign innocence, and that annoyed me even more.

How?

At this point, Wisp appeared in my mental realm.

"Take her soul."

"What?!" I mean, what? Like...how would one do that?

"I mean, make her surrender her soul to you when she dies."

"I can do that?"

"Yeah. You can mark her soul with a special process. She has to consent to it, of course, and recite a long phrase and agreement to mark that she wills her soul to you."

That...that somehow feels a bit extreme. And I didn't know I have that kind of ability.

"That sounds like what a demon does, I mean, take one's soul on death?"

"Well, it's actually the same thing. The contracts, in essence, are the same, but demons take the ideas to the extreme, of course."

"Why would I want her soul, anyway?"

"Well, all the souls you see are marked for their onward reincarnation or whatever the gods have planned for their next phase and stay in the realm at most for a year, usually six months. But if a soul agrees, they drop out of that process and belong to you...for a thousand years. And during that time, you may use the soul as you see fit."

"Like?"

"Well...anything."

I shook my head. Sounded exactly like what a demon or devil did. Not exactly what I thought a soul or spirit tree should be doing. I mean, how would it work?

"What else are you not telling me?"

"Or if you think taking away her soul is too much, tell her to give you a few of her levels or skills."

"What?" Another bombshell from Wisp. Wisp was hiding things from me.

"Ah, well, it's actually a fairly common ability amongst the ancients, high nobles, blue-blooded royalty, and high-level magic smiths, artificers, and crafters."

"Huh?"

"There are restrictions to the origin of your power, of course, and in your case, the person surrendering the levels must be at least level twenty, and they can surrender no more than twenty percent of their levels, and no more than twenty percent of all skills."

Okay, Wisp. Infodump there, but it sounded pretty important. I turned to Eriz and Yvon.

"Rest. I will decide your punishment in a few days. If you attempt to flee, I will kill you. And the refugees."

They gulped but nodded. Having seen the roots, they probably realized how easily I could do exactly what I said. Once they left, I went back into my soul realm to Wisp.

"You and I are going to have a long conversation on what else you haven't been telling me."

"Oh, I have plenty more, but the information I can provide is dependent on the progress you make on [Soul Forge], and if you want to know everything I know, you need an active [Soul Forge]."

"Can you tell me more about these soul contracts and surrendering of levels and skills."

Wisp bobbed around and then paused.

"Making a deal for the soul has been common throughout history. When a desperate man sacrifices everything to protect his family, he is making a request to the heavens or hell—or whatever natural aspect is watching at the time—in exchange for his soul. It is then up to the nature aspect to decide whether they want the soul, balancing the costs of assisting versus the benefits."

Huh. "Simplify?"

"Granting souls is super common and not forever. As a soul or spirit tree, having souls that won't move on is very useful. Just think of it as an employment contract."

"Can't I just make her work for me?"

"Well, that's harder to enforce than having a contract carved into her soul, no?"

"Oh." True, it would be like having a slave that couldn't defy you. Well, that was nice, but was that a 'good' punishment?

Death felt too...cheap.

YEAR 74, MONTH 2, WEEK 3

S pring had begun, and the beetles were out spreading
seeds.
   I finally decided on the punishment for Eriz and
Yvon.

"Thanks to your selfishness, Eriz, you've permanently
dragged us into this conflict. This is despite our hospitality to
you these past months. Your punishment is that you are to
surrender your soul to me and serve us for the rest of your life."

"My...my soul?"

"Yes, your soul. You put us in danger, even when we helped
take care of Roma. This is for putting our lives at risk."

She paused, too stunned to respond.

Then it was Yvon's turn. "Your punishment is that you will
now have to protect this forest for the rest of your life. And I'll
enforce that by not having you leave this forest. If you try, I'll kill
your people. In exchange, I'll allow your people to share and stay
in this valley with me, though, as you're probably aware, I have
rules I want followed."

She stopped.

"I didn't think taking your soul was necessary at this point,
and I am of the opinion that your combat and management abil-

ities will be useful in managing the coming refugees. But I will be watching you closely."

Yvon paused, thinking. After about five minutes, she sighed and nodded. "I can accept that." I guessed she figured to have me as a protector of the refugees was worth the cost.

She dragged me into this conflict, I may as well make the most of it. If this was going to end up in war, I'd better have more bodies to throw at the enemy.

I wanted to fight the Salah Kingdom, so this accelerated the entire process, but I was hoping for more clandestine, stealthy methods, by way of sneaky subsidiary trees, but oh well...

"How...how are you going to take my soul?" Eriz looked puzzled.

A magic ring appeared around her—an ability I didn't know I had until recently.

[Spiritual Contract - Judgment]. It's essentially a soul contract but in the form of a judgment. Demons, devils, and the dark gods got a lopsided version known as [Unfair Contracts], which was...well, unfair, but then it was less robust as a result. It had also sneaky abilities like concealing terms and conditions, but all of these resulted in a reduction of the ability grade to a lower-tier (relative, of course).

"Accept."

She shook. She looked at her mistress, and then back at Jura, who was watching her. "I-I..."

"Are you testing my patience, Eriz?"

I wondered whether there was undue influence in this world.

She gulped. "I...I'm sorry. Is there any other way?"

"No. For the fact that you've dragged me into this conflict, and the kingdom knows of this forest, you've made life difficult for me. Therefore, this is an adequate punishment for you. You could have told your mistress to meet you elsewhere, but here we are."

Yvon tried to defend her subordinate. "Her soul... It's too

much, isn't it? Can't she protect this forest like I do?"

"No. Her soul, or everyone dies." I probably would not actually kill everyone, but an ultimatum it was.

Eriz cried.

She glanced at Jura, but he just shrugged.

After she finished crying, she accepted the punishment, and the magic ring around her glowed, expanded, spun around a while, and then entered her body.

It was done.

[Eriz Maforlas's soul is now leased to you for a thousand years. Soul lease will commence upon death.]

Lease? Wasn't that like renting?

"Uh..." She looked around. I thought she must have been preparing for something more gruesome and painful.

And after a while, she looked at Yvon.

"Am I still here?" Eriz seemed to think she was going to die instantly.

"Yes." Yvon nodded, and she, too, looked puzzled.

"That's it? I don't feel anything different. Have you taken my soul yet?"

"Oh, not now. When you die, Eriz." I wanted to say, "So don't die," but then I was sure she knew that.

Now that her sobbing had stopped, she looked at her mistress. "Oh. Oh! That's all?"

Y'know...I was starting to think 'on death' wasn't that great a term. After all, it still meant this person got to act out their life for the remainder of their days, which was by no means shorter. It was a painless punishment. Nothing had changed, unless they cared about their soul.

Oh, well, I guessed I would take levels next time. Though having seen Yvon's combat abilities, having her around would be useful against the fighters this Salah Kingdom might deploy.

"For the soul part, yes. Also, from now on, you serve me."

YEAR 74, MONTH 3, WEEK 1

I loved spring.

Thanks to the hard work of the beetles and the regrowing bounty mojo, the normal tree count in the valley surged to three thousand eight hundred. That was a huge climb, but I guessed the season of spring counted toward that. If that continued, I might hit ten thousand a bit faster than expected.

Other than that, nothing particularly concerning happened. The kingdom didn't seem to be sending anyone at us...yet.

As for the refugees, Yvon's group of refugees set up camp along the right side of the slopes. All the refugee camps started building more permanent structures now that winter was over.

The centaurs, now given a certain allotment of trees that they could chop down, started to construct basic houses that resembled stables. Some of them engaged in wide-scale planting, of a plant known as the shrub of the fours. It was largely inedible to anyone but centaurs, minotaurs, satyrs, and their kind—it was their staple food. It seemed centaurs could survive on this plant alone, and once the plants started to grow significantly, I wanted to analyze them.

The treefolk were incredibly fascinating to observe. Their abilities resembled an inferior version of mine in many ways.

They enjoyed being in the sun, and clearly, their abilities were affected by the season, their steps faster, their skin and body more...vibrant. Their feet had an ability to connect to the earth, drawing energy, nutrition, and even mana. The treefolk used their innate affinity with trees to weave the branches of trees into more structures, and it seemed it was their preferred way of construction, bending trees into shape. It was like large-scale bonsai sculpting. I suspected they had the ability to boost tree growth as well, but I would ask them about it some other day.

Yvon's elves, being the most exposed of the bunch, started with building a mix of houses and fortifications from the earth. Stone walls, stone houses, I was quite amazed at the speed at which they managed to build with the rocks and dirt. They had to cut some of the trees down for the rest of the materials, but with the outburst of trees in spring, the loss was acceptable.

The last group of elves were split. A group, about three-quarters of them, were leaving. They only wanted to stay through the winter. The remaining quarter were going to join Yvon's group.

No matter.

YEAR 74, MONTH 3, WEEK 3

There was no movement from the Salah Kingdom. We initially wondered why, but then the olive oil traders came. For olives, of course.

"War has broken out," they explained. "The Kingdom of Nung and the Kingdom of Takde have declared war on the Kingdom of Salah. Their civil war and slaughter were an opportunity, a weakness, so both of them are trying to take a bite out of Salah Kingdom's territory."

Well, that was a wonderful coincidence.

Some cash changed hands, and olive oils were sold.

"The merchants guild would not be trying to sell information about me, no?" Yvon popped out at the trading post.

"Ah...the mistress herself." The merchants grinned. "Well, the kingdom is occupied now, but they are offering good money to find out who is backing your rebellion."

"Oh, any leads?" Yvon laughed.

"The merchants guild has our own theories, but if you mean to share..."

Yvon shook her head. "How is the guildmaster doing?"

"Ah, he is fine. No one would dare touch the guildmaster of

the merchants guild, even if he is half-minotaur, if that's what you are asking."

Yvon nodded. "That is good." She handed the merchant multiple letters. "I take it the merchants still offer delivery services, even to me?"

A merchant smiled, grabbed the letters, and shoved them into a box of some kind, coins exchanged.

"I take it you know the terms."

"No worries, it's to the other kingdoms."

"Ah."

"Sorry..." Laufen butted in. "Do you mind...helping us buy some things?"

"Like?"

"Oh, one of my friends wants exotic fruits and books about trees. Can you help us procure some? We'll pay you."

"Ah, I'll look out for some."

YEAR 74, MONTH 4, WEEK 1

The young chieftain and the elves left.

I was at five thousand three hundred normal trees. The surge was down to an awesome combination: the hard work of the beetles, this wonderful season of spring, and better mastery of this bounty ability I had.

Within the inner circle of subsidiary trees, I finally felt confident enough to start growing my first ginseng tree.

Life for the refugees was starting to stabilize. With homes built, their focus turned to defense, preparing for the next winter, and potatoes and all the other plants.

[Subsidiary tree leveled up. You can now have one hundred eighty subsidiary trees.]

YEAR 74, MONTH 4, WEEK 3

I spread more subsidiary trees farther out as a form of surveillance. And this was when I noticed my increasing inability to manage such a vast area of subsidiary trees. It was too far.

So, although the subsidiary trees were giving me vision, it wasn't functioning as an early warning system, and I couldn't camp there to watch over it personally. There was also a hill a distance away, and I wanted to somehow get my hands on more unique minerals and materials.

The essence production at this point was still slow because most of my energy was focused on growing trees, which now numbered six thousand.

Other than that, there were more refugees, more non-humans, and they all joined Yvon's camp. There seemed to be around two hundred of them. It seemed Yvon knew they were coming and had prepared extra buildings to house them, so Yvon's side was becoming quite lively. There were centaurs among the new batch, and they went on to join the existing centaur group instead, but it was a small bunch, only about thirty or so.

YEAR 74, MONTH 5, WEEK 1

S pring was almost ending, and it seemed the growth of new trees started to slow down again. It was now about five hundred new trees every two weeks, so I stood at six and a half thousand now.

To help support the elves, centaurs, and treefolk, I created subsidiary trees that produced cotton. The deal was that they would pay me twenty percent of the proceeds should they be sold to traders. But if they made it for personal consumption, there was no tax.

Yes, I am taxing the refugees. I call it the cotton tax.

In addition, the treefolk and centaur camps committed to providing thirty warriors each to the valley's defense. Yvon's group naturally committed the most, being the largest. They put two hundred of their people forward for the valley's defense. They mostly focused on the small monsters and creatures that spawned naturally in the region.

And Jura, being the chief coordinator and communicator of the valley, gained a new class.

Diplomat.

YEAR 74, MONTH 5, WEEK 2

More refugees. Seriously... The invasion by the two kingdoms into the Salah Kingdom seemed to have displaced even more people, sowing more death. I knew of the deaths with my wider reach, as I was collecting more souls. My soul realm was filled with little sparks of light, of humans, of non-humans, all the souls making the journey to the other world. They would stay for about six months to a year before moving on, so the constant death was currently adding a lot of little lights to the soul realm.

"It is good that you are approaching an active [Soul Forge] soon." Wisp bobbed around.

"Tell me about...other soul-manipulating creatures." I got straight to the point. I had questions I wanted to ask.

"When you get a [Soul Forge]."

"Ah..." I sighed. "So, do I have a limit on how many souls I can store?"

"Nope. The soul realm can store as many souls as you can possibly have."

"How's that even possible? Doesn't that break some rules or something?"

"It...it just does." Wisp couldn't answer, but oh well. Magic. Like how the secret hideout was far bigger than my actual tree.

YEAR 74, MONTH 5, WEEK 3

More refugees! After two weeks of more arrivals, Yvon's group was touching almost eight hundred, and they were accepting some humans as well. At first, my initial response was to reject them, but then their location, at the edge of the valley, and the assurance of Yvon and her group meant I relented. More bodies to throw at the Salah Kingdom was good.

So Yvon and a lot of the earlier elves and humans now took the role of enforcer, and they seemed to have come up with some kind of norms.

They also had an unofficial name for their growing part of town, which was located a little farther from where Freeka was.

New Freeka.

At first, they wanted to name it after their benefactor, Prince Galan, so the name floated about was Galansburg, but I rejected that idea as it stepped on the history of this place, of Freeka.

So it was fine, then. That new settlement they were working on could be the new town, and the area my main tree was in would be the old town of Freeka.

I also gained a random level, after almost six months of not gaining one.

[Level 117.]

[Timber Farm.]

[Produce average quality timber, at a much faster speed.]

"Ah."

YEAR 74, MONTH 6

A small scouting party from the Salah Kingdom was spotted. Their enmity with Yvon had not ended after all. The skirmishes with the Nung and the Takde were just minor distractions. Salah was one of the larger states in the region, and they had sufficient resources to hold both fronts and still pursue their...vengeance.

For Yvon, this came as a disappointment. Their earlier hopes of making peace in this land were dashed. It wasn't going to be as easy as they initially hoped.

I decided to let Yvon deal with it. If they were to make a life in this valley, they had to show they were up for the challenge, so they captured the scouts, interrogated them, and then killed them.

I supposed they would be suspecting something when the scouts didn't return anyway.

Later in the month, the traders came along, traded some oil, and brought us some exotic fruits. It seemed the olive oil prices had gone up slightly during the wars, so we were paid a little more, though the merchants' share was obviously higher.

It seemed Salah's claim over our valley and a few other territories was disputed by the Nung—their point being that Salah's abandonment during the demonic wars rendered their claim moot. The past few months had consisted of a mix of skirmishes and high-level diplomatic meetings, so the disputed area had been declared a temporary no-go zone.

But that was ending, as neither budged from their claim, so Salah was coming. And so were the Nung.

Ah, peace is but a temporary lie, the outcome of two nations bickering with words.

[Harvestable products upgraded. Papaya and grapes obtained.]

[Normal tree count: 7,800.]

YEAR 74, MONTH 6, WEEK 4

More refugees! Yvon's group was expanding their walls, and a second layer of walls were being built to protect the additional houses now. With the help of timber, some of their earlier buildings were being rebuilt taller, denser.

Yvon's group was actually fairly talented. One of them was actually a mayor, and he had taken the role of mayor of New Freeka. He was in charge of construction and absorbing the refugee influx. With him were a few councilors and several paper workers, experts at setting up and managing paperwork. It seemed they even got started on making some paper from all the branches and leaves.

Another of Yvon's group was a military trainer, and she was in charge of managing the defensive aspects.

I suspected the whole conflict stemmed from Prince Galan's skilled retinue, and this somehow threatened the elder prince.

[Skill obtained: Growth Surge.]

[Creates patches of normal trees, shrubs, and grasses. Affected by weather and seasons.]

YEAR 74, MONTH 7, WEEK 2

There was a fair bit of movement at Yvon's side. People were moving in and out. Other than that, everyone was getting ready for another round of winter.

Laufen and the elves dropped by each of the camps, though I kept watch whenever they did. The last thing I wanted was a kidnapping.

Though they were new and strangers, it made them happy. They were in a society after all, and elves who stayed alone for too long lost that social connection.

Especially the kids. There were more kids to play with, kids their own age. Lausanne in particular found another girl her age, and they played catch in the small town of New Freeka. In New Freeka, multiple subsidiary trees kept watch. These were so I could look and keep myself aware of what was happening.

But I was struggling to keep track of so many things happening at once, especially now that it had grown to almost one thousand two hundred people, not counting the treefolk and centaurs.

YEAR 74, MONTH 7, WEEK 4

Army spotted. Ten thousand strong. They bore the flags of Salah. This was a proper army, with swords, armor, knights, and mages.

They marched toward New Freeka, and as they approached, one man on horseback yelled, "We demand you surrender!"

"No!"

I had insufficient [Root Strike]s to kill that many people. At best, I could take out about...a thousand? And that left nine thousand men.

The refugees were worried, of course. It was a large force. They talked about running, but Yvon somehow convinced them to stay. Over the past months, they had built a wall to act as a defensive fortification, preparing for this day.

Ten thousand was a lot, but not all needed to die. If I could get a hit on the leaders and deliver a visible smacking of their morale, perhaps they could be convinced to flee.

"I think the core group of about four hundred are professionals. The rest look like conscripts."

"Mages?"

I had in mind a similar strategy to the earlier fight. I wanted to take out the mages first, but they saw how we fought the first time, so they might know that we would try the same.

And indeed, there were no obviously visible mages. All of them wore armor, so the suspected mages were likely those wielding staffs or sticks. They would probably show themselves once the battle got into close range.

The army closed in. The number of cavalrymen was a lot less this time.

The refugees could field about eight hundred fighters in total —seven hundred from the camp itself and a hundred from the centaurs and treefolk.

Arrows started to fly, and the enemy's leader activated a shield barrier, deflecting the arrows. Some of the arrows, though, were from actual archers, with shield-penetrating abilities, so some still got through. The treefolk used their ability to throw rocks and boulders at the army, and their size and energy meant they were able to pierce the shield.

Ten thousand mostly soldiers? Something wasn't right.

They entered into some kind of turtle formation to reduce the impact of our projectiles.

And they drew nearer.

Around the walls were my subsidiary trees, and they walked past them. I took this chance to take a closer look.

Mages. I knew some of them were, but with the bodies flanking and blocking, I couldn't see them very well.

A few of the refugees were also mages, and two fireballs flew toward the army, smacking right into a magic barrier.

It was at this time a long-range projectile smashed into the refugee mage, killing him instantly.

I quickly turned my attention to them.

Far away, there were three men, one holding a long barrel gun—a sniper? However, it was a lot cruder, made of forged crystal, and seemed to use magical bullets. Another one looked like a mage, with the whole wizard gear going on. And the last man was an old man in a complete set of knight's armor. He had a faint, authoritative presence, and the ornaments on his person were magical, which made me suspect that he was probably a lord or noble.

"Did you spot the supposed archdruid?" the old man asked.

"No," the sniper answered.

"Deploying ten thousand men is a little overkill. It's probably those treefolk," the mage said.

The old man nodded. "I wouldn't count Yvon out just yet. She's probably got something up her sleeves. The fact that she so brazenly set up a physical camp here suggests she has some kind of backing."

The sniper shook his head. "Seriously, there are none of the unusual mana signatures."

The wizard shrugged. "Maybe she's just overconfident or tired of running."

"Maybe."

The sniper turned his barrel around. "All these trees are... annoyingly tough." He fired, and the projectile pierced through one of my subsidiary trees. But it slowed the crystalline projectile down significantly and softened the blow.

The wizard paused, seemingly realizing something. "[Detect Presence]."

He paused and turned to the lord. "We should...leave."

The lord looked dumbfounded. "Huh? Why? Don't we have good odds?"

"I sense an ominous presence that stretches this entire valley...not something...not something an archdruid can do. The trees...they are looking back at us." The wizard pointed. "I feel them watching us."

The lord stared. "How sure are you?"

"These trees...they have a faint killing intent. This is no ordinary forest."

"Hmm. That explains why the refugees are stuck. They dare not venture through the valley, so they may as well make a stand here."

"We might still be able to defeat Yvon and her band of rebels. But whatever else is here, it's not going to fall to us, not to what we have here. If Yvon is somehow working with or trying to control whatever lurks in this forest, we may not stand a chance. It's a trap, milord."

The lord paused and looked at the sniper. "What do you think?"

"I trust his judgment. If he says we should leave, we should." He fired another shot, this time intentionally hitting one of my subsidiary trees. It punctured a whole through it and sent a jolt of pain through me. "Normal trees would explode on impact. I agree that this forest...has secrets. I'll need explosive weaponry."

The wizard nodded to the sniper.

"It is best I report this to the wizard's guild. A deployment of a much larger group of wizards may be necessary."

The lord nodded. "Very well. There is no shame in retreating to fight another day. Call the army back. If this is a trap, we will not fall for it. We would be better placed if we can tap some rangers and shamans for the next fight."

And so, the army of ten thousand retreated.

It was surreal for the refugees, who thought they would be goners or lose most of their people. The casualties on both sides were relatively small—about twenty to thirty—and for Yvon and her group, it was a huge victory.

[Skill: Haunted tree upgraded to haunted forests.]

Ah. Did I just scare away an army? I was pretty sure the army couldn't kill me, but I probably wouldn't be able to kill all of them, either.

Still, it looked like they would be back with a vengeance. So I needed additional countermeasures.

YEAR 74, MONTH 8, WEEK 3

Ten thousand normal trees reached!
Firing up [Soul Forge].
All the trees in the valley abruptly emitted a faint glow, and it scared the refugees.

I felt power surging into me, my roots, all of them overflowing with power.

And then a huge thunderbolt from above landed on me like a constant electrical connection. It caused everyone to jump, and the secret hideout shook like it experienced an earthquake.

The ground shook, my entire body of tree glowed in a bluish light, and the thunder, like a chain linked to the sky above, trembled and flickered.

"What is going on?" Jura asked. "Tree-Tree, are you okay?"

They didn't know.

The treefolk seemed afraid. "Is the tree suffering through a magical crisis?"

The centaurs wondered whether this was some kind of divine punishment.

The normal trees pushed more energy through their roots, and all of that energy flowed into the once inactive [Soul Forge].

There was a spark, and a small blue flame popped out and

danced in the middle of the soul forge. The [Soul Forge] actually looked like a massive circular jar, and now, there was a blue light emitting from within.

And then, a shockwave followed. The outer bark of my body was shredded by the bolts of lightning as they hopped in and out of my body like a short-circuited set of electronics.

[You gained 4 levels.] [Level 121].

[Skill obtained: Magic suppression: All hostile magic abilities below tier 3 are absorbed.]

[Skill upgraded: Root surge. Covers a wider area and use limit increased.]

[Skill upgraded: Subsidiary tree increased to 250.]

[[Soul forge: Blue] is active.]

[Soul forge: ForgeTree.]

[The physical realm's link to the soul forge.]

[Soul forge abilities unlocked.]

[The power to repair, mend souls. To strip souls apart and put them back together. The ability to add souls to your abilities, familiars, items, trees. The ability to push souls to their limits and beyond. The ability to rank up a soul. The ability to fuse soul fragments whole and create artificial sub-souls from ordinary soul fragments.]

Wisp shook, and then he split into three wisps.
Two then circled around the soul forge, orbiting it.
"You've done it. An active soul forge."
"Where do I start?"

"I suggest, given your now expanding reach, you need...assistants."

"Okay, lead the way."

"Not all souls were suited to make the journey to the after-life, the aether dimension where souls returned," the wisp explained.

Souls, though extremely durable, did fracture, crack, and decay from the presence of the outside world. Some souls were torn by the magic of men, between life and death. Some souls were stuck, lingering, seeking vengeance or salvation. Whatever it was, some souls couldn't make the journey. And for these souls, they decayed into fragments.

But it wasn't the end. Eventually, in the eternity of time, enough of these fragments would pool together and form a soul-body, one able to make the journey into the afterlife, where the administrator of souls could restore them and send them onward, to continue the eternal duty of souls. To reincarnate into the next life.

A [Soul Forge] assisted in this repairing and renewal process. It fused the fragments of ordinary decayed souls into a soul body, and the soul body then made the journey to the afterlife. But it left behind a "frame."

It was an artificial thing, not possessing the limitless, self-sustaining life force of a soul, but yet, it was close enough.

To use an analogy, the soul was comprised of a car (an outer layer) and a driver (an inner layer). The decayed souls were broken cars, unable to continue their journey to the other side. The [Soul Forge] forged the broken parts of multiple broken cars together, such that, together, they could make that journey. But, once that journey was made, the inner layer, the driver, disappeared, but the outer layer, the car, remained.

This outer layer was the "artificial soul." Like a person without a heart, it was close but not the same.

And with this artificial soul, we upgraded one of my very first abilities.

[Soul-forge is fusing autopilot with an artificial soul.]

[Autopilot has transformed into Forest Mind, Level 1.]

[You may now name Forest Mind.]

"Trevor." I wanted Treevor, but never mind.

"I am Trevor, Level 1 Forest-Mind. Greetings, Master Tree-Tree."

It speaks!

"I can handle the administrative, defensive, and organizational aspects of the valley on your behalf, and as I gain levels, you may select the skills and abilities I gain. Please assign me a duty."

YEAR 74, MONTH 9

It was as if I was playing a strategy game, and now, I had unlocked the radar, giving me access to mini-maps, live indicators, and numerical representation of all the things going on before, just now with much better detail.

An example would be the normal trees. Previously, I had data indicating how many trees were connected to me via rootnet, but now that data was a lot more granular, like how many of those trees were producing seeds and fruits, the average age of trees, the estimated fertility of the ground, and estimates of how many trees would be added.

"The merchants have been spotted to the southwest, sir." Yes, I thought I preferred sir over master.

And my alarm system.

"Good."

"The elves are on their way. With the olives."

There were certain things innate to Trevor, things that didn't need to be taught because they came naturally. Things like tree management, boosting growth rate, checking for new 'foreign' objects, and managing mining and essence extractions.

"Master, I gained a level."

"Yes, good." He was now level five after a month of practice. There was a limitation with artificial souls, though.

Artificial souls started off with a level limit of twenty, and to break that, I needed to upgrade the artificial soul or fulfill certain set criteria.

As they got upgraded, their abilities grew, but according to the wisps, so would their tendency to...misbehave. So, in a way, artificial souls generally became less stable as they grew. But this was also influenced by various factors, such as the skill of the soul forger, the power of the soul forge, and various other unknowns.

Another was that Trevor leeched off my knowledge and fused it with its innate knowledge of 'tree-stuff.' So, while it could handle forest-related matters superbly, it struggled to even talk about...communicating with its inhabitants. In fact, that communication it had with me was due to the fact that it was synchronized with me, and therefore, it could relay its message to me specifically.

So...in a way, I had an assistant no one knew about. That wouldn't matter to the elves, would it?

"How about me?" Meela popped by. Her soul was damaged by the journey, but I had used the [Soul Forge] to repair her. Still, it wasn't a complete repair. It seemed I would need to find additional upgrades for the [Soul Forge] to fully get back her power.

"I-I haven't thought of how to best use you. And you are due for reincarnation, no?"

"Oh, I spoke to Nobuo last night. He said I can stay for a thousand years before I return."

"Who's Nobuo?"

"Oh...the reincarnation god."

"Huh." I thought his name was Mozart? Or were there multiple reincarnation gods? "Why?"

"Oh...he assumed my soul was destroyed by the demons and would take a longer time to get back into the system, so he didn't arrange a subsequent reincarnation for me yet, so he says I can hang around for a thousand years."

"That's awfully long for him."

"Oh, time flows differently in the aether realm—it's like super-fast there." Meela's soul bobbed around.

"Really?" Well, I supposed it was like saying flies had short lives, and perhaps to these gods, our lives were like flies'.

"Trevor, any suggestions?"

"No, sir. Souls are not my area of expertise."

"Would you like a combat role?"

Meela's soul spun. "No. I did a lot of fighting with the stupid demons, so...I could help with defenses if you need it, but... something more...domestic?"

"What do you like?"

"I like dancing, I like...kids. I used to volunteer as a kindergarten assistant, playing games and stuff."

"Ah...anything else?"

Meela seemed slightly annoyed. "Why can't you just pick something? Can't I change it if I don't like it?"

Hmm.

"Wisp, is the [Soul Forge] fusion reversible?"

"For artificial souls, no. The disentangling process will shred them to a soul-frame (outer layer). For normal souls, yes, but the normal souls have a 'cooldown' period."

"You are right, Meela. It looks like you can change if you don't like it. I was afraid that it was an irreversible effect, in which case a mistake would be...terrible."

"Aaaahh. I see, I see. Well, I do like exploring places, eating food, and talking to people. You know, like a tourist. I think that would be nice."

"A tourist, eh." *I can't create human bodies, so too bad. At most I can make a wooden puppet...wait. A wooden puppet might be a good idea.*

"Is that it?" I asked.

"Hmmm...I also like to draw and paint. And hang out with my siblings."

"Sorry, I suddenly thought of it. Don't you miss your family or whoever where you came from?" I suddenly missed my nephew, too.

Meela paused. "I do. But like I said, time moves differently for different places... Relativity, interdimensional time-space and all that mumbo jumbo. This one thousand years is not going to be a thousand years in my home. Nobuo say he can send me back, without my memories, to the exact moment before we had the bus accident, and that accident would then not happen. According to him, the only thing I will get from this world once I return...is strange, unusual dreams."

"Ah."

"Yeah. Things will be back to the way they were, and all I get is a dream."

"Like primary school essays, eh. Where you wake up and realize it's all been a dream."

"Exactly."

...

...

"Do you like doing...research?"

"No."

"Hmmm... How about you just pick something?"

"I don't know."

"Seriously?"

"Yeah."

"Any ideas?" I looked at the original Wisp, and he turned away. I took that as a no.

"Ah. Can you just be my secretary then?"

"Sounds lewd. No."

YEAR 74, MONTH 9, WEEK 3

There were patches of [subsidiary tree], with grapes and papaya in all the different refugee groups as a form of dietary supplement.

The refugees of New Freeka had swelled to two thousand, boosted by the "victory" over the large army. So New Freeka was bustling with activity as they tried to cater to the needs of a growing town, with Yvon and her group of advisors the unelected leaders. Most of the new refugees were mostly escapees as the war with Nung and Takde continued to devastate that region.

"I bring...troublesome news, tree spirit." Jura nodded and sat at one of the tables in the inner circle of trees. He sipped on tea made with leaves and then continued. "Yvon's group is planning to send a delegation to Salah. To negotiate a truce, for coexistence."

"Oh." How was that troublesome? Was it not worth trying?

"The refugees themselves, though, don't think that is a good idea. Many lost friends and family to the brutality of the Salah Kingdom, like us, and enmity is not going to accept a truce. Personally, I think Yvon still wants to coexist peacefully with humans."

Hmm.

"So...the mood amongst the refugees is a bit conflicted. They are aware their options for revenge are limited, but they feel injustice and dissatisfaction at 'peace.'"

And?

"Some of them think you should decide whether a truce would be a good idea."

"Yes. Do you think Salah would hold on and honor a truce?"

"Well..."

"So, a truce is a good idea because it buys time. It gives us just cause to retaliate."

Jura paused and then nodded. "Yeah. Maybe."

Now that it was decided, I turned my attention to artificial souls.

"Thinking of making another?" Wisp asked, clearly knowing my thoughts.

"Yes. But I have much to think about...considering I have only sufficient fragmented souls to make...four more, for now."

"People die, and over the eternities you will gather thousands, maybe millions of souls. Life in this world is so fragile after all."

"Ah, true. Do these artificial souls die?"

"Yes, if they get destroyed."

Kinda like computers, then.

It was then we directed our attention to the [forge tree], a large tree located on the outer ring of my circle. Black in color, as if the tree itself had been scorched, it was split into five from top through the middle of the trunk. At the bottom, there was a big, black hole into a pitch-black screen.

And Jura gulped as he stepped in.

[Soul Forge activating...]

[Merging artificial soul, tree familiar, essences of earth, and 50 essences of bear.]

[Familiar has transformed into a Bear-shaped Tree Eidolon, Level 1. You may name it.]

"Bamboo."

Jura walked out of the forge feeling a little dazed, wondering what happened. It was then that a smoke-like thing started to appear out of his skin. It then accumulated, spun, and swirled before transforming into a bear made of branches, twirling and spinning together.

"Hi." A loud, hoarse voice broke the soft rustling sound of the forest.

Jura jumped. "What?!"

The bear took a few steps and stood on two legs like a grizzly. "I was once your familiar. With the blessings of the tree spirit, I have now transformed into an eidolon."

"Eidolon?"

I would let Jura figure it out.

Next was a giant war beetle. The [Soul Forge] took a whole day to merge a war beetle with an artificial soul, but when it was finally complete, a large war beetle emerged.

[War beetle has transformed into beetle knight, Level 1. You may name it.]

"Horns."

"Master," it spoke to me telepathically.

"Great. Horns, you shall lead the beetles."

"As you command."

[To assign more artificial souls, additional trees are needed.]

Ah. It seemed each of these artificial souls derived some form of control and energy from me indirectly.

[You obtained a beetle commander. Each tree with [insect warriors]
has expanded to 5 beetles per tree.]

[You leveled up. Level 122!]

[Poison field upgraded.]

Ah, man, I was hoping for some greater AoE abilities. Between
all the other boosts and support I got, I probably had sufficient
[Root Strike]s and [Root Surge] to kill two thousand men. If all
died at a single [Root Strike], the remainder would depend on
the beetle army I oversaw.

If a large army of ten thousand came along again, the citizens of the valley would be done for.

YEAR 74, MONTH 10

Traders came by and brought news and money.

Salah was winning the war against both Nung and Takde, so they might soon turn their attention back to us again.

The traders also needed another load of olive oil. It seemed it was a rather popular product. They asked the elves whether the olive oil production could be expanded, and they replied, "Maybe."

New Freeka was growing, and a further big influx of refugees resulted in a growth to almost three thousand. Food shortage was a problem, and so these refugees started engaging in hunting the nearby monsters, but Yvon directed them instead toward the open fields and lightly forested areas, where the less hostile animals and monsters spawned.

"We need food. Winter will be here soon."

Jura paused. "Food?"

"Can the tree spirit help?"

"The tree spirit is not the solution to everything." Jura shook his head. *Thank you for speaking up for me!*

Yvon and another of the senior New Freeka leaders looked at each other. "Surely, he can do...some things?"

Jura paused. "Hmmm..."

"Perhaps help with some...fruits?"

"Fruits don't grow in winter." That was a lie, some fruits did grow in winter. Especially with my [winter resistance]. Perhaps someday I would even get a [Greenhouse]-like ability. Hah. It sounded like a farming game then. Perhaps sprinklers, too.

Would I be a farmtree then?

"Hmm...I will speak to the tree spirit."

Yvon nodded. "Please. If the refugee situation grows even further, we will have a food crisis over winter."

"Then why are you still accepting more?"

"I can't turn them away. I made an oath to the gods when we started this fight, before this, to accept the non-human refugees, to offer safe haven to those who sought us out."

"Ah...a god's oath?" Jura asks.

"Yes. To Morya."

"Ah. That's one of the lesser, minor gods? Not Gaya?"

Yvon didn't answer, and Jura took the hint.

"Hmm..."

"So please ask the tree spirit for help."

"I will ask." Just as Jura was about to walk away, Yvon stopped him.

"Also...can the tree spirit create a tree in New Freeka? We can cater an area where a quiet sanctuary can be created."

"Oh. Why?"

"The refugees have...spiritual needs. A place for prayer, ceremony, and faith."

Jura nodded. "Ah, I see. I will speak to the tree spirit."

It seemed Yvon and her team still couldn't identify which trees were actually my subsidiary trees. [Camouflage]?

Oh, well.

"Can you let us know the tree spirit's decision tomorrow?"

"I will try."

Later, once they left, Jura sat on a wooden stump right outside the secret hideout.

"What do you think? Did you hear what they said?"

I paused.

I supposed if we did assist, they might soon expect it annually. There must be a cost to it, so they must bear a price for my assistance. Power and abilities should not be given freely as there were consequences.

"Potatoes. Offer them potatoes. But it comes at a price. I demand a magical item in exchange."

Jura paused. "Ah...what sort of magical item?"

"The number of potatoes I will nourish depends on what magical items they offer me."

"Oh."

"As for the tree for New Freeka, I am fine with that."

"Ah."

"How's the eidolon coming along?"

Jura stood, and then suddenly, wooden armor surrounded him, and that armor looked like a grizzly bear, his arms and claws made of wood.

He took a few steps, and his posture and gait were like that of a giant bear.

"This is my new form. [Ursa Mode]."

"Ah, so how is it?"

"Not bad. I feel stronger, faster. But without a real opponent, I will not really know how well it performs."

"Get Yvon."

Jura paused. "You want to show this to her?"

"It is fine. It is not as if she can do anything about it."

Jura nodded and left for New Freeka to inform Yvon of the decision. Later that evening, a clearing was made in New Freeka that had been designated as a space for a subsidiary tree.

And indeed, overnight, a tree appeared in the middle of that space.

YEAR 74, MONTH 11

The artifacts offered were...uninteresting. Rings, daggers, all with mild enchantments. The possessions of the refugees were...not spectacular.

Or perhaps they were not hungry enough to offer what was truly valuable.

But they did offer quite a few, about thirty, so as a result, they received about three thousand large potatoes, which spawned right next to their town.

This level of precision was made possible by Trevor.

Other than that, the month was...quiet. The cold was coming again. Winter was starting.

Lausanne, now almost six, was starting actual combat training since she was still holding on to that hero idea. Brislach and Wahlen were old enough and yearned for social contact, so they demanded a move to New Freeka, even though Laufen had been a great caretaker.

I guessed even elves went through that teenage rebellious phase.

Belle and Emile, though, seemed to remember the destruction a lot more vividly than the younger kids, so they were staying put.

Maybe they wanted to do work other than preparing olives.

Jura shrugged and let them go. I gave both Brislach and Wahlen a regular tree familiar, just for protection, and Trevor would help me monitor them.

Elsewhere, my beetles explored a bit farther, just to get a sense of what was out there beyond the valley. Once again, this was made possible by Trevor and Horns.

Beyond the valley, farther down south, were the ruins of Moton where I once stayed. It seemed after the demonic wars it was never actually rebuilt.

Even farther south was a region under the Nung Kingdom, known as Rufas, and it was where the region's temple of Gaya lay. Rufas was also a border city with Salah, and Moton in times past had frequently changed hands between Nung and Salah. A small town with few defenses, they often just surrendered when threatened. I suspected the temple of Gaya I once was in was there, but I couldn't be sure. Perhaps there were many, and I wondered whether the caretaker and Gewa's body were still there. Rufas was large, heavily fortified, and I had little insight to its interior, beyond a spying beetle.

To the east and west were large fields, now populated with wild buffalos, goats, and some smaller animals. There were also monsters, but they didn't attack the regular animals.

On the eastern side, as we headed farther, there were the ruins of multiple different forts. Some were being rebuilt, but most remained as ruins. The damage and ruins looked fairly new, and the fields were littered with the dead.

After that, the eastern terrain deformed even more, and it looked as if the area had seen some really serious demonic battles.

At that point, the beetles returned. It seemed that was as far as they would go from home. It seemed there was a maximum range available to them, even with Horns's extended range support.

On the western side were first the fields, then some

regrowing forests, and then some more ruins before the mountains. Moving on, there were some hot springs, then some lakes, and after that, a chain of active volcanoes.

On the northern side was where the demonic rift used to be. It was still mostly barren, and the beetles were frequently attacked by rather fearsome monsters that appeared there.

Horns advised a larger squad of beetles, should I intend to actually explore the areas closer to the demons.

YEAR 74, MONTH 12

Winter. Potatoes. The beetles slept—even Horns was operating at half-strength.

Winter was even colder than the previous year, but thankfully, most of the refugees were well prepared now. With some decent housing, heat retention from thicker walls, and a good stockpile of firewood, all the refugees were having a much more comfortable winter.

The centaurs, over this whole year, had constructed multiple large tents, with multiple layers of cloth and skin that helped slow down heat loss. They also built, with the aid of the treefolk, some drainage to help manage the rain that occurred frequently during the winter months. Potatoes, of course, were there as a reserve food.

The treefolk apparently also had a habit of storing food underground—apparently, they had a kind of magic that made a kind of fermented vegetable. It was their version of the winter cache, using cabbages mixed with all kinds of chili and vinegar.

Oh, and during the month, I gained an additional food variety.

[Harvestable crops: Apples]

[Winter resistance upgraded.]

The essence generators extracted all sorts of essences from the surroundings. So now that my roots extended the entire valley, it seemed it extracted from all the deaths in the valley.

YEAR 75, MONTH 1

Snow. Cold, cold snow.

Jura had a few sparring matches with Yvon. Yvon was stronger in pure swordfighting, due to her past experience as the right hand of the prince.

But then, once Jura activated his [Ursa Form], his speed, strength, and natural defenses shot up, and Yvon was no match.

"Bear form? A summoner's ability? Or perhaps a beastmaster?"

"Ah...I have no clue," Jura replied, being honest. *I doubt Bamboo knows that much about his abilities, either.*

"Hmm."

Other than this, the delegation they sent to Salah had returned. One of them, at least.

And the leaders all rushed to meet him.

"Milady, the kingdom has agreed to a truce."

Everyone was happy, but then this was too easy, so they asked further.

"What...what are the terms?"

"We are to take in all of the non-humans in the kingdom. In doing so, we have to pay a compensation of ten thousand gold coins a year for the next ten years."

Yvon paused... "All?"

"Ten thousand gold coins?"

"They are extorting us, these terms."

Yvon paused again. "Any more?"

"Your life, madam. They want your head."

YEAR 75, MONTH 2

Yvon agreed to the truce, with a few modifications. Her death came after two years of peace. She didn't see herself as being so valuable that her life mattered more than the security and safety of the non-humans she swore an oath to protect. In fact, she felt it was a fitting way to die, a martyr's sacrifice, a trade of her life for two years of truce.

The second modification they proposed was to have the gold payment reduced, paid quarterly, and the first payment commencing after a year of peace.

The Salah Kingdom accepted the modified terms.

Why?

One was that they still managed to get rid of all the non-humans under this truce plan, and giving this space for Yvon to integrate the non-humans was ideal. In fact, it was probably their main goal, to create a human-only environment. There was racial tension, and getting rid of those 'troublesome' elements was worth it for Salah, from a unity perspective. If they wanted to create a united kingdom, this might be one way to do so. The loyalties of these non-humans was always suspect, even though there was no evidence showing non-humans as more disloyal than humans.

Money was hardly an issue for a wealthy nation like Salah, and perhaps there were factions within Salah who saw additional benefits of getting rid of the non-humans. Salah no longer had to maintain multiple prisons, detention camps, armies, and soldiers to patrol their lands. In fact, to be able to reduce their logistical load and manpower need was probably what they wanted, so they could direct these resources to their current, ongoing conflict with the Nung and Takde. It was a concession they agreed to make, to deal with what they saw as a 'larger' enemy.

As for Yvon, the very fact that they still got to kill her, even if after two years, without having to resort to war was a net save for their military. They got to focus on other fronts that gave them just cause. In fact, her agreement either way was as good as an admission of guilt. So even if this New Freeka decided to wage war someday, Salah was the one that was right. The neighboring kingdoms would be less likely to come to our aid, and they would be able to use overwhelming force, and even underhanded methods, without losing support of the humans.

Thinking it through, Yvon may have signed herself and New Freeka into a tough truce deal. But this was a positive outcome for her as she got peace, and she could better ensure the safety of the non-humans.

Anyway, it was a decision Yvon made for New Freeka, and it was probably a good decision. For me, I was initially a little peeved, but then as I pondered the issue, perhaps this would allow me to better investigate the culprits of Freeka's destruction and focus my vengeance. After all, if they had less reason to suspect and enter into battle with us, I could keep my abilities hidden, unknown, and I could use that as a surprise attack. If they realized someone was constantly using roots to attack, they might well chop all the trees down as a defensive measure.

Also, the traders brought news of the demon king's corpse. The location had been discovered, but approaching the daemolite had proven to be exceptionally challenging as the location's gravitational field had been disrupted, and so the entire area was floating in the sky. Add to that, the place was crawling with fire elementals.

But most importantly, the traders brought something I had been trying to find for a long time—a register of recorded spirits and magical places in the region, in addition to a rudimentary map where the nearest magical ley line was located.

A ley line!

I wanted one.

The nearest one was actually close to the ruins of Moton, so Horns investigated, as Jura refused to leave the valley. The beetle squad took about three days to get there, only to discover that it was actually...a small dungeon.

Dungeon, eh.

Conventional thinking. I would need to break the dungeon core to get to the ley line, but I wondered whether it was possible to hijack the ley line without having to mount an assault on the dungeon. In either case, having confirmed the location, I started spawning subsidiary trees in a line. This process took sixty subsidiary trees, as the gap between each tree was about one-and-a-half kilometers, and now I had a string of subsidiary trees that formed a link all the way to the dungeon.

Somehow, this reminded me of those strategy games where I sent a scout in a straight line, cutting through the fog of war...

The dungeon was pouring out a ton of monsters—mostly low-level ghouls, zombies, and skeletons. The beetles and Horns had to constantly fend off the group of marauding skeletons and zombies, but with a subsidiary tree nearby, they were able to regenerate and hold back the horde.

This was where I discovered I had...a problem. My war beetles were big, the size of rhinos, but the dungeon entrance was only big enough for three of them, side by side. And having so little space also meant the beetles lost a few of their combat advantages—i.e., their charge attacks. They did have very strong armor, but if there were stronger monsters in the dungeon, these beetles were kinda sitting ducks.

"Sire, I suggest we stay put and control the area for now," Horns telepathically communicated. As an artificial soul linked to me, he could transmit his message to me directly, though he lacked any mouth that was capable of speech. So, even though he understood language...he could only speak to me...and the other artificial souls.

"We could set up defensive positions?" Trevor asked, also interested in this new expansion.

"It's a dungeon..." Meela poked her head in, seeing what I saw. It seemed she was able to share my vision... I wasn't sure how she was able to do that.

Outside, in the open, the beetles could crush and ram the undead easily and render them useless.

But as an experiment, I sent a few beetles into the dungeon anyway, and as expected, they died once they were trapped. Dungeons with narrow passages were not the best places for oversized beetles.

So...I needed a different strategy.

[Achieved long-distance connected roots. Unlocked new skill: Far-reaching roots.]

[Subsidiary tree has leveled up! Limit expanded to 400.]

YEAR 75, MONTH 3

The truce between Salah and New Freeka was signed. Refugees were expelled.

More than three thousand new refugees came that month, and New Freeka soared to seven thousand in population. Massive construction was happening, but thankfully, it was spring, so there was a huge surge in new tree growth by myself and Trevor, and then there was also the dedicated timber farms (which produced no energy, as all of its energy was used to create more wood mass) meaning an ample supply of wood.

The new people were a mix of elves, centaurs, dwarves, and some humans, as there were some families where the humans intermarried with non-humans. Mostly humanoids, as they were the most 'acceptable' to the humans, but still not enough. Yvon and her team were busy, and they expanded the town right next to the valley.

The forest was off-limits to the newcomers as there were monsters appearing. They were insect types, but they generally hunted the animals. It was also to prevent the newbies from... breaking the rules that had been set up. Of course, there were those that tried anyway, so...that was when the war beetles scared the shit out of them.

Anyway, back to the undead dungeon. The stalemate was still ongoing. I couldn't get into the dungeon, but they couldn't get out, either. Using additional subsidiary trees, I created a defensive line outside the dungeon, and any of the undead that appeared were instantly killed by Horns and their team.

Horns hit his level limit of twenty, and I was sad. His combat and support skills were quite interesting, but he had nothing useful in tiny...dungeons.

"How do I upgrade their level limits?"

"For who? Different unit types have distinct things." Wisp bobbed around.

"Let's say Trevor? Trevor has also hit his limit."

"A forest mind would require a 'brain.'"

"Huh?"

[Unlocked special tree type. Root-Brain Complex. Requires special minerals to grow. Special minerals required are 10 x Blood Crystals, and 50 x fresh animal heads.]

The...what?

"Guys, I got a task for you," I told the elves.

"As you wish." Jura found some of his skills upgraded recently, and strangely, it made his behavior a little weird.

"How about me? Can I help, too?" Lausanne asked. She followed Jura everywhere these days—he was her combat mentor, after all.

"Uh...it depends whether you'll be in danger."

It later emerged that the blood crystals could be bought, and they weren't overly expensive. But Jura would have to raise some money for it, so we needed to either earn it or get it via other means. The olives sold provided a good sum of money but it was insufficient to afford blood crystals.

"Is there any loot from the dungeon you found?"

"Loot?"

"Things that are dropped by the monsters or creatures."

"I-I don't know. I can't actually see it that well. Trevor, Horns, is there any?" My vision was mostly on living things and items made of mana. Inanimate, mana-less objects appeared as outlines, and frankly there were so many of these objects, I couldn't tell if they were any different.

"Yes, sire. There are some items dropped by the zombies and skeletons. We didn't pick them up, as...we don't have hands. But they look like ordinary items, sire."

Horns! Tell me next time!

I later sent Emile and Belle, with a protective group of beetles, to pick up the loot. It turned out zombies and skeletons did drop some low-quality loot, but loot was still loot, and it could be sold for cash.

And then I realized I asked the wrong question of Wisp.

"Uh...how do I upgrade Horns?" I mean, if I did want to do more things around the valley and the region, Horns was the best candidate...

Wisp paused "Hmm. I don't know, actually."

I was stumped. This must be a deliberate challenge. The system wanted me to figure it out myself, so when Horns returned to the valley, he went into the [biolab].

Under the microscope, the warbeetle knight's body was unlike any other.

The body was dry and flaky, and there was a tiny spring of mana in the middle, which I thought was from an artificial soul. Unlike normal souls who poured out clear mana, the mana from this spring was light blue, as if somebody mixed flour and blue coloring into it.

The body, the vessel of said blue mana, was dry and...cold?

[Body - mana type compatibility is low. Body absorption ratio is low.]

Ah, the biolab had tooltips and indicators.

I focused on the spring, and another set of tooltips emerged.

[Mana generation ratio hampered by low synchronization with external environment.]

It looked like a lot of work was needed. I didn't recall seeing this many tooltips before, or was it because of the upgrades? Or the soul forge? I could do with a lab assistant, so I wondered whether I could fuse the biolab and an artificial soul?

Ah. Maybe I should do that next...

Anyway, back to the body. I recalled there was a freshness, a softness when I looked at Meela's body. It seemed like the mana poured out of the spring, and the body lapped it up. Even with all the other bodies I had seen, the body lapped up and absorbed all the mana it produced.

Was this because I forced this creation? The body didn't absorb this foreign soul suddenly thrust into it?

Ah...if that was the case, did I need to begin a phase of introducing the artificial soul's mana to the vessel before performing the merge?

[Soul forge annex added: Mana-soaking facility and compatibility tester.]

[Biolab upgraded. Additional lab tools obtained.]

Ah.

Sounded like the answer was yes.

Still, I had a problem now. In Horns, the body and mana had low compatibility, so how did I fix it after the fact? Was there some kind of medicine I could make? Or maybe I needed to find some way to modify the body so that it absorbed and became more compatible with the artificial soul it housed.

Ah. Never mind. At the way things were going, I would find out.

I wanted artificial souls and assistants...and that ley line.

"Trevor, how many trees are growing this month?"

"We are on track for almost two thousand, sire." At the current rate, the normal tree count would stand at around 13,850 at the end of the month.

If ten thousand could support three artificial souls, would twenty thousand support six?

"Sire...we require some precious gems—like emerald, topaz, or diamond."

"Huh...why?"

"The rootnet will hit max load at twenty thousand and needs to be upgraded. There is an energy transmission capacity, and these precious gems can be used to upgrade the roots."

Ah. Like power cables?

Damn. I had so many competing priorities! Could I mine these minerals somewhere?

"Are there any mines or locations where this is available?"

"The map says there are some abandoned mines closer to the demon rift. There is no data available on the resources available or whether anyone lives there."

Hmm.

"How many of these gems do you need?"

"About 10kg worth, in any mixture, sire. It is sufficient to upgrade the main eight-directional roots that form the backbone of the rootnet. We are already consuming copper to upgrade the existing root networks."

"Fine...let's send Horns and the beetles there."

"But what about the dungeon?"

Ah, true. Damn it. Could I get the refugees to do it?

"Hey, I am still trying to get money for the blood crystals, so...I am busy." Jura shook his head. He wasn't keen on the dungeon or the mines, either. He was just planning how to sell all the loot.

Laufen, Belle, and Emile were not fighters, so they were out, too.

"Can we try to buy them like blood crystals?"

"If we produce more olive oils, maybe we can buy them?"

"I think it won't make a dent. Such gems are expensive, no?"

As we all discussed the matter, I asked, "Hey, Trevor, what's considered a precious gem?"

"Emeralds, diamonds, topaz, rubies, pearls, aquamarine, garnet—almost anything crystalline."

"Ah." I wondered how Trevor knew such things sometimes.

"I leech off your knowledge, sire. When we are created, we take a snapshot of what the [Soul Forge] thinks is relevant to our roles, and periodically, we get additional knowledge from you and Wisp."

"Wait, are you saying the [Soul Forge] is…sentient?"

Wisp suddenly popped up. "No. The [Soul Forge] has a certain categorization of information that it needs for each kind of role—i.e. combat, support, administrative, magical, and social. Your memories and knowledge are also classified into such categories, and the forge will match those roles to the knowledge."

"How about you?" I mean, Wisp knew shit I didn't, so it must have come from somewhere.

"I have inherited knowledge, granted to the wisps of all soul trees. From the nameless mother herself."

The nameless mother.

I wondered whether I could meet her.

Maybe I should dig really deep; maybe she was hiding deep underground in the heart of the planet.

YEAR 75, MONTH 4

Yvon and the leaders of New Freeka came to beg for aid. Their population had now boomed to ten thousand, and they had a real problem feeding and housing them all, even with the massive buildings they were assembling. There seemed to be some observers from Salah there, too, to ensure the truce terms were complied with.

Their problem was multifold really. Housing, food, how to make money for their truce obligations, and how to control such a large, restless, and unhappy population.

As they lived on the periphery of the forest, building and farming on the lands that were not yet forested, I left it to them. As long as they didn't encroach on the forest, I could allow space for Yvon's group.

"I offer my soul." Yvon kneeled, begged, really. "Anything, tree spirit. At this point, you are the only one that can offer us hope."

"No." One tiny soul to aid so many refugees? What did she take me for, a charity?

Then her entire council of fifteen men kneeled. "We offer our souls as well. We have fought long and hard together, for the dream of Prince Galan and Lady Yvon's non-human state. Here we have a great chance to achieve it, and with the powers of a great tree spirit, we can achieve it."

"Sixteen of your souls, for more than ten thousand refugees?"

"Yes."

"Is that a good trade?" I asked Wisp.

"No idea."

The sixteen kneeled. "Everything we have to offer and our remaining lives. Please, to house, to feed, to protect a fledgling city; a great tree spirit can do more than we can."

Uh, well, that was because your levels are so low. If one was a high enough level, one would get tremendous OP abilities—would they not?

"No. Not good enough."

They looked at each other and decided to go back to New Freeka. New Freeka, at ten thousand inhabitants sprawled across the entire southern valley, essentially blocking off access to the forests that I lived in.

Ah, no matter.

As the [Ginseng] grew, it seemed that stranger, more powerful monsters spawned in the forests. Things harder for the Beetles to defeat, on some days, larger groups of monsters appeared.

[Ginseng has reached stage 1 maturity. You may direct its next stage of growth.]

[Stage 2 growth choices are:]

[Mana growth and mana pool size. (Your mana will reduce by 1% for the entirety of the stage 2 growth period.)]

[Physical stat growth (Tree growth reduced by 5% during the entire growth period.)]

[Grant unique skills (Stronger monsters will appear during the entire stage 2 period.)]

[(Environmental choice) Grants title [Survivor of the Valley]. Title provides high-tier natural regeneration and increased defense.]

[There are twenty stages to the ginseng. Each successive stage increases monster spawn and stronger monster types, that will try to consume or destroy the ginseng tree.]

Uh.

Uh...

Was this a [protect the tree] mini game?

I picked [unique skills] because why the fuck not?

YEAR 75, MONTH 4, WEEK 3

The stalemate continued. There was a dungeon I wanted to invade, and yet I sucked. Repeatedly attempting to charge into the dungeon seemed to have created stronger zombies and undead, so if I wanted to get to it, I had better attack with a strong force able to wipe it out in one go.

Meanwhile, [Far-reaching Roots] increased the distance between the subsidiary trees further, essentially doubling it. I was now trying to explore alternative means of locating the stuff that I needed to grow.

Back at the ginseng tree, a couple of strong monsters appeared this month. They killed a few beetles before they were defeated, so I increased the number of beetles defending it to fifty.

The treefolk and centaurs were relatively content, being like suburbs to the booming New Freeka.

Yvon and her group returned again for another round of begging, and once more, I turned them away.

And yet, in New Freeka, it seemed quite a few people—elves, humans, and dwarves—prayed at my [subsidiary tree]. And talked about their issues. Some of these refugees had taken on the role of a 'priest,' limiting and controlling the sessions each one had to talk to that subsidiary tree. Even though I didn't respond.

Strange, but I supposed faith was needed, even when one was a refugee.

Some of these humans and dwarves had a culture of praying to the deity that controlled the land where they lived, even though they may not be a devout believer. It was an animistic kind of approach, to worship the land, but it was charming.

[Special tree unlocked: Tree of Prayers]

[Tree of Prayers has a calming, relaxing effect on its surroundings. Has the ability to passively soothe and comfort. Comes with naturally calming background music of rustling leaves and wind.]

Oh. This was like that time Brislach and Wahlen played hide and seek.

YEAR 75, MONTH 5

A massive tiger attacked my [ginseng tree]. It killed thirty beetles and managed to pull the ginseng tree out of the ground.

Then Trevor alerted me to the sudden attack.

And I killed it with multiple [Root Strike]s.

[Ginseng tree has been killed.]

Dammit.

Well, the ginseng tree was still lying on the ground, but it was dead. This fragile little thing.

I later had Laufen brew it into a soup, using tiger meat and ginseng—kind of like traditional Asian herbal soups.

I had Jura, Laufen, Emile, and Belle eat and drink the soup. Apparently, it tasted like roots.

They reported feeling strange but nothing else.

Maybe not so quickly? Or perhaps the ginseng was too young?

YEAR 75, MONTH 5, WEEK 2

Yvon came and begged for something again. This time, it was for us to create grapes. The [Harvestable crops: grapes], and the idea was that they would make wine with it, to raise enough money to pay the terms of their truce.

Good idea, really. "So, what's the offer?"

"My soul. I am marked for death anyway, so take my soul."

A soul for a vineyard of grapes? It was quite a good deal.

"Fifty grape trees," I said.

"Only?"

"Fifty confirmed grape trees, and I will use my abilities to boost a dedicated patch of land of four acres for grapes for the next ten years."

"Hmm..."

"Your soul for a grape farm."

One of her advisors shook her head. "No, it's too little."

"How about ten acres?" Yvon asked

"Twelve acres, then. But I get a ten-percent cut of all wine sales," I returned.

"Okay.

The deal was done. [Spiritual contract - barter] completed.

The denizens of New Freeka would build the necessary grape trellis for the grapes to grow.

As agreed, fifty subsidiary trees designated under [harvestable crops] to produce grapes, in an area twelve acres wide, the rest of it just ordinary grape vines, boosted by mine and Trevor's growth mojo.

A wine industry in New Freeka. Fairly innovative of them, wanting to make high-value items for sale.

[Level up! You are now level 123.]

[Skill: Reinforce defensive structures obtained.]

Huh. How was that supposed to be a skill I learned at level 123? Sounded crappy.

YEAR 75, MONTH 6

The New Freeka inhabitants worked fast, using the grapes produced from the subsidiary trees. The first batch of wine had been made and was undergoing testing and tasting. One of the senior leaders was an old man who was apparently a wine connoisseur and had skills in [wine-making], [wine-ageing] and so on. With his abilities, wines aged three times faster and were more resistant to spoilage. The [timber farm] produced a few varieties of fragrant wood types, and these were usable as wine kegs. Apparently, they could imbue additional texture and taste to the wine.

Huh. I kinda felt sad that I was a tree now. When I was a programmer, I drank occasionally to feel better about my stagnant career.

Maybe I should get them to pour some on my roots. I might still taste some...

Though I doubted alcohol would have any effect on a tree.

YEAR 75, MONTH 6, WEEK 3

Thanks to booming New Freeka, they were now at almost fifteen thousand non-humans, and more were expected. There was now a constant flow of merchants, and so the first set of the wines were given to them free as "samples," for them to bring back to their hometowns and cities, hopefully to entice some nobles or wealthy merchants to support these products.

In either case, this burst of growth meant Jura could sell the loot collected, and the olive oil could be sold once ready—the benefits of an active market.

But we still didn't have enough money for the crystals to create the [root brain complex].

How could a tree game or manipulate the economic system of this world anyway?

YEAR 75, MONTH 7

With an additional two thousand normal trees added to the valley per month, I hit twenty thousand normal trees this month. Thanks to this, it also triggered Trevor gaining a skill called [Explosive Regeneration] that he could use once a month. It allowed for a sudden regrowth of an entire section of forest that had suffered damage. The valley's trees were getting denser and wider, but really, Trevor providing oversight allowed me to focus on the big picture stuff. It was kinda like that moment where you could delegate menial tasks that one didn't like to a robot.

The higher tree count also granted two additional artificial souls, but I had yet to think of what to do with them. I did have the biolab assistant idea, and going by the way Forest Mind helped tremendously in research, I suspected a biolab assistant might end up being an automated testing system—which was cool. It was like having a science officer reporting back with new stuff every now and then—kind of like those RTS games, where we would select something to research, pass a few turns...and *ping!*

"How about me?" Oh. Meela. I sometimes forgot she existed since she went to sleep often. Apparently, non-physical souls like herself had the option of putting themself into 'stasis' or a 'sleep mode.'

"You actively reject every idea I put to you, and you still ask me for opinions..." I could use a secretary, but Trevor might get jealous. Or could he? I frankly had not understood the degree of sentience these 'artificial souls' displayed.

"Because I really, really just like lazing around. I have done a whole lot of thinking, and this whole hero thing is bonkers. Maybe Max would be a hero given the choice again, but me, no."

"You have a sense of good and evil, do you not?" The gods selected her, so...she had to. Or maybe the hero power kind of messed with her mind a bit. It wasn't beyond the god's ability to cause her to feel a strong compulsion to fight evil...

"That's because of my upbringing. I had great parents, but driving myself into doing hero things, all this fighting demons and monsters...no. I would rather be a bartender or an artist. Alexis would have been a teacher or a scientist."

"Too bad she's dead. Too bad they are all dead."

"Ah yeah." Meela made a noise that made me think she was frowning. "I wonder whether the rest of them... Where are they?"

"If they had a similar experience to you, maybe their souls are still drifting around."

Meela paused. "What?"

"I mean, your soul got shredded and damaged so badly that you couldn't even move on to the next world. And somehow, you followed the familiars here... Your friends were there with you, so it would not be strange if their souls got shredded, too—don't you think so? Because they have no real attachment to this world, maybe they ended up just...floating around or something."

This posed some interesting thoughts about the nature of the fragments I received when these heroes died. What exactly was I getting when I got the fragments? Their soul or something of an 'attachment' or 'extension' of their soul?

"Hmm..." Meela's spirit bobbed around in the soul realm. She did that when she was bothered about something.

"What are you thinking?" I asked.

"Can you make an altar?" she replied.

"An altar?"

"Yes, yes. An altar."

"Uh...okay."

I later had the elves do it since my ability to manipulate stone and rock was fairly limited.

It was a simple one, created next to the site of the Tree of Prayer. Essentially, it was just a flat rock, like a prayer or offering table, with a few rocks stacked on top of each other into a...totem?

"Is there a priest amongst the refugees?" she asked.

"Huh. Where are you going with this?"

"I met a priest once who said that it was possible to offer a prayer to the souls of those still wandering, to lighten their load, to send them...away. I'm hoping to pray to my friends' souls, so they find solace and peace, so they...they go peacefully."

"Huh."

I relayed the request to Jura, and Jura then asked Yvon. They needed some time though as there were a lot of new refugees, and they didn't have a register of their respective skills.

"You want to pray so they can move on, eh?" I asked.

"Yeah. That's the least I can do, to help them along, no? They are my friends; I wouldn't want to see their souls stuck wandering this stupid, war-crazy world anyway."

"War-crazy, eh?"

"You don't think so?" Meela sighed. Somehow, I heard that, even though she was a floating light. "I didn't realize it when I was alive, but...this world is obsessed with fighting."

"An output of the world they live in. Demons, monsters... If your world had creatures like this, you would invent weapons to kill them, too."

"I wish it wasn't so."

"Bet plenty of people do, too."

Other than that, the refugees were doing surprisingly well. With the first crates of wine sent out for deliveries, it seemed they were making good progress on winemaking. I had to give them credit for their entrepreneurial spirit, making such goods.

The stalemate with the dungeon continued, but if the refugees asked for help again, I was gonna ask them to help raid the damn dungeon. They could keep the loot, for the money, but I wanted the core. I had actually yet to decide what to do if I got it, but I knew I wanted it.

Lausanne followed Jura everywhere these days, and even though Jura was initially reluctant to take her as his apprentice, her persistence and cuteness somehow won over his old man's heart. He was aging, after all, and I supposed people mellowed as they aged.

"Tree-Tree..."

"Huh, yes." Jura jolted me out of my overhead valley vision. "Yes..."

"It's Lausanne."

"Oh. What about her?"

"She's...she's not talented, but she keeps trying."

"That's good." I liked hard work.

"No. It's bad."

"Eh? Why?"

Jura paused and walked a few steps around my main tree, took a deep breath, and then sat. "Combat or fighting requires talent. It is the way of the world. Learn to fight to your strength, not pursue an idol whom you can never match.

"Think about it. If you are good at fighting with a sword, you learn to fight with a sword. If you have talent to be a mage, you learn magic."

"Hmm..."

"What I am trying to say is...Lausanne's wasting her time by doing what she isn't naturally disposed to doing. But I don't know what else to teach her."

"That seems kind of fatalistic," Meela popped out and said to me. "Do people of this world believe that they should only hone their talents?"

Jura continued, unaware of Meela's comment. "Maybe I can test her for other things and teach her self-defense, but perhaps she is best suited for...more non-combat chores, like her mother..."

"Ew." Meela groaned.

"So, Tree-Tree, can you talk her out of her silly dream of becoming a hero? She may lose her life pointlessly pursuing a dream that is...erm...futile."

"..."

"Isn't she too young? How does one know of talent?" I retorted.

"In most societies, by the age of six it is already possible to identify what one is talented in. And in Lausanne's case, she's displaying a total lack of talent for fighting."

I didn't like this conversation. At all.

"Please, Tree-Tree. I'm trying to look out for her, so I think she needs to find something else to do. Something with a better use of her time. One doesn't teach a fish to fly or a bird to swim. Lausanne's trying, and I too admire that hard work, but it'll set her on a path she is not meant to walk."

Really.

"I'll...I'll think about it."

I felt terrible even saying it, but I wanted to speak to Lausanne first, even though she was just a child. I wanted to hear her thoughts, and I thought it wasn't right, just because one wasn't talented, it didn't mean one couldn't pursue their dreams. But I did recognize Jura's comment, that if she was classed in a way that didn't fit her natural abilities, that was a bad thing as well.

"What do you think, Meela?"

"No. The girl has the right to do whatever she wants."

"Even if she can do better elsewhere?"

"Yes. And can't you help her along?"

When Lausanne returned home later that evening, I spoke to her as she lazed on her bed. She had her own bed now that Brislach and Wahlen had moved to New Freeka, where they found work.

"Lausanne?"

"Ah, Tree-Tree!" She rolled over and squeezed a bolster.

"How's your training going with Uncle Jura?"

"It's hard! But I like it!"

"Really? Do you ever wonder if you should be doing something else?"

"You're really asking her?" Meela poked in.

"I like it. I want to be a hero that can save everybody! A hero must know how to fight so I can protect everyone!" Did Lausanne's experience with the reincarnated heroes spawn this desire to be a hero? Was it because she still didn't fully comprehend the nature of the heroes' divine gift?

"I see..." I chickened out. I just didn't have it in me to tell her to stop.

Was this my idealism that would somehow cross with the reality and cruelty of this world?

"Good. Encourage her!"

"Ah...is that not making it worse? Maybe she will realize as she grows older. This is perhaps a phase."

Meela stopped. "Y-you're kicking this problem down the road."

"Look, we don't know what the future holds. Maybe Jura is right, but maybe he is not." I thought it was too early to tell.

"He's wrong."

"Maybe. I hope so. But what if he isn't?" This world could be...brutal. And mistakes were costly.

"She's six. I didn't know what I wanted when I was six."

Lausanne leaned back. "You know, Uncle Jura says I should learn how to do other things. And I think he is also right. Do you think there's a way I can learn everything? But Mommy say I should not be greedy."

I paused.

Meela paused, too, and after a brief moment, she laughed.

"She's right. Do you have any skills that do that?"

"Hmm...maybe my [Dream Tutor]?"

"Then it's settled!"

The little episode I had with the dream tutor also led me to wonder whether I could fuse an artificial soul and dream tutor, thereby creating a teacher-type character. Of course, I only had a few slots, and if anything, I had to think about them carefully since I was unlikely to be able to upgrade the rootnet as quickly to support the higher normal tree energy transfer, even though I could still grow the trees without any inhibitions.

So much to think about.

I wondered whether trees losing their leaves was a result of overthinking.

"A dungeon raid."

"Yeah," Yvon explained. The group gathered was about a hundred and fifty strong, comprising of the best fighters, mages, and healers the entirety of the valley had to offer, even Jura, who after some convincing, finally agreed to participate.

Even adventurers were not spared from the whole non-human eviction notice. Salah wasn't taking chances—all non-humans, no buts, no exceptions.

In a way, adventurers had it better than the other refugees since their skills were needed everywhere, and some neighboring nations were willing to accept non-human adventurers into their lands. They were skilled, mobile, usually self-sufficient, and were already somewhat nomadic, so this eviction hardly stung. If there was one less country, there were still many others.

"Are you our employer, Mistress Yvon?"

Yvon paused... "I guess you can say so. Our goal is simple. Grab the dungeon core, and if we can't, destroy it. The dungeon core, whether whole or broken, as you know, is worth a fair bit of money, and it will help us with our truce obligations."

The gathered fighters chattered, prepping themselves for the raid, and then off they went into the dungeon.

I had no idea what was happening from the moment they went inside, but I waited, my beetles outside in case anything happened.

To be fair, I couldn't do anything if shit went down inside, but hey, I could cover them externally. Dungeons, from what I sensed, had similar 'space distortion' abilities like I did, so just because I had them 'surrounded,' it didn't actually mean they were.

So, in a way, all I could do was pray.

A full day and a half later, I got a ping via Bamboo.

"Master, the dungeon core has been obtained, but the dungeon-space is crumbling." It seemed that after the dungeon core had been dislodged from the dungeon itself, the barrier that shielded the dungeon from the space beyond disappeared, hence why Bamboo was able to then telepathically communicate with me.

"How much time do you guys have?"

"No idea. We might be trapped in here."

"Oh, no, you're not."

The entrance to the dungeon vibrated and shook like an earthquake was happening.

"Are they going to die inside?" Meela seemed worried.

"How far in are you guys?"

"It's a lot deeper than expected. It'll take us at least three hours to get out of the main chamber."

No. This wasn't going to work. At the rate the dungeon was crumbling, they wouldn't make it. *Hmm. What can I do, what can I do?*

Ah.

[Rootnet attempting to connect to dungeon-space.]

"Trevor, help me out here."

"Yes, sire. Synchronizing roots into the walls…"

With the dungeon core out of the way, the invisible barrier preventing me from spawning [subsidiary tree] within the dungeon's area of influence and entrance was also gone, so I spawned a few trees next to the entrance, and on top of it, and I guided my roots into the dungeon.

It sort of worked.

As the roots mixed in with the walls that were crumbling, it seemed the roots were taking over the distorted spaces, giving it the stability it needed.

[Energy draining. Passageways reinforced.]

It seemed some of the energy generated by my normal trees and subsidiary trees was being used to support this additional dungeon-space. It felt like a magically supported structure, centered around the dungeon core, which drew additional energy from the space and also the ley line beneath it. Now that centerpiece had suddenly disappeared, so it was as if an electrical circuit was without electricity and, oddly enough, I was coming in as the 'backup' power source.

"The vibration is stopping," Bamboo pinged, and as my roots reached deeper and deeper into the dungeon, I soon crossed paths with the escaping adventurers.

"The walls…" Yvon said. I could now hear her as my roots now covered the entirety of the labyrinth.

Dead. There were dead bodies. Adventurers, not all had survived. As they streamed past, I saw some carrying the injured, some carrying the dead.

"My roots can now extend into the labyrinth. You guys can calm down now." I spoke to Jura directly as he came into range. He was fine, bleeding in some places, but relatively speaking, he was unscathed.

He immediately slowed down and told everyone that the

tree spirit's roots were now stabilizing the dungeon, and so it would not collapse.

And with that, they took the chance to turn back and retrieve the rest of the bodies for a proper burial.

Yvon, too, had gotten her hand on the dungeon core, which she would let me examine in my [biolab] first before she arranged for a sale on the magical artifacts market.

[New structure obtained: Root Dungeon.]
[Root dungeon: leftovers of a dungeon that happens to be stabilized by the roots of a tree spirit. Doesn't spawn monsters or loot.]

[New skill obtained: Root-tunnels.]

[Root tunnels, as the name suggests, are tunnels made from roots. Good for smuggling, transporting, storage, and hiding.]

Sadly, the dungeon core was unscannable in my [biolab]. It was a biolab, not an everything-lab, so dungeon cores didn't register. Oh, well.

Anyway, that wasn't the purpose of me getting the dungeon core. That was the prize for Yvon's group, as they would get to sell it. Of course, the agreement was such that some of the proceeds went to the treefolk, centaurs, and then Jura, who also contributed to the expedition.

The objective for me was the ley line.

And so, with a few subsidiary trees now above the ley line, I extended my roots down, attempting to reach for that ley line. It was my first exposure to a ley line, so I didn't really know what to expect, but according to Wisp, it was some kind of fourth dimension thing, so it popped up in places, disappeared, and then popped up elsewhere, still part of the same 'line.' Every time it popped up, the things in its way would then be influenced by it, thus forming things like dungeon cores. The dungeon cores would then 'anchor' the aether line, such that they didn't move elsewhere, though what was more likely to happen, was that a new dungeon core would often re-appear nearby.

[Ley line connection initiated.]

I felt instantly dizzy. It was as if I had drunk a whole keg of alcohol, and the entirety of its punch just hit me in one go. Was this magic intoxication?

"Yes..." Wisp popped in. "At least you didn't knock yourself out yet. Then again, you are quite high level, so this is to be expected."

[Ley line connected. The subsidiary trees above the ley line are merging... The three subsidiary trees have merged into a Special Structure - [ThreeTrees of Mana].]

[ThreeTrees of Mana].

[Created when one subsidiary tree couldn't handle the energy of a ley line, so three of them merged. An artifact of the ley line, this structure serves as the 'conduit' of the ley line, so protect it as it is your connection to the ley line, in place of the dungeon core. Serves no other function.]

ThreeTrees. *Did the skill just do what I think?* And, seriously, why did they make that tree so...visible? It was like a big blue tree growing out of nowhere, telling everyone of its presence.

Come on, first the ginseng tree, now this. The system was trying to paint me as a target. Or was this some kind of subliminal messaging saying that trees were always targets, and we should always protect them?

"Uh..." I felt the dizziness slowly drain away from me, and my mind started to regain its senses. Then, even more updates!

Ley lines were awesome after all.

[Due to the additional energy types supplied, [Soul Forge - Black unlocked].]

[Soul Forge - Black allows for the conversion of undead spirits back into regular souls, reversing the effects of necromancy and the removal of the dark energies of a soul.]

[Additional repairs of damaged souls now possible.]

[Creation of Soul Harvesters now possible.]

[Soul Harvesters.]

[Some call them the grim reaper, some refer to them as Valkyries. These are traveling collectors of souls. They extend your soul harvesting reach and can be directed to specific places, such as battlefields and graveyards to collect souls. Souls collected have a higher chance of containing 'transferable experience.']

[Due to the presence of two colors, the following fused abilities are now available.]

[Nightmare collectors.]

[A special ghost type that steals nightmares.]

[Memory collection.]

[Using the dark arts, a small percentage of memories of the dead will be converted into skill essences.]

I was already losing the leaves on my branches thinking about so many things, and now I had more to think about. First of all, the [Soul Forge] had different color types, which supplied different abilities. I had blue and now black, and that was like pure control deck archetype, wasn't it? But I was a tree...so did that make me...a blue-black-green deck?

Anyway, it was time to ignore that little snippet about trading cards.

How many colors were there? If I was to hazard a guess, the black came from the fact that this was specifically an undead dungeon, so there was probably some linkage. If I went to the volcano, would I get red? And in a magical glade or something, would I get green?

That was another thing to add to the to-do list.

Next was to further repair Meela's soul. This second repair didn't do much, other than allow her to stay awake and active more often. Also, I was really tempted to fuse her soul with a soul harvester. She'd be a Valkyrie! Or a ghost! But she said no, though she promised to think about it.

She should be a nightmare collector then. Kinda like that *Saw* guy, no? Or was that the guy with the spiky nails? Once again, she vehemently rejected the idea.

"I'm a cute little girl. I ain't becoming your haunted ghost."

"But cute little girls make the best scary ghosts!" I pleaded.

YEAR 75, MONTH 9

The month started with rain. Rather heavy rain, though it was nothing damaging as there was natural drainage within the valley itself. As the clouds dumped water into the valley, the roots rejoiced. The trees all craved water, so the roots lapped it all up. The water released was absorbed by the growing number of normal trees and subsidiary trees, and it sated, for a moment, the valley's ever-increasing demand for water.

For New Freeka, they had to work harder. Yvon and team had to quickly repair and setup additional drainages. They had expanded so quickly to accommodate the large quantities of housing that the existing drainage was just not adequate. Flooding occurred in a few spots, but with some construction-type magic, temporary drainages could be built rather quickly.

The centaurs had some tents run off in the sudden downpour. Because they lived on hills and slopes, they were trading off flooding for mudslides and rockslides.

Even so, a few of the refugees drowned due to the sudden flash floods. There was nothing like a bit of death and destruction to teach a lesson about infrastructure planning, as morbid as that sounded.

And after the event, there was usually some kind of death ceremony, a burial or cremation, or for the first time, I witnessed a real oddity—the death ceremony of a treefolk, where the treefolk was cut up into many pieces...and served as a kind of soup, for the kin to consume.

"For our loved ones live forever in us and as a part of us. We are treefolk, and we carry the memories and lives of those who passed away before us."

Strange, but I supposed the ceremonial, ritualistic aspect of life was very much well preserved.

Lately, I had been getting more...prayers. It was similar to the conversations I used to have in Freeka, with the elves, where they would come and sit next to me and talk. It had to do with the [tree of prayer] and their belief that [soul trees] were a way of communion with their ancestors, gods, or whoever they worshiped.

So, in some societies, a [soul tree], a [shamanic totem], or a [spiritual rock] had a similar function as a church or temple— like some kind of merger between druid beliefs and conventional religion.

"Oh, tree, oh, tree, make me rich, and make me free."

Huh, a refugee praying for money. As if the trees had the power to grant someone a fortune.

"Actually, you do have some limited power to do so," Wisp interjected, and I brushed him off. I wasn't going to make somebody rich. Otherwise, I'd have people praying to me for winning lottery tickets.

"Oh, tree, oh, tree, let me be free of my stupid husband."

Ah...one of those. Did I have powers over domestic happiness?

"In some ways, if you are creative, you do!"

Damn it, Wisp.

"Oh, tree, oh, tree, make us safe and stop all of this running. Let us find a home, where we can live in peace of the rest of our lives."

The common prayer of refugees, sick of running away, and looking for a final place to stay. I totally sympathized. I recalled being evicted as a tenant, and that was a horrible experience.

"Oh, tree, oh, tree, kill the humans. Kill those who make us go through this suffering."

Ah, the vengeful, too. Such was the anger from those who lost their families or friends. Vengeance was a common prayer topic. After all, refugees all had plenty of grievances from the experiences they went through.

And my [Tree of Prayer] responded to such energy, absorbing some of it and converting it into [Essence of Mercy], [Essence of Hope], [Essence of Anger], and [Essence of Vengeance], and in doing so, it also helped to reduce that anger and emotion in those who prayed. That said, the rate of conversion was really low. Perhaps as it was just a prayer, the energy within that prayer was minimal.

Or maybe the absorption ratio improved as I leveled up this skill. Who knew? Maybe I should consider merging a [Tree of Prayer] with an [Artificial Soul]. Maybe that would create a [Tree-priest].

This month, the traders also brought in news about Salah, concerning their ongoing wars with the Nung and Takde Kingdoms.

Salah was winning, and so Nung and Takde had now formed a coalition, with possibly other nations that had historical grievances with Salah. Of course, in Salah's eyes, this was treated as an escalation, and Salah was now trying to get its own allies in, so there were hints of a bigger regional conflict brewing. If additional nations joined the war, New Freeka might end up being right smack in the middle of the war, instead of being on the other end of the battlefield.

This was of little concern to me. If Salah got owned in a battle, that wasn't my problem. But this news worried Yvon, so she and her council scrambled to send people to all the nearby nations to declare some kind of neutrality toward this conflict.

New Freeka, as a young nation, was still trying to comply with its truce terms and safeguard its new citizens. It was deeply concerned with any disruption to its growing trade and food supply.

Personally, my ideal outcome was for the battles to be fought around me, without affecting me, such that I gained the souls from all this...conflict.

But this conflict also exposed the [ThreeTrees of Mana]—as in it was a big blue 'shoot me' sign in the area. It was huge, it was obvious, and it did nothing else. It was also quite far from me, as that was where the ley line was...

At that moment, I was uncertain whether anyone would react to the presence of the [ThreeTrees of Mana]. Perhaps the nearby nations would ignore it. Perhaps they would think it was some kind of strategic asset and seize it...or anything, really.

So, if a conflict did happen, protecting the ThreeTree would also be something I needed to do. If the nations turned hostile, defending it was my priority.

Theoretically speaking, the location of the ThreeTrees of Mana was already contested territory. Abandoned during the previous demonic battles, its last owner was the kingdom of Salah, but historically, that plot of land had changed owners a few times. Unlike the valley of Freeka, which was somewhat legally under the truce arrangement, a part of this new nation of New Freeka.

Even if Yvon managed to get some kind of neutrality declared for the valley, that neutrality would likely not extend to this newly claimed area of mine. In fact, it might even be seen as a hostile act from New Freeka in claiming that dungeon. So I might have invalidated the truce already!

But I would not part with the ley line. That was a fact, so if a battle did pop up, I would defend it, and unfortunately for the New Freekans, I would have to drag them into the battle if I had to.

Ah, there were so many moving variables, though...so many ifs. If only I had eyes and ears in all the nearby nations...

Hah.

"You're overthinking." Meela popped up, poking her head into my thoughts.

"Why? I'll end up dragging the refugees into battle...which is bad for them. So I should be thinking about what to do next carefully, no?"

"It hasn't happened yet, right?"

"That's not how I see it." Not planning for things was how I got into trouble the last time. I should do better, right?

"I think you're getting a bit too into that whole long-termist tree thinking."

"Uh, and that's wrong because?"

"Uh...how about the here and now?"

"It is just reality that I have to plan a bit more into the future. I'm a tree. I can't just wing it."

I also discovered that Meela had experienced some changes from the additional repair in the [Soul Forge - Black]. She gained a bit more 'awareness' of my thoughts, and to some extent, she knew what I was thinking. It was unnerving as I didn't enjoy having my mind read. She denied it anyway. She just said she had a very good innate sense of what my thoughts were, but she wasn't reading my mind.

But all souls got their minds read...a little. According to Wisp, a soul tree could very well read and rummage through the memories of the souls that passed through it, if certain conditions and abilities were met, and this exchange was...mutual. Of course, for most souls, this didn't really matter because when they reincarnated, they forgot them. Heroes, however, retained their memories, and if they carried knowledge of a soul tree into their next life, that made them rather...dangerous. Frankly, the mechanism was still confusing. Apparently, some reincarnation gods would wipe the memories clean, but some didn't.

Someday, if I met Mozart again, I needed to ask him about this memory wipe thing. How did it even work?

Ah.

"Meela, so, what would you do? If this war happens, my ley line is under threat."

"Fight them off, then."

"So, you agree with me."

"No. How does anyone know that bunch of trees is related to New Freeka anyway? Most people can't even tell two trees apart!"

Meela's spirit bobbed around and twirled.

"So, act as if the two sides are separate, unrelated camps," she continued. "Find a way to delink the two, visually. If they look different, nobody's gonna suspect the two tree groups are related. Don't you have some kind of ability to make it as if they look different...or you don't? Perhaps a [Camouflage] or [Illusion] skill? And do you have a way to remove the straight line of subsidiary trees, so that it's not so...erm...obvious?"

I paused. That was a good idea. "When were you this smart? You've always given me the happy but slightly mentally retarded hero girl impression."

"Uh. I'm a designated reincarnated 'hero.' I get like super-boosts to my intelligence stats."

"Really!"

"Yes! Apparently, all heroes get like 'tactical genius' as a perk."

Really, that sounded like rubbish. I didn't recall them being tactically smart at all, and in fact, they often relied on their cheat ability to get themselves out of tough situations.

"You sure don't act like it all the time."

Meela pouted. "Okay, I lied, there's no such perk! But I mean, I can think if I want to. We're not exactly idiots."

"Then?"

"That's me rejecting the need to work hard and refusing to think too hard through my solutions. I live life with the Pareto theory. If twenty percent effort is sufficient to get an eighty percent score, I'll do it, and I'll leave the eighty percent effort for fun stuff. Anything that pops up, I wing it with my natural talent and ability."

Mental slap, please.

"I mean, that's the best you can do," she concluded. "Cut the connection, and if they are under attack, defend it. They might not even pay attention, and the location of the battle might not even be there, and you've just prepared for nothing. So do what you can and then don't worry about it."

"Fair, fair. Are you still considering my offer as a secretary?"

"No."

"Trevor, did you catch Meela's suggestion? Are you able to alter the look of the forests around the ThreeTrees of Mana?"

"Yes, sire. The energy and mana from the ThreeTrees of Mana contain certain specific aesthetic variations—courtesy of the [Soul Forge - Black]—that we can apply to the florae in that locality."

"Good, next is, how about...hiding the line of trees that link this valley to the ley line?"

"We can create subsidiary trees that are mostly hidden underground like a kind of small tuberous plant, with only a small shrub appearing above. That way, while there is still a portion of trees that are above ground and can be spotted, they would not stick out as obvious, and they could be easily disguised by a thick overgrowth of other shrubs and weeds. But the trade-off is that they lose their customizable branches function, and our line of sight in that area would be significantly reduced."

"Well, it's worth it, I think, so do it." Ah, things were going smoothly!

"Yes, Sire. As you command."

"Wisp, your turn. Are we able to merge an artificial soul with the [ThreeTrees of Mana]?" The logic of me doing this was simple. If it could level up, it would be stronger and with some sentience, so then ThreeTrees could defend itself better.

"No. That is actually a connection with your [Soul Forge - Black], so you cannot merge it. It's like a forge trying to forge itself."

That made sense. "Fine, so I need some kind of defensive unit at that location then…"

I turned to Meela.

"Since you have so much to say…mind being some kind of defender?"

"I like talking with you, so no thanks. I like being here a lot more."

"Come on, you're the best! Besides, you can still talk to me—"

"Master!" Trevor and Horns both butted in.

"Yes?"

"Riders spotted on the horizon, heading toward us at high speed. They will probably close in on the treefolk village soon. They all have a rather significant magical presence."

Ah, how strange. It was as if they advertised that they were powerful mages, so I hovered over to check them out as they passed by some of the subsidiary trees.

"How far is it?" I heard them say, riding. It was a group of five, all on horseback.

"No idea, but its ahead."

"The horses are exhausted, and I am out of [Vitality Restoration]."

"We'll arrive by nightfall. Hang in there, horses." One of them patted their horse, trying to encourage them to keep riding.

"Should we interfere?" Trevor asked.

"Wait. Watch." I didn't think they were hostile, at least, not yet.

They soon arrived at the forest, but the treefolk were not their focus. They headed straight to New Freeka and demanded to meet with their leaders. Were they some kind of magical emissary?

Thanks to a subsidiary tree right next to the meeting place, I could somewhat eavesdrop on the conversation.

"Hi, who are you people?" a man asked. He was one of Yvon's inner circle and one of those involved in the dungeon raid. He was armed and stood in front of the rest of them. He was the first to appear from the leader's house.

"We are representatives of the King of Baroosh. We come seeking a great healer, wizard, and magician to aid our ailing princess."

"Oh. There's no—" the man started to respond.

Yvon stepped ahead, signaling for the man to let them keep talking.

The Baroosh man, the leader of the five of them, continued. "The princess is gravely ill, and we seek the aid of the great healer to come to our capital and heal our princess."

"Yes, we heard that. But why would the great Baroosh come to our town in search of such a great healer? Surely, the great cities have far more talented mages, wizards, and priests..."

"Ah, I am afraid the disease our princess has is...unique. Our great oracle has had a vision that here lies the cure, the solution to that disease."

"I am afraid there is no such great healer here." Yvon shook her head. "You may ask every one of us if you don't take our word. You may walk and explore our town and knock from door to door, but we know not of any great healer or cure."

The man paused, perhaps thinking of some kind of retort. "Hmm...is that so? Never mind. May we rest in your town for a few days or weeks? Perhaps among the refugees are some hidden geniuses in the art of healing."

Yvon smiled. "Certainly, please do feel free to make use of our guesthouse."

Later in the guesthouse, the Baroosh men spoke. Once again,

courtesy of a conveniently placed [subsidiary tree], I could catch some of their conversation.

"Is she lying?"

"No. My [Truth Detection] didn't trigger, nor did my [Detect False Statements]. They are being honest when they say there are no great healers here."

"Hmmm. Maybe they don't know."

"Exactly. This place is a hive of refugees—so many that run here—easily a few thousand of them. Some of them may be hiding their talents, and the leaders know not of their talent."

"But Salah never had a great healer, either."

"Indeed. It is strange that the oracle guides us here."

"You know how oracles are, they will answer your question, but it may be because our question is not correct," one of the men said while munching on some potato salad. "Maybe it's a trick answer, and we need to look for something else."

"Whatever it is, we can't go back without the healer. We'll get our heads chopped off. We start our search for the healer after we rest tonight."

YEAR 75, MONTH 10

My ginseng tree got attacked by a flying creature. It pulled it out of the ground before a [Root Strike] struck its head. So, once again, I had to restart my ginseng tree. My constant failure to cultivate and protect my ginseng tree reminded me I still had a problem with airborne monsters. Maybe I could get flying leaves as a weapon, kinda like Pokémon.

Right?

Or maybe I could shoot seeds as a projectile like the rapid-fire machine gun in PvZ. I already had fruit bombs, so launchable fruits would turn them into fruit-artillery and fruit-flak cannons? Come on, system, give me something similar or a skill like that?

A fruit cannon. A seed cannon would be fine, too. Something to shoot at all these flying monsters that were starting to really bug me.

System? Give me a skill, please?

[Insect warrior variation unlocked: Web-trap Spiders.]

*[New customizable branch option: Web-trap spider nests. Home to 3
web-building spiders.]*

*[Web-building spiders have few direct combat abilities except for their
poisonous fangs, but they are able to build webs between your trees,
laced with paralyzing poisons, and build trapping cocoons.]*

Uh.

Not exactly what I wanted, but I supposed a spider able to build traps was still better than nothing, so I designated one.

A spider crawled out, and it was really rather tiny, about the size of a small dog. Each of the spiders could build and maintain three sets of webs, one branch had three spiders, and so there would be nine webs.

The first spider quickly demonstrated its ability, building a massive web between the branches and trees, about ten meters across and wide, and it counted as 'one' web. For anti-air, it wasn't exactly ideal, after all, if a dragon or something came up, a trap like this wasn't going to work, was it?

Ah, a tree couldn't decide which insects would live in it, so fine...webs and spiders.

"There's a spider!" Jura shouted and pulled out his sword. He had just come out of the hideout and was surprised to see a spider so near to the main tree. I guessed having a bunch of webs right above his head kinda shocked him, too.

"No. Stop. It's my minion."

"Really?"

"Yes."

"The girls are not going to like it. At least the beetles kind of look like giant armor, but this spider looks like a fuzzy...monster. And it's dark brown and black."

"I frankly didn't realize it was creepy."

"EEP!!!" Belle screamed when she, too, stepped out of the hideout and spotted the spider.

"It's one of my new...minions. They are...my anti-air defense."

"Can we not have them near here, at least?" Laufen too had come out after hearing Belle's screams.

Hmm...I mentally commanded the spiders to build their webs higher up, perhaps between the canopy layer of trees. That way they didn't come across the refugees or elves so often—except for the ginseng tree area, which I would cover in multiple layers of webs, just to prevent airborne monsters from pulling the tiny ginseng tree out of the ground again.

With that, the spiders hid away in the treetops, and the elves went on their way. Except Jura.

"Bamboo has been rather talkative lately since he hit level twenty and capped out."

"Oh, how is he?" I asked as a bear made of wood appeared next to Jura.

"I am fine, Master. I recently acquired this wood-form summon that allows me to take this rather weak form, but at least I can act independently."

"Yeah, he's been telling me about having to 'upgrade' from an eidolon to unlock more powers..."

"Yes, Master Tree-Tree." Bamboo approached and stood next to the [Forge Tree]. As he did, a prompt appeared.

[Bamboo, Woodbear Eidolon, has reached his level cap. To upgrade (i.e. to Level 30), the following options are available:]

[Blue - Armor path - 50 small copper ingots & 5 medium red rubies needed.]

[Black - Claw path - 50 small iron ingots & 5 medium onyx needed.]

Ah.

For artificial souls, they started off with a level twenty cap, and if I had a single-color [Soul Forge], I could unlock one upgrade—i.e., level thirty. Each extra color increased the upgrade by one, so, if I had all the necessary resources, I could upgrade twice to level forty.

It seemed the colors of the [Soul Forge] represented something lacking in the artificial souls. Each color added an effect and made a more 'robust' artificial soul.

"Tree-Tree?"

"I'm afraid we need to acquire some resources to do this. Can you get five medium red rubies and five medium onyx and a lot of copper ingots?"

Jura paused. "Is this like the blood crystal thing?"

"Yes. Where are you on that, anyway?" Ah, yes, Trevor also needs an upgrade. All three of my first artificial souls had reached their level cap.

"It's being shipped here. After the dungeon raid, I'd gotten enough money to buy it, but the trader said the supplier was really far away, so it will take some time. Maybe next month we'll get it."

"Fine then. Are the visitors bothering you?" I asked.

"Yeah. They seem to be looking for some great healer or some great magical cure, but we don't know of any. But they are still here, claiming that their oracle never lies."

"Should we be afraid of them?" Lausanne then popped out, asking the question of Jura.

"Well, not really. But Baroosh is one of the larger kingdoms around—at the same level as Salah—so they are a respectable force. Making allies of them would be ideal for Yvon and gang, but we really don't have healers to offer." Jura's response was actually meant for the elves, but it was also an education for me because the names of all these nations did tend to slip by me.

YEAR 75, MONTH 11, WEEK 2

A great battle broke out in the conflict between Takde, Nung, and Salah, and a great, cursed spell was cast—one that sacrificed the lives of twenty-five thousand soldiers and with it, created an exceptionally harsh winter in that area...and beyond.

The spell was so powerful that it summoned a vortex, a magical vortex of ice and frost, and then the region transformed into a snow-covered land, one of blizzards, snowstorms, and strong gusts of wind.

That spell extended to the entirety of the valley, overnight, from what was normally a light rain, into snow and ice. Thick snow. A terrible cold snap. A few of the smaller streams even froze over.

This stunted the growth of the region's crops, already reeling from the earlier mild winter.

Everyone was prepared for winter, so a huge stockpile was already here. New Freeka's efforts to vastly expand their farmlands and crop cultivation meant they were facing this intense cold with at least a few warehouses and silos full of harvested, preserved vegetables and grain. What was meant to be their solution to a migrant surge became a solution for an exceptionally bad winter, though I wondered how long this stockpile would last.

Since it was a great battle, I figured there must have been a lot of death, a lot of souls still lingering in the battlefield, so I decided to send my many soul harvesters there. They were like faint ghosts, and so they could travel really far, but it would take a while for them to come back. With the soul harvesters, they expanded the range of my soul absorption to almost the entire continent, which was massive.

Massive!

Also, the group from Baroosh expanded, after about two weeks.

"I am disappointed, Apprentice." A wizard stepped through the portal, escorting the sick princess and followed by a healer and a paladin. They were surprised by the sudden cold, but they came well prepared and put on thick jackets and shawls. I supposed their princess had waited a bit too long.

"My sincere apologies, Teacher. We have tried to ask every single one here, and yet we couldn't find one that we think has potential. That's why we asked the oracle whether the healer had moved or gone away."

"Excuses." The wizard was old, had flowing white, wrinkly hair, and, I noted, also a typical wizard's hat with a pointy tip.

The man bowed and didn't respond.

The princess followed behind. She had a very faint presence, and her steps were soft and light, the healer supporting her every step and movement. I also noticed the healer using some kind of potion on her, at regular intervals, especially when she started shivering.

The wizard talked with the existing group for a while and then stopped.

"Well, let's find that healer." He cast a strange magical spell, and then from a small metal case, a magical arrow appeared and spun in circles. It kept on spinning, even pointing downward at times.

The wizard then paused and looked at the man. The man looked equally dumbfounded.

"This..." The wizard seemed stumped, and the paladin stepped up next to him.

"Wizard, what's the meaning of this?"

"This artifact is the Compass of Oracles, and it links and augments the oracle's ability so that we can locate whoever or whatever the oracle learns..."

"Get to the point, Wizard. Why is it flying everywhere?"

"I-I don't know." Yet the wizard's initial confusion turned into a strange smile. The earlier group looked puzzled.

"Whatever. It's cold. Let's continue this conversation indoors. The princess cannot take this weather for very long," the healer insisted, and they retreated to the warmth of their guesthouse.

"So...what's with this cold?" the healer asked as he tended to the frail princess in the guesthouse.

"Aftermath of the Salah wars. Someone used a great blizzard vortex spell, with blood sacrifice..."

The wizard, though, seemed laser focused, analyzing the Compass of Oracles. It still spanned everywhere.

"Any ideas, Wizard?" one of the men finally dared to ask.

"Maybe. Maybe the land is a nourishing factor. I will need to test it out."

"The land? This freezing place?"

The wizard ignored the man.

Next, the wizard ran outside and cast a few spells I couldn't quite identify or observe. He did that for a good half a day, constantly casting spell after spell, though nothing in particular seemed to be happening. At this point, I was feeling a little bit... defensive. A wizard had come to New Freeka and started using a whole bunch of spells...that felt a little too close for comfort, so I kept watch.

A group of high-powered people in search of something, casting weird spells? That was just ringing all the bells.

"That's really odd," the wizard mumbled.

"What's odd?" one of the men, who seemed to be the wizard's apprentice of some sort, asked as he came out to accompany his master.

"The readings and compass all point through this entire valley, and yet I don't detect any kind of magical presence from the earth—or is it muffled or suppressed somehow because of this stupid blizzard effect on the weather of this entire place?"

The apprentice shrugged and shook his head. "I did tell you this place is...rather unusual."

"That cannot be. Magic still flows in this entire valley, and yet there is something that also envelops this valley like a large piece of cloth hiding furniture..."

"If it is so, then the healer picked the best place to hide."

"No. I doubt the healer knows. There is more to this. Tell me, are there any magical structures? Is there a holy relic or artifact here?"

"You know, if you say it's the entire valley, that kind of reminds me. Some of the people here worship a tree, you know. Do you want to go and see it?"

The wizard nodded. "At this moment, there are few other leads. Let's go."

They braved the snowstorm, that was almost perpetual now, to go to the [Tree of Prayer], the courtyard now coated in a layer of white snow, which actually wasn't the only color of snow, surprisingly. In some parts of the world, there was a kind of magical aberration that turned snow into different colors—like green, blue, yellow, or purple. Anyway, I digressed.

"So this is the tree they pray to," the apprentice said.

The wizard then cast a spell. [Detect Magic].

And nothing happened.

"Hmm..."

Next, the wizard paused and cast [Fire Spark] at the Prayer Tree.

Again, nothing happened.

"There's a hostile magic suppression aura here. It's present throughout the entirety of the valley, and that's why a few of my spells seem to be not responding, particularly those of the probing type," the wizard explained to the apprentice.

"But it is no denser here, so I doubt this tree is the source of it."

"Huh, maybe that's because the tree is everywhere." The apprentice shrugged. "I hear the locals say the entire forest belongs to the tree that rules this valley, and entry would be at our own risk."

The wizard smacked the apprentice. "So that sounds exactly like where a healer would hide. Did you check out the forest?"

"Yes, we have, Master. There's just a whole load of trees and a lot of monsters."

Oh. Wait. At this point, their earlier conversation about magic suppression rang a bell.

Was that me? When I leveled up and unlocked the soul forge, I did get an ability called [Low-Tier Magic Suppression].

The wizard looked at the apprentice, shaking his head. "Anyway, let's do more tests on the type of suppression here, whether it is tier-restricted…"

He then cast [Fire]. Once again, nothing happened.

Then he cast [Blue Fire], and this time, a blue ball of flame appeared in his hands. "Hmm, tier-four spells are not suppressed."

"So, does this mean we can find the healer?"

"I think we already have a good clue. Whoever is powerful enough to create a tier-three suppression aura throughout this entire city is probably the one able to heal the princess, or they would at least know the person that can heal the princess."

Yup.

These guys were looking for me! Ah, so this was interesting; if that was indeed the case, I thought I could use this as a bargaining chip, and so I quickly summoned Jura to explain the plan.

And the next morning, despite the snow outside, Jura and Yvon went to the guesthouse.

"Oh, Lady Yvon, what brings you here?"

"Ah, I have good news for you all. I think we have finally discovered who the healer you were looking for is."

"Really? Have you been lying to us the past few weeks?" The apprentice wasn't happy.

Yvon shook her head. "I thought you were referring to a person."

"What—"

The wizard spoke over the apprentice. "Never mind that. The princess comes first. Bring us to the healer."

"Not so fast." Jura paused. "There are a few things the healer wants to know and wants from you before they are willing to have a look at your princess's condition."

"Name them. Quickly," the paladin and healer insisted. "The princess's condition worsens by the day."

Jura handed over a list I had him write. The paladin and healer looked it over and then passed it to the wizard. "This is extortion, isn't it?"

Jura smiled. I could tell he was enjoying this. "It's the terms the healer proposes, in exchange for his aid. You can choose not to. And he did say if he can't improve the princess's condition, he won't take payment."

"Fine. We'll give these things. Great powers don't come cheap, after all," the wizard said. "Bring the healer here."

"Good. But I am afraid you have to go to him."

All the Barooshians looked at each other, but then they nodded in acceptance. It wasn't as if they had a choice. So, together with the princess, all of them ventured out into the snow, making the slow walk through New Freeka and into the forest.

"Where are we going?" They clearly didn't like walking in the snow.

"We'll reach there soon. Anyway, what's the princess suffering from?"

"I am afraid...even I don't know. All we can do is keep supporting her body so she doesn't die." The healer shook his head. "It's almost as if her body wants to kill itself."

Soon, they arrived at my main tree, where the beetles and spiders were sleeping, dormant.

"Eh..."

"Wait." The wizard turned to Jura. "A spirit tree?" It was as if he was struck by a realization.

"Yes. This spirit tree rules over the entire valley."

The wizard nodded in understanding. "That explains why the compass is confused... I am guessing this massive spirit tree extends its roots everywhere."

"Bring the princess inside," Jura said, ignoring the question.

The healer carried the princess, and Jura then stopped the rest of them from entering. "I'm afraid I can only allow the healer into the tree from here. The rest of you must wait outside. The tree's rules."

The wizard paused and looked at the paladin, and the rest of them nodded. "Fine. I can trust a spirit tree." And so, the frail princess was escorted into the [biolab].

Once I started examining the princess using the biolab, it was immediately apparent what her problem was.

As with all living beings with mana, there was a spring in their body, and in the princess's case, that spring was almost entirely destroyed. That spring appeared like a regular fountain to most, but the princess's spring was charred and dark, and the structure around it had somehow turned into rubble. There was still some mana flowing out, but it was irregular, inconsistent, and at times even corrupted. And when the corrupted mana flowed out, it interacted with the body and created a rotting effect.

It was as if the tap that supplied water to a body was broken, and because of that, while there was water flowing out, it was polluted water, and that polluted water 'poisoned' the body.

The body tried to fight back against that corrupted mana, and as a result, her body turned blue, kind of like a mana-gangrene.

So I looked deeper. My biolab was of a higher level now, so I got more visibility, tools, and even pop-ups to explain what I was looking at.

"She did something forbidden, or perhaps not her level to do." Wisp somehow popped up. "All this points to an attempt to summon a higher power."

"Oh?"

As I looked into the spring, a small indicator appeared. *[Outer-shell destroyed.]*

"Huh. Outer shell destroyed?" This seemed to mean she was like the reverse of an artificial soul, or perhaps similar to how Meela was previously. A regular soul comprised of an inner and outer layer, whereas an artificial soul was only the outer layer. So she had somehow managed to destroy her entire outer layer?

Hmmm... That was really strange, and I asked Jura to ask the men what the princess had done.

"The Spirit Tree wants to know what the princess did. She has somehow destroyed a large part of her soul..."

The wizard and healer seemed really shocked, and they turned to each other. The healer started first. "The princess was last spotted in the wizard's tower. What was she doing?"

The wizard stared back. "I...I don't know. She was going through the ancient tomes and then..."

At the same time, as I kept looking into the princess's body, I discovered another thing. Exposed to Void mana.

"What the hell is void mana?"

"Oh, I can answer that one. It's raw mana form. Primordial mana, so to speak. It's the most powerful of mana types, but...it is also the most dangerous. The normal body of a mortal is not fit to handle void mana. Even heroes can only handle it in small degrees. That's why they only get the second-tier form—star mana. If one distills and processes star mana further, one would then get the normal kinds of mana."

Heh, this sounded like the big bang, then the formation of stars, and then the heavier elements? If mana was an element that existed in the birth of the universe, it was akin to primordial quarks, and then they would form protons, neutrons, and electrons, and those would then fuse into regular atoms.

"This surely begs the question, why would this princess somehow be exposed to void mana?"

"Ask them what was in the tome that the princess was studying," I mentally spoke to Jura.

The wizard paused. "I think she was looking into a tome on..."

He stopped.

"I don't think it's relevant. Can the tree heal her or not?"

The healer and paladin turned to face the wizard. "I think it is relevant. What was the princess actually trying to do?"

"She might have been looking at a tome about otherworld heroes...and theories on how to summon them. It was one of the crazy tomes left by the Mad-Hero, Arsene Emir..."

The paladin then grabbed the wizard's hand. "What? Why was the princess allowed to be anywhere near a tome by the mad hero?"

"I was doing research on it, and I didn't realize the princess had snuck in."

"Excuses! So all this was your fault, Wizard!" The paladin was mad.

I let the Barooshians continue their argument as I turned my attention into figuring out what I could do about this princess's damaged soul.

The [Soul Forge] would be able to fix most of the destroyed outer layer, but the exposure to void mana was going to be harder to remove. In a way, it was like Meela's [demon poison], but only from another source, a rawer source.

It took about another hour, but I had looked at all I could, so Jura and the healer helped to carry the princess to the forge tree. She rested on a platform inside the forge tree, and once ready, both Jura and the healer had to go back outside.

As I attempted to repair her damaged soul, I got a prompt that some personal items belonging to the princess needed to be sacrificed.

"Does the princess have any...items or personal belongings that she cherishes?"

The paladin took out a small hairpin and passed it to Jura. Jura then threw it into the forge tree.

Not enough.

"Another one."

The paladin checked his backpack, and the healer checked a bag that contained the princess's, pulling out a small comb. "Her mother, the queen, gave her the comb."

And into the forge tree it went.

The logic of it was essentially, to repair a soul, especially one still in a bodily form, one would need to 'harvest' remnants of the person's soul that were sometimes residing in their cherished items to then use them to patch the soul. It was like soul-organ-transplant surgery but with personal belongings, unlike Meela's case, who wasn't constrained by a body any longer.

So the quality and relationship one had with the item determined the value for the repair. And the comb qualified. In fact, the comb itself was sufficient, so the hairpin flew back out.

"The comb itself will do."

After it was melted by the [Soul Forge], it then fused into the princess's body. And while a snowstorm blew outside, in the immediate vicinity of the [forge tree], multiple lightning bolts rained down on the forge tree itself, each creating a connection of lightning to a branch.

"This is rather scary," one of the men commented outside.

"I've never seen anything like it." The men, waiting in the

snow, were watching lightning strike the forge tree multiple times whilst their princess was inside.

About an hour later, Jura and the healer went back inside the forge tree to retrieve the princess, putting her back into the [biolab] for monitoring.

Under the [biolab], the spring itself had been repaired. But an indicator still existed on top, still saying [exposed to void mana]. I was unable to remove this status as I didn't have enough power to do so. It seemed that I needed access to a few more [Soul Forge] color types before I could.

At least I actually got to see an explanation of what it did.

[Exposed to void mana—will have occasional nightmares of otherworldly horrors. Overuse of mana will result in fainting. Cannot use mana potions as will result in a void-mana flaring and will cause hallucinations and seizures.]

And indeed, it seemed this was as far as I could go, so the princess came out of the biolab and back to the worried Barooshians.

"The spirit tree says this is all it can do. The princess's body should not be killing itself anymore, but she will still have nightmares, and don't give her mana potions. Overuse of mana also will cause fainting."

The princess's hands and legs, once blue, now gradually regained some color, and she no longer felt an intense weakness and pain through her body, so much so that she was actually able to talk.

"Food," was the first word she said.

The healer and paladin quickly took out some kind of bread from their pouches for her to eat. They seemed happy because she was visibly recovering, and so, rather than eat in the snowstorm, they walked back to the guesthouse to rest.

"What did you do back in the tower?"

"I-I tried to summon a hero." It seemed the princess had not been able to hold a proper conversation or even explain what happened because of the intense pain she was in.

"WHY?"

"I-I...I wanted a hero to be my husband—rather than that stupid old duke."

Ah, at this point, I stopped eavesdropping.

Their conversation went on about Barooshian court politics, international relations, political marriages, and power balance stuff—which frankly wasn't my cup of tea at all.

Later on, they all used some kind of portal magic to return to Baroosh. They said they would find some way to deliver the promised goods.

[You leveled up! Level 124!]

[Subsidiary tree limit increased to 700.]

[Biolab leveled up.] [External Biolab unlocked. Customizable Branches can now create biolabs!]

[Winter resistance upgraded.]

[You learned a new skill: Winter-adapted crops.]

Ah, so I gained crops that could grow in this stupid snowstorm.

D espite this horrible cold weather, the traders delivered the blood crystals. And once they did, I quickly got to it. Ah, thanks to the new ley line and soul-forge color, I also discovered there was a new upgrade choice for Trevor as well.

[Trevor, Forest Mind Level 20]

[Upgrade choices:]

[Blue - Root-Brain Complex. Requires special minerals to grow. Special minerals required are 10 x Blood Crystals and 50 x fresh animal heads.]

[Black - Skull Shell - Requires special minerals to upgrade. 10 x Bone of a wyvern, 1 x heart of a lion, and 50 x Bones of a lizard.]

Huh. Oh well, let's go with the immediate upgrade. The blood crystals and the heads of the animals were put together in a pile, and then I triggered this upgrade. A few dozen roots appeared and drilled into each of the heads and then the blood crystals, creating a rather messy haze of blood in the area. They twisted, they turned, they tangled, and sparks flew. It was a bit like watching a dozen snakes mate, with added fireworks.

And when it was done, a brain-like jumble of roots was formed. It was really just roots folded and twisted many, many times over until it resembled a brain.

[Trevor's level limit has been increased to 30.]

[Trevor has gained a unique passive ability - Hive's Guardian.]

[Hive's guardian - gains limited control over the lower-tier monsters and beasts that spawn in the valley. Doesn't override their natural instincts.]

Ah, fairly useful then. But then, as I turned back to my usual view of the valley, I noticed some changes. The interface was now more...game-like? The mini map extended farther, and there were more layers to the views available. The granularity of the view was also much better, and I could see more colors.

"If you desire, Master, I can customize the views for your viewing pleasure. Each of the trees in the valley sends back a ton of data through their roots, and it's a matter of processing them into usable information. With this upgrade, my processing capacity has increased! I will be able to provide better alerts and better forecasting ability!"

Sadly, the affected area was centered around that new [Root-Brain complex], so the farther I went, the less data available. But it was still sufficient to cover the entirety of the valley. When I went as far as the ThreeTrees of Mana, the data available in that region was close to none and still lacking in terms of defenders.

Therefore, it was time to create my second forest mind, one for the ThreeTrees of Mana's area, which I would call the Southwest Forest.

[In order to house your new forest mind, three subsidiary trees will be merged.]

[New Forest mind has been created. Do you want to name it?]

"Dimitree."

"Greetings, Master," Dimitree responded, with an accent. Was that intentional? Well, if it was, please continue. Russian/Ukrainian voice presets, please.

"You're tasked with defending my connection to the ley line and the vicinity of the Southwest Forest. Ask for help if you foresee difficulties."

"Acknowledged."

Afterward, I set up a few dozen subsidiary trees in the area, all with war beetles, and I placed them under Dimitree's command. Still, because of the freaking unnatural cold, there was practically no army movement in the region. Instead, this harsh winter brought a lot of death. Even in New Freeka where there was housing, it was insufficient protection, and the Treefolk had to construct additional barriers, actually starting fires indoors to keep themselves comfortable.

So cold. I feel like my branches are getting frostbite.

"It's just your imagination, Master."

YEAR 75, MONTH 12

The cold just got...colder. Some parts of the terrain turned almost ice-like as if it was an eternal winter. If such a spell was possible, and I thought it was, this felt very much like it.

I supposed this was how Arendelle felt when Elsa did her winter thing. I thought on how Elsa would be a rather fascinating reincarnating hero.

Nothing much happened this month because everyone was just really trying to wait out the cold. The effect of the spell, added to the natural turn of the seasons, made this so crazy cold, the elves all ended up hiding in the secret hideout, where it was warm and temperature-controlled.

The New Freekans attempted to build underground structures at this time as a way to get a bit more comfort out of this ridiculous weather.

YEAR 76, MONTH 1

I thought last month was cold. This month, it somehow proved me wrong as it got even colder. There were days where all that happened was ice flew through the air as any water froze instantly.

It even caused my tree barks, that were normally winter resistant, to feel brittle and flaky.

Since last month, Trevor, Dimitree, and I had used our abilities to support the rest of the normal trees, so that the cold didn't kill off the trees in the forest. They were already in some kind of 'winter-hibernation' mode, but this excessive cold would normally kill them. Even in this magical world, death by cold was still possible.

It would be bad if I lost my normal trees, so this was when that energy was consumed from [tuberous storage] to create a warm flow of nutrients and energy supplied to the normal trees, preventing freezing and keeping them alive.

This little episode with high-tier magic also reminded me of my vulnerability to such powerful magics. If somebody was to cast a [meteor] or magic of that caliber, what countermeasures did I have? If I was a tree stuck in the blast radius of the Tsar Bomba, what could I do?

[Winter resistance upgraded.]

[Winter-resistance aura obtained. All trees connected via rootnet are more resistant to the effects of cold and ice. Beetles and webspiders also gain some winter resistance.]

[Warm Winter Fruit obtained. A fruit that helps to keep the body warm.]

Uhh, that helped a bit, I supposed. With the winter, but not the Tsar Bomba. Or wait. Was the system saying this was the magical equivalent of a nuclear winter?

"This winter is unbearable. We need to do something." The villagers were now trying to get Yvon to do something about the winter, but what could she do?

Good news was there was absolutely no fighting in this sort of weather. The bad news was people were still dying—bad for them, not me. So my soul realm was packed with souls due for their reincarnation within the next six months, from the returned soul harvesters and, just generally, from all the death in the vicinity.

And from the fragments of the souls harvested, I obtained my fair share of interesting essences, also my first [Experience Seed], a product of the [Soul Harvester] ability. The experience seed was used to create a [Level Fruit], each seed, to create one fruit. The effect was to increase one's level by one, up to the level cap of said person.

Yes. A fruit equivalent of rare candy.

BUT! The creator of said level fruit (me) couldn't use it. Again, it was similar to that soul contract where I took a person's level away or where they surrendered their experience to me. It would get converted into [transferable experience], which could then be processed into [Experience Seeds] and [Skill Seeds]. In fact, even [Skill Essences] could be further processed into [Skill Seeds].

A single level wasn't much, for those in the lower levels. But I would imagine such an item being more useful and valuable to those at high levels since it was harder for them to level.

YEAR 76. MONTH 2. WEEK 1

The cold was letting up. By a tiny bit.

It was still snowing every day, with some days having ice storms. Not fun. Again, I was burning through my [tuberous storage], trying to feed and support the forest so that it didn't freeze to death.

I had actually become a little positive out of this. I mean, at least it was just ice, right? I could still keep the trees alive by giving them warm energy by consuming the stored energy. It was kind of like winter and summer. You could constantly add layers of clothing to keep yourself warm, but it was kinda hard to strip down to cool yourself off when the air itself was cooking you.

If, say, the entire air was cursed under a massive heatwave, I would need to find ways to cool down the forest, and I thought the only way I knew at the moment was to pull up cool water from deep beneath the ground. And there wasn't much of that. There was a fair bit of thermal energy coming from deep beneath as well.

This was despite me being fire-resistant, but for a drought or prolonged heatwave? I wasn't sure.

Maybe I needed to find some kind of 'cold-water' source

from far away. A massive root could then supply cold water from there to regulate the temperature of the valley's trees.

And the opposite would be to find a hot water source?

Maybe that volcano that Horns surveyed a while ago might be able to supply that.

"All this talk about the cold..."

"What?"

"I don't feel it."

"That's 'cause you are blob? A floating soul with no ability to sense temperature?"

"But some of the souls were telling me about how cold they felt. Or maybe that's just their final moments, carried over..."

"Wait. You can talk to the souls?" I didn't know why I had the impression that only hero-grade souls could talk, but I supposed I was wrong.

"Uh...only some of them. There seem to be a few that still retain their ability to talk...but all they do is repeat the same thing. Kinda like machines."

Oh. This soul thing could be...confusing. Why could some talk and some couldn't?

Anyway, New Freeka was in a state of emergency. Food supplies were running low as they didn't expect such severe weather and much higher consumption of their stockpiles. That led to rather ingenious solutions as some of their farmers actually had rather interesting skills. One such ability was indoor farming, and that led to multiple greenhouses being built and a few attempts at underground homes.

Speaking of underground...

"Dimitree, have you taken over the labyrinth?" The leftover labyrinth of the dungeon, now supported by roots, was located in the Southwest Forest.

"Yes. The inner labyrinth remains warm, though the entrances are covered in snow."

I thought I could propose that as an alternative location for the refugees to live, protected from the cold. But it was too far.

The journey there took at least two days, maybe more in this snow.

Then there was the old tunnel, left by the giant demonic centipede. It was located quite deep underground, so as to minimize tremors and detection, but because of its relative depth, I had found little use for it. But now that I had the [root tunnels] ability, I could think about creating more feeder tunnels to connect to that big underground tunnel.

"Suggestion."

"Speak, Trevor."

"There are certain kinds of vegetation that grow in tunnels. We can grow those there, and they would provide additional energy output. Variants of subsidiary trees."

"There's no sunlight in there. Can the subsidiary trees survive?"

"Not trees...more of a...fungi."

"My powers extend to that of fungi?"

"Uh, no. But if we extend our roots into the underground cave, we can create an environment for symbiotic fungus to grow, which can produce energy."

"Hmm, is the output worth it?"

"No. Fungi produce minuscule amounts of energy, but it has the effect of creating the base of an ecological system that can support certain kinds of farmer ants and insects."

Hmm. Underground fungi.

But I did want ants. I thought ants would be interesting warriors.

"Are beetles insufficient?" Horns asked.

"Ah, that is not my point."

"There are many kinds of beetles. I am sure you could have some kind of facility to research beetles that would help."

[Biolab - Beetle unit research tree obtained]

[This massive tree allows research and development of various beetle

types, such as flying beetles, armored beetles, poison beetles, fire beetles, water beetles...]

Uh.

"Yes. I think beetles are better than ants."

"I get the point, Horns. But I still want ants."

"No. Beetles are the best. We are already sharing the space with spiders. Please don't neglect us beetles."

"Ants?"

"Beetles. We have dung beetles. We have dancing beetles. We have colorful beetles. Beetles are superior."

I sighed. "Okay."

YEAR 76, MONTH 2, WEEK 3

"How long is this stupid blizzard going to last?"

"Forever, or at least until someone manages to disable or dispel the vortex?"

"Not forever—such magics have a natural decay to them. Over time it will go away, but we are talking about years..."

Troubling news came from Yvon's informants and diplomats. None, not Salah, not Nung, not Takde, had claimed responsibility for using a blood sacrifice spell, and in fact, all of them were now not-so-secretly launching their own internal investigation into the cause of this catastrophe that brought severe blizzards to an area the size of a country. All three nations were affected by this massive spell, and all three capitals were within range, though Salah, being the largest of the three nations, was least affected.

Well, to be honest, if that was all there was to it, it wasn't really that troubling. I mean, a hurricane was a country-sized disaster, no? Nobody jumped when a hurricane or a massive earthquake rattled the world, right? (Though I may be wrong...a perpetual hurricane would be equally horrible.)

The troubling thing was some of the more sophisticated intelligence claimed that it was a secret demon cult at work. A cult that aimed to summon and control the demon king. They call themselves the Circlebreakers. A demon cult that, as the rumors started to emerge, manipulated the nations and took advantage of the massive battle to somehow sacrifice at least twenty-five thousand to test out some kind of blood magic.

It sounded bonkers; which nation would want to publicly admit it used such a drastic measure, one that involved blood sacrifice? So naturally all of them would deny their involvement, even if they did do it. Besides, I presumed everyone in that battlefield was dead, and any evidence they could gather by magic was being corrupted and distorted by the presence of that blizzard magic vortex, and with each passing day, the evidence vanished. Perhaps if some of the souls and spirits could talk, I could find out a bit more, but until then, this theory sounded absurd.

So...I still assumed one of the countries did it. Or maybe it was a mix, and one of the countries collaborated with the cultists to activate such a spell.

Anyway, those were distant affairs that unfortunately affected me. It went to show that turtling strategy didn't work when there were large area-of-effect spells and abilities.

The merchants were quick to adapt, though. Money really had a way of making the world go round, even the magical ones.

This month we had the first visit of the 'cold-resistant caravan.' Essentially, they were a delegation of about a hundred, with dedicated mages and special carriages that were magically reinforced to provide protection from the cold and snowy weather.

Of course, the goods were expensive. They needed a markup on such special services, after all.

Oh, well.

The Barooshians, though, the wizard at least, came back to New Freeka, with the agreed rewards, most of them the upgrade materials I needed for the root system and Horns' claws.

Apparently, the wizard's punishment for exposing the

princess to forbidden magics...was exile. And the delivery to New Freeka was his last task by the king.

Surely, the wizard couldn't take responsibility for the princess's recklessness? But such were feudal societies—you got your ass handed to you even if you didn't have anything to do with it.

"Surely, we would welcome a wizard like yourself to our town..." Yvon was quick to bring him over to her side.

He sighed, nodded, and reluctantly accepted Yvon's offer of hospitality. "I guess I will stay for a while."

They soon got him to work on some kind of anti-cold weather spell.

Meanwhile, I was expanding my territory toward the volcano that Horns surveyed. Most of the beetles were inactive in this weather, and that was a weakness with having insects.

But as we approached the volcano, my subsidiary trees were slowly dying, so I couldn't extend them farther. This was despite my own heat resistance, but the death wasn't due to heat alone.

The surroundings of the active volcano were filled with sulfur, and there were active lava flows, forming rivers in the area. And, at every eruption, a blast of energy swept out from the caldera, and the shockwave created a gust of wind. All this, cumulatively, created a hostile environment for the trees.

One of the external biolabs (only one so far) next to the inner ring had a menu prompt. Kind of like those alerts when I unlocked a secret mission.

[Biolab research option unlocked: Volcanic adaptation. Estimated time required: 3 months. Materials needed to start research: 100 pieces of sulfur.]

Uh. Okay! Now I'd like to check all the other kinds of environmental adaptations...

That kind of put my plan to use trees to crawl into the volcano on hold. Thankfully, though, the area around the volcano was still relatively warm, such that I could deploy my beetles and task them with venturing into the volcano area to harvest the sulfurous minerals.

At about the same time, I created two beetle research trees to research winter adaptation. It was annoying to have so many of my beetles going into hibernation in this weather, and I was hoping to have some beetles that had the ability to function in the cold.

It was really hard to do much when my beetles spent so much time hibernating in their cozy trees.

YEAR 76, MONTH 3

The nations were now starting their work on dispelling or weakening the blizzard vortex, with spring returning, and the intensity of the blizzard reducing slightly. Slightly. Because it was still snowing.

And that meant crops were not growing. Luckily for the New Freekans, their indoor farming experiments were working, so they now intensified their efforts to build additional indoor farms in an effort to combat food shortages. But the cold also meant my timber farms were not as productive, so they very quickly used up the entirety of the timber farm...

"We've got a problem. Food supply is low—we probably have enough for another month—and the indoor farms are not producing enough food."

"Hunt. We hunt for the foxes and winter creatures."

"Okay. Let's do that, but we are talking about almost twenty-five thousand people in New Freeka. Is there sufficient meat to feed that many?"

"Maybe not, but better to have meat than not."

"Some of our watchtowers spotted a large group of yaks that spawned. That would be ideal for us. Their furs can also serve as warm clothing for the men."

Yvon paused and nodded. "Fine. Take fifty men and go hunt."

The warrior nodded.

"Still, we need other food sources. Meat is good, and we still have storage... Perhaps the truce is suspended?"

"Huh. The hell with the truce, Lady Yvon. Salah won't be able to retaliate in such circumstances."

"Salah may well figure out how to dispel this magic," another of Yvon's advisors chimed in. "Though, depending on how we word it, we could perhaps get some leeway..."

Yvon pondered that for a while. "Can you arrange someone to visit them to convey our intentions to suspend the truce requirements, given this...disaster?"

"Certainly."

"Back on topic. Food. Food and warm shelter. We had sixty-eight of us die of cold last month. We need to find a solution or something to stave this cold off until summer. Hopefully, we will have some plants growing then."

The discussion was held in one of the large halls in New Freeka, and all the leaders were invited. It comprised mostly of Yvon's comrades back when they were with Salah, but they had also gradually brought in the refugees to join the leadership team. After all, with twenty-five thousand of them, voices of rebellion and dissent would rise quickly, especially when it was cold and people were hungry.

"Can we buy them?"

"The merchants do sell food, but their prices are...extortionary. They know we need it."

"Still, if we have to—"

"Then we will. But let that day come only when we have exhausted other means; our coin is our hard-earned money."

"We should set up our own merchant corps, get out there and buy food from the unaffected nations."

Yvon nodded. "That is a good idea, though the merchant

guilds won't like it that we bypass them, but they'll come around. Anyone willing to volunteer to lead this task?"

A few men and women rose their hands, and Yvon nodded.

This level of eavesdropping was partly facilitated by Trevor's upgrade, which allowed him to process the data coming from within the valley and New Freeka in greater detail.

"So, one group to hunt food, one group to buy food. Anything else? Magic?"

"Would Baroosh be able to send help using that portal magic?"

"Uh, that is worth exploring." Yvon nodded and assigned Eriz to the task.

"Alternatively, is there no magic spell that creates a warm barrier to keep out such cold?"

"Hmmm. As far as I know, we don't have wizards at the level of entire towns here. We have been doing them at the building level, but the spells expire relatively quickly." Indeed, there were mages using their spells to create fire or generally warm up certain places, but spells like this lasted short periods, sustained by mana, and they did run out.

The warming effects of certain skills, such as [Comfortable House] or [Slow Burning Fire] that some of the refugees had lasted a bit longer, but that didn't work on a large scale and couldn't house everyone.

"Does...does the will of the forest have any way to aid us?"

Ah yes, the "Will of the Forest." It was one of the ways the refugees had come to refer to me, after the recent assistance with the potatoes. Apparently, those who visited the [Tree of Prayer] were those that would also end up using this particular phrase. They had been seeing my presence in their sleep, as a tree that somehow appeared in their nightmares and ate them.

Yvon didn't respond.

"I mean, the Will of the Forest is the one that somehow managed to heal the princess. Perhaps it has some way to aid us?"

Yvon sighed. "As you all have known, and I said this that day...the tree spirit doesn't give its aid freely. There is a cost to borrowing its aid, and is there anyone willing to sacrifice their soul for it?"

"Ask the elves. The will protects them. Perhaps they can figure out a way to sway his views?" one suggested, referring to Jura, Laufen, and the elves.

"Or Miss Eriz? Eriz was protected by it?"

Eriz shook her head then. "The tree has punished me for bringing all of you here, back then. I doubt it would listen to me now."

"If enough of us prayed to it, perhaps it might? That is what the churches tell their believers to do in times of hardship."

Oooooh...the religious kind.

To be honest, my ability to support the valley was also relatively limited. First of all, there were just too many of them. Twenty-five thousand New Freekans, and even with my new [winter resistant crops], I could grow about twenty-five hundred winter-resistant potatoes a day, and that was enough to make maybe thirteen hundred meals per day. That still left a huge twenty-three thousand seven hundred without food. I mean, I thought I was already pretty awesome to produce twenty-five hundred potatoes per day.

And add to that...fruits. I had the warming fruits and the winter-resistant healing fruits, which only my main tree could produce, and I could produce about a hundred each for the two kinds of fruits. That was maybe another hundred.

If I had the entire valley's trees, then yes, I could then tap on the normal trees to create food, but now, the normal trees in the forest were consuming energy, not creating them.

So yeah.

This weather was horrible.

"Perhaps they could make use of the tunnels," Trevor suggested. "Maybe they can grow mushrooms in there."

"If they have the right kind of mushrooms. And don't they need time?"

"True. Mushroom, as fungi, means they would benefit less from your 'bountiful growth' effect."

Well, it looked like the New Freekans were on their own. Too bad for them.

Beetles near the volcano then reported they had collected sufficient sulfur to start the research into [Volcanic Adaptation], which I did. Immediately.

Thankfully, research still functioned under such cold.

"Trevor. Are there ways to research winter resistance?"

"As your forest minds, we are able to perform research with the aid of [External Biolabs]. Though our research functions are relatively limited, and a dedicated research-focused artificial soul will be needed for high-tier research."

"Oh?"

"So if I assign you to do so, does it come at the expense of anything?"

"Yes, if you assign us to perform research on any of the external biolabs, our ability to support the valley's growth will be impaired by ten to twenty percent per research topic. As you have already selected [volcanic adaptation], I am already using fifteen percent of my available energy."

"I see. What other research options do you have?"

"Well...you'll have to tell me. There's no list to choose from."

Hey, that wasn't how I expected games to work. There should be clear tech trees, not I thought of something and then the biolabs figured it out...

"Uh, that's how it works in real life. Inventors do that," Meela chimed in.

"You want to volunteer? Can I fuse you to a biolab?" I actually knew the answer already.

"Fine, why not work on winter adaptation as well?"

"Sure..."

Oh.

My ginseng tree died from a pile of snow that somehow fell onto it and crushed it.

Dammit.

[Beetle winter adaptation stage I - two months remain.]

[Tree volcanic adaptation stage I - three months remain.]

[Tree winter adaptation aura - three months remain.]

YEAR 76, MONTH 3, WEEK 4

I had a visitor. An uninvited one.

"Hmm." A strange man appeared in my inner courtyard one day, right in front of my original main tree.

How did this guy get here? Right in front of me?

"Strange." He held a strange stick in his hand, and it bent toward me. It looked like some kind of prospector's stick or a diviner's item. Perhaps it was similar to the compass that the Barooshians had.

He looked up, and I saw he was alone, but he had a big cloak and hoody kind of set up, like an assassin. Somehow, if I had skin, I would get goosebumps. Something about his presence just...scared me. Could it be some kind of intimidation ability? Or was he perhaps a level-one-hundred assassin or something of that nature.

I woke Jura, who was asleep at the time, and he came out, armed and ready. "Hello?"

The assassin dude glanced at Jura and shrugged. "Sorry. I think I got lost. Do you know where New Freeka is?"

"No, you didn't," Jura said. "No one stumbles into this inner courtyard 'lost.'" This inner courtyard was actually specially guarded and protected, with the effect of my [illusion] and

[Camouflage] ability. So the odds of walking here and actually being lost were close to nil, so by way of elimination, that meant he was deliberately here.

The inner courtyard had the [forge tree], the [root-brain complex], and the other large, upgraded subsidiary trees that were converted into housing. He glanced around, looking, his eyes trying to find something. Perhaps someone other than Jura?

The assassin dude smiled. "Yes, you are right. I happen to be looking for...heroes. Do you know of any?"

Jura laughed and decided to joke to lighten up the mood. "None here. They're all dead. You gotta wait till the gods summon them again."

"Well, that's what the gods want the public to think." The assassin looked at me, and the stick kept bending in a strange way. He then placed the stick into some kind of magic pouch and took out a different kind of item, a metal divining ball.

"Eh?" Jura exclaimed. He was alert, but he too sensed the tremendous pressure from the man before him.

The metal ball didn't react. "Hmm...no heavenly blessing, so you certainly are not a hero..."

"Uh, of course—"

The assassin turned, and suddenly, Jura fell to the ground. He was alive, but it was as if his legs suddenly lost all strength.

Two very tiny needles almost instantly pierced his legs, and they were laced with some kind of poison. But before Jura could scream, or I could do anything, the assassin was right in front of him, tapping a strange golden metal rod into his head.

"Sorry, this won't kill you, but it'll make you forget all about me and this entire thing."

And Jura lost consciousness, but I detected that he was still very much alive.

I speculated my chances of killing this person were slim.

I felt this assassin could probably dodge my [Root Strike]s easily, so even if I tried, I assumed it would take multiple shots for it to work. I would need an AoE ability to get him, or some way of slowing him down, if I wanted to hit him on my very first strike.

The assassin then looked and walked around my main tree. "Hmm, the otherworlder locator points here, though...meh. Too many false positives with all the things the heroes leave behind."

I continued watching. I supposed he might try something on Jura, but my instincts told me to wait. Jura's unconscious body shook a bit, and the assassin walked over.

"Ah yes, it's still freezing cold." He covered Jura in a thick blanket that he pulled from his pouch. "Sorry."

He looked around, then gave a big sigh.

"I guess he didn't come here then. Dammit."

He lifted his fist to the sky and shook it.

And then the assassin vanished. Just like that. Without a trace. Despite me and my roots covering this entire valley, I didn't pick up his presence after that. I still wondered how he just slipped in and out of the entire valley like that.

"Apologies, Master, but I have no idea how he slipped past all our detection and patrols," Trevor apologized, but I couldn't blame him. He could walk in a straight line at me, and I still wouldn't see him coming. That was just how absurdly powerful his ability was.

"A skill, obviously. Very, very high-level stealth and camouflage. But add that to our list of weaknesses." I somehow suspected my own [Camouflage] and [Illusions] also worked on him, so he didn't suspect much.

"He feels like a friend, though," Meela said.

"Really?"

"All good over here," Dimitree reported, explaining the status of trees in the Southwest Forest. The cold was less severe there this month, benefiting from a strong warm current.

New Freeka managed to buy some food from neutral nations, so they staved off a bit of the hunger situation. And as the seasons changed, a bit of the cold and snow from the bloodspell was counteracted by the natural warmth of the spring.

However, it was still snowing, so the crops were still not growing.

I also learned that I overestimated the refugees' dietary requirements, as they actually had skills that made them better able to withstand cold and hunger. Some of them had skills like [Minimal Diet], [High Efficiency Body] or [Endure Hunger], which allowed them to make the most of what little food they had. Their experience being on the move, frequently with little food as well, gave survivors these skills, which made them tougher.

One of the most impressive of such abilities possessed by refugees was [Ascetic diet], where they survived on one meal per week without looking worse than a normal person.

In fact, if all the refugees possessed such abilities, my potatoes would actually be able to feed a lot more than I initially calculated. Perhaps by a multiple of five.

"It's hard out there..." Belle sat, all snuggly in her bed. "Tree-Tree, is there not much we can do to help them?"

"Well, there is, but let them figure it out themselves."

"I think some of the refugees are jealous," Emile explained. "They wonder how we can still be so comfortable here and not extend a hand to help them. They think we are being selfish..."

"Wahlen told me they have been getting weird stares, and some of the men actually cursed them openly..."

"Huh." Well, I'll let it slide, but if any of them make a move, I will not hesitate to punish them. I mentally made a note to Trevor to put increased surveillance on Brislach and Wahlen, who now lived in New Freeka.

"It is the way of the world." Laufen sat with Lausanne, working on some cotton clothes. "It is our luck that Tree-Tree watches over us."

"Well, some of them were driven out of their homes, too, so they feel that they have suffered much," Belle responded. She was really cozy with a thick blanket wrapped around her. It was actually warm in the room, as the main hideout and the nearby subsidiary trees had temperature-controlled spaces.

Lausanne then pouted. "Tree-Tree, maybe you should help them. Give them potatoes? I think they will like potatoes."

"Hmmm. I don't want to assist them so easily. Aid breeds complacency..."

"But they are in need. Heroes help people, no?"

Hmmm... How could I tell Lausanne that I honestly didn't care about the New Freekans all that much? Sure, they were useful, but...that was about it.

"How is your practice coming, Lausanne?" I tried to change the topic, after all she had been receiving [Dream Tutor] from me for quite some time.

"Oh, it's okay. I have been learning a lot, and those dreams where I learn strange skills are really, really cool."

"Why can't we get those dreams?" Emile and Belle complained.

"Because Lausanne's young mind is surprisingly receptive to it."

"We are not old!"

"Uh...I mean her mind is still growing, so the skill-dreams seem to work better."

Then Lausanne nodded, and she ran around for a while.

"Tree-Tree...are you going to help the refugees?" Ah dammit. I thought children easily forgot topics. *Why does she recall it so well?*

"Uhm, Lausanne, I cannot use my powers so easily, and there is always a cost for any other ability that I use. If the refugees ask for help, then, depending on what they offer, I will consider it."

Lausanne paused and then nodded. She seemed to accept that power wasn't something used so freely. "Maybe you are right. Uncle Jura likes to say that power needs to wait for the right time."

Heh, that was surprisingly insightful from Jura. Perhaps that new [diplomat] job had given him new mental perspectives.

"They must first help themselves."

A few days later, Meela spoke to me, her voice serious. "Tree spirit?" Wisp was next to her, and we were in the soul realm.

"Hmm."

"I have a strange dream, or...well, maybe it's not really a dream. But like some kind of mental whisper. But I think it means something. Something...important."

Important? What could be important? Oh well, let's go with it. "So tell me."

"I-I saw Alexis."

"Okay. What about her?"

"She's not dead."

Oh. That is good, I suppose.

"She... Somehow my prayers to the heroes reached her."

Hmm, then again, that didn't sound so good.

"Her body is currently consumed by demonfire, after she used [Fireform] to avoid the destruction of the demon king's core... She is battling it every moment now. It seems the demon-fire, when there is a sufficient amount of it, gains some kind of consciousness...or some kind of innate instinct."

"Oh, okay." Didn't sound good, but so? She was really far away, right?

"And...erm...I think the demonfire that consumes her body thinks that a hero is still around, and so... It thinks the source of the prayer is...a hero."

Oh, no. I mean, I kind of figured that was what Meela meant. It was just...just so typical of communications to lead to such actions. "She's headed this way."

I mean, how did a demon know where to go? I guessed there were ways for that to happen.

"Yeah."

"When will she get here?"

"I don't know."

Uh. "What else did she say?"

"Not much... She mumbled about how she is a fire elemental since she's stuck in her fire-body form, and that fire body is controlled by the will of the demonfire."

Well. Shit?

Hmm, let's see what measures I can take against a fire-crazy demon.

A fire elemental and a perpetual blizzard. Not exactly what I imagined to face, but here I was.

The demon-fire Alexis arrived a lot later than expected. I initially thought she would arrive perhaps within two to three days, given the heroes overwhelming cheat powers, so I scrambled to prepare myself to face a hero, but then again, her body was controlled by demonfire, and that demonfire wasn't exactly...intelligent.

Her arrival was easy to spot, as the demonfire was a lot flashier. Despite a snowstorm that engulfed everywhere we could see, her glowing, flaming body just shone through all that snow like a lighthouse in a storm. Her body was a huge, glowing fireball shaped like a woman. She reminded me of a female version of the human torch, or perhaps phoenix, but there, under all that fire, was something that looked like a solid core.

She arrived with a bang, shooting fireballs and firing beams of fire through the entire valley.

"This is the monster the tree spirit warned us about?" Yvon's immediate reaction was...well, one of shock.

After Meela had the revelation, I quickly cascaded the alert down to the people, that a powerful monster was likely coming our way, so that they could prepare. But I would realize all my preparation was for naught.

Jura nodded. "Yeah. Some kind of...fire-creature."

"That is a whole lot more than just a 'fire-beast.'"

Alexis floated in the sky, surrounded by a dark, maroonish fire that raged violently. The remnants of the demon king's fire, it looked unaffected by the effects of this magical blizzard, or even if it did, whatever effect it had was probably minuscule.

Yvon looked back at Jura and shook her head. "Whatever that is, it is flying. There are very few ways to engage that thing unless it comes down to the ground. Our arrows are not going hurt it, and I doubt fireballs from our mages will, either!"

As Yvon and Jura discussed, Alexis clearly didn't consider them to be a threat; instead, she still continued to shoot fireballs at the forest, blasting up a whole section of the valley, one fireball at a time. The first impact vaporized any snow or ice that had built up, and the second impact instantly set the normal trees on fire.

Indeed, given the monster was...a fire elemental, the best option was to use opposing elemental weapons or destroy the elemental's core.

"So?" Jura looked at Yvon. He entered into the bear-armor mode, a black-colored wood wrapping his entire body, and it made him look like a giant bear as he leaped into combat, charging in the general direction of Alexis.

The fire elemental noticed and directed the fireballs at Jura. Each time, he activated a wooden shield to parry those fireballs, but the shields were only able to absorb two fireballs, so Jura had to constantly reactivate the wooden shields.

"Well, how are you going to hit it?" Yvon wondered, activating a magical arrow. The fact that it was a fire elemental meant Yvon quickly reorganized the team she prepared for this. Not everyone was suitable to face a high-tier monster of this sort, so some of the guys retreated back to New Freeka and set up defensive positions.

Jura's bear-shaped legs contorted, and the wood armor twirled into a spring-like structure, propelling him high into the air, close enough to come into contact with the fire elemental...

He got blasted with a point-blank inferno. It exploded right in front of him, and he got thrown far away to the ground, the wooden armor already black, but now charred and smoking. The impact was enough to knock Jura out but thankfully not kill him, as the armor took most of the damage. I sensed Bamboo going offline. Jura would likely need to be in bed for a few days.

"Jura!" Yvon shouted, but she quickly turned back to face Alexis, who now noticed the rest of the men and retaliated with a few more fireballs. I activated my [wood shield] to protect them from the fireballs.

Well, that went horribly well, I thought as I activated multiple wood shields to block the fireballs. Their effectiveness was pretty good, blocking multiple hits before getting destroyed.

"Master, they won't be able to harm that monster," Trevor quickly summarized. True, with enough wood shields I could significantly reduce the damage Alexis dealt, but we couldn't hit or hurt the elemental much.

And this was when I noticed Horns charging toward the monster. "For the master!"

Uh. What?

"I shall defeat the foe!"

I assumed he somehow forgot that he couldn't fly, so I wasn't sure what possessed him to attempt such a move and what he was attempting to do.

"What's he doing?"

"I think he may have some skills, Master."

"Really. Let's see, but I think he's gonna lose." Alexis was a hero, and that fire was from the demon king itself...

Horns charged toward Alexis, his beetle shell coated with some kind of resin, which was actually pretty good at absorbing the fireballs. And then when he finally got beneath her, he dug into the ground and shot spikes at Alexis from his shell.

[Spike-attack]

"Oh. I didn't know he could do that."

But it was too low tier a skill, and the spikes burned up before they harmed her body. And so Alexis lobbed a few fire-balls back at Horns.

He would have been a crispy-fried beetle if not for a few [Wood shield]s.

"Retreat, Horns. Not your match—"

Alexis waved her hand and shot out a continuous jet of blue fire, and it incinerated everything in its path, including the wood shield. I instantly tried to activate a few more shields to protect Horns, but it wasn't good enough, the blue flame burning through the wood shields rather quickly, also burning half of Horn's back body before he managed to run out of range.

"Master, I failed—"

I sensed Horns going offline. He was...probably not dead yet, but I would need to repair him after this.

"It's fine. Hibernate mode."

Yvon, very smartly, chose to retreat all the way to me. I guessed the fact that she survived so long out in politics was no fluke.

"We're no match for this monster."

At this point, I knew. Alexis had a fire aura that burned any lesser object that got near her, and she had almost limitless quantities of fire-type magic—and that blue flame was really powerful.

"Any suggestions?"

"No, sire. I think our chances against it are quite slim." Even now, her very presence was melting all the snow into water, then steam, and then the trees were catching fire. It was ridicu-lous how she could be a one-person weather changer.

"Is there really no way we can reach her?" Meela sighed. She felt upset that Alexis was burning up the forest, and she had created a path of destruction that led her right to me.

[Root Strike]. A root flew up and hit her. The damage was

low as the fire aura incinerated the root partially, so reducing the impact.

I thought I could do a repeat of my earlier strategy by using multiple [Root Strike]s, but then I noticed that fire soon regenerated the damage. The [Root Strike] barrage would need to deliver a fatal strike, or I may just be wasting time.

Meela tried the friendship route, so she prayed and attempted to mentally communicate with Alexis to convince her to stop attacking us.

I tried a few more [Root Strike]s, just to be sure, and like the earlier ones, they did hit, but the damage I dealt wasn't much. I threw a few fruits at her just to be sure, but they burned up in midair, without achieving a thing.

"Yvon, can you evacuate the elves? And stay out of this." This was not going to be easy, and I suspected the mages would be useless.

"Ah...yes. Certainly." Yvon quickly took the elves and ran. A few fireballs went their way, but I blocked them with the [wood shields]. The [shield generator] trees also had been trying to block the fireballs, but as the shield generators were independent of me, their strength was inferior, and they could only block two to three fireballs.

"She's in there, and she says she's in great pain," Meela actually managed to communicate.

"How?"

"It's a thing heroes of the same generation can do. A kind of... telepathic link over short distances... Anyway...she can't help us. The demonfire is too strong, and her soul is too weak to resist or take back her body."

"Okay, no friendship-no-jutsu route."

Alexis burned up a few more of the subsidiary trees and then sent a few fireballs directly at my main tree, and they exploded right on my trunk.

My historical experiences with fire had made me very resistant to them, so the fireballs didn't even leave a scratch on my main body. My main body, unlike the skill extensions, enjoyed the full benefit of my [Tree Heart], and this prompted Alexis to aim blue flames at me.

And they didn't hurt. The blue flames couldn't burn me, either.

This seemed to be a stalemate. She could burn up the entire forest, and I would still be standing, but I couldn't hurt her, either.

This outcome wasn't what I wanted, so I needed to find a different strategy.

Irritated, Alexis sent out a wave of fire from her body and pretty much burned almost all the normal trees around my main tree. The subsidiary trees, forge tree, and root-brain complex shared quite a bit of my fire-resistance abilities, but the flame was strong enough to let Trevor experience pain.

"Master, I don't feel so good." Trevor was housed in the root-brain complex, and the blue fire was slowly getting to it. It inherited a smaller percentage of my godly fire resistance, and it would be invulnerable to most fires. Except one from a hero or a demon king.

"Shut down and hibernate. Horns, you, too!"

"Acknowledged." Rather than lose Trevor and Horns from the constant barrage of fire, it was better to pull their artificial souls back from their bodies and house and hibernate their souls within me.

"This isn't ideal." I shook my head. Alexis still blasted the forest, and I was doing my best to block as many of the fireballs as I could. Which worked and, as a result, it irritated the demon-fire-Alexis more.

Meela shook her head. "Alexis's trying to take back control, but it's not working. The demonfire's will is too powerful."

At this point, the elves had managed to evacuate to the 'relative' safety of New Freeka, and it was just me, the spirits, and Alexis. Yvon managed to haul Jura away from the battlefield as well.

It was strange to be feeling so hot when just a little farther away was the cold blizzard. Too bad I couldn't channel the blizzard's power and direct it all at Alexis.

"We can't defeat her." Meela sighed. "All you can do is stall her, but she's free to run elsewhere."

I paused and tried to think.

If I couldn't defeat her, then I would attempt to contain her. The logic to me was simple. She couldn't hurt me, so if I contained her such that she couldn't hurt anyone else, that was a win, too!

Alexis lobbed a few more fireballs and released multiple firewaves, and what was once a green valley turned into a blazing inferno, with me the sole untouched tree in the middle, as the blue flame was strong enough to burn even those with higher fire resistances.

"What's your plan?" Meela asked.

"Well, remember my extremely crazy demon and fire resistance? I am going to exploit it."

"How?"

"I am going to eat her."

[Constrict] x 30. Sixty roots and vines shot out from my main body and attempted to reach out to Alexis's fiery body. Thanks a little to her target being me, which I supposed was due to her sensing the presence of Meela, or perhaps those fragments of heroes, she was now really close to me, trying to burn me.

I wasn't sure whether Alexis got the point that it wasn't working, but hey, if all it wanted to do is keep trying...well, go ahead.

The fire worked to a limited degree on the roots and vines. Her fire aura burned up a few strands of roots and vines, but there was enough of the constricting vines and roots to form a thick net. I had taken inspiration from Horns's body to coat the roots and vines with a layer of fire-resistant resin, and as they touched her fireform body, some of them burned.

With the resin-coated, fire-resistant net around her, I pulled and managed to grab her flame body, pulling her toward me, into me.

"You're actually going to..." Meela looked surprised.

"Eat her..." Yes, I was.

Alexis's body seemed to panic and released a continuous stream of blue fire, and even stronger black fire, but closer to my main body, the root and vine's fire resistance increased, so she was trapped. Fireball after fireball exploded as I pulled her even closer.

Alexis's body now almost touched my trunk, and she released a huge chain of fire-waves, the acts of a drowning man, flailing, in an attempt to escape, but she still couldn't break through my vines. However, that fire scorched the surroundings, the forge-tree and the root-brain complex were burning, the ground now charred black.

Then, as she closed in on the trunk, the main body of my trunk opened up, revealing a biolab pod. The vines then pushed her inside into the biolab. The demonfire attacked the biolab, and now, I felt like I was in a sauna. Or like an arctic monkey sitting inside a hot spring in winter.

That didn't stop Alexis. She kept trying, releasing wave after wave of fire. Perhaps she thought my resistance was due to an extreme regeneration and I would run out of mana, or somehow, she hoped that the fire would eventually get through.

But it didn't.

I was kinda thankful that its only power was fire, and so its only response to any threat was to burn the shit out of it. I mean, if it had Alexis's brains, she'd probably try lightning or perhaps ice. *So yeah, when you're a hammer, all you can do is hammer.*

"This is insane," Meela said. She was clearly rather amazed to see me drag Alexis into my main body and figuratively drown her fire out.

"Well, it works."

I then began the next step, trying to battle the demonfire's presence. It was strangely...familiar. Like the [Fires of Baal] that used to burn on top of my trunk, the fire even felt rather pleasant. This time, I wasn't the same tree I used to be, and so I would defeat the demonfire myself.

I drew on all the mana I had, from the ley line, from the normal trees, from the storage, from...everything, and with it, I flooded Alexis's body with my mana, driving out the demonfire and the demonic mana that now ran through her body.

It was like attempting to do a blood transfusion, driving out the dirty demon blood and replacing it with my clean blood.

Unbeknownst to me at this time, from New Freeka, by putting Alexis's body into me, it seemed like the entire valley's trees appeared to be on fire. The heat generated from the trapped demonfire was released through my roots, my branches, like how a kettle vented out hot steam, and throughout the valley, my branches and roots would periodically spit out the trapped demonfire.

From afar, my main trunk was like a furnace. There was a reddish glow from within, that trapped demonfire, a fire inside a paper lantern, and this lasted for weeks as I battled.

Single-mindedly focused on beating the demonfire, I had no idea what happened other than my long, laborious battle for control of Alexis's body.

I kept at it, and I continuously flooded her with my mana. Gradually, I made progress. Like my experience with the hellhounds—how they, after I overwhelmed their body with my mana, transformed into a woodhound.

Everything I had, I poured into Alexis's body. Though I doubted I could take 'control' of Alexis, my theory was that it was all I needed to drive out the demonfire.

After a week, I gained ground, and I pushed the demonfire, perhaps by half. The demonfire tried and gave its all, releasing all the fire it could, trying to destroy me from within.

After the second week, I had made even more progress, and the fire-elemental form was starting to subside like a body that had finally stopped burning. And in my biolab, I began to see something resembling a soul again. Its black-colored body, a 'charred' body, was starting to emerge from what was once a body almost wholly made of fire.

But that didn't look good for Alexis as it meant she was probably going to die.

So, as I fought the demonfire, I also looked into her body. I saw a spring tainted red, burning. A body that was parched, cracked like baked dirt, like a lake that was drained of water. A bloody red mana flew out from everywhere as my mana flowed into it, slowly pushing it out into the beyond.

And after the third week, I finally drowned the demonfire with all the mana I had.

I won.

YEAR 76, MONTH 5, WEEK 3

"You did it..." Meela nodded.

The demonfire was gone—finally—and Alexis got her body back. Well...what was left of it. It couldn't have happened soon enough, as all the ejected heat from the demonfire meant the entire valley was literally like a minefield. Any second a tree would emit fire or hot steam, so all the inhabitants of the valley tried to stay as far away from trees as possible.

But this meant the treefolk had to go out in the open, to New Freeka.

Alexis's body had been in the fireform for too long, and her physical body was completely burned. Now, it crumbled right before our eyes like a collapsing sandcastle. It was evidently not an ability that was meant to be used for so long...

"Help me, connect to me."

"What?"

"Please. Just do so." Alexis coughed. Her body, even though there was no demonfire anymore, was of no use.

To be honest, I found something strange about that request. But I did, my roots and vines entering her body and attempting to provide her with nutrients, the way a feeding tube would. But her body was a goner, unable to receive nutrients anymore.

And then Alexis mumbled something...a spell that I couldn't quite understand. It caused her body to crumble, then turned into a paste, and then, it...mixed into the vines and roots in her body. And then those vines and roots mixed with the rest of the biolab, and that pod transformed into a chrysalis of some kind.

"What..."

[New subordinate consciousness, hamadryad Alexis detected.]

[Integrating...]

[Integration failed.]

[Soul condition is in extreme damage. Extensive repairs required.]

[Attempting to repair using soul forge.]

[Soul forge is offline. Expected downtime 2 weeks.]

[Subordinate consciousness will be put into stasis.]

[Alexis has died.]

[You gained a fragment. You have 67 fragments!]

[You have gained 4 levels. You are now level 128!]

[Biolab upgraded three times! Biolab resistance to attack increased. Biolab modification options increased! Soul-forge-linked abilities increased!]

[Constrict upgraded! Vines now are able to drain mana and lifeforce! Vines now able to ensnare magical creatures.]

[Natural Mana Overwhelming upgraded!]

[New tree variant obtained: Carnivorous plants.]

[New ability obtained: Heat transmission root systems.]

With Alexis defeated, I could finally take stock of the damage. And it was quite bad.

From all the fireballs, and the inferno that raged afterward, the valley lost over seven thousand normal trees and about a hundred of my subsidiary trees. Both the forge tree and the root tree complex were damaged by the blue flame, and they would require about two weeks to regenerate. Horns was also in a kind of 'repair' mode, and he was holed up in one of the beetle subsidiary trees, recuperating from the damage.

Trevor was also offline, and it would be two weeks before he was back on, so my range and detection ability was back to what it once was.

The elves, New Freeka, and most of the refugees stayed far away from the forest, and so when it finally stopped, everyone looked incredibly cautious. Of course, I went and checked on the elves first to find Laufen, Jura, and gang resting in one of the rest houses.

"It's finally stopped." Laufen looked out the window, noting that the fires had stopped for a full day. With that, it meant the snowstorm was going to return as well. From snowstorm to blazing inferno and now back to a snowstorm again.

"Yeah." Jura was awake, but his entire body was suffering from burns. He was recovering, though, as the healers tended to his wounds. "Wonder how Tree-Tree is doing..."

"The monster is inside Tree-Tree?" Belle nodded. "If so, do we still want to go back and stay there, if Tree-Tree is still there?"

Laufen nodded. "I trust that Tree-Tree will take care of us and keep the monster separated from us."

"Hi," I mentally spoke to the elves.

"Oh!" they all shouted in delight!

"What have I missed?"

Laufen paused and then soon elaborated on how the entire valley was on fire for a good three weeks. The heat from the burning forest helped warm the entire area, but it also made it dangerous for anyone to get near the forest as there were periodic firebursts from my roots and trees.

But other than that, all else was normal, as the refugees were still hungry and cold, so I turned my focus back to the forest.

"I'm still around, boss," Dimitree said, reminding me that he was spared from the damage because he was just so far away.

"Ah yes. Great! All well in your part of the world?"

"Yes, boss. You've been draining a lot of mana for the past three weeks, so we're on low-activity mode. Now, we can get back to our usual routine again."

Well, that was good. I then turned to the research trees. A few of the biolabs were damaged during the entire battle, and with me draining all the mana, and Trevor being out of commission, the research on the volcanic and winter adaptation was all suspended.

[Beetle winter adaptation stage I - two months remain.]

[Tree volcanic adaptation stage I - three months remain.]

[Tree winter adaptation aura - three months remain.]

"Dimitree, can you continue the research?" I mean, I did have another forest mind, so he could continue the research, right?

"Certainly. Please create a few biolabs in the Southwest Forest." Ah yes, that made sense as the lab should be near the Forest Mind for it to conduct research.

Once Trevor woke, I wondered whether it would be possible to get both of them to do research. Would that speed things up?

YEAR 76, MONTH 6

The past two weeks kind of zoomed by as I focused on restoring the damage from my battle with Alexis. The valley's damage was severe, and some of the blue flames continued to burn, so I had to find a way to put them out, such as throwing a pile of dirt at it. The residual fires did end up burning a few more trees, but eventually, I got to them, thanks to the snow.

"Ah, good to be awake. I'm back. Seems like I've slept..."

"Yes, Trevor. Time to fix our valley." Indeed, our valley was heavily damaged by the fires, and Trevor's restoration abilities would be much needed.

Trevor's presence sent an update to my entire point of view and interface, and more data flooded in. He was clearly getting into it. I sensed him checking on various trees and quickly using his abilities to regenerate some of them. Well, this fixing thing would take some time since the cold weather was making it hard for us to do much.

Next, I checked on the elves. They were back now, living inside the secret hideout once more. They actually appeared to just miss the warmth of my secret hideout, where the temperature was always constant, and there was always some fruit or potatoes to eat, so they were delighted when I told them they could return to the secret hideout.

The girls were exceptionally happy to get their beds back and quickly snuggled in.

"Ah, I am so tired of this cold." Belle jumped on her bed. "So glad that my bed's still here!"

"The blizzard's gonna just get stronger after this. I wouldn't want to be out there." Emile sighed. "I hope the rest of them are doing okay. I feel kinda bad hiding in comfort here."

"That sucks. But... Oh, well?" Belle shrugged. "It's kinda amazing that all this is undamaged despite how crazy the fighting was."

That's partly because the secret hideout is pretty much fire-resistant?

Meanwhile...

New Freeka's new hunter corps and merchant arms success-fully acquired food, in exchange for furs and wines. The under-ground and covered farms were also in full swing as more and more of the refugees acquired the skills necessary to manage their underground and indoor farms.

But politically, things were not going so well for New Freeka. The three nations resumed their mudslinging, as talks broke down on who was responsible for the blood-sacrifice blizzard spell.

So Salah came up with a strange ultimatum to New Freeka: Side with the kingdom of Salah and the truce conditions would be waived. Choose not to and bear their wrath.

"This is an insult," the advisors said.

"I know, but what choice do we have? We have no military power to stand up to Salah." Yvon sighed.

"But they expect us to forget that we were expelled from there? That we were massacred, our long escape from Salah, and the countless lives lost as they go about their bloodthirsty ways?"

"..."

"Our people will insist we have a bit more spine." The advisor shook his head and tried to convince the rest of the advisors. They too felt really mixed about this.

"Are the lives of our people less important than some principles?"

"How do we know? Salah may well be the one that cast the spell, then if we side with them, we would be wrong, too!"

"If so, the answer must be to insist that Salah prove their innocence, then we stand on their side?" one of the advisors suggested, and it was quickly attacked by the other advisors.

"That still won't go down well with the people. Remember, we are expelled from Salah, many of us. Now they demand we stand on their side? Even if they are truly innocent in terms of this accursed spell, I—and I speak for many others—cannot accept it. We'd rather go to war with Salah."

"But war leads us to a lot more death, and that's what we're trying to avoid. We shouldn't go to war and put our people's lives on the line," another advisor said. "Our people are tired and are finally starting to rebuild their lives here. Do we want to throw them into the fire again?"

It was a tough choice for the New Freekans, so they couldn't come to a decision.

YEAR 76, MONTH 7

"Meela!"

"Alexis!"

The two girls jumped happily when Alexis's damaged soul finally received its first layer of repairs. I had to wait for my [Forge Tree] to recover and some of my energies to return before I could get down to the business of fixing her and waking her from her stasis. Like Meela, the damage her soul had taken was extensive, and it spoke of the incredible resilience of the heroic souls that with just a single layer of repairs, she was already able to speak.

The kind of damage was a mix between Meela's and those of the princess who experimented with void magic, so I was more than able to repair quite a bit of the damage her soul suffered, but there was still some damage that needed different-colored soul forges to fix.

"I would hug you if I could." Alexis shrugged, her soul now appearing in my soul realm after the repairs.

Meela laughed. "I don't think ethereal spirits can receive hugs."

"Yeah...I feel a lot better after the tree fixed me. None of that crazy demon voice anymore."

Meela's soul bobbed happily.

"The demons have been reading my mind."

Well, that's a bombshell that came from nowhere.

"That means they know what I know. Of gods, of our technology, of...home."

"Oh." Nothing worse than the magic this world had to offer. Look at this world. They had nuclear blizzards.

"I doubt it's their first time." Meela shrugged. "Heroes have been summoned to this world time and time again. I'm pretty sure demons have captured heroes a few times before."

Alexis sighed. "Well, that's out. Feels good to finally say it." It seemed to be a real sigh of relief, of a weight finally released from her shoulders. "Having my brain read all the time isn't a pleasant feeling."

"Well, you're...sort of dead, so I doubt that's any better?"

"I'd rather be dead, honestly. I'm really relieved that the tree spirit was able to defeat me. I initially feared being the vehicle for more of the demon's destruction."

"Well, luckily, I have just the set of abilities to counter you," I jumped in.

"Yes. Interesting set of...operations you're starting here," Alexis mused.

"You like it?"

"It's...not bad." Alexis's spirit floated around.

"See, someone appreciates it for a change."

Meela shrugged.

"Anyway, what spell did you use in the end?"

"Oh...it's a reduction-to-spiritual-form spell—something I learned from being stuck in the fireform for too long—since my body is disintegrating—and then a merge-self spell."

"Merge?" That's when I realized Alexis might have tried to hijack my body.

"Yeah. I tried to merge with you, but your soul was far too strong, and instead, I got absorbed..."

"Don't do that ever again."

"Ah...I'm sorry. I just wanted to still somehow live..."

Anyway, I still had to figure out some alternatives, so I spoke to Wisp, separately. "Wisp, any way I can control what the souls do against me?"

"Well, in their soul form they have no ability to harm you—at least directly. They are, after all, souls that existed with your soul realm, and the soul realm is a contained 'other' space. Once confined and merged into a vessel, their ability to harm you depends on the vessel."

Hmm...lots to think about there.

"But there are safeguards you can perform, such as entering into a soul contract. Such an act would constrain their actions for the next thousand years." Ah yes, I was an idiot, but I supposed I would have to, if I ever wanted to give them a vessel.

"There's a vessel already developing inside the pod, which the lady Alexis used. It seems to be a woman made out of wood, but it will be some time before it is ready."

"How?" I mean, how'd Alexis do that?

"Her spell managed to only take control of the pod, and so she used it to become a cocoon to grow herself a new body. But because her magic is decayed, the new body that is growing is now under your control." I therefore took the opportunity to have a look at the body she's growing—it's essentially a body made of wood. But the limbs and joints were all made of some kind of soft vine.

[[Hamadryad Body – Developing]. The body is made from the nimble wood of a soul tree, and the soul that lives in this body derives energy and life support from the soul tree. So the body will die when the soul tree does.]

Hmm, but at least this body aligned hers with mine, as she would die when I did. But then, she could just hop bodies, and she might still try to take over me, rather than become attached to me. For now, though, she was still in my soul realm, so I needed to take some precautions. She failed previously, but that was because her body and soul were in terrible shape. If she was in her best shape, might she succeed?

"Alexis." I returned to the two ladies, who were happily chatting away.

"Yes, tree spirit?"

"Do you plan to stay in this world? Or do you plan to move on?" The soul realm was where souls prepared for their onward reincarnation after all. If she left, then my fears would be less.

"Ah...if what Meela tells me is right, I might see Nobuo in the next few weeks. They're a bit slow to catch up on such matters. I'll see what he says first, but I think I'll stay."

Oh. That was a disappointment.

"Because the price of my failed attempt to merge with your body...is that my soul is now subordinated and shackled to you for a thousand years."

Just to be sure, I checked.

[Alexis]

[Status: Soul-contracted to Tree-Tree.]

Ah, so the variant of her attempt to merge with me ended up backfiring and turning it into a soul contract. That was...rather weird.

So I went back and asked Wisp more questions.

"Can a body have two souls?"

"Maybe, but one is always the 'master.' In your case, you're the soul tree, and you're the undisputed master of your own soul. The lady is reckless to have attempted to take over as 'master' of your body. After all, there is nothing in the world that can remove a soul tree, one able to manipulate the souls of others, from its own body."

"Nothing?"

"Nothing. Even a god can't touch a soul tree's soul until the soul tree dies, in which your soul then becomes any other soul. Think about it. How can a being able to repair, create, and upgrade souls lose control over their own body to another soul? The power to manipulate souls comes from the soul tree's innate structure, and to kick you out involves tampering with that innate structure."

Hmmm. "But you said earlier that she could harm me?"

"Well, yes. She could cast spells at you and physically attack you if she so desired. Both Meela and Alexis, if they were combined into a vessel, would be their own persons, and they could attack you if they choose to. But chasing you out of your own body is not one of the things they could ever do."

Ah, I misunderstood a bit. I supposed that changed the type of precautions I would have to take.

Hmmm...

YEAR 76, MONTH 7, WEEK 2

Everyone was busy doing farming, especially of the underground or indoor variety. Those that couldn't were busy hunting. It was going to enter the really cold months soon, and if the magic behind this snowstorm didn't weaken, it would just mean colder days ahead. So, although there was the threat of a re-escalation of the war between the three kingdoms, the people of New Freeka were just single-mindedly focused on preparing for more harsh winter.

It was really the only thing on most of the people's minds.

On my side, I did my part by growing potatoes. I mea ...I could grow a lot of potatoes, so that was what I'd do. And then there were those fruits of healing and warming fruits as well, which I got the elves to store in the secret hideout.

The elves purchased vinegar from the traders and used this to create pickled fruits, so these pickled fruits, kept in large wooden containers, were what they stored for winter. It seemed the effectiveness of the healing and warming reduced by half, but in exchange, we got much longer-lasting fruits that didn't rot so quickly.

By now, the valley's damage from the fires was gone, but of

the many trees destroyed, only twenty percent of them rejuvenated. After all, the weather was too cold for trees to grow.

It seemed there were actually a few groups of wizards
attempting to dispel and weaken the blizzard; after all, for some
wizards, this was a chance to level up, try to do something that
few other wizards had done before. At the same time, they could
earn brownie points with the rulers of the three kingdoms.

I hoped they were successful. This stupid winter had gone on
for far too long.

"Fear not, Master. The winter research is going well, and
once that is done, we will be able to regrow even more trees."
Trevor and Dimitree both tried to comfort me, but I still felt a bit
annoyed.

Aside from that, my soul harvesters returned! I got a lot more
souls. It seemed the winter was really killing a lot of people, so I
had enough to create one more artificial soul. The only problem
was I didn't have enough power for it.

YEAR 76, MONTH 8

[Beetle winter adaptation stage I - completed!]

[Tree volcanic adaptation stage I - 1 month remains.]

[Tree winter adaptation aura - 1 month remains.]

Ah, yes. My beetles could move now. After the first stage of beetle winter adaptation, I noticed the beetles now had some kind of internal-warming system, where there was some kind of warm sap pumped to their joints and limbs to keep them warm. However, the sap was only produced in the subsidiary trees-beetle nests, so they had to periodically return to the trees to restock on the saps.

This gave them an effective operational time in winter of about two hours, which wasn't that great, but at least they could now move and function in winter, which was a whole lot better than them sleeping in their nests!

I wondered...if this got taken to the extreme, would the beetles actually gain functional warm blood–pumping hearts?

"Interesting stuff you have there." Alexis was a lot nosier than I expected. She was extremely interested in the kinds of research and actions I was taking, and thanks to the repairs she'd gotten, she and Meela could now both be nosy.

Still, the fact that she tried to merge with me made me a little defensive around her.

"You're feeling suspicious of me because of what I did before I died. And I can understand that, and I would like to apologize again. But let me be useful to you. After all, there are still many ways you can use me."

Well, in this respect, Alexis actually wanted to be useful, but Meela just...seemed rather happy loitering around. But you know, this little incident did make me wonder how...loyal Meela would be. "Paranoid?" Meela chimed in.

"Yes."

"But as long as we are in our soul form, we are stuck. Here, as souls, we have no ability to take action. But, if we are to earn your trust, you need to first take that first leap, to let us be of assistance to you."

Well...Alexis was right there. Ah, it was a risk I had to take. All I could do was task my artificial souls with keeping an eye on them and use the existing spells and contracts to keep them under control. But for now, I would put that idea off.

The weather was experiencing some oddities. On one day, the weather suddenly got better, but then it got a whole lot worse the next day. I suspect it's the wizards trying to meddle with the magic of this snowstorm.

The New Freekans were still busy digging in, building large storage facilities to store the hunt, and they had even started curing meats so that they could be stored for longer. To be honest, this blizzard was proving to be a boon for them because they were developing more unique food-storage abilities, which would last them through future hardships.

Politically, they had yet to decide who to side with on the whole Salah ultimatum, and that had gotten them a rather stern warning letter from Salah, who insisted that they pick a side and do so soon—or else.

I turned my attention back on the elves.

"How are you feeling?" I asked.

"Better."

I started work on Jura's wounds after the elves returned to the secret hideout. His wounds were mostly a whole lot of broken bones and a few burn marks. Bamboo, being wooden armor that protected his body, absorbed most of the damage from the explosion, but that meant Jura still had to deal with the fall damage.

"Good." His burns were now fully healed, but what was left were the broken bones. The bones had fused together but were still in the healing process and would take some time before they regained their past strength.

I foresaw Jura should not join in any combat related activities for at least two months, or those repairs might break.

YEAR 76, MONTH 9

[Tree volcanic adaptation stage I - complete!]

[Tree winter adaptation aura - complete!]

Hell, yeah. My trees were growing in the muthafooking winter. With the completion of the winter adaptation aura, trees near me all gained some resistance to winter and were now able to grow in it.

This meant a return of growth!

This feeling of finally being able to grow after not growing for so long kinda felt like being able to taste food after losing your taste buds for weeks. Ah, how glorious it was to be able to grow after being stunted for so damned long.

At this point, I realized that I was somewhat of a growth addict. I really enjoyed watching another patch of snow-covered dirt produce a bunch of green shoots, which then transformed into a proper tree. And the central trees, those closer to me, were even able to feed energy back to me.

It was kinda like being sick for so long that you forgot what being healthy felt like, and now, *woosh*! Hell yeah.

Grow, grow, *growwwww*!!!

"Is the tree always like this?" Alexis asked.

"I think he's gone a little crazy." Meela shrugged. "But that's normal."

Also, there was still the volcano thing. The first stage of the upgrades meant my trees could now approach the volcanic area without dying, but I was still a distance away from the volcano itself. There was, however, a lake that was being warmed by the volcano's magma, and since the valley did need some hot water, I placed a few subsidiary trees next to it and activated my heat transmission system. It was essentially a kind of root system that pushed the hot water from the heated lake to the valley.

[Secret Hideout upgraded! Hot water now available.]

[Hot volcanic bath obtained!]

Oh. Did I really have to go that cliched route of getting a damned onsen inside my own secret hideout?

Although there was some transmission loss, it was good enough that I could get the valley's trees a bit warmer, too, so there was a bit of steam and mist now emerging in the valley as the hot water interacted with the cold weather above it.

[You've acquired the skill: Mist.]

Oh.

"I like hot springs." Alexis shrugged. "Now I want a physical body."

"Me, too. I haven't had one in ages," Meela also commented.

"Which one? The hot springs or the body?"

"Why not both?"

Were these two ladies going to commentate on all my actions and achievements?

"I find their banter amusing, Master." Horns, too, had finally recovered from his injuries, and he too shared a bit of the winter upgrades, so like the other beetles, he had a sap in his body that acted as a heater. "Will they be useful?"

I shook my head and changed my train of thought. The main volcano itself was still farther in, and to get there I needed to work on my next stage of the volcanic adaptation research, which also involved getting more materials from the volcano.

[Beetle winter adaptation stage II - 6 months remaining.]

[Volcanic adaptation stage II - 8 months remaining. Requires 200 x sulfur.]

[Tree winter adaptation stage II - 8 months remaining.]

Ugh, the higher stages were going to take more time, or I would need to increase the number of biolabs working on them in the future.

"Assign me," Alexis volunteered. "I volunteer to do research."

Her dryad body was fully developed now, and if I wasn't mistaken, it was designed with herself as the template, and so it was going to make her a dryad, who then undertook research in the biolab. "I'll think about it," I replied.

"Oh, come on. You can cast spells on me if you want to keep watch. I won't do strange stuff, I swear!" Alexis pleaded.

Hmm...

YEAR 76, MONTH 10

Oh, more growth. I loved growth.

This resurgence in growth was most keenly felt by the New Freekans, who were amazed to see the bigger trees sprout, even in this snow, and it applied to the potatoes as well. Thanks to my newfound powers, the potatoes produced daily increased to two thousand! Double! All because of the winter resistance!

I hid all my potatoes, using beetles as my carriers. There was really no need to let the New Freekans know there was a huge stockpile of potatoes underground.

This made me think of the poor chap so many years ago, the one who asked me for a healing fruit, but I couldn't give him one because I still didn't have winter adaptation back then.

Ah, well.

Speaking of which, when did the demon king die again? About three years ago? Was there going to be a ten-year gap again this time?

"Generally, ten years."

"I wasn't asking you?"

"I know, but I wanted to answer it."

She was being a bit of a smart alec and maybe a bit chunni.

"And I think it's important," she continued. "When I was researching the ancient text, it seems the ten-year cycle is just a rule of thumb. There have been occasions where the demons choose to delay their invasion although the supposed time was up."

That was a whole lot more long-winded than I thought it would be. But I supposed it would be useful to know, somehow.

"I still don't know why, though, and what exactly the other-worldly demons want."

Huh. What do the demons want? Don't they just behave on instinct and act out their directive to kill all lives?

"I mean, so far, the demons from the other worlds can't be reasoned with, so we don't actually know what they want... unlike the local demons." Oh, there were factions in the demons, too; well, when I thought about it, it figured, creatures of evil were not equally evil or evil in the same way.

Anyway, back to the growth thing. With the warm waters from the volcano, areas where the hot water was released turned into something of an oasis in the cold, and the area there was a little more fertile. The hot water was also mineral rich, so I noticed the potatoes I cultivated were a little larger and different in color.

"Actually, Master, if we use the minerals extracted by our roots and infuse them into the potatoes, we can achieve a similar effect."

Yes, thanks for reminding me that I had a huge pile of minerals I didn't use while simultaneously hinting I was a dumbass. At the same time, maybe this was why I needed all these assistants. I was clearly not making the most of my resources and abilities.

YEAR 76, MONTH 10, CONTINUED

So...

Now that things were returning to normal for me—somewhat—my focus was on the volcano. The volcano was clearly of great interest to me as it generated so much heat and energy—something I would need for my valley.

But the next phase involved defeating the magma monsters that spawned near the volcano while protecting my trees. And from the initial skirmishes between the beetles and the magma monsters, they didn't fair too well at all. It took about five beetles to beat a single magma monster because the magma monsters were able to burn the beetles when they got near, and the beetles attacked by ramming the magma monsters with their horns.

So it was a bad matchup, really. That was one problem I needed to fix. I couldn't manually go in and use [Root Strike] on the magma monsters—okay, actually I could, but it was just that, if I did that personally, then I didn't have the time to do other stuff, so I needed the beetles or whatever solution I came up with to be able to act somewhat autonomously.

"Horns, any ideas?"

"Research fire-resistant protective shells and magical horns for more power!"

"That'll take three and six months, respectively, Master," Trevor added, giving the numbers. "And that would also delay our other research on further enhancements to the tree's resistances."

"Ugh." I wanted all the research. This felt like playing those games with huge tech trees, and you just wanted to choose all of the available options because in some ways, you did need them all. "Recommendations?"

"We could spread out our time on both," Trevor and Dimitree said in unison, "but it'll be a two-month delay for the other two projects."

"No. I want them, too."

So the next step was more forest minds, but clearly, I was limited in this aspect.

"Are you willing to consider my help, now?" Alexis spoke up.

I'll think about it.

YEAR 76, MONTH 11

Winter! Well, it was rather comfortable this winter, thanks to the hot water piped in from the lake—and my new winter resistance aura.

The New Freekans were doing well, fortifying themselves, and they did manage to build up a large stockpile of food. It seemed their indecision led to Salah denouncing the truce, and now they even accused the New Freekans of collaborating with their enemies. So the truce was off!

But, even though the truce was off, it didn't descend into war directly. After all, Salah was still tied up in their conflict with Nung and Takde, and the winter also severely impaired their ability to wage any assault on New Freeka. It was actually a normality in the world, that war was declared but actual fighting didn't happen until sometime later, and for certain human nations, there were even rules of engagement that the rulers followed, or they found themselves having awarded cursed titles, for falling out of favor with the human war gods.

Gaya, apparently, was one such god that demanded certain rules of engagement: that battles were fought on open fields, each battle started with a commander leading the charge, there was clear publicly declared casus belli behind the conflict, and that a prayer was held before each large war.

Strangely enough, despite how restrictive it sounded, Gaya, as a god, participated rather directly in terms of larger conflicts, often granting commanders tremendous gifts. It was said that if heroes, the singular most powerful humans in the world failed, they would turn to the commanders of Gaya to defend the world, though, in reality, there was still a huge gap in their power. Gods in the world interacted with it in a few ways, namely through gifts, and there were rules around such gifts, that all gods followed, even the dark gods native to the world.

I partly learned this from Alexis because one of her first acts when coming to this world was actually figuring out how to go back, so she went head-on into books on gods, magic, and all that. But, of course, there were restrictions on going back, and one of those restrictions, placed by the million-headed hydra that watched over Earth, was that the souls returned clean. In short, they returned without their powers or memories, though they might still experience dreams that reminded them of their past lives.

So...back to war. The New Freekans were, of course, annoyed by the development, but knowing that Salah's engagement wouldn't happen soon, they decided to fortify themselves, to prepare for the coming conflict. Despite the cold winters, New Freeka's population was now a respectable thirty-five thousand, and so they had the ability to field close to thirteen thousand fighters in the battle, which was a decent fighting force.

Salah might easily have sent fifty thousand, perhaps even a hundred thousand, but they were a far larger state with more competing priorities, with their ongoing war with the Nung and Takde. So, unless Salah really provoked them, they might just let this little conflict carry on for a bit longer.

Yvon, though, was still trying to avoid war, so her negotiators instead focused on who was the real culprit of the Blood

Blizzard, which, increasingly, was pointing toward the acts of a terrorist group that had infiltrated the senior army leadership of all three nations, in order to carry out such a large sacrifice.

In short, even if they did find who was behind this, the emerging fact still pointed to all three nations contributing to the blood blizzard, and none of the three nations would want to implicate themselves in the spell, so...the war was just going to go on.

So...too bad.

This week, I converted one of the large subsidiary trees into a training room at Lausanne's request. The weather outside was now far too cold for combat practice, so their sword-fighting practice headed indoors.

She was going to turn eight soon, and despite her earlier lack of talents, she somehow managed to pick it up. Perhaps through a combination of [Dream Tutor] and [Power-leveling], she acquired sufficient sword fighting skills to have simple sparring sessions with Jura.

She had also started to gain levels. There seemed to be some kind of barrier preventing very young children from gaining levels, but this level barrier was inconsistent and varied across races. Out of curiosity, I had her dip into one of the biolabs, just to check on her. I had a theory previously that young children's 'spring'—that connected their body to the soul and vice versa—wasn't yet fully mature, so that person was unable to gain levels. Prior to this, I didn't even have an assessment of Lausanne's estimated soul rank, but now I did.

My intuition was right. Indeed, her 'spring,' the fountain that produced mana, now had a consistent shape. This raised a big set of questions, as in, what exactly influenced the size and shape of the fountain? I also had a few thoughts about this—one was whether all souls were the same, but there was some other thing that acted as the link between the soul and the body, and that then influenced a person's full 'potential'—or, if the souls were different, then there should be a way to manipulate and change the qualities a soul had.

"Master, you're using my root-brain to augment your theories again..." Trevor grumbled. Ah yes, it seemed I sometimes unknowingly tapped into the processing power of the trees to think. But this had the effect of taking away processing power from Trevor, which then impaired his performance. I needed to think of the root-brain complex as a computer processor, and if I was using it, Trevor couldn't.

"I should have more root-brains." It was logical, no? I came from a world of quad cores and more. It would be fascinating if I somehow stitched all these root brains together into some kind of collective super-brain, no?

[Special project unlocked.]

[The Grand Mind Tree—significantly boosts tree-related research output and grants wider understanding of soul magic. Gains additional psychic-type magical abilities.]

[Requires 10 x root brain complexes and 1 ton of gold and 1 ton of quartz crystals. Once all prerequisites are complete, construction will take 1.5 years.]

Ah. My own supercomputer. Well, kind of.

"Alexis, you're redundant if I get this."

"Noooooooooooooooooooooo." Alexis sighed, but then she paused. "But you're not going to get it soon. It'll still take time. So assign me to a biolab, please? You're going to have to wait probably two to three years before you can achieve it. Maybe more."

She was right. It was going to take a while. Construction of the root-brain complex itself required 10 x Blood Crystals and 50 x fresh animal heads, and so ten root brains meant a whole lot of blood crystals, and that meant money, which we probably didn't have.

"You're right, Alexis. But I still don't really trust you, so I've decided that I will merge you with a biolab someday, but you will be watched and observed."

"That's okay. I'd rather tinker in the biological structure of trees and beetles than be stuck in this dark and dreary place. Can't you do something about how gloomy your soul realm is? A biolab it is then."

"It's a transit lounge for souls to reincarnate. It's not helpful for it to be a pleasant place to be. I can't have too many souls not wanting to move on." Well, to be fair, the souls only lingered around for six months to a year, and after that, they would move on. The soul realm, whether pleasant or not, had no influence in this.

I got sidetracked again. I mumbled to myself and resumed watching Lausanne. Her body was really young, after all she's only seven turning eight, but the [Dream Tutor] had given her a rather varied set of skills, and so she was actually pretty versatile as a person.

She still wanted to be a hero, but lately she was starting to understand that there was a gap between herself and the true heroes that could change the world with their power, though somedays, she still believed she could stand up there. She would have to gain a lot more levels if she wanted to. Only with levels could she even think of standing up to a hero, one who was blessed by the heavens.

"Tree-Tree, do you have powers to you know...make me stronger?"

I did. The ginseng tree, and it granted a permanent boost. But the problem was that they just kept dying—usually after their first unlock. If I grew a ginseng tree inside me, maybe that'd work. It also didn't help that they died within two to three months in this cold weather, so I would have to wait until the wizards actually managed to weaken or dispel this cold weather before resuming my replanting of my three ginseng trees.

"I do, but you'll have to wait."

"Okay! I'll need all the help I can get!" Lausanne raised her hand like a hurrah. "Uncle Jura says heroes are super, super strong, and I'll need all the blessings the world can give me to be as strong as them."

Hmmm...

That was actually possible. Perhaps throughout the world there were various 'permanent' blessings, similar to ginseng trees. If a person could gather enough of them, they could be as strong as the heroes.

"I think I should go on a journey someday, with Uncle Jura and Mom, to get those blessings."

"That's a good idea, Lausanne..."

Jura had healed, but his bones still needed to fully recover. So he was just doing simple exercises and relying on Bamboo to provide training for Lausanne. Bamboo and Jura actually managed to achieve some kind of bond, and Bamboo now manifested itself as a flexible wooden arm for Jura, so Jura was back to being two-handed.

It was kind of like a prosthetic but with a summon. Quite a cool outcome actually; I frankly never thought of that. It wasn't as good as a real arm, of course, but as workarounds went, it was pretty good since Bamboo and Jura as a familiar had a mental link.

"Bamboo is due for an upgrade, too." Yes, so was Horns.

"I think I'll go on a journey when I turn fifteen. That's when they say we're old enough to start traveling. Then Uncle Jura can go with me."

I nodded. Lausanne talked to me a lot, and that meant she listened to my thoughts about the future. Strangely, I thought this meant I'd influenced her to think about what she wanted to do, unlike the rest of them who tended to look at things on a shorter time frame.

"How are Brislach and Wahlen doing?"

"They're working in New Freeka. I think Brislach's working in a shop selling potato breads."

"Ah..." Wasn't she doing something else? Ah well. Not everyone had ambitions of the grand kind, and that wasn't a fault.

"Wahlen's working in the treasurer's office as an administrator. He's learning how to read and write, too."

Literacy. It was mix and match in this world. Most of the time they were taught by a village elder in the small villages, and to some extent literacy was a valuable skill, useful in government matters and trade. Some cultures had stronger emphasis on reading, some less. Elves surprisingly didn't place much emphasis on writing and reading, as their long lives tended to mean they would just pick it up over the years. They also seemed to favor oral traditions, having an appointed old one in every village to remember the traditions and ceremonies—certain subtleties that the written word couldn't capture.

"I should learn to read and write, too. A hero must be smart!"

"Knowing how to read doesn't make you smart, Lausanne."

"Doesn't it? But at least I'm not stupid!"

"Not knowing how to read doesn't make you stupid."

"Less stupid," she mumbled. "I can work if I know to how to read and write. Good for traveling."

"Good point." Writers were useful. They were often paid to write letters and messages. Some writers doubled up as messengers, and sort of mailmen, and this was usually a relatively good way to gain admission into a merchant association or guild. "Ever thought of being a merchant? That's a good way to travel the world without involving yourself in too much fighting."

"A hero as a merchant?" Lausanne slumped, but then she actually thought about it.

"Yeah. Why can't heroes be merchants?"

She was seriously thinking about it.

To be fair, I hadn't heard of a merchant hero before. Their

neutrality kind of made it hard for them to play the role of a 'hero'—someone who had to take a side.

"Lausanne, rest time's up. Practice," Jura called, and he picked up a wooden practice sword and shield. Thanks to Bamboo's augmented limb, he could now teach Lausanne the standard sword and shield method of fighting.

"A hero as a merchant..." It was still on her mind, but then she stood and rejoined Jura in the middle of the training-tree. Essentially, it was a large empty room in a tree.

As Jura and Lausanne resumed their regular practice, I turned my attention to the volcanic area once more. Some of the magma monsters were getting a little bit aggressive, and I had to periodically kill them to protect the subsidiary trees located nearby.

The volcano was an active volcano, its caldera partly blown apart, so there was a part where there was liquid lava flowing out. As was the norm in the world, this led to magma monsters spawning, and from what the beetles had seen farther inside, there were larger magma monsters closer to the caldera.

So far, they were territorial, so they didn't seem to attack us if we didn't approach.

"Master, it is time I got an upgrade," Horns suggested. He was fully recovered now, so he was due for an upgrade since he capped out at level twenty earlier. Bamboo, too, so I took the chance to review their upgrade requirements.

[Horns, Level 20 Beetle Knight]

[Upgrade options available:]

[Blue - Baron Beetle - 5 x blue crystals, 30 x almost-complete skeleton of a large animal.]

[Gains commander effects, which grants nearby beetles increased abilities.]

[Black - Beetle Dark Knight - 10 x obsidian rocks, 20 x large claws.]

[Gains combat skills.]

[Bamboo, Level 20 Woodbear Eidolon]

[Upgrade options available:]

[Blue - Armor path - 50 small copper ingots & 5 medium red rubies needed.]

[Gains defensive abilities.]

[Black - Claw path - 50 small iron ingots & 5 medium onyx needed.]

[Gains offensive abilities.]

[Trevor, Level 27 Forest Mind]

[Will be unlocked at level 30.]

[Black - Skull Shell - 10 x Bone of a wyvern, 1 x heart of a lion, and 50 x Bones of a lizard.]

[Gains a ghostly projection.]

All these upgrades imposed a lot of resource requirements. So I would need more resources.

"You require more minerals," Dimitree chimed in, with his Russian accent. It reminded me of a wraith. Or was that a terran goliath?

Ah, yes. "You've been taking in a few too many of my game references."

"Ah, whatever. If I want these resources, I'll get them from New Freeka."

————

"The tree spirit demands what?"

The advisors look concerned when Yvon shared my resource demands with the rest of her council.

"Blood crystals, gold, quartz crystals, copper and iron ingots, rubies, onyx, and blue crystals," Yvon repeated, but she clearly understood their concern.

One of Yvon's closest advisors then clarified, "It's more of a... request than a demand, right?"

Yvon shrugged. "I'm not too sure if I understand the tree spirit correctly, but I think it sounds more like a demand than a...request."

"Should we?" One of the advisors looked really worried. "It feels a bit like extortion."

"I believe most of you have seen the tree spirit's combat abilities, and it's incredible abilities throughout this valley... The recent hot water spring around the tree of prayer is a recent addition."

"It's hard, though. Those goods are not regular stuff. They are jewels or crystals... I mean, even the cheapest of those are the blood crystals and the quartz. The tree's asking for a lot."

"Well, the recent burst in natural growth and the hot water in the valley helped us a lot, too."

It quickly seemed clear that it was divided into two camps— one who thought that my demands were reasonable given my assistance to their survival, and then a bunch who thought it was excessive, and they should only give what they could manage.

Yvon mostly stayed out of it, asking the council to decide as her soul was contracted to me. She said she wasn't a 'neutral' party to the decision.

Of course, from my point of view, I knew that these people need a bit of...encouragement.

So I decided to withdraw all the hot water piping into New Freeka, and so in this cold month, they had a *really* cold week. After that week, they met up again and agreed that it was best not to offend me, so they decided to support my demands. Between Salah and me, they decided to be on my good side.

[Monsters slain. You've gained a level. Level 129!]

[You've gained a new skill: Training Treehouse.]

[Training treehouse improves experience gain, skill gain chances, and reduces injuries significantly.]

U h. This sounded like an extension of my training room. Seriously, this system leaned heavily toward the nurturing, growing side of things, really sparingly granting me offensive abilities.

I supposed that if I wanted to work around the tree, I needed to think like the system. If I was designing a system for a tree, what would I think about?

My suspicions were that a system in which a soul tree was at the center, focused on a few core principles. Again, this was just a theory that I had, based on my experiences so far.

'Grow, nurture, and endure.'

This was the first, core principle with any tree. The logical driver behind any tree was to grow, to expand, and so I should get a wide range of abilities that promoted growth and allowed me to endure a wide variety of damage and still recover. With it, I would need the ability to 'support' young things and also build an ecosystem with the tree as the foundation.

'Enhance and adapt.'

A tree that expanded would need to adapt to various environments and react to the challenges that were unique to this world. This was the evolutionary, research side of what I suspected was a natural inclination. If trees were unable to react in a world where magic was native, then trees would quickly go extinct. So I believed the trees in this magical world had natural adaptational abilities superior to that of our world, and the system supported them.

Then there was the 'Soul abilities,' which arose as a 'soul tree.' These were not natural tree abilities, but they existed because I was a soul-related kind of entity, and so the system had to grant me abilities that were natural for a soul-tree to have.

Thinking along those lines, if I intended on getting more offensive abilities, it would grow as a result of working toward more 'enhancement' and 'adaptation' as a result of a tree being forced to defend itself.

In other words, to 'game' the system to give me offensive abilities, I must put myself into a situation where self-defense was a required adaptation.

Now how did I go about doing that...

...

...

Never mind. I quickly upgraded that empty training room into this 'training treehouse' so that Lausanne could benefit from it.

Oh, and I tested out those carnivorous plants that I got.

They functioned more like traps, really, and they sprang out to eat anything about the size of a wolf. This was pretty good, but the drawback was that the digestive period was quite long, so essentially, if a huge swarm of demon hounds came along, they'd be full very quickly.

So useful under certain circumstances, but its use in a large-scale combat situation was probably limited.

If anything, what I would need was a fire-breathing tree. Imagine it. If a tree could breathe fire, or even poison, that would be pretty useful. And such options were indeed available on my research options.

Being frustrated at how slow my research was, I eventually decided to take a chance on Alexis.

"If you try anything funny, I will kill you," I warned.

"Understood, but I am soul-contracted to you, so don't worry about it. We're aligned, trust me."

"I can't, but I'll give you the opportunity to prove me wrong."

I initially would have preferred Meela, but the soul-contract was an additional layer of protection I had, so after some thinking, it was actually better to use Alexis first. If Meela had gone rogue, I might find that I had fewer means to retaliate.

[Initiating soul forge.]

[Combining Alexis with an external biolab.]

[Combining...]

A bolt of thunder struck the forge tree, and from it emerged a glowing blue seed. It was as large as a dog, and it floated over to the external biolab I'd chosen, embedding itself in it.

[Alexis has successfully merged with an external biolab!]

[Alexis is now a laboratory spirit, level 1.]

"Oh, wow," she mumbled before manifesting herself as a

glowing blue ghost inside the laboratory. "There's so much data. So much...data."

"Uh."

"I'm fine. I'm fine! This is amazing." She seemed to be looking at some kind of interface, tapping into my stored records of all the biolab scans I had done in the past, including herself. "Even my own records are here. I've never realized what you'd been looking at!"

At this point, I decided to just observe her for a while.

"This is amazing."

The external biolab that she now possessed, and was a part of her, was actually a tree with a hollow interior, filled with pods and various equipment for testing. It had a 'transportation' system, in which a beetle delivered any of its required materials for research.

"Your visual way of representing the soul and the body-mind connection is incredible. I've read books on the theoretical basis of magic, and how the souls interact with the body, but this...this is mind-blowing. It's amazing how intuitive it is, representing it as a spring and a field that spring nourishes. All those magical theory books make life difficult by overcomplicating the terminology and using difficult to understand words. This. This is concise!"

Oh. Okay. She's really dived into the deep end. I honestly didn't think of it as that...unique, but I supposed humans with no access to the [biolab] would find it that way.

"Alexis, are you okay?" Meela asked, sounding a little concerned.

"Oh, more than okay. This is amazing. This is exactly what I was trying to find when I was trying to research magic! You should see this."

"You know I don't like that kind of stuff." Meela shrugged.

"Ah yes, but I'm fine. I'm really fine."

Meela sighed. "I sometimes forget how much of a nerd you can be."

"Hey!" Alexis floated and looked at other stuff. "The representation of the demon's presence as a parched fire with a dried field is also fascinating. It seems to imply the demonic energies are antithesis to our own, and it opens up so many options on how we can counteract their presence. What's this, a data set on our star mana and those floating vases pouring out star mana? Holy cow, this is like...mind-blowing, too! What else do you have!" Alexis was constantly floating about the biolab, looking at more and more of the interfaces.

Meela turned to me. "When she reads a great book, she can't stop talking about it. I think she's in that phase again."

"Meela! Seriously! This information can advance magic research by decades!"

At this point, I decided to cut in. "Alexis, your task is to research the beetles and the countermeasures necessary to conquer the volcano. Don't get sidetracked."

"Ah yes, yes. But can you give me a week. Let me just have a look at this huge pile of data you have. I'm sure there's some other amazing stuff in here."

"No. I will not tolerate disobedience on your first day as a biolab spirit. Get to work."

She sighed and then nodded. "Okay, okay. I'll do it, but give me daily free time, all right? I work eight hours a day, all right? The remaining hours are mine for rest and my own activities. I really want to look at all this data!"

"Twelve hours. And you will be monitored."

"Ah fine. I know." She then gained a level. Although her god's blessing was lost when she died, she still retained quite a few perks, one of which was the experience perk.

[Beetle winter adaptation stage II - 4 months remaining.]

[Volcanic adaptation stage II - 6 months remaining.]

[Tree winter adaptation stage II - 6 months remaining.]

[Beetle volcanic battleform - 3 months remaining (may complete earlier).]

[Beetle volcanic defensive armors - 2 months remaining (may complete earlier).]

On the New Freeka front, they received an envoy from Nung and Takde. It seemed that Nung and Takde now wanted to aid New Freeka in their 'resistance' against Salah, but the person sent by Nung was slimy beyond belief, so Yvon and the advisors found it hard to agree with them.

There were no 'good guys' in this war between the three nations. All of them had their own goals, and all three wanted a piece of each other, though Nung and Takde were now 'allies' as a result of their mutual enemy.

Under other circumstances, they would probably attack each other.

So, once again, New Freeka's council couldn't decide. They didn't really want to turn down their aid, but at the same time, these two nations weren't the most upstanding and honest of nations. One of the key skills a leader needed to have was the ability to decide. Sometimes picking a choice was more important than evaluating which one was right. But Yvon's style seemed to be more concerned on what was right. She had a need to be 'morally' correct—at least from her perspective—and that clouded her ability to sometimes make tough, probably cruel decisions.

Ah, well.

YEAR 77, MONTH 1

A new year began. It was still as cold as ever, though—not like the wizards had gotten to the point of weakening it yet. There was still a fluctuation in the coldness, so I supposed whoever they sent to undo that cursed spell was still tinkering with it.

That little moment with Alexis and the whole database of my past research brought up a point about my data access rules. As a tree, I shared the information freely with my artificial souls, and all the biolabs, so it initially seemed natural for me to do the same. In fact, I didn't even think about this data security issue until Alexis did what she did.

But I guessed that now it was a bit too late. Oh, well. She was doing all right as a research spirit anyway.

"I think I'm near a breakthrough," Alexis mumbled. "I think I've figured this thing whole lab work thing out. All I've got to do is press some buttons and the lab itself will just keep trying different combinations of materials to change stuff."

She was already level ten as a lab spirit. It was rather unfair how these hero-reincarnators still retained some of their perks, even after death.

Alexis floated over a few beetles, each in a clear pod with a light green liquid, kind of like how most people imagined large, glass preservation cylinders to look. The lab itself did most of the work, as in making changes to the beetles that it experimented on and then producing the results for Alexis to interpret. The length of the research essentially was an automated number crunching exercise, derived from an estimate of X percentage likelihood of a favorable outcome divided by time taken per 'test' per biolab.

In a way, since we were on the security topic, it was really like a machine trying to break a password by trying to key in a combination.

Therefore, by adding Alexis, a sentient mind of the mix, she could look at the data and make educated guesses, which narrowed down the options the biolab had to crunch, so we were more likely to make progress on a research topic.

So, when a biolab was tasked to research 'volcanic' endurance, it would try different combinations of trees and then see what worked. As such, my own guess was that providing the correct environment, and sufficient resources, would actually enhance the research output of the external biolabs.

"It's a lot more mechanical than I thought it would be. It's really all about looking at all the output and datasets and just deciding where to go as a next step, and the biolab just does it for you...most of the time." Alexis frowned. Now that she was a spirit confined in the biolab and its immediate surroundings, people could see her, and they saw her as a blue apparition that haunted the biolab.

"What are some of those words..." Meela frowned.

"Mumbo-jumbo." Alexis laughed. "Really, just talking about research results and choosing what's more likely to work based on the testing results. I know you understand it. Don't act dumb."

"No, no." Meela sighed.

"You're just trying to avoid my fate of being made into a research spirit, aren't ya? It isn't so bad, actually. I get to float around and look outside of the tree. Have you noticed how starry it gets at night?"

Meela didn't answer.

"The moons are gorgeous at night, and one of them never truly turns dark. And I think the other one's on some kind of three-month cycle, instead of the one month we're so used to."

Well...the moons were different after all.

"Meela, seriously. Take a leap, do something, see the world with me. Again. Don't just hide there in the comfort of Tree-Tree's soul realm..."

"No..."

Alexis paused, and then she floated up to the top of the biolab tree. She sat on one of the branches and looked out. "Well, the sunrise's going to be gorgeous." There were some things I couldn't see, given the limitations of my tree vision. And what I couldn't see, those in my soul realm couldn't see, either.

I too wished to see how the sunrise truly looked, instead of an augmented version pieced together by the collective data formed through Trevor and Dimitree's gathered sensors and receptors throughout the valley.

Maybe I should actually have...eyes.

[Eye-Tree Stage I research option unlocked - 24 months needed.]

Whoa. The word itself was kind of scary, and I tried to imagine myself as a tree with eyes. No matter how I did it, it still came out as a little freaky—probably the kind of stuff that belonged in a Lovecraftian epic.

Heh. Why didn't I just give myself the eye tree? I supposed certain kinds of abilities now had to go through research. I was a bit confused actually. Did the system actually have a way of saying what I could research or what I could get through my skills?

There were discussions that said leveling granted skills on a random basis. Essentially, there was a big pool with skills in it, where skills you were more likely to get had a higher probability, and then you essentially drew. Research was what happened when you failed to draw the skill you wanted, and as a consolation, you could still work toward the skill. Perhaps?

Anyway. These were mysteries of the system. For all I knew, it was just one person dare deciding what to give me, and what not to, just rolling a die every now and then for the fun of it.

YEAR 77, MONTH 2

S trangely, I assumed the wizards succeeded. On the eve of
the second month, a strange lack of cold swept through
the land, and the cold didn't come back.

"It's probably just a reduction, not a complete removal,"
Trevor spoke. "We can still faintly detect the presence of the
spell, just...in much smaller amounts."

"Huh."

"Probably a reduction in the power of the spell's effects, so
the valley being so far away experienced a significant
improvement."

"You know, if you have a lab that focuses on magic, you
could find out..." Alexis said, butting herself in.

"It's a biolab, with magical sensors that focus on living
things. It's not a magic lab."

"Okay, but why not make a magic lab? It will help since there
are so many magical unknowns out there."

"It's not as if I desire for a magic lab, then I will get a magic
lab."

"Research?" Alexis tapped a few screens in the biolab.

Alexis floated into the middle of the lab and used a skill,
[Research Planner].

"We'll need to first unlock material testing, then materials lab, then into magic-attunement, and then into magic-sensitive equipment, and then a basic magic lab. Probably about a year and a half's worth of research. But you'll get a material lab within six months!"

I'm thinking.

"What do you say? I think it's a good idea!"

I'm thinking.

"After your volcano research. I want to be able to secure the volcano first."

"Aww, man, come on. I think magic can help you fix the volcano problem, too."

"No. Biological solutions first. I have Horns to help me manage the beetles if I can get those upgrades."

Alexis sighed. "Okay..." She pouted and went back into her biolab-tree. Somewhat unnervingly, this biolab-tree derived its energy from Alexis, not me, and so it gained new equipment and abilities as and when Alexis leveled.

Alexis was now level fourteen, and her most recent skill was [Probability Charts], which produced an estimated likelihood of outcomes for a test before actually going for it. In short, her skill simulated testing, a bit.

Her biolab-tree had a small chamber that functioned as her personal room, where there was a bed that actually interacted with her spiritual form, so she could sleep. Actually, the entire biolab-tree seemed to be able to react to her as if she was a solid, real person, and at the same time, she could switch it off, and then pass through things.

Alexis went back to her room and decided to take a nap instead. Maybe she wasn't that happy with my decision.

Anyway, now that the snowing stopped, it was a great chance for me to boost my growth!

GROW!

Expand!

My tree instincts were driving me a little crazy.

EXPAND!!!

Yeah.

So we had more trees. After losing close to seven thousand trees to Alexis's demonfire, thanks to this month's returning warmth, and my newfound winter resistance, we were back up by three-and-a-half thousand trees. So yes, more trees. MORE. TREES.

The trees were also now starting to feed energy and resources back into the [Tuberous Storage].

[Tuberous storage upgraded.]

[High density tubers unlocked. Tubers will be naturally upgraded.]

Oh. Yay? They stored two units of energy now.

Back to expanding...and food!

And so I decided to try my luck with the damned [ginseng tree]...again.

"Alexis, can you also keep watch?" The ginseng tree's right next to the biolab, with a lot of beetles and web spiders protecting them.

She covered her head with a pillow. "Didn't hear you."

I knew she did, and I knew she would—because her soul-contract compelled her to.

Anyway, the New Freekans were happy. Warmth meant a return to regular farming, stockpiling, and less burning through their stockpiles.

Yet it was also bittersweet because the opportunity for Salah to now attack them was returning. The winter sort of gave New Freeka a natural 'terrain deterrent' from war. Even in a world of magic, not everything ran on magic, and so the terrain still had a huge influence on logistics, resources, and even petty things like warm clothing and all.

The council decides to reject the Nung and Takde offer, as they decided to state that they had no claim in this war and would prefer to stay out of it. It was a way of not pissing off Salah too much, as this gesture would suggest that New Freeka was genuine in not participating in any conflict.

"If Baroosh were to endorse New Freeka's independence, do you think that'd go well?" One of Yvon's councilors was speaking to the exiled wizard of Baroosh. They seemed to be rather close acquaintances, perhaps, even friends.

"Knowing my king, I doubt that'll ever happen. He has never endorsed or supported any allied nations, especially one as far away as New Freeka. He is not a man of many friends, and he believes each nation should stand on their own strength."

"Ah..."

"But I suppose you could convince some of the lords to lend some assistance from their private armies. The fiefdoms themselves act mostly independently of the king, anyway..."

The councilor nodded. "Ah. I'll need to get this message to the trading corps. Let's start with a trade."

"That's a good idea. By the way, I heard about the tree spirit's demands..."

"Yeah. It's kind of extortion, isn't it?"

"I don't see it that way. Strangely enough, I now come to view the tree spirit as the guardian 'beast' of this valley, and supporting it is probably the best insurance you can get against Salah."

"Really? You think the tree spirit is willing to step in? From what I hear from Lady Yvon, the tree spirit is flighty, inconsistent, and acts rather irrationally at times."

"Such are beings of another plane. Their minds are...different."

"True. Can't expect it to think like we do."

"And I doubt it ever will. Its concerns are different, and my view is, New Freeka best align itself to the tree spirit's desires. I think from the fire-demon encounter alone, the tree spirit demonstrates far greater destructive power than it usually lets on."

"Hmmm. Some of the councilors will find that a hard pill to swallow since we are supposed to be an independent state, not a puppet of a tree-spirit."

"Convince them not to see it that way. Think of the tree-spirit as a potentially friendly dragon. It has its own thing going, generally lets you do what you want, and if you make it happy enough, it can sometimes help you. Perhaps get the treefolk chieftains to speak to them. They revere the tree spirit after all, as their deity of some kind."

"It'll just sound like preaching. The other councilors will hate it. Maybe you should speak to them."

"You know well enough that they look at me with the same eyes of suspicion. I am an exiled wizard from another country. What weight do my words carry?"

The councilor sighed. "There must be another way."

"Maybe you don't actually need to give the tree spirit actual jewels, you know."

"Huh?"

"It's a tree spirit, right? Perhaps all it wants is a nearby location that contains those jewels, even if it's hidden or buried under mountains of dirt and rock. Or, maybe, it doesn't even need it in the processed, polished form we are so familiar with. I highly doubt it wants it for the same reason as our nobles and royals do. Maybe it just wants raw...jewels—so be it if it's mixed with rocks and whatnot."

The councilor rubbed her chin. "That's actually a good point and worth clarifying with the tree spirit. We've gotten so used to noble's expectations to have jewels in a certain condition that I didn't think that a tree may not need it in a similar...state."

Certainly, raw, unprocessed gems were worth far less than processed ones, which needed special equipment and skilled gem craftsmen.

"Yes. Tell Lady Yvon we would require more information. If we can glean an understanding of the tree spirit's intent, we can act accordingly."

"This room is awesome." Lausanne jumped. Apparently, she had leveled up.

"Indeed." Jura nodded, holding a set of wooden weapons. "The passives to your training remind me of the effects of a skilled military drillmaster. Such rooms would be useful in preparation for any war."

Lausanne blocked the wooden sword. She was gradually getting better at all the combat skills Jura was passing on to her, and Jura's complaints had been getting fewer. It seemed the term 'late bloomer' was real, or perhaps it was just the influence of [Dream Tutor], constantly feeding the combat-skills to her.

They practiced for about two hours. "All right, enough for now. How are you feeling?"

"Sore!" Lausanne talked about her muscles aching from all the blocking. Jura was pulling his punches, after all Lausanne had only just turned eight, so her physique wasn't comparable to Jura's, who had years and years of training and the body of an adult. Lausanne was at least ten years away from her body standing up to Jura at full strength.

Jura passed her an ointment made of preserved healing fruits. Laufen's experiments in preserving the healing fruits granted her some basic ointment-making skills, as it seemed the juice from the healing fruits mixed with the vinegar to form some kind of basic pain-relieving liquid. It wasn't a potion, though.

Lausanne sat on one of the chairs in the training room and applied the ointment to her sore joints.

"I expected to find you here." Laufen walked through the door.

"Hi, Mom. Just finished practice..."

"I spoke to some of the merchants in town, and I found out there's a proper teacher for Elvish writing. Do you want to go?"

Lausanne nodded. "Oh, really. Good. Can he come here? This training room has training boosts. Maybe I will learn better here."

"I'll ask the teacher about it. Anyway, come, we need to go work on the olives now that we're finally getting some fresh batches."

"Aww, man..." Lausanne pouted.

Jura pushed her along, making hand motions, chasing her away.

Next stop, Volcania. Okay I came up with that name, but the volcano area was a mouthful, so I decided on Volcania.

Volcano research was complete, so I tasked Alexis with researching more volcano-related countermeasures.

[Beetle winter adaptation stage II - 1 month remaining.]

[Volcanic adaptation stage II - 3 months remaining.]

[Tree winter adaptation stage II - 3 months remaining.]

[Beetle volcanic battleform - complete!]

[Beetle volcanic defensive armors - complete!]

[Beetle - anti-magma weaponry - 3 months remaining.]

[Beetle - basic magical lances - 6 months remaining.]

With the completed research, the beetles near Volcania gained a special armor, and their head changed significantly, such that it was enveloped in the new special armor. With these changes, three beetles could take on a single magma monster.

So, with the improved status, the beetles attempted to head farther, closer to the volcano, and find a bit more information about the inner volcano...

They failed.

Too many magma monsters.

Undeterred, I created more subsidiary trees, all designed as beetle-nests. Each beetle-nest housed five beetles, and with an additional thirty subsidiary trees, I sent the larger beetle army into the volcano.

And still they failed because there were just way too many of those magma monsters inside.

Fine. If it was a game of numbers, I was a tree-spirit with the ability to spawn multiple subsidiary trees.

So I spawned another seventy of them.

[Subsidiary tree limit increased to 1,500.]

Hell, yeah. Power to the tree swarm. I was an invasive species of trees about to take over this volcano!

"Horns, you take command of the beetles and do some recon, all right?"

"Got it, boss."

Over the next few days, Horns mounted several expeditions into the inner volcano area, only to encounter stiff resistance from large swarms of magma monsters. It seemed that the inner volcano area was crawling with giant magma monsters, large enough to be buildings on their own. Magma golems.

If not for their lack of horns, they would actually look somewhat demonic.

"We can't get past the magma golems. They are far too powerful."

"I see." It seemed the upgrades were still insufficient to take on the larger monsters. So I would have to wait for more upgrades.

"If Alexis could do some research..."

"I am already doing that."

"Ah, yes."

"It'll take time, even with my skills." Well, she wasn't lying, and I foresaw materials being my next bottleneck, higher-tier research required exotic materials, which would be harder to get.

An expansionary approach was necessary, at least to secure additional materials that I would need. My current [Root Extraction], [Mineral Refining], and [Essence Harvesters] reactivated now that I no longer had to be in 'winter' mode, and they were producing iron, copper, and a few other commonly found materials, and for essences, the common ones. The nightmare and soul harvesters brought me two experience seeds, so I had a total of three now. It seemed this was an incredible rarity, a gift that even kings desired. A fruit that guaranteed a level? That was worth a ton. It was something I should use to make a trade someday, for something of equally great value.

"I wonder whether I can detect the demon king's coming," Alexis mused, tinkering with the lab. "You sure you don't want magic labs? And sensors?"

"You still hung up about that?"

"Yes! There are so many things I want to know. Can we reliably predict the demon king's arrival? Is there a magical fluctuation in the world that we can pin on? What are the kinds of magic that create the demon rifts? Don't you ask yourself those questions?"

"I do, but my priority is the volcano."

"Why?"

"Because it is a volcano. I want to expand there. I want to gain the volcano's powers. My instinct tells me a volcano, as a natural force of nature, is similar to a ley line."

"Okay, that makes sense." Alexis paused and then floated onto some branches. Her biolab grew over the month, adding another branch that housed more pods, smaller ones, which were used to run smaller experiments, which then helped to speed up the entire research process.

"I mean, that's what I think. My gut feeling is there are natural energies in the ley line, magic of the world, and perhaps I need to find a way to tap into it. Gain new research. Perhaps its raw form is not so easily accessed as a ley line, but it is a kind of 'native' ley line. So I want it. Happy? Will you help?"

"Huh." Alexis paused, and I assumed she bought my explanation. "So you want some kind of permanent establishment on the volcano, which allows you to tap into its strength like some geothermal power plant?"

"Yes." Well, yeah.

"At least I now understand your obsession with the volcano. And I see why it takes priority over magic...sensors."

"Good." I was a tree spirit, and gaining more powers for my [Soul Forge] was logical. I could even say it was something that drove me.

[Research planning.]

"Ah."

"I checked. It wasn't clear yet. I couldn't see a clear path to it, but having [magma tolerant roots], [tremor resistance], and [natural energy harvesters] seemed like the few basic precursors to collecting energy from volcanoes. What else you needed... well, it was still unclear."

"That's a good start. We can start work on that after we are able to reliably expand and hold a position on the volcano. We are in this for the long haul."

"Still, you're not worried a demon king might pop up and ruin your project? I think he's about...what, five or six years away? The first of the rifts should open within the next few years."

"I am betting on the chance that he spawns on some other continent. Demon kings don't always appear in the same place."

"Then?"

"The heroes will come along and save the day. As they always do. I hope..."

Alexis sighed. "I guess you have a point. Even heroes are just gears in this system. One that just keeps on churning. So much for...heroes."

"I think heroes are a stopgap measure to solve the demon king problem." Well, that's how I saw it. Maybe the gods hoped some heroes became so powerful that they could beat multiple generations of demon kings, but so far, that had not happened. The best was a generation of heroes surviving three demon kings, according to Yvon's knowledge of history.

"Has it always been this way?" I asked.

"Ask the gods." I mean, that's really the way, right?

"They don't say shit. The reincarnation gods know nothing about the history of this world. All they know is the gods of this world ask for reincarnators, and their job is to give them to it."

"What's in it for the gods? What's their stake in keeping the world this way? Can't gods just snap a finger and make things go back?" My personal guess was that they couldn't. Perhaps their abilities of intervention were...limited. So they resorted to heroes.

"I have no idea."

YEAR 77, MONTH 4

I was level 129 a few months ago. When was I going to get the next one?

I decided to go to the volcano and [Root Strike] a lot of magma monsters. However, it proved to be less effective than I thought it would be.

I mean, they still destroyed the magma monsters in a single hit, but near a golem, it still took easily fifteen shots of the [Root Strike] to kill it.

And that was way too much.

I wondered whether it was because of my super effectiveness against demons, so I previously didn't feel my [Root Strike]s were that weak, or if it was that these magma golems had a special defense against [Root Strike]s. Might just be a passive that went, "Reduce damage from nature or tree-based sources by fifty percent."

Or perhaps it was some 'pierce damage reduction.'

Or perhaps I was really just weak.

"You know...rather than constantly theorize about what exactly the problem was, you could just consider using [Inspect]?" Meela suggested. "That's what Alexis would do."

I paused.

I felt like an idiot.

Idiotree.

I mean, it was seriously basic, no? Use [inspect] on monsters. I even had the inspect skill.

Had I been a tree for too long that I forgot such basic monster hunting...basics?

Did I lose common sense somewhere along the way?

YEAR 77, MONTH 4 (CONTINUED)

[Inspect]

Dammit.

The magma golems had pierce resistance, nature element reduction, and physical damage reduction. So all those skills together meant my [Root Strike] was less effective than it would be on any other monster.

Less effective, but still, fifteen [Root Strike]s...

Okay, actually any other monster of a similar 'tier' would have skills and passives that provided a similar level of resistance. It was how higher-tier monsters, just like how higher-level people, were exponentially stronger because of the cumulative effects of stacking different abilities.

So any other monster of such a tier would be just as difficult, in their own way.

"So..."

"Research more weapons, of course."

"Might I suggest killing the golems anyway?" Horns butted in. "You know. Because they killed so many beetles, I would like to see them die."

Ah.

"I would like to have vengeance, Master."

When did he learn the concept of vengeance anyway?

"You know what? Yes. Let's go hunt golems. I need the damn level."

And off I went. I spent the next few days attacking every golem I saw with [Root Strike]s, and then I would crawl up to another golem and continue.

It was kinda like how a zerg base used creep colonies to get close to the enemy and then attacked them with sunken colonies. And I did that, many, many times.

Spawn subsidiary tree near golems, unleash a rain of [Root Strike]s, kill golems, repeat.

And I saw Horns crying in joy. Seriously. He must get enjoyment from having a bigger badass kick the butt of the badass that kicked his butt. Actually, I had no idea whether that was a cry or a shout because it just sounded really...insecty.

Anyway, kill golems.

And after maybe about fifty golems, I leveled up!

[You gained a level! You are now level 130.]

[Upgrade initiated...]

The entire valley shook as a thunderstorm suddenly appeared out of nowhere. Lightning hit each and every subsidiary tree, and each and every branch on my main tree.

Was this like the starting sequence of some superhero transformation?

A hole opened in the sky, and from that darkness, massive black lightning struck my main tree.

"What...what is happening?" The elves seemed afraid as the massive black lightning continued to strike my main tree.

"I suggest all of you leave...for a while."

Indeed, they all ran as fast as they could to the town of New Freeka, and well, it seemed they too could see what was happening from a distance because there seemed to be a massive hole in the sky.

"Any idea what's going on?" I asked the rest of the souls and Wisp.

"Not a clue." Alexis shook her head, but she looked rather amazed by it all. "And how are you still talking when that black thing is striking you like that?"

"Uh. Good point." Am I supposed to feel pain or heat, or...I don't know...anything?

Lightning after lightning struck down on the trees, but yet they didn't do any damage. It was as if they were just making a connection.

Was this the fate of trees in a storm?

"Are you evolving or something?" Alexis asked.

"Yeah. I think."

"Ah, man. Level one hundred?"

"Ah, secret." Some things should be a secret, no?

The lightning strikes continued, and then, all of them stopped. The hole in the sky widened a bit farther to reveal something that looked like a rift, a small fissure in space.

And then black lightning emerged, larger than any other, and it zapped my main body.

[Void energy collection completed.]

Oh.

Oh, now I felt pain. It felt like every single part of my body was cracking, like a snake trying to change its skin or a sea creature replacing its shell.

My branches, barks, and trunks started to swell, and the leaves all dropped from my main tree, leaving me looking like a bare but bloated tree, all the bark expanding to reveal cracks and seams like stretchmarks.

[Upgrading...]

And then those cracks expanded as a new layer of skin emerged from underneath, a glossy, dark-colored bark. This cracked and expanded, and then the older layer fell away from my main body over the next couple of hours.

The hole in the sky was gone, but the ground was still constantly rumbling as my body expanded. I believed the same was also happening to my roots, and that caused the ground to constantly shake for those two hours.

And then I was done!

[You have now transformed into the Starsoul Tree.]

[Starsoul Tree]

[Able to tap into and access the wisdom of the past, from exposure to ancient bones and fossils.]

[Gains access to a special type of leaf. Able to collect starlight and produce star mana in small quantities (maximum number of leaves capped). Also gains access to a star mana storing organ and special star-mana abilities.]

[Stats improved, various collection, various skills upgraded.]

[Soul management and access rights and restrictions unlocked.]

Ah...yay?

Star mana.

As I read that update, coming across that word, I just paused and took a moment to realize what just happened. Star mana. The supercharged fuel of the heroes. And I could make them.

In small quantities, perhaps incomparable to that of the heroes, like the massive amount that Alexis used to have, a gift she now lost since she died. It was an odd thing, of course, since I thought heroes could 'resurrect' with the right spells, but as it turned out, it was only a gift that unlocked under certain conditions, and it expired when the demon king died.

Anyway, star mana. I could make it...I could make it.

What did this mean? Had I taken a small step toward being a hero? One chosen by the gods to do battle against the demon king?

I-I couldn't wrap my head around that. I was a tree, and if a demon king...if Alexis's description of its power level was true, I was still very far away.

Just because I had star mana, it didn't make me a chosen hero.

So, no. I didn't think so. And somehow, a part of me rejected the idea of fighting the demon king...so that was also not the path I wanted to go. It went against my natural strengths as a tree.

I was a tree. And a tree was a nurturing, protective force.

So how could I use star mana? Did the other great spirit trees have star mana, too? I assumed so. Maybe with star mana they managed great escape-like feats like an entire vanishing forest.

Star mana. A great power. And a secret.

YEAR 77, MONTH 5

A small branch grew above me, at the very top. A few leaves grew, almost black in color—the star-leaves. They were even shaped like stars. It was my secret experiment in star mana gathering, and I was excited to see what I could find at the end of that path.

Then I moved my attention to the research happening through the biolabs throughout the valley.

"Well, beetle winter adaptation is complete, but it's not cold anymore. Maybe I should direct my attention toward volcano research as well, together with Alexis?"

Right now, with Alexis, Trevor, and Dimitree, we could run about six research topics concurrently.

"Hmmm...indeed. The volcano is the biggest priority at the moment."

"The resistance in the volcano's inner area is indeed much higher than expected, so we do need stronger, or at least, more specialized beetles to counter the stronger magma golems."

"Giant beetles."

"Thanks, Horns."

"Golems are big. If beetles are big, beetles can win."

"That's a good idea, sire. Our small size is a weakness. A large beetle may be a good solution."

"Trevor, you're agreeing with that idea? Giant beetles?"

"I do believe Horns is right to suggest that, and he has the combat experience to support that sort of view."

"How *giant* are we talking about?"

"As big as the golems."

"Are there some biological rules in this world on the size of insects?" I mean, there should be a limit, right? Though I kinda felt stupid, even my current war beetles were the size of rhinos. So actually, there were probably no rules on that.

"Uh, probably if we had the right materials and components, a massive beetle would be possible."

"Alexis, any input?"

"Sure." Once again, she used her [research planner], and I swore I saw her smirking from the corner of her face. A short moment later, she nodded and came over to join in the conversation.

"Presently, there are no obvious paths to beetles the size of golems."

"Giant beetles. Maybe half the size of the golems?" Horns sounded a little sad.

"Ah, I wasn't finished. But beetles about half the size of golems is possible. We would need to research enhanced exoskeletons and enhanced interior structures, and then we would then be able to research a large-beetle-pod, and then a large beetle."

"Large beetle."

"Not giant, but bigger than what it is now. So large's a good word."

Horns nodded furiously.

"Seems like everyone's keen on the idea?"

"I still think magic is better."

"Giant beetle."

"Yes, sire. Giant beetle is a good path. I believe massive war beetles can do a great deal of damage on the battlefield."

"Very well then. Let's go with it."

[Beetle winter adaptation stage II – complete.]

[Volcanic adaptation stage II - 1 month remaining.]

[Tree winter adaptation stage II - 1 month remaining.]

[Beetle - anti-magma weaponry - 1 month remaining.]

[Beetle - basic magical lances - four months remaining.]

[Eye-Tree Stage I research option unlocked - twenty-two months remaining.]

[Enhanced exoskeletons - four months remaining.]

[Enhanced interior structures - not started.]

[Large beetle pods - not started.]

Well, I already had six concurrent research topics, but next month, I could add enhanced interior structures to it once the volcanic adaptation and anti-magma weaponry were complete.

Anyway, with that, I returned my attention to the elves and the New Freekans. The evolution I underwent last month, that one day of the great, black lightning storm, faded from the memory of the elves quickly. After all, to them, it was just one of those scary days, and I didn't appear any different than I did before.

That's because of [Camouflage]. My true appearance was unseen by anyone, except the artificial souls and Alexis.

A sense of gradual normalcy was returning, now that the effect of the blood blizzard was slowly fading from the air itself. Crops were growing throughout the farmlands, and the valley's trees were surging in number, surpassing the number of trees destroyed. For New Freeka, it is war preparation time, as Salah issued a formal war declaration. They considered New Freeka as an enemy nation, and as a result, all direct trade routes between Salah and New Freeka were cut, legally.

Then followed posturing and nasty, threatening letters demanding surrender.

Which we all ignored.

Although that was the collective decision of the senior leaders, the councilors, leaders of the standing army, and the higher-ranked mages, it was still stressful and highly worrying for them. The town was now fully gearing up for war, their magic builders working overtime, building massive walls and other defensive positions.

Guards were on full alert, and all visitors to New Freeka were thoroughly screened, as there were also fears of assassination attempts.

"Jura, it's not a good time." Jura stood in the middle of the council room. Yvon and the rest of the councilors sat around the table.

"The tree spirit wants an update on the demanded jewels, which was agreed upon earlier."

"We are in a state of war, Jura." A councilor stood.

"And the tree spirit is your best chance of defending New Freeka successfully." Jura glared back at the councilor.

"And what exactly would a tree spirit bring to the table if Salah invades with a large army?" the councilor responded. "Some trees? Potatoes? Hot water?"

Yvon almost intervened, but another councilor next to her stopped her.

"The tree spirit has been making demands, and where we

believe it is a mutually beneficial trade, if the circumstances allow it, we will support those demands."

The councilwoman next to Yvon leaned in and whispered. "The tree spirit needs to know where we stand. It's about time we make clear our position to its representative."

Yvon sighed.

"But these are tough times. Resources, whatever we have, are all focused on our existential threat—the Salah Kingdom—who recently threatened to wipe us off the map. We need all our resources for more men, more weapons. Not the whims of a tree spirit who claims ownership over the entire valley."

Jura listened and then laughed. And he laughed like a maniac.

Jura laughed for a good three minutes before all the councilors, them staring at him like he was some kind of madman.

When he stopped, he looked at Yvon. "Ah, Yvon, are the councilors aware of the extent of the tree spirit's powers?"

She paused before responding. "I did tell them."

"What did you tell them? Perhaps your knowledge too is incomplete."

"Uh, the tree spirit has the power of an archdruid, many very powerful healing powers, some ability to repair soul damage, abilities to absorb fire, abilities to control beetles, abilities to create hot water, spawn various trees and use root attacks, the ability to boost growth rates and spawn different types of trees..."

Jura nodded. "Not bad but let me ask you, how many beetles does the tree spirit control?"

"Three hundred? Maybe four hundred?" Yvon answered.

"Any other guesses?"

"Seven hundred?" a councilor decided to humor, saying it as a joke.

"As more recently advised, the actual number is about three thousand. Led by a beetle knight."

The councilors all stared at each other.

"Tell me, if three thousand beetles go to war, how many men would Salah need to field?"

One of the army leaders, a captain, sitting in the council room did some mental math. "Twelve thousand, perhaps fifteen."

"Do you all believe, for a moment, that New Freeka can protect itself from the tree spirit's wrath should those three thousand beetles turn against you?"

The councilors looked at each other.

"Would three thousand beetles be an existential threat, I wonder..."

One of the councilors stood. "Are you threatening us?"

"No. I believe from the tree spirit's point of view, you all are threatening him, by challenging his dominion over the valley. So, Councilor, you better retract such words and pray the tree spirit doesn't hear it directly."

The councilor paled and took a seat.

"Yvon, I believe you recall the agreement when the tree spirit consented to your new settlement in New Freeka."

One of the older councilors stood. "That our presence is at the tree spirit's grace and mercy, and we are to acknowledge the tree spirit as the rightful master of the valley. We are not to encroach on the forests more than the tree spirit allows."

"It is but a phrase, no?" Another councilor, a younger one from the refugees, stood. "Such phrases exist in the founding documents of many nations. A...formality to acknowledge a benefactor."

"Not when the phrase refers to that of a tree spirit, an actual magical being who resides in and controls the valley."

There was silence in the room as everyone stared at each other.

"Back to the jewels. I have been authorized by the tree spirit to let the council and everyone else in the room know that the jewels are meant to fulfill the evolutionary requirements of the beetle champions, and various other beasts that live in the depths of the valley's forests. Obtaining them will further enhance the combat abilities of the beetles."

"If we get them. Can the tree spirit lend us his aid? With those three thousand beetles?"

"Yes. He is prepared to summon the three thousand beetles, deploy whatever other beasts he can gather from the valley to do battle, and he also has various other abilities at his disposal. But he will do all of this only in a defensive battle against Salah or any other attackers, and not for an offensive attack."

That was simply because it was easier to control the beetles when they were nearby, as Dimitree and Trevor could both assist in coordinating the beetles' movements.

"W-we need some time to discuss this."

"You've been given a week to talk it out; the tree spirit expects a positive response."

"Acknowledged."

Jura walked back to the valley with an air, a kind of smugness, around him. He seemed rather pleased how it went.

Also, Jura understated the number. I told him three thousand, but actually, with my most recent evolution into a starsoul tree, the maximum subsidiary trees I had increased to a mind boggling four thousand. So, with five beetles per subsidiary tree, the actual maximum beetles I could deploy would be...twenty thousand.

But, of course, I wasn't going to have them all as beetle-trees. I also needed essence harvesters, material processors, crop producers, biolabs, homes for the elves, surveillance trees, and so forth, so the actual number of 'free' trees available was about two and half thousand. That still represented a massive army of twelve thousand five hundred beetles.

There were already about two thousand beetles full-time defending the volcanic area from the magma monsters, another two thousand in the south forest around Dimitree and the ley line, and then another two thousand hidden throughout the valley and its forest. The current actual deployable beetle force was...six thousand five hundred.

I liked to have some unused subsidiary tree capacity to spawn additional subsidiary trees as and when I need to, in an emergency response to any possible changes, or to reinforce new areas when necessary. So that would mean setting aside about four hundred trees.

So four thousand five hundred beetles were the actual end number of new beetles available. Nine hundred subsidiary trees.

"How did the discussions go?" I asked.

"I believe it will be positive, Tree-Tree."

"Glad to hear that."

"Oh, Bamboo is asking for an upgrade."

"I am aware, but I need those jewels first."

"Ah. Yes. I guess I have personal interest in wanting those jewels, too." Jura laughed. He seemed rather happy.

———

"Do you think he is lying?" a councilor asked during their private meeting.

"I think not," another replied.

"Three thousand beetles. That's a massive number."

"Indeed. My initial projections factored in four hundred beetles in any defensive fight against Salah." Two army advisors turned to take the stand—captains, both of them.

"How does this change the battle?" a councilman asked.

"A war beetle, as Jura referred to them, is actually equal to two elite soldiers. Salah would have to deploy specialized forces to deal with the war beetles, as their thick armor and massive horns make them difficult to kill using regular weapons. It's possible to swarm one of the war beetles and then attack its weakness—their joints and the gaps between their armor—if they are scattered throughout the battlefield, but numbering three thousand, there would be a very low chance of catching any of those beetles alone."

"Captain, I understand none of the technicalities of combat. What I want to know is what does that mean in a war for us, and would the price of the jewels be worth it?"

"I believe, if the numbers are true, it is our best chance of beating Salah, multiple times. Three thousand war beetles essentially means Salah must field at least thirty thousand men just to even hope to have a good chance of winning against the war beetles alone."

"You said twelve to fifteen thousand in the earlier meeting with Jura and then two elite soldiers in your earlier sentence."

"I fudged the numbers with Jura to understate the value of the war beetles."

"Then the two elites?"

"Salah's conventional army composition comprises of one elite for every ten regulars. Thirty thousand men is then reflecting three thousand elite soldiers and twenty-seven thousand regulars. It's what I would need to deploy if I was asked to defeat war beetles of that number. And mages. At least a hundred mages."

Yvon paused. "Remember our first battle here against Salah? The one led by Waysorious Moffard, the Purple Blade?"

"Ah...why?"

"The beetles back then hid underground or in the trees. They then sprung up behind enemy lines."

The captains nodded. "If so, that makes their defensive value even higher, and I believe there isn't much to discuss. I strongly request the council fulfill the demands and get assurances from Jura, and the tree spirit, that those three thousand beetles will assist us. I would pay ten times the demanded amount to get the defensive services of three thousand war beetles."

The councilors looked at each other before they eventually all nodded in agreement. The wizard of Baroosh nudged the lady next to him. "As I predicted, the tree spirit is truly the guardian beast of the valley."

The councilwoman turned and nodded her head. "Certainly. Even I underestimated the number. You're right, I should have brought it up earlier."

The wizard smiled smugly. "Glad to be proven right."

The councilwoman shrugged. "Ugh."

YEAR 77, MONTH 6

[Tree - volcanic adaptation stage II – complete.]

[Tree - winter adaptation stage II – complete.]

[Beetle - anti-magma weaponry – complete.]

[Beetle - basic magical lances - 3 months remaining.]

[Eye-Tree Stage I research option unlocked - 21 months remaining.]

[Enhanced exoskeletons - 3 months remaining.]

[Enhanced interior structures - 4 months remaining.]

[Large beetle pods - 6 months remaining.]

[Beetle - anti-magma armors stage 2 - 12 months remaining.]

I t was time for more volcano smash. With the volcanic adaptation and anti-magma weaponry, the odds of beetle versus magma monster were now three to two. So, with two thousand beetles in the area, I attempted another round of volcano invasion.

And yes, I was a little bit closer. With upgraded weaponry, we could easily take on the regular magma monsters and claim additional territory since fewer beetles were needed to successfully defend one area, but I still couldn't hold the areas with the massive magma golems, so I had to avoid those areas, but that was about it. I was a step closer.

The trees in the volcanic area were black, reddish in hue, reflecting their adapted trunks and roots, which were highly heat-resistant and able to extract their resources from the dried magma that formed the earth around the volcano.

It was progress, but now consistently holding position against the magma golems would be the next hurdle for an actual 'volcano' base, and then I would need to move on to finding ways to extract the energies from the lava beneath it.

A part of me realized that was probably the point where I needed a magic lab of some kind since extracting magic from lava was probably out of the scope of the biolab. Oh, well. Alexis would be happy then.

As I mulled things over, the first batch of jewels from New Freeka arrived, with a request for a demonstration of my three thousand beetles? Hmm.

I guess seeing is believing.

YEAR 77, MONTH 7

"I got to level twenty yesterday."

Jura paused and looked at Lausanne. Laufen was next to him, and the little girl then said, "I got a passive ability, it's called [Blessed by a Soul Tree]."

The two adults glanced at each other. In a way, they were now like her father and mother, and there was a mix of pride, worry, and confusion when Lausanne said she hit level twenty.

Most children never leveled so fast, with most around level five to ten at age eight. It was most likely due to the presence of my continuing involvement, the constant essence infused [Dream Tutor]s, [Power-Leveling], and most recently, the upgraded [Training Tree].

"Well, what does it do?"

"Erm, it doesn't say much, it just says I'll get certain...blessings?"

"Tree-Tree, any idea?"

Well, the first thing that was clear when she gained that ability was that I could now see her much more obviously than everyone else. It was as if she was glowing in my vision. She had a constant tooltip hovering over her—one that just screamed: 'Look at me.'

"Well, rather than conjecture, would you mind coming into the biolab, and we can all find out?"

"Yeah. Good idea."

As Lausanne walked to the biolab inside the secret hideout, Laufen and Jura both looked at each other.

"She's growing very quickly," Jura said with a sigh. "I fear for her."

"Me, too. But I also feel I should be proud. It is what Ricola would have wanted for his daughter, to be strong."

Jura paused and then nodded. "I suppose so. Ricola would want his daughter to be competent, even though he himself wasn't much."

Laufen ribbed Jura. "Hey."

"I mean, his talents were in being a village chieftain. Combat was never his strong suit."

"I suppose it's Tree-Tree's influence then."

Well, I had been giving Lausanne every single combat-related essence I generated through [Dream Tutor], so it did, over a long period of time, give the necessary improvements toward her understanding of combat tactics.

Lausanne walked into the pod, and the vines wrapped around her body. I then took a look.

"May I?" Alexis asked, and I shook my head.

"Sorry, let me have a look first."

Alexis sulked. "Okay..."

And...frankly Lausanne's body appeared normal. She was a regular elf after all, though I could see right next to her usual soul spring, there was a small flower.

[Blessed by a Soul Tree.]

[Due to long-term exposure to Soul Tree's abilities, the body is naturally accepting of its influence. Grants additional compatibility with various Soul Tree abilities, spells, and skills, and so they last longer and have stronger effects.]

"Oh. Sounds okay." At this point, I thought it wasn't much. I couldn't see anything else different, so I let Alexis in on the view.

"Hmm." She, too, looked at Lausanne's young body. Her soul spring was normal, and the water coming out of it was clear and smooth. The body seemed well, normal, the shores covered in a thin layer of grass nourished by the mana from her soul spring. It looked like there was still some ways to go.

"It's generally normal," I said. "The skill isn't much."

"I don't think it's a bad skill."

"How so?"

"I think her growth rate will be even faster since it means your training room, [Dream Tutor], and [Power-Leveling] will be more effective on her."

"Oh. That's a good point."

"You have plans for her, don't you?"

"What do you mean?"

"I mean, you have been investing a lot of your essences into her—more than any other elf. It feels like you want her to be something. Or are you preparing her for something?"

"Huh..." Frankly, I didn't know why I was doing it. Somehow, I got so sucked into the narrative that Lausanne wanted to be a hero that I just went along with it. But thinking about it, I did think that it was worth trying.

"Maybe a hero would be too hard. To stand at our level she would need access to a lot of star mana, gain the various divine blessings, and unlock a cheat ability."

Well, yeah, duh, that's way too high a wall. It was like trying to climb K2 after a successful hike up a gentle hill. I was foolish enough to send Lausanne up such unreasonable...walls.

"But...I think creating a champion is a good idea. Reaching the level of the demon champions I think is a realistic target. Perhaps she can get there when she's...thirty? I think she needs to learn magic next. A magic lab would do so."

Ah, Alexis trying to sell the magic lab idea again. To be fair, I did appreciate the need for one, once we made progress with the volcano. But I would keep that to myself for now. "You want to be her tutor?"

"I don't mind. I think I'll gain different skills, compared to all these research-linked abilities I have now. It would help if I regained my magical abilities somewhat."

I felt a little threatened by the idea of giving Alexis her magic...again. She did—though it wasn't really her—burn down slightly less than half of the valley.

Oh.

Volcano occupation was now a stalemate. I would attempt again once we unlocked the large beetles—twice the size of rhinos. Hopefully, then the odds would be better. At present, it took about two hundred beetles to kill a single magma golem, and I only had two thousand in that area. Two hundred per golem, and there were a lot more than ten golems. I was hoping the odds changed to about ten or so large beetles per golem, then the chances of a successful occupation of the volcano would increase.

My thoughts then changed to New Freeka. They asked for a demonstration in exchange for the jewels.

Luckily, it went quite well. They had never seen three thousand beetles march out of the forest before.

YEAR 77, MONTH 8

"Salah is coming. With a force of fifty thousand men!"

"Huh?"

"That was quick," Jura mused, but to be honest, I thought I knew why that had happened, and it was also why I held my cards back.

I suspected there was a mole within Yvon's council. Someone close to them was a Salah informant.

I didn't know who exactly, but among the twenty-five senior leaders, all of them were talking about the beetles. Apparently, none of them could keep their mouth shut after they witnessed three thousand of them, and this news somehow reached Salah, who, for whatever reason, felt threatened by these beetles. Maybe they saw me as a threat they needed to crush quickly, and so they came to crush me before I got even stronger.

"It could be there is just some kind of surveillance magic happening," Alexis mused. "As far as I can tell, there are no scrying countermeasures or spell barriers in New Freeka, except the forest itself, which gets some scrying protection from your massive [Camouflage] and [Mist] abilities."

Jura, on the other hand, thought different. "I think they just wanted to fight New Freeka, and this is a convenient time since they are still in the stalemate with Nung and Takde. I doubt they know about the beetles. The traders and merchants I speak to seem to say Salah has been itching for a fight for some time, since the blood blizzard has significantly weakened. They just want to find someone to suffer for the punishment and misery of the blood blizzard."

"Fifty thousand men. What are our odds?"

"I think we can win." Jura shrugged. "But it will be a hard fight. And it also depends on who is their general."

During this conversation, Trevor pinged me personally. He was my surveillance officer, after all.

"I see the enemy army in the outermost tree rings. I don't think they are suspicious, as they left the outer trees untouched. Also, they have siege weapons, Master."

"Are you sure no suspicions? Or are they just playing the part?"

"Any mages?"

"Yes, sire. I counted a mage corps of at least one thousand. There are multiple individuals exhibiting a rather strong presence as well."

"Okay, bring me there."

"Certainly."

With that, my vision zoomed to the incoming army. Thanks to my wider coverage of subsidiary trees, I had trees really far away now, and Trevor even went through the process of decorating each tree such that they looked like natural growths in the area.

And indeed, a large army was marching, comprising mostly of foot soldiers—around forty thousand—a section of cavalry—about two thousand—and then the rest being a mix of the mages, healers, siege weapon operators, and their elite forces.

"New Freeka has spotted us," a commander said as he rode up to a man who looked like the general of this army, thanks to his elaborate armor and uniform and a long, flowing magical cape.

"Good. It seems we can go with our initial plans for now. Bombard the town with our siege machines and mages, and force them out of the town, into the open where we can slaughter them," another man said, and he too rode up to the general. The general just smiled in return.

Heh. I have the countermeasure for that.

"We spotted the beetles that Waysorious fought during the last battle."

"How many?"

"Five hundred, perhaps? They are really well hidden within the trees, and only our rangers can spot them with any accuracy."

"I recall Waysorious also suspects the presence of an elvish archdruid."

"You agree with that assessment, General?"

Ah, the chief was a general.

"Lord Rosul's earlier expedition claims the presence of a living forest. His wizard says there is a presence that stretches the entire valley."

"I-I've never heard of that." The men around the general seemed surprised.

"It was something Lord Rosul shared only with our senior leaders, and it is why we have been treating New Freeka with such caution—and also why there are one thousand mages."

Realization appeared on all the senior leaders around the general. Perhaps they suspected fifty thousand was overkill.

"Yes, now that the battle is near, it is time I tell you the actual strategy of this army."

"The king and the high council suspect the presence of a magical beast—something like a great earth tiger or a king grandbeetle—that Yvon has somehow managed to convince into an alliance. It is likely to be a defensive pact, else Yvon would be more...offensive in her dealings with us. The recently observed magical phenomena in New Freeka from our spies supports this theory. A firestorm, then countless black lightning, all points to magical beasts, of a very high tier, that likely have experienced a high-level evolution recently."

A gulp.

"Now, now, we're going to try to talk to it. First—"

It was then a ranger appeared. He appeared to be very old.

"This is Master Ranger Falklay. He's very good with magical beasts; he has the ability [Commune with Magical Beasts], [Locate Magical Creatures], [Beast Talk-no-jutsu], and [Charm Magical Beasts]. He'll sneak into the forest first and find the magical beast. Our invasion of New Freeka will commence only after he gives us the signal on whether he can convince the magical beasts to withhold or ignore their defensive pact. Else, one of the alternatives is that we will have to bomb the shit out of the forest as well, then fight the beast. But we will weigh our chances when that happens."

"Siege weapons against magical beasts?" a captain asked.

"Not ideal, but if we have to fight it, we best weaken it first. High-tier magical beasts are powerful, but siege weapons and magic will still hurt them."

"Now that we are near, what do you think, Master Falklay? Confident that you will succeed?"

"I think our chances are good. There are magical creatures, and I sense a few in the forests. My senses tell me of a fairy of some kind or a forest sprite. Charming fairies will be a huge challenge, but I think I can succeed in convincing it or them to break the pact."

Ooh, Ranger. Interesting...

"How will we know?"

"Falklay will fire a flare. Green flare for go, red flare for bomb, or blue flare for run. He's also equipped with a speaking stone."

"Run?"

"If the magical beast is a lot more powerful than we currently suspect, we would be better to retreat than attempt an invasion. No point wasting our lives, right?"

"What if there's no flare?"

"Then we wait. We wait for a week if we have to. Communion with magical beasts is going to take time, and we will give Master Falklay the time to talk. But after ten days, if Master Falklay is alive, we will expect a flare. If Master Falklay is dead, we will run. But that's unlikely, right?"

Master Falklay grinned. His face was really wrinkly.

"Run?" one of the younger captains asked.

"Of course. We must know exactly what we are facing. I will take calculated risks, but magical beasts are a category of monsters that is best dealt with...by powerful adventurers." The rest of the men nodded; the general was a highly conservative man.

———

Falklay made his way toward the valley, under the cover of various stealthing abilities, such as [hidden amongst trees] and other such effects, which made him close to invisible to other men trying to spot him...except the tree itself.

So, yeah, I saw him sprinting, alone, into the valley. Despite his age, he was still clearly a high-level ranger and had the stats and abilities to back it up. And as he got closer, I noticed he would stop every now and then to use some of those abilities.

"Strange...the reading is confused," he muttered, touching the trees, some of which were subsidiary trees.

As he made his way into the valley, he came across a few beetles. The beetles spotted him and attempted to attack him, but he had a skill where when he just lightly touched them, and they fell into a kind of 'sleep.' I seemed to be a kind of 'disabling' ability he had.

"He has an ability to make us 'docile!'" Horns was shouting in my mind. "We must kill him! Kill him! He is a threat! A threat!"

On the other hand, I was very curious about this Falklay, and I wanted to see exactly what he had.

"Horns, go hibernate. Beetles, retreat as well."

With that, the beetles quickly hid and stayed out of his way... which the ranger noticed.

"Huh. The beetles have gone. It's watching me, eh? A king-beetle with some kind of 'domain' abilities or a fairy with 'glade-watch?'" he considered loudly.

He walked closer, his senses sharp, and as he followed them, it led him right up to the main tree.

"Huh." He looked around, wondering what he was seeing. "The beast is asleep?"

He then turned his eyes on Alexis's biolab. He glanced up and down, and then he used an ability: [Identify]

"A forest spirit...of the academic kind?" His face paled somewhat. "Something's not right..."

[Eye of the Ranger].

He looked around, confusion evident on his face.

Then he looked at my main tree.

"It's not a magical beast..." He withdrew his arrows. "No, this is a lot more complicated."

At that moment, I too used [inspect] on him, but it got... repelled. It seemed he had some kind of skill protection.

He lifted his bow and arrow and aimed it at the sky. It was going to be a flare. I wondered whether he was going to bomb the forest, but then again, I had countermeasures so I decided to wait and see.

"I wouldn't fire that yet if I were you." Jura stepped out of the main tree, ready for combat.

"Oh?" The ranger looked like he was about to shoot, but then he decided not to.

"So, who are you, and why are you here?"

"Hmm." The ranger paused. "Might we settle this over a cup of tea, instead?"

"Oh, tea?"

A set of four chairs and a table magically appeared before the ranger, and he sat down. Then he started to brew a pot of tea. "Yes, tea. Clearly the proper way to speak to magical beasts is invite them to tea, no?"

"Magical beasts?" It was Jura's turn to be confused as he took a seat.

"Worry not, elf. The tea is laced with a fragrance that magical beasts will enjoy but does nothing to us. I mean you no harm, so here, I'll drink it. You can use [identify] and [detect poison], too. I won't feel offended." He swapped teacups with Jura and took a sip.

Jura laughed. "So, Ranger. What magical beasts are you speaking of?"

"The forest spirit there, and the beetle lord hiding somewhere in that tree." The ranger pointed. "And these trees right around me." He then pointed to the [root brain complex], and then my main tree.

He then paused before shouting, "I know you are watching! You can join me for tea if you want! It's good stuff, made with tender young tea leaves collected from the Sifar Mountains."

"He's dangerous, Sire. We should kill him!" Horns shouted in my mind. "We should!"

"I agree. But my curiosity is piqued, so I will humor him and watch what happens first."

"I feel a bit of a headache coming on," Alexis complained. "I think he used some kind of skill on me. Sucks when I lose some of my magic resistance..."

Hey, you retained your overpowered ability to level. That counts, right?

Anyway, we focused back on the little tea party between Jura and the old ranger.

Jura decided to take a drink.

"So, old man, what do you want?"

"I work for Salah, and I am here to help with General Akbar's destruction of New Freeka."

Jura, strangely, didn't react to the news. His diplomat levels had been rising, and such news just didn't faze him anymore. "Oh. Why?"

"Well, Salah and New Freeka are at war. I am a servant of the king, and a soldier of Salah, so I am here to help Salah win."

"I see. And so how does that lead you to this little forest?"

"Well, can you interfere if we attack New Freeka?"

"Unfortunately, no. We have an agreement with them. They are under our protection."

"Why? Perhaps there is something Salah can offer you."

Jura grinned. "Ah, well, do you know the tale of the original village of Freeka? I still remember the day almost seven years ago."

"Hmm, has Salah transgressed against Freeka in some way?"

"Yes. Salah's army burned this village, killed many elves living here, and if I remember correctly, their soldiers skewered the bodies of the dead on this tree behind me. Those who survived fled far and wide."

He paused. "Ah. I see that's how it is. Surely, it is time for bygones to be bygones."

Jura's face contorted. "I still remember the faces of those burned to death. The screams, the shouts. The loss of the village scarred me, haunted me for years, and it is only with great blessing that I stepped out of that shadow."

He sipped his tea.

"So I believe I am not wrong to say my grudge, rightly, runs deep."

The old ranger sighed. "The acts of a vast nation like Salah cannot all be attributed to the nation. There are many actors in any country, and not all are aligned in terms of our values and principles."

"You're an old man. I'm sure you have seen many battles and know very well such statements do nothing to my grudge. This grudge, anger, and hatred are not something a quick talk can relieve. And now you, and that large army of yours, are here to destroy New Freeka. Does that not sound like Salah intends to repeat that incident?"

The old man paused and nodded. "Well, you are right. But, in war, there are no good sides. Only victory matters."

"It is as you say, only victory matters. This is not the first time Salah has tried this, and we won the previous two battles. Do you think you can win this one?"

The old ranger nodded. "Indeed. That is why fifty thousand warriors are here."

"Well, you've made your intentions clear, so you may leave now."

The old ranger grinned. "Well, I am deep within enemy territory. Do you think I will leave without taking all of you out first?"

[Root Strike].

That was the moment a few [Root Strike]s surged from the ground. He dodged and shot a few explosive arrows, but my wood shields blocked them.

I followed up with a few more, as Jura, transforming into his Bamboo-armor form, gave chase. Trevor released a poison field that covered the entire forest, and frankly, there was no chance of him escaping.

Unlike the assassin from before, I knew exactly where he was because his [hidden by trees] ability didn't protect him from...a tree.

He ran and simultaneously fired numerous magical arrows toward Jura.

"General. This is Falklay. Please, arrange bombing of the forest. Bomb the forest. I repeat, bomb the forest now! I am engaging with the inhabitants!" he yelled through the speaking stone while he ran. "Ah, dammit..." he added. It seemed the spiders' [hidden presence] natural ability was a bit harder for him to detect as he had run into some spiderwebs.

He cut through the webs, but it slowed him down enough for a [Root Strike] to hit him, which was parried by a small buckler shield. I supposed it was magical since it actually managed to absorb the impact.

"Ah, roots." He ducked the arrows Jura shot at him, but that gap allowed Jura to catch up.

"So why not stand and fight?"

"I reckon we are about the same level, but given my skill mix, I will lose." The old ranger shrugged. "So...no."

He smashed a potion on the floor, and it released a bright light followed by a thick smoke. It was a flashbang, essentially, and it briefly stunned Jura.

A few arrows hit Jura's wood armor, and then the old ranger resumed fleeing. "General, where are the bombs?" he shouted at the stone. "No, you don't have to worry about me. I'll find a way out."

And so the siege machines and the mages got into position, and they started to hurl rocks and spells at the forest.

"They have started the bombardment..." Yvon looked on from the new walls they had built, but as they braced for impact, they noticed the curvature of the projectiles driving the boulders and fireballs toward the forest.

"Uh..."

"The forest..."

Right before the projectiles were about to make impact with the forest, my subsidiary trees, of the hundred or so designated as [shield generators], kicked into action.

Massive wood shields surrounded the trees, so the boulders and ordinary fireballs just collided against the shields, leaving some scratches and burns on the shields. Compared the demon-fire-powered fireballs of Alexis, these fireballs and boulders were really basic, so some damage was taken, but it was well within our limits.

The army tried again, and the second and third volleys similarly left only some small damage on the shields.

"What do you mean the bombardment is not working?" the ranger shouted through his message as he continued to flee. He seemed to be getting caught in more spiderwebs as his concentration strayed, but he was much faster than Jura, so Jura struggled to catch up.

The old ranger was halfway out of the forest now, but frankly, I didn't plan to let him live. So the next moment he slowed down, when a section of spiderweb caught him, I unleashed a few [Root Strike]s at him.

Again, they were blocked by that small buckler, the leg guards he wore, or the magical chainmail he wore under his shirt.

It was nothing fatal, but I was wearing him down. Each of my [Root Strike]s were filled with paralysis and poison, and the entire forest was releasing its own poison—a mix of Trevor's abilities and my [poison field]. It was nothing lethal, especially over such short periods, but every little bit of the poison and paralysis was slowing the ranger down.

Unfortunately, he managed to swallow a few antidotes, which rejuvenated him momentarily.

Another volley came from the siege and mages—again to no effect, thanks to my shield generators.

"General, it's not working. Strong wooden barriers are blocking our attacks around the forests, and those shields can take one hell of a beating."

"Ahhhhh!" There was slight panic in the camp as a group of beetles, about three hundred, emerged behind them, attacking the siege machines and mages. They managed to destroy a few siege machines, but it was a trained army, so some soldiers were already onsite to protect them, and they quickly reorganized. The mages redirected their attacks on the beetles instead. Each beetle, with its thick armor and the recent volcanic adaptation (which granted tiny amounts of fire resistance) could endure one fireball, so the mages needed two shots to kill them.

Additional fighters rushed to protect the mages and siege machines, and the numbers were sufficient to overwhelm the three hundred beetles. However, it was enough to delay and distract those ranged attacks, giving Trevor and myself some breathing room to regenerate some of the weaker [shield generators]. There was some variation in the enemy's siege machines— those operated by higher leveled men and some stronger mages, who accordingly dealt more damage.

I continued to send more spiders after the ranger, and he demonstrated his competence as a forest ranger, cutting through the spiders as if they were nothing. But he was increasingly exhausted, and he realized it, knowing what my plan was.

Every time he slowed down, a [Root Strike] would appear somewhere, and I knew I was gradually wearing him down.

"Going somewhere so soon, old man?" Jura said as he finally caught up again.

"Tell me, those [Root Strike]s, are they from you?"

"Ah. No." Jura attempted to slash at the ranger's head, but he ducked.

"That's a shame." He somehow dodged and put some distance between himself and Jura, throwing some small knives. They hit the wooden barriers around Jura and then exploded. "They're not going to stop, are they?"

It knocked Jura back a little. "I really hate explosive attacks. Keep getting them." He jumped and tried to close the gap with the old ranger, but the old man was still too fast. "And no, you'd be a fool to assume those [Root Strike]s will run out."

He shot a few arrows, but Jura gave me the opening I needed, and two [Root Strike]s flew toward the ranger as he tried to aim in midair. He managed to react in time, but the [Root Strike]s broke his shield buckler and armlets.

"Oh, dear." The old man flinched from the impact of the

[Root Strike]s, and he smashed into a tree. Before he managed to recover from the impact, I quickly activated [Constrict].

Vines emerged from the tree he was against and entangled his legs, and then they injected a poison through his skin.

"Oh, no." He realized he was done for as the vines quickly wrapped around his entire body.

Jura landed right in front of him. "Well, it looks like the bombardment stopped. I think they might be busy now."

"Kill me," the old man said. "As a soldier, I knew this day would come eventually."

"Oh? That's not for me to decide."

He stared at Jura. "You...deny me this right?"

"Oh, come on. Your country burned my village, and you want to play at being honorable? Please, did you somehow think I was in charge?"

"Then who is?"

Jura paused. "I almost answered you there, but that...is a secret."

A root appeared, grown with the strongest paralysis and sleep poisons I had, and it stabbed him right above his heart, through the damaged chainmail. With that, the poisons spread quickly, and he lost consciousness within a few seconds.

———

The mages and soldiers, after a long two-hour battle, defeated the group of three hundred beetles, but there were quite a few casualties.

"General Akbar, Falklay has lost consciousness." An adjutant reviewed the magical artifact linked to Falklay's arm.

"What?" The general was deep in thought.

"Should we resume the bombing?" another of the general's assistants asked.

"My gut tells me there is no point. You saw those shields. They take just a little damage from regular attacks and ordinary fireballs. We'll just wear ourselves down doing the same thing. Get the mages to group together for a [Grand Fireball] and fling some oil barrels into the forest."

Well, that's no good.

So, before that happened, I launched my attack. Multiple tunnels appeared throughout their camp. It was a function of my [Root Tunnel] ability, and from them, thousands of beetles streamed out, horns blazing, charging into the soldiers.

From above, they appeared like a horde of ants that just got triggered, and a black tide swept out of those holes.

Then [Root Field], [Poison Field] and [Root Surge] followed. The field of roots slowed down the soldiers, the field of poison weakened them, and the sudden surge of a wide area of sharp roots from beneath the ground killed hundreds of unprepared regular soldiers, while harming some of the elites.

"General, we are under attack! By a massive beetle force!"

"How many?"

"Maybe three thousand? It's throughout our position, and I have not gotten a good count. Even our lookouts are under attack, and they've not respon—"

Before he finished the sentence, a [Root Strike] emerged from underneath the camp and pierced the man through his chest, splashing some of his blood onto the general's face.

The general was armored with enchanted gear and probably had numerous abilities to protect himself, so I decided to first pick off the rest of his men. It was probably too much effort to kill the general now.

He drew his sword and lifted it up; it glowed with lightning. He then pierced the ground with it, and I felt an electrical zap. It stung a little, maybe nothing more than a small numbness. But, no matter, I had plenty more to go.

Another adjutant ran over. "General, the siege machines are under heavy attack from roots emerging from the ground, and almost all of them have been destroyed."

Together with Trevor and Dimitree, we unleashed multiple

[Root Strike]s on various positions in the enemy army, picking on the mid-tier 'elite' forces—those who were stronger than regular soldiers but had limited defensive abilities against multiple [Root Strike]s.

"Retreat and stay away from trees!" the general shouted, with some kind of skill that carried his message to his entire army.

"General, our elites are falli—" Another [Root Strike] pierced the assistant's legs, but it failed to deliver a lethal blow.

"I know. The enemy's targeting those stronger than the beetles. This is a trap, and the longer we stay, the more we are going to lose!" he shouted and activated a skill.

The skill spread out over the entire army, all the soldiers, those lightly wounded and even the heavily wounded, experienced a sudden rejuvenation in their energy, their bleeding stopped temporarily, although the wounds remained, and their steps turned into large, quick strides, unhindered by the [Rooting Field] or the [Poison Field].

They retreated.

Our kills—mine and those of the beetles combined—numbered probably three to four thousand, though many, many more were injured. The beetles got most of the kills, but they also suffered the most casualties as I focused on the mid-tier forces. I got about four hundred or so kills.

Frankly, if the battle had gone on, it would probably have resulted in heavy casualties on both sides. The beetles were less effective than I expected, but that was due to the general's passive buffs for his entire army.

They fled for as long as the general's ability lasted, and that brought them quite a distance from New Freeka.

For now, the battle was over. I had no doubt the general would return with more firepower, but that was a worry for another day.

[2 levels gained! You are now level 132!]

[You gained a new skill: Serpentine Root Strike.]

[Poison Field and Rooting Field upgraded.]

[Shield Generators upgraded.]

Oh. The best part of any battle.

YEAR 77, MONTH 8

A few days had passed since the battle, and it was time to check out the loot. Since the beetles did most of the fighting, New Freeka had no right to any of the loot or remains, so the beetles collected all the remaining armor, weapons, and more to put into my [Tree-asury]. I'd trade them for something someday, though, there seemed to be some magical items in there...

Next was my prisoner. Frankly, I didn't think he was going to talk, and I personally didn't really feel like interrogating him. I felt it was going to be a waste of time. After all, Salah was an enemy, and we were playing defense. The things he could tell me, I predicted, would be quite worthless.

So I didn't waste time interrogating Falklay in the end as my interest in him was more...academic in nature. After stripping him of his remaining magical items and storing them in my [Tree-asury], I turned to my main objective.

Drugged with all kinds of paralysis and still fast sleep, I put him inside a biolab where I could investigate him. Eventually, I would suck him dry with my vines and feelers. I wanted to see how a high-level person looked under the hood—just to compare. I had seen the heroes, Jura, and Yvon, and now I had this ranger. I wasted no more time before taking a look.

There were some notable differences, mainly in where the mana and life force was strongest. The eyes, nose, and ears were more pronounced than others—probably due to his need to be sensitive to his surroundings—and his soul spring, with all the stones around it, combined to create a nice fountain. Taking a good look at the fountain, there was a kind of wooden frame around it, in between the stones, and as I reached out to touch the stones, little tooltips came up, telling me what skills he had.

I tried to yank at the wood and stones. It was just something I always wanted to try, but I never attempted it with people whom I considered my allies. I had always wondered what would happen if I took one of those rocks out.

So I yanked it. And it didn't move. *Ah, well.* I kept trying, but instead, it just hurt the ranger. It seemed it was magically 'tied' and 'intertwined' with his soul, via some kind of force.

So I stopped and rested for a while. Maybe I just needed more power.

After drawing a bit more mana and energy from the trees around me, I tried to yank a rock from the fountain, again. It shook, and I sensed a huge amount of pain, but he remained unconscious and strapped in. Thank goodness for the paralysis.

The rock shook, but then something pulled it back again. It was as if I was trying to pull a piece of metal away from a very powerful magnet. I could, a little, but then the magnet pulled it back once my strength let up.

Uh...

It wasn't working. Borrowing the root-brains for some processing power, I calculated that the amount of energy I needed to break that 'magnetic' pull of the soul spring seemed really, really high, so I decided it was probably not going to work, no matter how many times I tried. Maybe this was like the atomic bond of souls, and that was why I needed a huge amount of energy to break it.

"It's only if you're trying to break things. Fixing things is a lot easier since those same forces work with you." Wisp whispered his wisdom. *Thanks, dude.*

I let the ranger sleep a day inside the biolab, and then I resumed my testing the next day.

There had been quite a few other things I wanted to test, and it just so happened I had a high-level person whose body was suitable for it.

Once again, I entered the ranger's inner realm, and this time, I flooded his body with my mana. It had been something I was curious about since I did it with the hellhounds, and then with Alexis's body when she was contained within me. What if I did it with a living 'normal' person? What happened then?

His body vibrated intensely, struggling in the biolab, as my mana, like a green tide, washed into his inner realm.

[Specimen's compatibility with injected mana is low. Specimen body is resisting. Prolonged exposure may result in mana poisoning.]

Ah. Did this happen before?

I kept it up anyway; I still wanted to see what happened. The body flailed inside the pod, kinda like a fish struggling to escape from an octopus.

[Specimen body is experiencing mana poisoning.]

Okay, I decided to see what happened when I healed him.

[Mana poisoning reduces magic and ability effectiveness.]

Really? I tried injecting his body with the healing liquids from my [Healing Fruit] and also the [Paralysis Poison]. It was a conundrum, I supposed, but the healing just repaired the damage; it didn't cure the status ailment.

[Mana poison is still in effect. Specimen body's organs are starting to suffer damage.]

Heal? But I noticed the healing was slower.

Two full days passed as I constantly drowned the ranger's body with my mana. He wasn't dead yet because one of the vines continued to supply his body with nutrients and air to stay alive, so I could continue to observe what was happening.

I was actually curious. Did the body actually gain compatibility over time? Or did the body continue to naturally reject my mana?

[Specimen body's organs are failing.]

Ah. *Heal?*

[Healing effectiveness is significantly reduced due to high levels of mana poisoning in the physical body. Specimen's body is dying.]

Oh.

I couldn't stop it. The decay in the body was surprisingly quick as the mana poisoning somehow made the body turn on itself. It was as if the body was rejecting itself, and strangely, I kept watching. A part of me realized this was a rare opportunity to witness death under a microscope, and then some.

And where I paid attention to the most...was the soul spring.

I saw the land surrounding the river and lake that formed the person's mana start to break apart as if a great earthquake was shattering them into small pieces. Then the 'water' in that river and lake started to leak out into the nothingness, and it revealed a crumbling 'riverbed' of some kind, filled with unusual marks. I couldn't see much as the crumbling went on rather quickly.

I wondered if it was because he was dying quickly.

But I didn't wonder long because I had to focus. I wanted to see what happened to the soul spring then.

As the crumbling 'riverbed' closed in on the soul spring, the spring started to dry up, the height of the spring falling and, eventually, stopping. Then the rocks and the structure surrounding the soul spring started to break up, too.

This was something I waited for, so I reached out to it and tried to grab hold of the rocks. As I touched them, they... vanished, poofing into dust. All the rocks did the same.

All that was left was a bare, empty hole floating in the nothingness as all the land and 'riverbed' had crumbled away, the background changing into emptiness. In a way, it was like a black hole sitting solitary in space. Perhaps in that empty whole, there was once a star, once a 'soul' there.

"The soul has gone," Wisp whispered to my imaginary ears again.

"I see."

[You've managed to salvage some of the decaying skills! Due to the decay of death, the salvaged skills are of a lower quality than the original skills possessed.]

[You've received the following, which can be used to create [seed-infused skill fruits]!]

[class seed - ranger] x 3.

[class seed - beast tamer] x 2.

[skill seed - archery] x 2.

[passive seed - spark of brilliance] x 1.

Oh, man. All these skill fruits were useless to me. But I

guessed I would find a use for them somewhere. Maybe Lausanne.

[You've witnessed death as it happens in the inner realm.]

[Familiar contracts upgraded - skill salvaging chance increased!]

[Biolab upgraded - post-mortem equipment, death sensors, death-delaying equipment, and body preservation added!]

Hey. That's something good. Finally. The physical body of the ranger stopped flailing like a puppet with its strings cut off. Lifeless, the body was pale and greenish from the damage of the mana poisoning over the last few days of experimentation. I later arranged for the corpse to be burned.

Meanwhile, the victory over the Salah army had made a lot of New Freekan devotees. A few days after the victory, they held some kind of feast in the courtyard of the [tree of prayer], where the leaders of New Freeka thanked their lucky stars for the protection of the valley's spirit and their victory.

It had free food, drinks, dances, and performances, some kind of prayer, and also worship led by the treefolk, things like that.

I felt somewhat flattered that the citizens thought that way, but the words of the leaders did feel quite hollow. Despite all the praise of their guardian and the so-called will of the valley, they somehow managed to worm in a word or two on their supposed contributions.

Perhaps it was a thing with politicians, even in this world.

YEAR 77, MONTH 9

"Tree spirit," Yvon said. It was rare for her to come alone to the main tree's courtyard, but the fact that she did meant there were probably changes in the way things were organized on the New Freekan council.

She presented jewels and other items I had previously requested, stored in some kind of magical bag.

"As you requested."

"What is it that you want?" Jura sneered. "For Lady Yvon herself to deliver the jewels, surely there is more to this than just...delivery."

"The freeloader!" Horns shouted in my mind. Only to me, of course.

Even I knew that.

She sighed and nodded. "It is as you say, Jura. After the victory over the Salah forces, we have been receiving letters, messages, and...envoys."

She then showed a few of these letters and passed them to Jura.

"Some of the smaller nations nearby are greatly impressed by our successful defense. And they would like to form some ties."

"Freeloader! And now they take credit for the beetles' sacrifice!" Horns shouted. He wasn't too happy that the beetles were the ones who suffered as it would take a month or two to regenerate their numbers.

Jura somehow seemed to be synchronized with Horns, and he sneered. "Such opportunistic behavior. It is only after such a grand display of power that you get offers."

Yvon nodded. "That's how anyone would see it, but look at it from their perspective. They wouldn't dare anger a country the size of Salah, so naturally, they would avoid any association with us. But that changed when that army of fifty thousand retreated. Now, we are like a new power in the region—a force able to stand up to Salah—and so these smaller nations now view us more positively."

"Us? Us? They had no casualties in combat! Put your men in combat, then you can say us!" Horns was rather grumpy. He wasn't too fond of the New Freekans—mainly because he felt some of the dead beetles didn't have to die had New Freeka lent some help.

I personally thought the beetles were just a self-replenishing mob, but Horns clearly cared for his hive.

Jura sneered again, also somehow synchronized. "I don't appreciate the 'we' and 'us' being thrown around. New Freeka did absolutely nothing. We only assisted once we found out they were first targeting the valley."

Jura was hiding some details about our own checkered history with Salah there, but hey, he was the guy with the [diplomat] job.

Yvon gave out a long sigh. "Indeed. And that is why I'm here. We are in an awkward position as New Freeka is clearly relying on Tree-Tree's ability for defenses to hold Salah off, and yet the outside world—our neighboring nations and Salah—don't know that. They are under the impression that New Freeka is the one controlling all the...forces."

"Master. They are freeloaders!"

Horns, I think you need to stop shouting. I get it.

"Then clarify. Tell them New Freeka did nothing, and it is the valley's protector who did," Jura retorted. "You don't want to overstate your military prowess and face the consequences later."

Yvon sighed. "I wish it was so simple. But the people of New Freeka, too, want to believe that the tree spirit is on our side."

"Yvon, you, of all people, should know that Tree-Tree cares very little for New Freeka. It's a transactional arrangement, one out of favor. It is about time you let the people of New Freeka know this as well."

"I-I can't. I can't snuff out their hopes like that. The tree spirit is their newfound pride, their source of stability in this world. If I tell them that, I-I am afraid a riot may break out."

"Then crush it."

"Permission to let them run riot. Then we may have beetles running riot, too!" Horns interjected in my mind.

"Even the councilors want to believe it, and they want to believe that Tree-Tree will protect them. It seems it was my mistake, for being vague and unclear about the real relationship between New Freeka and Tree-Tree."

"So?"

"I...erm... Can Tree-Tree officially be our guardian and protector?"

"Shameless!" Horns commentated. "Freeloaders! These beggars want to demand our master's protection?"

Oh, shush now. I'll think about it.

"What do I get in exchange?" I spoke into both their minds, and Yvon paused.

"Uh...our loyalty?"

"Rejected. I care not for that, and you have no way of ensuring loyalty. I demand servitude. I have need of minions to carry out my demands."

"Uh..."

"Make Jura and the elves royalty of New Freeka. Jura and

Laufen will be my two spokespersons, and they will play the role of the new joint rulers of New Freeka, and the rest of you can be advisors. From henceforth, the ones who rule will be Jura and Laufen. All citizens of New Freeka are to acknowledge their position as your new joint monarchs. They will be the voice of my will, my elven avatars."

Jura seemed surprised by that. "Tree-Tree, that..." He clearly didn't expect that, but seriously, I had been wanting to give Jura direct ruling powers for some time. The arguments and issues we had with New Freeka over the past few years, especially the last few months, really solidified that view, that Jura deserved a seat at the council, such that my demands were heard and known, and my needs were respected and complied by these people. Unlike the treefolk, who seem perfectly content living in their small villages, or the centaurs who are similarly happy to have their hillside slopes, these New Freekans had been creating problems.

Yvon herself also seemed shocked, and her mouth just gasped, a little too dumbfounded to respond, and she took a few deep breaths just staring at Jura and my main tree before she finally managed to respond.

"Ah, we...we are founded to be a council, a collective rulership, such that everyone has a say. To...to return to a monarchy would be against...against our founding principles. It... The council and the people will not accept it."

"Then be gone. New Freeka stands alone," I responded. It wasn't like I really needed them. It was really more of a mutual coexistence since they had the ability to partake in trade to acquire materials that were not available locally.

"Ah. Please, wait, tree spirit. Let me have some time to discuss this with the wider council. It is such a crucial decision. I alone cannot make this decision. I will summon a meeting immediately."

Jura, too, seemed to be taken aback. "Ah, Tree-Tree, we may need to discuss this."

"Later." And then I turned to Yvon. "Go, gather your council."

And so Yvon ran back, leaving the jewels behind.

"Horns, we got the jewels already. Let's break your first level cap."

"Tree-Tree, wait. About that proposal earlier, to make us the monarchy, are...are you serious?"

"Yes." Well, not really, but if New Freeka agreed to it, I didn't mind at all.

"Please reconsider." Jura shook his head. "It is a position I'm not willing to bear, a weight I cannot carry."

"I must have my position heard and respected in New Freeka. Let's see what they are willing to give."

Jura gulped. "Surely, there is room to compromise with them, something that doesn't involve usurping the entire ruling council? Even I think that sounds a bit too much, although they've been absolutely deadweights in the past two battles with Salah."

"Well, I am willing to compromise, but let's see how sincere they are in their counter-proposal."

———

Yvon quickly gathered her council for an urgent meeting.

"The tree spirit wants to make Jura and Laufen monarchs?"

Yvon gulped and nodded.

"No. Absolutely no monarchs!" Quite unanimous was the decision from the councilors. None of them wanted to have a king and queen over their head. New Freeka modeled itself after the elvish republics.

"Then we lose our protection. We were all on the walls when the battle happened. You've seen the fury and damage the tree spirit can bring."

"I still can't help but think this sounds a lot like a criminal gang's extortion," one of them said.

"The tree spirit has no reason to help us, so quash that

thought." Yvon glared at the rest of them. "But, at the same time, I too disagree with having a king rule over our new nation. It is not something our people wanted, and I believe most of them are happy with the way things are."

New Freeka organized itself into multiple districts, and each district elected three councilmen to the high council. So, in a way, there was a fair bit of representation by the people, which did help in making the locals feel somewhat connected to their rulers. It was a partly democratic structure, though the title of councilmen often passed from father to son, due to the family's influence, even in such a young state.

"Then..."

"So what are we willing to give?" Yvon asked.

"Give?"

"Look, if we are to negotiate this with the tree spirit, we better be prepared to offer some meaningful concessions or give some rights away. Without the tree spirit's protection, New Freeka's chances of survival are rather slim. The tree spirit's annoyance at us was very clear in that previous meeting. I frankly don't want to have that annoyance turn into outright hostility. I hope everyone now understands why this meeting is so urgent."

All the councilors glanced uncomfortably at each other.

"Unfortunately, I agree with Lady Yvon's assessment, and so..."

"A king and queen are totally out of the picture. The people like the leadership the way it is now. Even if the tree spirit turns against us, I think none of our people would agree to have a king and queen."

"And if we tell them this is to secure the tree spirit's protection..."

"No. I know our chances are slim without the tree spirit, but we are a sovereign nation. If we agree to have someone else rule over our heads, that's against what we have fought for all this while."

"Oh, cut the political bullshit. We didn't fight one bit," one councilor said. "All the fighting so far has been done by the tree spirit's minions."

"I meant the fighting figuratively, as in...our struggle so far. Anyway, are you on our side or the tree spirit's side? You really want a king to rule over us?"

"That's not what I meant. We must know exactly what we are dealing with here, and to do so, we must recognize the fact that we are very vulnerable," the other councilor rebuked. It was a messy argument, with a lot of side conversations.

"So can we have some consensus? I believe it's clear we will refuse having a king. But are we willing to give Jura and Laufen a seat, and accordingly, authority?" Yvon tries to steer the conversation back to the topic. These councilmen tended to go off on a tangent sometimes.

There was an awkward look among everyone as they shrugged. It took one of the more daring councilors to finally say, "Yes," and then all the others started agreeing.

"Fine. Now that we agree to give them a seat, what will be their authority? Remember, it must be something concrete, with actual powers, or else the tree spirit will not agree."

"Then what are we willing to give?"

"Administrator of the valley? Forest master?"

"The tree spirit won't accept that. It's no fool. It's already master of the valley, and it doesn't need us to grant it that sort of authority. It must come from something only we can give. Our men. Our money. The ability to directly intervene in our affairs."

"Fine, let's go about giving Jura and Laufen combined voting rights over the military, diplomatic affairs, a share of our tax collection as 'tribute,' and smaller voting rights on domestic, trade, and policing."

The councilors went about debating the finer points of the proposed rights and powers of Jura and Laufen as politicians were often inclined to do.

"Okay, so...those are their rights and powers, but how do we give it to them without making the rest of the population feel that this is something arbitrary and without basis? As it was, some districts were already uneasy over their representation, and they were demanding more councilmen."

One of the rare centaur councilors then spoke up. "I believe the treefolk worship the tree spirit, do they not?"

The councilors turned, mostly out of surprise.

"If so, we can follow how some elven kingdoms have special positions for the senior members of the church."

"Are you suggesting elevating the tree spirit to a god?"

"In principle, yes. From the powers we have seen, he might as well be a local deity. So a spokesperson of a local deity surely can be given a formal position in the ruling council, with special rights reflecting the local deity's influence in the area."

"Ah."

"There is a precedent. The Dwarven Nation of Prummash, far to the north, gives the Great Forge Serpent's chosen a special position in their advisors' council."

"What matters then is how we convey this decision to the people..."

"*If* the tree spirit accepts it."

"If it doesn't?"

"We'll have to figure it out."

And with that, Yvon's meeting was over, and Yvon returned to meet us, this time with six other councilors.

"So have you agreed?" my voice spoke into their mind.

The seven exchanged glances before Yvon took a gulp and stepped forth. "Tree spirit, we...we are truly humbled that you've assisted us during the defense of New Freeka, and our words cannot describe the gratitude we have for sparing us from the bloodshed of battle."

"Ah, the freeloader has finally learned gratitude, eh?" Horns seemed to be happy.

"Spare me the flowery words. I take it you've decided not to accept my proposal." I'd been in enough meetings to know that what started flowery often ended in a refusal.

They paused. I wondered how I sounded in their minds sometimes.

"Ah, we...we have a counterproposal. Something that would be more aligned to our own founding ideals. We would propose to create a special religious role for both Jura and Laufen, whereby the tree spirit is elevated to that of a local deity."

Jura paused. He seemed to be thinking.

"In this way, Jura and Laufen gain a position as the Voice of the Tree Spirit, which will give them similar rights and authority to that of a religious leader. As the 'voice,' they will have significant authority in areas of the military, diplomacy, and external trade. We also commit that our military will be split into a few divisions, with one third of it under the command and rule of the Voice. They will enforce the demands of the tree spirit, within the framework of authority that the Voice has."

Hmm, a third of New Freeka's forces.

"They will be given a special name of your choosing, such to differentiate them from the regular military."

There was a silence, perhaps for a few seconds, before Yvon continued.

"We will formally set up a new institution under the Voice, and we will contribute a sizeable portion of our tax collection to this institution, which will also fund the force."

Oh, and tax revenues, too. "A third. Of all tax revenues and collections," I spoke into their minds, and they froze. The seven councilors exchanged glances, and then they nodded.

"Yes. A third."

"Anything else?" At this point, New Freeka was willing to offer a third of their military, and their tax money to me, so I was quite satisfied with the offer.

"Uh..." Yvon shook her head. "That's all we can give."

Well, in terms of land, I did control the valley, and that had been my right since day one. New Freeka only controlled the unforested areas further south, the large farmlands, and the town itself.

"Never mind."

An awkward silence followed. Perhaps they were waiting. Even Jura looked a bit worried.

"I agree to it, in exchange for my participation in New Freeka's defense." My thoughts behind this were fairly simple. I did intend to somehow rule over New Freeka eventually, but at the same time, I did realize that placing Jura as king over New Freeka was extremely sudden. Most likely, the New Freekans themselves—the now fifty thousand non-humans—were going to resist it, and I would then have a rebellion on my hands.

Not that crushing it would be an issue, but that would delay my ability to gain the necessary resources to further upgrade the rest of my artificial souls and research.

So this sort of transitory arrangement helped, and I assumed it would give Jura and Laufen the necessary experience needed to let them learn about managing a town before ultimately usurping New Freeka. It would be easier to boil the frogs of New Freeka gradually, so let them get used to having Jura as a member of their ruling class before, one day, taking them over entirely. Ruling the New Freekans by proxy wasn't a bad idea anyway—at least the nitty gritty of people-management was left to the appointed proxy, and the world would look at the town, not at me directly.

The tax revenue would also really help. I could buy more jewels and weird artifacts. I was eager to test out the ability I had gotten when I evolved to a [Starsoul Tree].

A few days later, I checked my updates:

[Beetle - basic magical lances - complete.]

[Eye-Tree Stage I research option unlocked - eighteen months remaining.]

[Enhanced exoskeletons - complete.]

[Enhanced interior structures - one month remaining.]

[Large beetle pods - three months remaining.]

[Beetle - anti-magma armors stage 2 - nine months remaining.]

[Fruit bombs - increased range and power - three months remaining.]

[Tree - volcanic adaptation stage 3 - eighteen months remaining.]

I would need to start working on the volcano again. The enhanced exoskeletons granted the beetles stronger, faster bodies, but this was at the expense of consuming my harvested metals and some essences and also a longer regeneration time if they died. The beetle magical lances, even though I completed the research, were not immediately usable as I needed to obtain some kind of mines before they could be infused into the beetles themselves.

Ah.

So I needed a mine, preferably one that would supply me with non-ordinary resources, such that I could further upgrade the beetles. There was a natural limit on how I could keep upgrading them with ordinary items, without giving them the ability to level via an artificial soul. Also, at the rate of my mineral harvesting from the earth, I had sufficient metals to support only four thousand beetles with the enhanced exoskeleton.

"Guys, what are our priorities?" I called on my artificial souls for a meeting.

"Take over the volcano! Kill all the golems!" Horns said. He had just had his upgrade as a [Baron Beetle], increasing his level cap to thirty. The upgrade granted the beetles around him extra strength, armor, and speed. Still, it wasn't sufficient to take on the golems. They were just far too large and tough.

"And?"

"Locate additional minerals, resources, and ley lines." It was Trevor's turn. "We're actively sending some beetles to scout on the far away locations."

"Upgrade? Spiders, fruits, healing. All require upgrades."

Thanks for the reminder, Dimitree. We do need anti-air. That reminds me, where the hell did I leave that airship from Salah?

"Were you not working on it the last time, then you broke it apart and dumped it in your treasury? I think you got stuck when the biolab couldn't look into the materials or decipher the runes." That was Trevor, digging through my memories faster than I could remember it myself.

"Really?" Was it that long ago? I tried to dig through my own mind... Oh, God, it'd already been three years. I thought I was also getting more forgetful.

"Trevor, can you do me a favor and help me track all my outstanding tasks?"

"Certainly. I'll create a task manager in your interface."

"And a calendar."

"Will do."

"Then mark when the date of the ten-year anniversary of the demon king's death is due. I want a countdown timer in my interface. I fear I may forget as I move onto all these lesser missions."

SIDE STORIES - ALEXIS AND MEELA

SOMETIME AROUND YEAR 77, MONTH 9.

"Looking at the skies again?" Meela's soul popped up in Alexis's mind. It seemed there was a kind of shared network that existed for all the souls and artificial souls under Tree-Tree's care. Perhaps it was the rootnet's ability.

"I always do." Alexis sat on the branch of her biolab. From the outside it looked like a very large tree, but inside it was filled with all sorts of unusual equipment. "I really like the sky. It's orangey today."

"I can somewhat imagine it. Isn't it nice, not having to run here and there, fighting all the time, just to gain levels?"

"It's not a bad change in pace." But her face was a bit sulky.

"But it's not enough for you, is it?"

Alexis looked up, noticing a small orange cloud floating overhead. "Yeah."

"Why?"

Alexis shook her spiritual legs. For those not attuned to magic, she would appear as a wisp, a faint blob of blue light on top of a branch. For those with the right affinity to spiritual magic, she appeared as a young girl, but ethereal, that was bonded and lived in the 'biolab.' She was, in a way, the biolab, and this 'ethereal body' was just a 'form,' a 'projection' from that biolab.

"I always thought we'd survive. Like heroes in all those stories. A happy ending for all of us."

"Eh? You were the one doing the most research and saying we'd all most likely die. The rest of us were just winging it."

"I mean, I had the data staring at me, telling me otherwise, but a part of me still, truly, believed in that fantasy, that all things would end well."

"You're just like all of us after all." Perhaps there's a smile somewhere in there.

"Yeah."

Alexis looked up again. The sun was gradually setting, and there were just a few clouds now. One of the moons was already visible. Its glow was faint, but as the sky darkened, it would get clearer and clearer.

"I-I thought of what I'd do after the war. After the demon king."

"Oh?"

"I'd go on a holiday. A world tour, properly, this time. Not our rushed city-to-city killing big monsters kind of tour. Take the time to hike the highest mountains and see the uncharted lands. Explore the world..."

"That sounds like being an adventurer."

Alexis paused and blushed. "Ah...yeah. I guess it does. But here I am, stuck here serving the tree spirit as a research assistant."

"Hey, that's what all of us end up doing, if we're still at home. Working in dead-end jobs."

They both laughed. "Well, that's a good point. This is a dead-end job, isn't it?"

"One that you have to work for a thousand years."

"Man, that's depressing to think about. And look at me, I'm this...tree."

"You should ask for a holiday. Ask for normal employment terms—leave days and sick leave."

"Uh...I highly doubt soul contracts have allowances for leave days and sick leaves." Alexis laughed.

"Eh, I think everything can be negotiated. Perhaps some kind of arrangement can be made. Look at Yvon, she's still out and about even though there's a soul contract attached to her."

"That's cause she's not dead yet!"

"Ahhhh..." Meela was probably making an embarrassed face. She didn't comprehend soul magic all that well.

"Anyway. I'm stuck here. And Tree-Tree doesn't trust me."

"Of course he doesn't. You tried to take over his body. Now that I think of it, he's being generous to give you this 'dead-end' job you're complaining about."

"It's my survival instincts!"

"Yeah, yeah."

An awkward silence followed for a moment.

"We probably should talk about something less...touchy."

"Yeah."

"What were you thinking of doing after the war, Meela?"

"Me? I didn't think about it much, but I thought I'd be a princess. Have high tea in some fancy palace, eat dessert, walk in pretty gardens and stuff."

"Doesn't that mean you have to marry some prince?"

"Uh, I suppose so. I'll have first choice, won't I? I'm a hero, after all."

"And doesn't that mean you have to...you know...sleep with them?"

Meela paused. "I didn't think of that. I'd pick a handsome one with no body odor, then. But yeah, I'd like to be a princess. This is another world and being a princess like those fairytales would be something I'd like to do."

"But it'll be you that's rescuing the prince because you're the hero, and he's not. He'll be the dude in distress!"

"What's wrong with that?"

"Uh, nothing, but it's strange, I guess."

"You're kooky, Alexis."

"Uh. You too, Meela."

"You know, I still really like one of the princess's gowns. It's so pretty. Remember Princess Alainas of the Faroah Isles? I really liked her sea-shell dress during the reception they threw for us. It really captured the essence of a mermaid."

"All I remember is her trying to hit on Max so hard. She was really trying to give herself to him."

"Oh, I remember that. What, were you jealous? Wait. You liked Max?"

"No, I didn't! But I just remembered how ridiculous the princess was." Alexis shook her head. "All the touching and flirting...it was just so horrifying to watch. It was like a train crash happening in slow motion."

"But she's really pretty. And if Max doesn't have [Immunity to Charms], he'd fall for her."

"I don't think it's the charms, though." Alexis shrugged. "Notice how none of us ever eyed any of the good-looking men or women we met throughout our journey? I think it's the effect of the hero title. Until our quest is done, we won't be sidetracked by such stuff."

"Oh, man." Meela sighed. "Did that mean I missed all the good men that could have been in my life, too?"

"Maybe. You could've been a princess if you weren't a hero."

"Oh, well."

"It's not fair..." Alexis sulked.

"Huh?"

"We spent years fighting demons, hunting them throughout the world, and we killed the demon king. And what did we get? No special reincarnation from the gods. No post-battle reward to thank us for our sacrifice, those years of constant gruesome fighting. Aren't the gods just using child soldiers in a way?"

"Uh. I never thought about it like that. I thought it was a

privilege, a responsibility for those with our gifts. And we are no longer the teens we once were."

"Just a few years, Meela."

Meela didn't say anything and just stared.

"But we have a second chance here. We're still in this world. We can still reap the rewards of our sacrifice."

Meela's spirit bobbed. "I don't like the sound of that."

"No. No, no, no. I mean...I don't have to be trapped in this dead-end job forever."

"The soul contract's on you..."

"Maybe Tree-Tree can release me from it. Then we can travel the world."

"Uh...we can travel the world if we wait one thousand years. We could just go and sleep in the soul realm and wake up one thousand years later."

"You can do that. I can't. So these one thousand years will be a lot longer for me. If I have to keep doing research for the next one thousand years, I might go mad."

"Well, talk to Tree-Tree? A bit of honesty, and maybe you can achieve something big for him. Then he can free you from your contract."

"Huh. I certainly don't plan to serve—" Alexis winced in pain. It was an intense one, and it sent Alexis into a kind of fidgeting shock.

"Oh, dear. You triggered it."

The pain lasted for a good ten minutes. Meela, a floating soul, could only watch as her friend suffered in intense pain.

"Ugh, man, that was a bad headache. What was I saying? Where was I? What were we talking about?" Alexis finally recovered from the pain and seemed to suffer from some kind of amnesia.

Meela paused before deciding not to remind Alexis of the discussion. "Oh, nothing. We were just talking about dresses. Remember Lady Alice's silver bling dress..."

SIDE STORIES - LAUSANNE

"Relax and be focused," Tree-Tree whispered into my mind. A small wolf. That was my real opponent today, and I felt a bit intimidated by the idea of fighting it as my first non-sparring opponent. But it was a monster that appeared all the time in the forest, so Tree-Tree said it was probably the easiest one around.

Still, not easy. It was still bigger than me!

It growled, baring its fangs.

At the back of my mind, I knew Tree-Tree was watching. So was Horns, the giant fighting beetle, and maybe even Jura somewhere. So I tried to relax, but it was different.

There was real 'anger' in the wolf, true hostility. Perhaps it was hungry. It growled again, and it changed its posture, looking at me with those angry eyes.

I looked at the spear in my right hand and the dagger in my left. I practiced for this, a long time, and so I believed I could do it. I had it engraved in my mind thanks to so many dreams of me just swinging the spear and the dagger.

No, I must do it.

A hero must do what a hero must.

The wolf charged, and our eyes met. My grip on the spear tightened, and I waited for the moment. It felt instinctive. I was one with the spear. It was a small one, and while I couldn't use a full-sized spear yet, it was enough.

The wolf entered my range.

And it pounced.

I ducked and instantly activated my ability [Powerstrike]. It felt natural like the times I practiced with Horns and Jura. The spear's tip pierced the wolf's hide, and it whimpered.

Our eyes met as the wolf looked at its wound, blood spilling. I saw the pain in its eyes. This might be the moment it died, I hoped. It whimpered, one of sorrow.

Like a dog.

A part of me wavered, and my spear shifted slightly. It was enough to change it from a fatal strike into one that would only leave a deep cut.

The wolf fell behind me, but it managed to get up and run away, leaving a trail of blood dripping onto the dirt.

And yet, I didn't give chase.

I froze.

My mind somehow replayed that pain in the wolf's eyes, the whimpering voice that sounded dog-like.

"You okay?" Tree-Tree whispered.

"I-I couldn't do it."

A part of me cursed myself then. Was this how my dreams of being a hero ended?

Was I not meant to be a hero? Heroes killed monsters!

"The first time you draw blood says a lot." Jura walked over, still holding his bow and arrow, ready if the battle went bad. "How do you feel?"

"I-I'm disappointed. I'm angry. Why couldn't I do it?" I looked at Jura, and he smiled. His big hands held my shoulders, and he gave me a shake.

"Why are you disappointed?"

"Because heroes are supposed to slay monsters! But...I failed. Didn't you tell me that some heroes started fighting monsters when they were six or seven? Does that mean I can't be a hero?"

Jura shook me again.

"Are heroes mindless fighting golems?"

"No..." I mean, heroes were supposed to be like gods in the battlefield, the power of the heavens made flesh, the fury of a hurricane made into human form.

"So why are you disappointed? Is it really the right thing to feel?"

"Uh..."

"The question is this. Why did you have to kill the wolf?"

"Because it's a monster?"

"Why do you have to kill monsters?"

"Because monsters hurt people?"

"Did it hurt you?"

"Well, not yet."

"So why do you have to kill it?"

"It can't hurt me?"

"Then you'll be killing everyone."

"It's very likely to hurt me and show aggression? If I didn't, I would be hurt."

"Good point but, in this case, you've wounded it and chased it away. Is that sufficient?"

"Uncle Jura, you're giving me the moral answer again. I can sense it when you're lying and don't believe what you say." I was young, but I knew it when I heard it. Uncle Jura would kill anyone that even scratched us. Maybe only Tree-Tree could stop him.

Jura shrugged and rubbed his head. "Heh. Well, it actually comes with experience, young Lausanne. When you meet more people, and meet more monsters, you will be able to better judge who do you spare, and who do you kill."

"So that was the morally correct answer?" I thought the

standard education that all elves, all 'parents,' tried to give was to be morally just. But I lived in a world of wars. Even eight-year-old children like me knew that morally correct was just words. I lived in a world where might made right. Where heroes could order nations because their powers gave them that right. Where demons could crush nations overnight because their might was stronger.

Jura paused, kneeled next to me, and rubbed me on the head. "Yes. I have to tell you what is morally correct to do. When you deviate from it, you must be able to answer to yourself about why you deviated from what was morally correct. I may not truly believe in it, but that is because I know what is important to me."

"Well, a hero should do what is morally just." Did they? Maybe there were other ways of thinking. Or I was trying to take the easy way out?

I sometimes thought being a hero was really hard. All these types of justice, fairness... How did they think about these kinds of things in the heat of battle?

———

A week later, I asked Tree-Tree to let me fight the forest monsters again.

I thought long about it. I mean, it was hard to really think about it. I was only eight, and I got headaches when I thought for too long, and when I did, I felt like going to the playroom and just playing with my wooden toys again.

"So why do you want to fight again?" Jura asked. Maybe a part of him wished I would stop this hero dream of mine. I sometimes still heard Uncle Jura say that when he talked with Mom.

"I don't know. I just want to. Maybe I will get better."

"That's not a good reason."

"I just want to," I insisted.

"Just because you want to, it doesn't mean you can." Uncle Jura frowned and gave me that look when I was being a bit...difficult.

"Okay. But I still want to fight monsters. I want to level up, gain experience."

Jura sighed. He probably knew I would run into the forest myself anyway since Tree-Tree was always there looking out for us. "Fine, be careful."

So I found another small wolf to fight. There were lesser animals, like those giant rats or big squirrel-like stuff that lived in the forest, eating whatever fruits and leaves grew here.

This time, I wanted to beat it, but maybe I didn't have to kill it. Would I still get experience that way?

We spotted each other, and the wolf sized me up. At least, I assumed that was what it was doing when its eyes seemed to roam.

"Hello, wolf. I'd like to fight you."

The wolf growled, and I growled back. Naturally, my growl wasn't really threatening.

It entered into a combat stance, and so did I, my spear and dagger ready.

It charged, again, the same movement as the earlier wolf. Somehow, the animals had set moves that we could learn.

I ducked.

[Powerstrike].

This time, I aimed somewhere in the side. It wouldn't kill it instantly, but it would do some harm.

The wolf winced in pain, and the dagger in my left hand swung in, landing a few cuts.

It swiped, and its claws managed to scratch me.

"Owwwwwww!" *That really, really hurt. I'm bleeding, a gash right on my left arm, from my wrist up to my elbow.*

Pain. I felt like my entire left hand stung. Mom wouldn't like that. I had better get back and hope it didn't fester.

The wolf was injured, too; the cuts and the stab from the spear were causing it to bleed. I thought it did to me.

"Lausanne, are you all right?" Tree-Tree spoke into my head.

"Fine. Bleeding. Can you help me later?"

"Okay."

The wolf charged, trying to take advantage of the time I was still talking to Tree-Tree. But my instincts, born from years of dreams and constant practice, managed to react in time, and so I ducked and stabbed the wolf again in the abdomen with my short spear.

It whimpered as it fell onto the dirt floor, and then its voice weakened. It was defenseless. The second stab drained its strength, and it could only limp.

It still looked at me. This time, its eyes were a mixture of anger and fear.

"Should I kill it?" I wondered.

My left hand was bleeding, and yet my grip on the dagger remained. The wolf took two steps back, limping.

"Should I? It hurt me."

What would a hero do? That depended on which hero, really. Some would kill this wounded wolf, some would spare it, if it shows no further hostility.

If I were a hero, what would I do?

My eyes met with the wolf again. It growled at me as it stepped back.

I'll take its life.

I thrust my spear at the wolf.

A loud clang sounded.

My spear was blocked by Jura's sword. He pushed my spear back, turned, and then shooed the wolf away, letting it slowly limp away.

"Lausanne." He turned and noticed the bleeding on my left arm.

"Why'd you stop me, Uncle Jura?" *Why did he block my spear?*
"I think you're not ready to take a life yet."
"Why?"
"Because you are not. Now don't argue with me, and let's go back to Tree-Tree and get that gash patched up before your mommy nags me for not looking after you."

I sighed. Oh, well.

Stats page

Lausanne Ricola, Level 20 (cumulative)
Elf girl, aged 8
Elf warrior (Level 11)
Skills
•Powerstrike.
•Basic evasive steps.
•Spear experience – medium.
•Dagger experience – low.
•Basic pain endurance.
•Improved reaction – basic.
•Shadow Stab.

Villager (4 levels)
Skills
•Disease resistance – basic.
•Cottonwork – basic.
•Olivework – advanced.

Generic/non-job specific (5 levels)

Skills

- Basic endurance.
- Advanced reading and writing – common tongue.
- Blessed by a soul tree (special).

YEAR 77, MONTH 10

Laufen, Jura, Belle, Emile, and Lausanne—even Wahlen and Brislach, who both came back—met in the main room of the secret hideout, seated in a circle.

"I called everyone here to discuss the announcement from the high council," Jura started, the high council having announced the arrangement a day ago after formalizing the necessary amendments to their rules and laws, to incorporate the existence of the new positions and institutions.

"How could we not?" Wahlen shrugged. "Everyone in my workplace is talking about it and asking me whether I get anything..."

Jura sighed. "First of all, you might have heard the story, but let's just go through why this is happening. Tree-Tree has decided that he wants a larger role in the affairs of New Freeka since Tree-Tree has been tangled up in multiple battles due to New Freeka's hostile relationship with Salah. Providing free protection without compensation or representation isn't what Tree-Tree considers to be an ideal arrangement. This will give Tree-Tree greater ability to choose the battles it fights and avoid those it doesn't want to participate in."

"But isn't that what...tree spirits do?" Brislach asked. "Tree spirits raised by elves protect their cities and capitals? Are they not benevolent spirits of the earth that protect the inhabitants and their surroundings?"

"That's a story often passed down, but the truth is not so simple. We don't know what price the elven nations pay to their tree spirits in order to obtain their assistance. If there are, I would think they are secrets of the kings and the royal court. Perhaps the tree spirits of those nations owe the elves some kind of favor, too. We cannot use the charity of other tree spirits as an expectation of Tree-Tree's demands and conduct."

The other elves nodded, prompting Jura to continue.

"A healthy ecosystem must have everyone playing their part. A New Freeka that doesn't contribute back to the system is not productive to the entire valley."

"Ecosystem?"

"Yeah, a word from Tree-Tree. It means the system of how each individual and creature in the valley interacts with each other."

An awkward pause followed.

"Right. Back to the announcement. Tree-Tree has decided to appoint me supreme counsel and Laufen as vice counsel of the newly set up Valtrian Order. Now, what this means is that both of us are now part of the high council of New Freeka."

"Some of them say it's a power grab." Wahlen voiced out the rumors from the ground. There were plenty of other such thoughts and rumors passing around.

"In some ways, it is." Jura nodded. "The fact is, a third of all tax collected is now under our control, and so is a third of the militia. A skeleton group of administrative staff and treasury have been assigned to assist the Valtrian Order as well. And that is a heavy burden we now have to bear, to fulfill Tree-Tree's will..."

Another moment of silence passed as everyone digested the meaning of this change. It was big, since the seven of them were named as the 'Selected' special individuals that Tree-Tree had commanded to be specially protected. In time, this might mean having guards assigned to each of them.

"Any thoughts?"

Wahlen grumbled, "Uncle Jura, to be honest, I-I don't really care what Tree-Tree wants to do. I am trying to move on, actually. We lived for years under Tree-Tree's care and protection, like refugees, like war victims, and now, there is a town that springs up next to Freeka, one of nonhumans like us, where we can return and live life as regular people again. A life, similar to the past. Before all this destruction. I even have a job now...and friends!"

Jura paused and looked at Wahlen. "Tree-Tree—"

But before Jura could continue his response, Wahlen continued, "I understand all this is actually possible because of Tree-Tree's presence and protection of New Freeka. But this pronouncement does make our life a little bit more complicated."

"I understand. After living so long in the shadows of war, all of us would really cherish these moments of normalcy and calm..."

"I would like to continue having a normal life like everyone else. Live a life in a town, working... Being a part of the ruling elite is something that never crossed my mind." Wahlen and Brislach moved to New Freeka to work and live some time ago, and frankly, I could see why.

"It is disruptive for the life you've tried to rebuild in New Freeka, but please, bear with us. There are bigger things at play here." Jura nodded. "We'll try not to disrupt your life as much as we can, so you can still live some of that normal life. But things will change, and not everything will remain normal."

Wahlen sighed. "I suppose that will be all I can ask."

It was Brislach's turn to speak. "We're going to be special, aren't we?"

Laufen nodded. "Yes. It is a strange twist of fate, but we are now a special group in this valley..."

With some reluctance, the seven elves accepted their fate.

The announcement was rather confusing to the populace of New Freeka, but to most of them, it was something they soon forgot since reorganization at the top happened frequently, and for refugees who lived through changes of power, such things were common. Every time a king changed, there was bound to be some restructuring.

So the new organization of the season was the Valtrian Order.

That was the name I came up with. Just a combination of the words 'valley' and 'tree.'

A few days later, the exiled wizard of Baroosh visited the inner courtyard of my main tree, surprising Jura who was taking a rest, a little overwhelmed from the sudden influx of matters requiring his attention. "Greetings."

"Ah, Wizard Madeus."

"I hear that you are hiring, Supreme Counsel." The wizard smiled and bowed.

Jura coughed at the title and the bow. Perhaps the wizard was mocking him. "Ah, yes."

"Well, good. Allow me to get to the point. I would like to offer my services to the tree spirit."

Jura coughed quite hard. Was he choking? After a few coughs, he recovered and looked into the wizard's eyes. "Surely, you jest."

"No. I mean it. I would like to offer my services to the tree spirit and the Valtrian Order. It's something I've been thinking about it for days since I found about the whole Valtrian Order's setup."

Jura couldn't answer, so he just paused.

"Accepted." I didn't let Jura say more.

I had a need for a mage's services, so the fact that he came and offered it was very much welcome. Whether he had the right motives...well, that could be sorted out later. As it was, I needed someone as a counterpoint to Alexis, to share knowledge of the magicks from a different source, and Alexis, as a 'foreign' hero, lacked the nuts and bolts of magick since her power over magic was likely to be innate—something of a gift arising from her cheat power. A regular mage like Madeus would likely have a more robust understanding of basic magic, as he had to explore it from a young age.

The wizard staggered back, having not spoken to me telepathically before. "Ah... Apologies. It is just a surprise to hear the voice in my head... So this is what Yvon and the councilors hear when they speak of the tree spirit."

"Welcome, Wizard. We have much to speak about. Jura, can you please summon the captains of the existing Valtrian Order? I wish to speak to them later."

Jura nodded and left, his cape fluttering as he walked. He had a special uniform made for him—one that identified him as supreme counsel—and everywhere he went, a few of the Valtrian guards would accompany him. There would be plans for a new set of uniforms for the Valtrian guards, but that was a lesser priority, so for now, their uniform remained as it was.

"So, Wizard. I believe your name is Madeus?"

He nodded.

"All right. Madeus, welcome to the team. First of all, as a tree who doesn't get to go out much, my knowledge about the wider world is very limited. So, tell me, what do you know about...the wider world? And heroes. And that void magic the princess encountered."

He paused and stopped. "That's a lot to go through, but...are you referring to my research back in Baroosh?"

"That would be a good place to start." I led him, using the vines, to one of the subsidiary trees' external rooms. Since some of the elves moved out, it had been repurposed into more of a study for Lausanne. She was out now, so we could use it. I was hoping to make a library here someday.

"Back then, I was researching the magics of the heroes...so I collected various books and writings left by the heroes of the past. One such item was the Mad-Hero, Arsene Emir, who... obsessed on summoning more of his friends."

"May I ask why?"

"The king was curious about the origins of their power. By discovering how they were summoned, perhaps we could glean a hint."

"Oh?"

"The high king of Baroosh is a very old man—he is close to a hundred this year. So he has met many generations of heroes, who all went on to slay the demon kings. When he was only a teenager, he met a hero who appeared in the Baroosh, freshly summoned by the gods. Our king offered him shelter and spoke to him at length. He came to understand that the heroes all come from another world very different to our own. But, at the back of his mind, he really wanted to know where the heroes' power came from and whether, just whether, there was a way to gain that power for himself."

Well, okay. The high king of Baroosh just kind of went up in the list of threats, but somehow, the wizard still spoke of him rather reverentially.

"Well, the hero didn't know much. He only knew that each of the gods gave a few heroes their blessing, and as such, that generation—there were ten of them—were scattered throughout the world. Anyway, the point is, the king saw the heroes when they were freshly summoned. The hero he met then, his name was Andrei, had the power of bending earth, such that everything was drawn to or away from him. He could make things heavy or light."

Uh...Madeus, are you going off on a tangent?

"When the king met the last generation of heroes, he was... rather disappointed. Their powers were still amazing by most measure, but yet, compared to Andrei the Earthbreaker, there was just too large a gap. So the king wondered whether there was a mistake in the summoning of heroes."

"The heroes still beat the demon king, did they not?" I

thought heroes should be judged on whether they beat the demon king. That was their purpose, right?

"The point I tried to make to my king is that there are just too many different types of heroes. Consider the story from two hundred and twenty years ago. There was only a single hero summoned. And that single hero became Emperor Taksa Moor Nungsari. That hero later founded the Darmoon dynasty, which later splintered into the Takde, Nung, Salah, and the now destroyed Moras and Fikris kingdoms."

"Sounds like there's nothing much, other than history." *I mean, so what?* If my own experience served as a guide, it could be their attempted 'extraction' of souls didn't work that well. Maybe the truck that was supposed to hit the bus missed, and the rest of the passengers survived.

"Well, yes." Madeus slouched, his head downcast. "My research got me nowhere. It seems a lot of it is on the individuals and some strange stroke of luck. And it's not as if the lesser number of heroes is always stronger than when more heroes are summoned. For every theory I came up with, there was always some other incident that proved otherwise."

"Okay. So heroes are random." *Actually, does he know about star mana?*

"Yes. If there's anything that I actually did find, it is that the heroes are getting younger. And I have no idea why."

"Huh?"

Okay, that was absolutely a letdown. I was hoping to gain some insight into heroes and the demon king, but it looked like I would have to try elsewhere. At least he seemed rather knowledgeable about history, so I decided to try a different question. "Anyway, since we are also talking a bit about history...is there a time before heroes?"

The wizard sipped his tea and thought for a moment. "Uh... there is supposed to be a time before heroes and demon kings... but it is millennia ago, and we don't have any records."

"When was the first documented demon king?"

"We also don't know. There was a demon king, Demon King Amadeus, who destroyed close to eighty percent of the world, and with it, most of the world's written records. So the information predating Demon King Amadeus is scarce, and the word-of-mouth stories are not reliable."

"Fine, tell me about Demon King Amadeus. How did the world defeat it from such a position?"

"Uh...the legends from that era are not very consistent. It did happen many thousands of years ago... There are a few theories, though... The most believed one is that a group of heroes were summoned in the scattered islands, and they later defeated the demon king."

"Has any other demon king come close to that level of destruction?"

"Not many, but a few notable demon kings did destroy at least a few continents each. Of those we know of, only Amadeus was successful enough to destroy all the continents..."

Hmmm... "Why didn't the heroes stop them?"

"Again, we have very little knowledge. My own understanding is that it was a case of the heroes being summoned too late and needing time to get stronger. In quite a few cases with other demon kings, overconfident heroes tried when they were not ready and got killed."

"How'd the world recover from something like Demon King Amadeus?"

"Uh, there were survivors, a lot of them in hiding. And the heroes who defeated Amadeus went on to defeat two more demon kings, so the legend goes. That gave the world some time to recover from the extensive damage, but all this is really word of mouth since written records from that era are rare. We don't really even know whether the destruction was really that extensive since the records are so rare."

"Have there ever been instances where...heroes were summoned twice?"

"Not that I know of, but...it is possible?" Madeus seemed totally clueless on this. *Fine.*

"Fine. Tell me about this...the ten-year demon king cycle." I mean, that's something that I wondered about. Why ten years?

"Oh. We have no idea why. Perhaps it's some quirk in the stars. It's not a rule, though. There have been exceptions a lot of times, and we have no idea why."

Okay, not helping. I needed to try other kinds of questions. "Why did the world leave all the fighting to the heroes? Why not the locals? Is there nobody at the level of the heroes?"

"Uh...it's...it's just the way it always has been..."

"Really?"

"But I would think it would be really, really hard. Even slaying a demon champion needs very high-level fighters and mages."

Once again, not helping. Was there some level wall or ceiling that existed for the locals, so that the world needed to rely on external powers? "Hmmm. Never mind, then. Thank you for sharing your knowledge. I will borrow your knowledge of history later."

"You are welcome. Consider it proof of my sincerity." Madeus nodded and took a sip from the wooden cup.

"Anyway, why do you want to serve me?" I asked.

"When you managed to undo the damage suffered by the princess, I realized that you must be a great and powerful being. To serve a great being would be a privilege, an honor, and I hope to be part of that greatness. Maybe the greatness will rub off on me." *Ah, a glory chaser. Hmm. I'll need to watch him a bit more carefully.*

"Hmmm, greatness may not be something I can offer. I can offer you fruits."

Madeus laughed as a bowl of fruits appeared before him. He smiled, grabbed one, and bit.

YEAR 77, MONTH 11

An envoy from Salah came, bearing strange news. One of...unconditional ceasefire. A truce. The offer soon riled up the entire high council, who managed to be outraged, happy, and greedy. Pretty much everything.

It was the first time Jura sat on the high council, with his thirty-three percent voting rights on such matters, with an additional right to veto certain decisions.

"We have the advantage; we should demand reparations from Salah!" one of the councilors said. "They are afraid, and now they want a truce!"

"I grow tired of war," another councilor said. "Perhaps we should just take it."

"No! Salah has caused us a great deal of harm. We should not take it without compensation!"

They argued, and they eventually settled into two camps, a group that demanded extra compensation, and another that wanted to accept.

So Yvon, as the chair of the high council, turned to Jura. "Supreme Counsel, as representative of the tree spirit, do you have any words to add?"

"Tree spirit is of the view we should accept it. Ongoing

combat is not productive for the valley. There are bigger concerns..."

My first concern was the demonic rifts. Those should start appearing very soon, as those happened well in advance of the demon king's arrival.

"But Salah's not exactly a trustworthy country to deal with? We could accept the truce only for them to break it!"

"So? We don't have any offensive capability at the moment. A truce is good for us since it allows to trade with Salah."

With that, the truce was accepted. Of course, this was rather shocking to Salah's envoy as well, who expected a rejection and were prepared to die.

YEAR 77, MONTH 12

"Here's the man you asked me to find, tree spirit. I'll leave the room now." Jura bowed and left the old man standing alone in the small room, right next to the [Tree of Prayers]. It was a 'special room,' more of a courtyard, with one tree in the middle and sunlight coming in from above. It was winter, so there was snow, too.

The old man, a half-elf, looked around and shrugged. "What's this..."

I spoke directly to his mind. "Hello, Wesley."

He paused and tried to see whether there was anyone else in the room. "Is this some trick? Or magic?"

I gave him some time and, after a while, he stopped.

"Fine. Who're you?" he asked.

"I'm Tree-Tree, the tree spirit of the valley."

He rubbed his chin. "Huh, so there really is a tree spirit. So what can I do for you?"

"I'd like you to help conduct some...ceremonies for me. Something a person like yourself, a former priest, can do."

"What kind of ceremonies?"

"Simple ones. I have a few in mind, for the dying, for death, and for births. Laufen will assist you, but she is not fit for the role of a master of ceremonies. Are you keen?"

The man paused. "What do I get?"

"A fair pay, accommodation, and some tea to help with the aches you have. Additional things can be discussed."

The man paced around the courtyard a few times. Clearly this was something he was thinking about a lot until he paused and asked, "Which god am I praying to?"

"None."

His face was one of shock. "So...what rituals are we actually doing?"

"I'll let you know, but first, are you willing?"

The first of the ceremonies happened a few days later. One of the older folk in New Freeka passed away. There, the population comprised of a mix of elves, dwarves, centaurs, treefolk, half-elves, some lizardmen, and quite a few more others, though elves formed the bulk of them.

So there were actually many ways to process a corpse. The few that I knew so far were cremation, burial, magical decon-struction, petrification, or transformation into a statue. The presence of magic added a large variety of possible ways a corpse could be 'sent off,' 'entombed,' or 'immortalized.'

Anyway, that was just how things were elsewhere.

"What's this?" an elderly woman, the deceased's wife, asked as the corpse of the old man was brought in by some of the guards on stretchers.

Wesley smiled, a calm, reassuring smile from years of training as a priest, and he warmly greeted the elderly woman. "New Freeka's welcomed the tree spirit into its fold, and this is one of the many ways the great tree has given us his gifts."

It was a large open space, and there was a curved, bent tree as if the tree grew straight up before heading sideways. Along its trunk, there was a large opening in it, filled with a greenish liquid. Multiple flowers dotted the side of the trunk.

Wesley nodded to the guards, and a few of the men assisted in placing the corpse of the old man slowly into the opening.

"With this, the dead will be one with the tree spirit, his soul on their journey to the world beyond."

The corpse slowly sank into the thick, greenish liquid, and for effect, the flowers around the trunk started to bloom a little bigger as a pleasant, calming, soothing scent was released into the room. There was even some wind and rustling sounds to add to the moment. And when the corpse fully sank and disappeared into the green liquid, the flowers glowed slightly.

The family cried for a good hour as Wesley spoke to each member of the family, giving them a blessing. He then picked the flowers from the side of the trunk and passed one to each of the family members.

"What happens to the body?"

"It is now with the tree spirit and has found peace, at last," Wesley said and, somehow, probably due to his past priest levels, it was really convincing. "These flowers contain the essences of your deceased father, and they will last longer than normal flowers, but they, too, will fade after a year. Think of it as a reminder of he who has now left us."

The elderly woman nodded. "Is there...something more permanent, perhaps a marker we can get? To remind us of our beloved?"

Wesley smiled, and he touched the trunk. From the greenish liquid, a small bone floated up. He carefully picked it up with a special spoon and placed it in a ceremonial wooden bowl.

"Ah, yes. This is the condensed bones of your husband. Keep it as you wish or make it into something." The elderly woman accepted it with tears in her eyes, and after a bit more small talk, the entire family left.

Wesley breathed a huge sigh of relief.

It was the first time this ceremony had been shown to the citizens of New Freeka, and even the guards themselves had not seen it.

"How'd it go?" Wesley asked when there was only Laufen remaining inside the courtyard of death. There were some proposed names for the courtyard, perhaps to call it the Garden of Return, to signify one's return to the tree spirit. I quite liked it, but I was still pondering other names before finalizing it with Wesley and Laufen since Laufen was going to play a larger role in the 'rituals' and 'religious' aspects of the Valtrian Order.

"Good."

"Is that really the bone of the deceased?"

"Yes."

"Ah, good. I've not lied, then."

"What'd both of you think of the ceremony?"

Wesley sat and smoked some kind of rolled-up leaves, nodding. "It's...easy. I believe the tale will spread soon, and more families will ask for this ceremony."

"Any views on how to improve it?"

Laufen shook her head. "I like it, but let me sleep on it a little. Maybe I'll get some ideas later."

"Me, too. I was so nervous doing it for the first time. All I want to do now is just get the hang of it first."

"Very well; it was a good first time. Go get some rest." They both nodded and left the courtyard, and I returned into my soul realm to have a look at the results of the ceremony.

"The dead man's soul was in good condition and a state of calm. Reincarnation to the next world was going to be quite a breeze. It was actually an interesting modification of the elven tradition of burying the dead next to the soul trees, instead going for the route of direct absorption."

Well, that was fine, but my focus was on...collection, so I checked my log.

"Ah man, no 'seeds.' Well, at least there are some essences..."

This ceremony was actually derived from that little experience I had with both Alexis and, later, Falklay, and that exposed tree trunk was really a modified biolab 'pod.' The idea I had was really rather simple. I wanted more of the 'seeds' that came with

Falklay's death, and I was really keen to try and get more of those 'seeds' by way of 'absorbing' the dead.

By giving the citizens, the families, a pleasant experience, I was hoping to get fresher 'dead' and, with that, a higher chance of harvesting whatever I could get. A part of me felt a little tiny bit bad for desecrating the dead, but the bulk of me felt like it was totally fine since I was playing the religious role here! And besides, they would just end up burning the body, so that wasn't exactly any better than what I was doing.

The next ceremony was something where Laufen played a bigger role. A birth...and babies. In some worlds, there were rituals like baptisms, flower baths, or special chants to bless a newborn.

Children are our future. My future.

"Congratulations on the baby." Laufen bowed and shook the hand of the young mother, the father next to her watching. The little infant cradled in the mother's arms cried a little, and the mother quickly rocked and tried to soothe the baby.

"Ah...what can we do for you?"

"As the vice counsel of the Valtrian Order, I'd like to present a small present for the family, for the newborn."

Laufen handed over a basket containing a few bottles.

"That bottle contains a special liquid made from the sap of the tree spirit. It will boost the infant's strength and vitality. It'll also help with the cold weather." Made using the [Childcare corner]'s special syrup, mixed with some essences, some minerals, it should give a good boost to any weak baby, and it also gave a shot of 'warmth' to help the baby through the winter.

"That other bottle is something for the sick babies. If they have a fever or a cold, or just don't look too well." I had something given to Roma back when he was a tiny baby, so this was the same thing, just bottled up. Made from [healing juice] condensed into a thick, gooey, sweet syrup.

"That last one is if the baby's hungry, but the mommy's out of milk." It was a thick, preserved juice containing a mix of nutrients, meant to temporarily tide over the child's hunger. Again, made from the [childcare corner].

"Ah..." The father and mother seemed rather surprised, but the father seemed afraid to receive them, as was normal for gifts. Perhaps there was some expectation of payment or some kind of subtle extortion as refugees often encountered in their journeys.

"It's free. A gift with no strings. It is something the Valtrian Order wants to do for the children born of the valley." Laufen bowed and went to walk out, flashing a warm, motherly smile before leaving. "Please let me know if you have any challenges with the child."

Although Laufen's official title was now vice counsel, she wasn't exactly keen to participate in the political activities, so as with all quasi-religious, militant organizations, there needed be someone to spearhead the public service, charitable, social elements of the organization.

Laufen's duties were to organize the gifts for the newly born, set up a creche for young children and babies within the Valtrian Order's space, create an orphanage for the orphans, then a kindergarten, and finally launch a combat-oriented school for the older kids. Charity and such social services 'softened' the image of the Valtrian Order and cultivated a generation with favorable views of the order.

There were a lot of births—on average, about six or seven a day, so Laufen had many homes to visit. In time, Emile, Belle, and the workers would also play the role of delivering these gifts, but for now, the two younger ladies were helping out as her assistants.

Some of the parents would outright refuse the gifts, and that was fine. It was given at no compulsion, and Laufen herself would not push—after all, parents had the right to choose what they gave to their infants. Gradually, though, this was helping to build a positive reputation for the Valtrian Order, building public support for this 'new' entity that suddenly emerged.

As part of the transition to the newly setup Valtrian Order, a large patch of land around the Tree of Prayer had been transferred over, so a bit of construction work was going on to build all the facilities required, though we had to prioritize for the burial services first, which was fairly easy since it was mostly just setting up the space for the tree.

Also, I wanted to have the Valtrian Order earn some income independent of the tax collections, in order to fund all the other ideas I had in my head for my gradual takeover of New Freeka.

One of these ideas was to set up a clinic, or a healing chamber of some kind, using the biolab and the medical juices. With this, I could charge adventurers, soldiers, and whatnot a fee for using my healing services, similar to how it was for other healers all around the world. This wouldn't be much, but it would help subsidize the cost of staff.

Next, I would be looking to sell some special products. I had some in mind, perhaps even the ginseng, if I could make them of an acceptable quality. They would probably sell for a good price. Then higher-quality crops, directly to the market. But that would involve dedicating some of the subsidiary trees for that purpose. Maybe a special series of olive oils for ceremonial use and sale. I thought that could sell since people loved 'enchanted' stuff.

The processed, preserved healing fruits were also a potential product, but whether that was a worthwhile venture might depend on the price.

I also had my ability to make wood products using my wood-shaping magic, but I thought that was probably not a good use of my time unless I made them automatically.

Additionally, the beetles could go and kill monsters and bring back loot we could sell.

Oh, wait. My large beetle-pods were ready, too.

[Large beetle pods - completed.]

[Enhanced interior structures - completed.]

[Fruit bombs - increased range and power - completed.]

[Eye-Tree Stage I research option unlocked - fifteen months remaining.]

[Beetle - anti-magma armors stage 2 - six months remaining.]

[Tree - volcanic adaptation stage 3 - fifteen months remaining.]

[Roots - volcanic mineral harvesting - stage 1 - five months remaining.]

I had an epiphany one day, which was, there was sulfur in the volcano. Shouldn't that allow me to make sulfuric acid? Would I be able to have fruits with highly corrosive acid in it? Or beetles that spat acid? A ranged unit perhaps?

As a result, I just had to conduct research on the ability of my volcano-adapted subsidiary tree's roots to safely absorb sulfur through their roots. I thought that would be the first step in acquiring any sort of ranged unit. So I was going to have larger beetles, hopefully ranged beetles, and also flying beetles and acidic, corrosive beetles. Plenty of variation in the beetle family. Of course, this made Horns rather happy. I still hadn't figured out how to get that step from sulfur to acid, but I would figure it out once we got there. Perhaps it would be some kind of large, segregated tank where the sulfur was processed.

Oh, well.

I was starting to have a few more things going on than I could handle.

I needed help.

Time to create another artificial soul.

The Tree of Aeons will continue in Book Two.

THANK YOU FOR READING
TREE OF AEONS

We hope you enjoyed it as much as we enjoyed bringing it to you. We just wanted to take a moment to encourage you to review the book. Follow this link: Book 1 to be directed to the book's Amazon product page to leave your review.

Every review helps further the author's reach and, ultimately, helps them continue writing fantastic books for us all to enjoy.

———

ALSO IN SERIES:
Book 1
Book 2
Book 3
Book 4

———

Want to discuss our books with other readers and even the authors like Shirtaloon, Zogarth, Cale Plamann, Noret Flood (Puddles4263) and so many more?

Join our Discord server today and be a part of the Aethon community.

Facebook | Instagram | Twitter | Website

You can also join our non-spam mailing list by visiting www.subscribepage.com/AethonReadersGroup and never miss out on future releases. You'll also receive three full books completely Free as our thanks to you.

Looking for more great books?

One bad roll catapults a group of friends into a new world... Five friends gather for their usual game night like they have hundreds of time before. But when they use a strange new die, they are instantly transported to a fantasy world where all gaming ideas can come true. Together, the party must join forces to deal with the vile Necrolord whose plans will not only threaten this world, but Earth as well. Should be easy for a team of lifelong gamers. However, when gaming and real life collide, there are situations which can't be anticipated. Will Samo use science to solve all her problems? Will Wyatt always resort to violence? Will Bourbon discover lost treasure? Will Falcon restore his kingdom. Will Melf, the bard, find his pants?

Get One Bad Roll Now!

———

Kullen is the Emperor's assassin. The sharp hand of justice. The Black Talon. *Gifted a soul-forged bond with his dragon, Umbris, Kullen is tasked with hunting any and all who oppose the Empire. But when the secretive Crimson Fang murders two noblemen before his very eyes, Kullen must discover the truth of who they are and what they want. What he uncovers is a web of lies and deceit spiraling into the depths of Dimvein. Natisse, a high-ranking member of the rebellion known as the Crimson Fang, has no greater goal than to rid Dimvein of power-hungry nobles. Haunted by her past, fire, flames, and the death of her parents, she sets out to destroy the dragons and those who wield them as unstoppable weapons of destruction. Until she too finds herself buried beneath the weight of the revelations her investigations reveal... The Empire is under siege from within, and one man, dressed in black like the night, stands at the epicenter of it all.* **Black Talon is the first book in the Dragonblood Assassin Series from #1 Audible and Washington Post bestseller Jaime Castle & Epic Fantasy legend Andy Peloquin. It's perfect for fans of the Forgotten Realms, Joe Abercrombie, David Dalglish, and Kel Kade.**

Get Black Talon Now!

For all our LitRPG books, visit our website.

Made in the USA
Monee, IL
11 April 2023

31695931R00395